What others are saying...

"Mabel, a former lawyer forced into retirement at 49, stumbles into a new career as an amateur sleuth when she volunteers at a historic home that's the scene of both historic and contemporary murders. A twisty mystery that offers up plenty of suspects – including an eccentric group of historical society volunteers – as well as cute pets, a unique protagonist, and a budding romance. Sure to interest cozy mystery fans who enjoy small towns, unique characters, a touch of romance, and a splash of history in a contemporary story."

~*Victoria Gilbert, author of the Blue Ridge Library Mystery series and Booklover's B&B mystery series*

"When Mabel Browne gets canned by her law firm at nearly fifty, she decides to volunteer with the local historical society, conveniently next door to the house she inherited from her grandmother. The site of grisly ax murders decades ago, the historical society house is soon the setting for another one. Mabel, not known for her tact, but with a good legal mind, can't help getting involved. Readers will have fun following Mabel's sleuthing activities and her attempts to avoid ending up an ax murder victim herself."

~*Miranda James, NYT and USA Today bestselling author of the Cat in the Stacks and Southern Ladies mysteries*

D1287973

MABEL GETS THE AX

By

Susan Kimmel Wright

Mabel Gets the Ax
Published by Mountain Brook Ink
White Salmon, WA U.S.A.

The website addresses shown in this book are not intended in any way to be or imply an endorsement on the part of Mountain Brook Ink, nor do we vouch for their content.

This story is a work of fiction. All characters and events are the product of the author's imagination. Any resemblance to any person, living or dead, is coincidental.

Scripture taken from the Holy Bible, NEW INTERNATIONAL VERSION®, NIV® Copyright © 1973, 1978, 1984, 2011 by Biblica, Inc.® Used by permission. All rights reserved worldwide.

The Author is represented by and this book is published in association with the literary agency of Hartline Literary Agency, www.hartlineliterary.com.

The Team: Miralee Ferrell, Alyssa Roat, Nikki Wright, Kristen Johnson, Cindy Jackson
Cover Design: Indie Cover Design, Lynnette Bonner Designer

Mountain Brook Ink is an inspirational publisher offering fiction you can believe in.
Printed in the United States of America

DEDICATION

To my grandmother Blanche Kimmel—memories of
the hours we spent together have lasted a lifetime.

Chapter One

"WHY NOT SEE IT AS AN opportunity?" the career counselor told Mabel. "In a way, you're fortunate. You have a nice severance package...and that inheritance you were telling me about. A lot of people dream of retiring in their fifties."

"Forties." Mabel's voice sounded loud in the small office.

"Forties." The quirk of the counselor's mouth failed to match her pleasant, agreeable tone. Both knew Mabel was less than a month from the dreaded next decade.

"I'm a good lawyer," Mabel said. "With twenty-three years' experience."

"I realize that, and it's a shame the job market's so tight right now." The counselor, who couldn't have been much over thirty herself, smoothed the draped front of her ivory blouse. She had the kind of bony figure that could handle all those extra folds without looking like ballroom draperies.

Mabel's slenderizing pantyhose were losing the fight to stay up. She should have gotten the next size. "Maybe we should look at management positions." She shifted and heard her chair groan in agony. "Where a legal background would be an asset."

"I'm so sorry." The counselor glanced at her cellphone so gracefully Mabel nearly missed it. "I've already explored all those options."

She stood, letting Mabel know their meeting was over. "I apologize for having to stop right here, but I have another appointment in five minutes. Why don't you look into volunteering? Many seniors find a lot of satisfaction in that, and I'm sure you'll be making a valuable contribution."

Mabel got up too, almost tipping her chair. "Listen. I'm not a 'senior.'" As a rule, she despised air quotes, but she found herself making them. "I'm a forty-something professional in the prime of my life. You—" Here she stabbed her finger in the counselor's direction. "You advertise yourself as a specialist in 'second acts.'"

When she found herself air quoting again, Mabel lowered her hands and stuck them in the pockets of her navy suit. She took several deep, hard breaths. "I've paid you a lot of money."

The counselor smiled in a calming kind of way, but her lips were tight. "I know you have, and in return for that, I've given you hours of my best efforts. Please remember we got you two interviews. But I've exhausted every avenue. There isn't anything else I can do."

She opened the door, keeping a wary eye on Mabel. "Do think about volunteering. I'm sure you'd be an asset wherever you chose to lend a hand."

Mabel bent to collect her big, slouchy leather purse from the floor. Why did this feel so much like being fired, all over again? This time, she'd paid for the privilege.

She refused to thank this fairy princess for nothing. Instead, she gave her a small nod as she passed into the waiting room. "Good luck," she told a sixtyish man, briefcase resting on his well-pressed knees. "You're going to need it."

Was it her? Was she the problem? Twenty-three years as an associate attorney with Zimmer and Buehl, and she'd never gotten anywhere near a partnership offer. Everyone who'd started with her out of law school, along with squadrons of younger graduates over the years, had eventually either made partner or gotten an even better position elsewhere.

Mabel ducked into the restroom. She leaned on the counter, staring at herself in the mirror while she tried to figure out what came next. She pushed back her shoulder-length mass of chestnut curls. A few little laugh lines. Only a couple of gray hairs. She didn't look fifty. Did she? And wasn't fifty supposed to be "the new thirty," anyway?

All right. She wasn't petite. She never had been, though. At 5' 9", and big-boned to boot, it was no surprise she was looking at fifty from slightly in the overweight category—but only slightly. In other cultures, her figure would be the very ideal of womanhood.

Mabel didn't live in those cultures.

The day she'd been let go, Mabel had been late getting back from lunch. Her annual physical had run late, and her doctor had lectured her about her weight again. She'd dashed into the office with her greasy bag of take-out chicken, feet wet from the rain and a runner in the despised pantyhose and been met with a note to see the managing partner. She'd gone to law school with him, and he hadn't been the brightest set of headlights on the road to success. He'd passed her up, all the same.

When he told Mabel her services were no longer required, merely because one more client had complained she'd been a little bit too blunt, she threatened to sue the firm. "Age discrimination." She slapped her hand down on his mahogany desk when she said that. "Gender discrimination." Another slap. "Try me."

In the end, the firm had given in. While they might not have appreciated Mabel—and she had to admit she might have had a small tact problem in dealing with clients—she was a good lawyer and knew she had a strong case. In the end, she'd signed a release but left toting a big bag of money. The skinny counselor had been right about that.

Mabel slapped the restroom counter the way she'd slapped that desk.

"I'm moving on," she told her reflection. "Shaking the dust from my feet."

Volunteer, the counselor had said. All right, she would.

But Mabel was going to turn this volunteering gig into a new career. If the counselor couldn't help her reinvent herself, she'd have to do it herself.

Maybe she could turn a volunteer job into a real job, once people saw what she could do? No—she'd do something even better. She was going to have an exciting career, and she knew what it was going to be. Mabel dug around in her bag and found what she was looking for.

She steamed back into the waiting room. "Excuse me." She waved a crumpled magazine at the receptionist. "I slipped this in my bag when I got called for my appointment and forgot to return it."

The receptionist, a twenty-something with sleek red-violet hair, sharply angled a good two inches longer on one side, gave Mabel a vague smile and nodded, before looking back down at her phone.

Mabel waved the magazine again. "It's six months old. I'd like to take it if you don't mind."

"No prob." The receptionist didn't even bother to look up again. "Knock yourself out."

Mabel stuffed the magazine, Seniority, back into her bag, stifling a sniff of disdain. Apparently, some people were allowed to be rude to the client and still keep *their* jobs.

This was going to be fun. She'd felt this way when she was accepted to law school. Of course, that hadn't panned out quite the way she'd expected. But to tell the truth, law could be awfully boring. Especially being stuck for decades in a tiny associate's office, shuffling papers.

This time, Mabel knew she was headed for excitement. She wasn't going to have any managing partners or difficult clients to deal with. She would be her own boss. She was going to be a writer.

Mabel rode the elevator down to the ground floor and headed for her little gray hatchback, parked at the curb, with a spring in her step. The article she'd been reading had given her the idea.

The piece was about retirees' volunteering to do things like teach nursing in the developing world—and about "making a difference." It hadn't been much of an article—half a page, and part of that was a picture.

But Mabel would write a *book* about volunteering. Which shouldn't be hard. After all, she had spent all those years writing hundred-page briefs. She could knock off two of those and have a 200-page book. In fact, she could start by doing a series of articles and just combine them, once she had enough. She knew she'd be good at it.

She looked at the clock on her dash and realized she was going to be late feeding her animals. Besides her cat Koi, she'd also inherited Barnacle, a scruffy blue heeler mix, from Grandma Mabel, along with her house, a bit of money, and her outdated first name. Medicine Spring was a short thirty-minute drive, but she had to stop for more dog food. Barnacle ate way more than she'd expected, having been used to feeding a small cat. Mabel had only been in Grandma's house, God rest her soul, about six months. Already, Barnacle had probably gone through a dozen big bags of dog food.

Dusk had fallen by the time Mabel reached the single long block that was Carteret Street. Grandma's house—Mabel's house now, she corrected herself—sat at the lonely dead end, next to the woods forming the back acreage of the municipal park.

As Mabel swung onto Carteret, her lights washed over the imposing house that sat on the sprawling corner lot behind its tall iron fence and hedges. A gust of wind brought down a shower of golden maple leaves. Rain and wet leaves slapped the car.

Perfect. Now she was going to get soaked. The one thing this crummy day had been lacking.

Only five houses occupied the entire dead-end block—three on the right and two on Mabel's side, which included the mansion on the front corner and Mabel's at the end. Her weathered Victorian sat on an overgrown two-acre lot bounded by the park at the end of the street and woods along the back and across the street. Not for the first time, she thought how isolated her house was—and how dark.

The mansion's cast-iron fence and tall hedge marked her other boundary. The spotlight on its front lawn hadn't yet come on, nor the rewired gas lamps by the walkway. But a bit of light spilled over the hedges from the corner streetlamp, casting gloomy shadows, their edges wavering in the rain.

Mabel's headlights flashed on the small, hand-lettered sign by the gate. The wind swung the wooden rectangle wildly on its support hooks. *Sauer Mansion: Tours by Appointment.* A phone number followed.

Below that, another line added *Medicine Spring Historical Society Meets Second Tuesday, 8 P.M. Public Welcome.*

Mabel had walked past the mansion many times and knew what the sign said. It was all very tasteful but so small only a pedestrian—with good eyesight—could read it.

Grandma had been a devoted member of the historical society, and its long-time secretary. But what a snooty bunch most of the rest were. "Sauer Mansion." Mabel sneered. Though the house was famous, nobody outside the Medicine Spring Historical Society ever called it that.

The rest of the world—including Mabel, for as long as she could remember—simply knew the elegant American Craftsman variant as the Sauer Ax Murder House.

Chapter Two

MABEL PULLED INTO HER DRIVEWAY, A weedy strip of dirt and pebbles along the near side of the house and gathered her bags. The rain had picked up and clattered on the roof. After rooting around on the floors and all through her purse, she groaned and concluded that—sure enough—she didn't have an umbrella. Not that she could've held onto one in this wind, anyway, especially schlepping all these bags.

The dog food bag would get wet. She hoped she wasn't about to immediately ruin forty-dollars' worth of fancy kibble.

Frantic barking came from the house, rising above the rushing wind. After six months, Mabel wasn't sure if Barnacle still thought she was an intruder, or if he was merely excited, starving, or desperate to go kill more of the struggling shrubs around the back door by pottying all over them.

"I'm coming." The wind snatched the words out of her mouth.

Clutching the heavy, shifting collection of bags to her chest, Mabel ran for the shelter of the front porch. Grandma, as was customary in Medicine Spring, had used her back door, even for company. But Mabel wasn't going to stand outside, fumbling for a keyhole, in this downpour.

As soon as she reached cover, Mabel let the bags slide to the floor. Frantic whining, accompanied by heartfelt yelps and the sound of claws scrabbling against the nice old walnut door, came from inside.

As she shoved the door open, squeezing herself and the food bag inside, sixty pounds of stinky, gray-speckled fur almost propelled her right back out again. "Barnacle, down."

Instead, he jumped again, planting saucer-size paws on her chest. "Down."

This time, Barnacle obeyed, if only because he'd discovered the dog food, and started pawing and biting at the bag. Mabel hoped the plastic coating was as tough as it looked.

She flicked the switch, and weak yellow light filtered down from a single bulb dangling from the high ceiling. "Koi," she called. "Here, kitty."

A shadow separated itself from the darkness beneath the antique bench in the front hall where Grandma Mabel used to sit and pull off her snow boots. The big pouf of black fur, flecked with gold, meowed a question and twined itself around her ankles. Mabel didn't need to be fluent in cat to translate. Koi would not be inquiring about Mabel's day, but "Why is my dinner late, and where is it? Now."

Mabel pulled off wet shoes and socks and dragged the food bag away from her drooling dog. "Dinnertime, guys." Barnacle barreled past her, almost buckling her knees.

Mabel steadied herself and followed him into the cramped kitchen. She dumped the bag onto the big, round oak table that took up nearly half the room. Newspapers and junk mail slid to the floor.

Skating over the scattered paper, Mabel threw the lock on the back door and grabbed Barnacle's collar to clip him to the tie-out cable. Usually a happy camper in all kinds of weather, he hesitated in the doorway when the cold rain blew sideways at him. A sheet of water cascaded from the awning and splashed up from the puddle at the foot of the two stone steps.

"Go on." Mabel gave a shove, and Barnacle lumbered down to the yard and lifted his leg on Grandma Mabel's beloved mock orange bush.

She came back inside and closed the door, lest Barnacle come blasting right back in, shaking water everywhere and making muddy pawprints on the floor and all that fallen paper. Mabel began picking up the mess, but a wave of sadness washed over her, and she sighed. All of a sudden, the day had caught up with her.

Mabel dropped her armload onto a chair not already piled high with papers, books, and magazines. Then, she sank onto the one remaining vacant chair, and Koi leapt onto her lap. The cat rubbed her chin on Mabel's hand and purred. Hungry as Mabel knew Koi was, the cat had always been sensitive to Mabel's moods.

Mabel stroked Koi's soft head. The old house felt empty tonight and lonely—despite her furry friends. Here she was, facing down the barrel of fifty, with no job, no husband or kids, and…this. She looked around the overcrowded kitchen with its high, shadowy ceilings.

She'd loved the Victorian when Grandma was alive. Everywhere she looked, some little thing reminded her of her forceful forebear, whose gruff exterior was the protective shield over a warm and generous heart.

Now, Mabel looked around with a growing sense of despair. This house was so old—with so many things needing fixing. Not to mention its dark and gloomy atmosphere, especially at night.

Grandma, a child of the Great Depression, had saved *everything*—from old newspapers to empty margarine tubs and used aluminum foil. She'd patched things when they broke, even when the result was less than stellar. The house stood as a bulging monument to seventy years of recycling and stockpiling. When she'd developed dementia in her last couple years, things had only gotten worse.

At the sharp sound of barking at the back door, followed by a flurry of scratching, Mabel gently scooped Koi to the floor. The offended cat stalked away, tail in the air, to go sit next to her empty food bowl in silent disapproval. She seemed to say, "So much for my efforts to provide encouragement."

Though Mabel grabbed a rag to dry him off, Barnacle dashed inside and shook, sending an explosive spray of water over Mabel and everything else in his path. He grinned, tongue lolling, and plopped on his bottom next to his empty dish, as if to give her the hint.

Mabel filled the food bowls and the animals' shared water dish. Then, she steeled herself to light the temperamental gas oven. She'd picked up a family-size mac-and-cheese, as well as a fudge cake. Tonight was no time to start a diet. Right now, she needed comfort food—and strength to deal with the turn her life had taken.

After she'd managed to get the stove going without causing an explosion that would've eliminated all her house-related problems, she stuck the mac-and-cheese inside and sat down for an appetizer. Mabel stuck a fork into the still semi-frozen cake. Why make the effort to thaw and plate a slice when she'd be the only one eating it?

She'd left her counselor's office on a big burst of enthusiasm. It was one thing to hatch a brilliant idea, and something else altogether to make it happen.

Mabel hardly knew where to begin. Besides trying to launch a writing career, she had the estate filings to do, a cluttered house to clean, and a yard turning to wilderness. Already that sour old biddy on the property behind her had been complaining and threatening to call the authorities if the lot wasn't cleaned up.

"For fifty years I put up with your grandmother's debris in my back yard, and I certainly don't intend to suffer through another fifty with you, young lady."

And she'd had the nerve to say Barnacle, the gentlest, most laid-back moose of a dog ever to draw breath, had "menaced" her. That had been another call to the authorities the old lady had warned she was going to make.

Mabel had been tempted to tell her she was a resentful old shrew who still held a decades' old grudge over a court ruling in Grandma's favor, concerning that back property line. But it was hard to be very mad at somebody who referred to her as "young lady." Plus, Auntie Em's words in *The Wizard of Oz* had echoed in her head—that for years she'd wanted to tell evil Miss Gulch what she thought of her, "and now, being a Christian woman, I can't say it."

She'd swallowed hard and forced a smile. Still, here was one more worry to add to her lengthening list.

Mabel ate her mac-and-cheese directly out of the container, with Barnacle's steamy chin on her knee. When she got up and threw the dregs in the trash, he followed her with big, sad eyes.

"Sorry, buddy." She washed her fork and put away her leftover cake then stood at the microwave while her tea brewed.

Mabel realized she wouldn't start feeling better till her life had some positive direction again. For the past twenty-three years, she'd known where she was going, from 8:30 every morning until 5:30 at night. She had known she'd be paid every other Friday, without fail. Her medical insurance premiums had been paid—something else she now had to think about, and soon.

Her life had had a purpose. It might not have been the most exciting or meaningful purpose, but people counted on her to review those documents, do that legal research, prepare those pleadings.

Nobody needed her anymore. Maybe they never had.

It was important to get moving on this writing thing. Once she'd gotten her new career launched, she'd feel she had a plan, at least, and something to do.

What should her first step be? Mabel returned to the dim front hallway and dug through her purse for a notepad and pen. In the kitchen, the microwave dinged to announce her mug of Mountain Autumn tea was ready.

Back at the table, she flipped the notepad to a fresh page. *Exactly like my life*.

Pen poised, she thought. A writer would need a good supply of printer ink, it went without saying. She wrote that down.

And paper.

At that point, her brain seemed to stall. Once she had those basics, she guessed she was simply supposed to sit down and start writing.

Write what? Her idea about turning volunteering into a career had seemed brilliant, back at the counseling office. But what did she know about volunteering?

Mabel had never volunteered in her life...unless you counted the time she'd let herself get roped into being a vacation Bible school aide. To be fair, she guessed she couldn't count that, since she'd only volunteered the one day. She'd been told, "Thanks, but we won't be needing you the rest of the week." Mabel had always suspected it had something to do with her telling the three-year-olds that the next one to wet his pants would have to wear them that way, because she couldn't take it anymore.

She leaned back and lifted her mug, inhaling spicy cranberry steam, as she stared out at the night. Koi leapt onto the table and curled into a purring ball at Mabel's elbow. At her feet, Barnacle yawned. She felt herself relax. These two felt like family. Like her support team.

Maybe she should start by volunteering somewhere. Then, she could bring the voice of experience to what she wrote. With a sense she was making progress, Mabel wrote a heading on the next page—Volunteer Opportunities.

At first, she tried to think of what she might like to do—or be good at. When her list had remained empty for a while, she decided she should just suck it up and write down whatever volunteer jobs she could think of. She'd probably need a variety, anyway, if she was going to write an entire book about the world of volunteering.

Mabel had filled two pages by the time she laid her pen down and yawned. Barnacle got up and went to the door.

"Last out for you, and we'll call it a night." She set her empty mug in the sink and opened the door. The rain had tapered off, though the awning still dripped, and a heavy mist filled the air.

Barnacle disappeared into the fog at the side of the house. She could see nothing but the movement of the tie-out cable as he sniffed through the bushes, picking his spot. The fog had completely erased the bulk of the Sauer mansion beyond.

Mabel's feet dragged when she locked the door at last and climbed the stairs. All she wanted now was bed. Grabbing her notebook and another mug of tea, she plumped up her nest of pillows and settled deep into the saggy old mattress and soft-worn, handmade quilts. "Stay down."

Barnacle had been used to sleeping with Grandma, and the battle to keep him off the bed had been going on the entire six months she'd lived there. Most mornings, she woke up with him halfway on top of her. Despite his being a bed hog—and his breath could slay dragons—there was a certain comfort in that, when sleeping yards away from the site of the ax murders that had haunted her dreams for over forty years.

He rested his chin on the edge of the bed.

"No." Mabel averted her eyes from Barnacle's pleading face and opened her notebook.

She knew it would be hard to fall asleep. All the day's events—and the looming, devastating issue of her firing—crowded into her brain.

But a lot of her mood was due to that Sauer house. Ever since moving here, she'd tried to convince herself she was a grownup now. That what had happened over there behind those hedges was now ancient history, which had nothing to do with her. That those long-ago screams didn't still echo through her nightmares. But they'd been a part of her too long.

Grandma hadn't intended to scar her for life, she knew. In all fairness, Mabel used to beg her to talk about the murders. Even though she'd always seemed very matter of fact about the whole thing, Grandma had probably had some deep-seated issues with them herself. After all, she'd only been about ten when the killings had happened—old enough to be well aware of the most horrific crime ever to rock the small town of Medicine Spring. But still too young to process what had happened.

"Stop." Mabel pushed the murders out of her mind and tried to concentrate on volunteer opportunities.

The church choir was a logical starting place. That would mean a couple of hours every Tuesday night, though, and no sleeping in on Sundays when she was tired. Plus, with her husky voice, she'd have to be an alto. Since she struggled to read music, they'd probably stick her back next to old Almeda Blair, who—next to Barnacle—had the worst breath in Medicine Spring.

Half an hour later, having gone down the entire list several times, Mabel sighed. Despite her feelings about the Sauer house, she concluded her choice would have to be the historical society. The society had been Grandma Mabel's charity for many years, so in a way, she'd be carrying on a family tradition. She could prove to herself the Sauer mansion was no more than a house—that she was a grownup who could handle anything.

After draining the last bit of her now-cold tea and switching off her lamp, however, Mabel pulled the covers over her head. When Barnacle scrambled up onto the bed in the middle of the night, she didn't push him off.

Chapter Three

THE EVENING OF THE HISTORICAL SOCIETY meeting, Mabel dressed in supposedly slimming black jeans, topped with a black pullover and gray tweed blazer. She sat on the bed to tug on black boots. She'd planned to try to blend in with the staid older crowd by wearing one of her business suits but at the last minute, simply couldn't face putting on the costume of her former life.

She and Koi, who'd jumped onto Grandma's dresser next to her, stared at Mabel's reflection. Since she wasn't a lawyer anymore, Mabel decided she'd never pull on another pair of pantyhose as long as she lived. Maybe she would even give all her suits to Goodwill.

She was a writer now. She should dress cool and "artsy."

Mabel tried to look at her backside, wondering if black had been a mistake with all this pet hair. Oh, well, too late now.

She remembered Grandma always took a contribution to the refreshment table at these meetings. Mabel wasn't a baker, though she did sometimes throw together a mean batch of crispy rice squares. At the last minute, she'd decided to go with Halloween-themed chocolate cookies with bright orange creme filling. Easy, and everybody liked them. At least, Mabel did.

She slipped a cookie out of the bag. Nobody would miss one.

"You two are on your own," she told her pets, turning on the TV and one lamp for them. Another quick look in the mirror. "Hi," she practiced. "I'm Mabel Browne's granddaughter, also Mabel." She smiled at her reflection and was treated to a display of chocolate-studded teeth. Clamping a quick hand over her mouth, she hurried off to brush cookie crumbs out of her teeth.

The Sauer house was well lit tonight, and the clear sky pierced with silver stars and a shiny tin-foil moon. Mabel sucked in a deep, calming breath before heading up the broad front steps. She followed a small, bent-over woman, who clung to the railing with one hand and a cane and big purse with the other.

Mabel wasn't a middle-aged, unmarried, failed lawyer. She was a successful writer-to-be and the granddaughter of one of the pillars of the historical society. There was no reason to feel nervous.

Mabel approached the lady ahead of her. "Hi."

The woman startled, jerked around, and nearly lost her balance.

"Easy there." Mabel smiled as she put out a steadying hand.

The old lady scowled. "Good grief, young woman. There's no need to bellow at close range."

"Um, of course not. Um, sorry." Mabel shifted her cookie bag. "May I help you with that?" She gestured at the enormous handbag.

"No." The scowl became a full-out glare. "Thank you."

"All righty then," Mabel hated herself for the nervous giggle that came sort of snorting out. She coughed. "I'll, uh, follow along and spot you. My name's Mabel. Mabel Browne's granddaughter."

The woman's scowl relaxed a shade as she looked Mabel up and down then cleared her throat. She opened her mouth, closed it, and managed a small smile. "Yes. Well...welcome, I'm sure." She turned to climb the rest of the steps.

It wasn't until then that Mabel realized the other woman hadn't introduced herself. She hoped the rest of the group would be more inviting.

Even with lights ablaze, the entryway was less than cheerful. Mabel froze, cookie bag in hand. She was standing in the belly of the beast—inside the ax murder house.

"Hi," said a pleasant male voice at her shoulder. "I don't believe we know each other."

Mabel spun around, so startled by a friendly reception she nearly dropped her cookies. "Oh, hi. I'm Mabel Browne's granddaughter, also Mabel." She stuck out her hand to shake.

"Darwin Carmody." The slender man with silver at the temples of his dark hair smiled and took her hand. "I do know you then—or at least who you are."

Mabel smiled. "Yes, I remember you. You sing in the choir at Grandma's church." Mabel's church now too, she guessed, though she hadn't yet formally joined and still hadn't gotten to know everyone.

What she did remember, squirming at the recollection, was her mother's once suggesting she might try flirting with him a bit. He was pleasant and professorial looking with geeky glasses, a worn suit, and only a bit of salt-and-pepper, but he must have been twenty years older than she was. She remembered hearing that, like her, he'd been forced into painfully early retirement after he hadn't gotten tenure at Branch State College.

"I do." He released her hand. "You inherited the house. You're planning on joining us, I hope?"

"Thinking about it."

"Wonderful." He gestured at the bag. "Refreshments? Here, let me show you where they go."

He led her to a dining table topped with a vintage lace tablecloth. In the center sat a green bowl full of silk autumn leaves and jewel-colored mums, surrounded by silver trays and crystal and china platters laden with the most beautiful display of treats Mabel could imagine. Shortbread and apricot-filled cookies. Tiny cream puffs. Miniature scones sparkling with sugar. Cheeses and crackers and puff pastries bursting with mushrooms and asparagus. On an oak sideboard, covered with an embroidered runner, sat a coffee urn, electric hot water server, and delicate cups.

"I guess I should have brought a serving plate."

"Don't worry. Wait right there." Darwin stepped through a swinging door and came back with a small, rather dented aluminum tray.

Mabel poured out the cookies and spread them around.

"The meeting will soon be starting," Darwin whispered. "We'd better get in there. Helen—our president—will likely ask you to introduce yourself. We don't get many new members—especially youngsters like yourself."

Mabel couldn't help smiling. This was a wonderful, unexpected perk. Here, she was a youngster.

"I'll take you around personally during the social time." He motioned her toward the pocket door. A murmur of voices, mostly female, drifted out from the room ahead.

Mabel couldn't resist grabbing a savory pastry and a couple of cream puffs. "I didn't have time for dinner," she explained, popping the pastry into her mouth.

Darwin winked. "I don't blame you. They're always my favorite part of the meetings, and whatever's left over will be my dinner for the weekend."

A chandelier, fringed floor lamp, and several leaded-glass table lamps shed warm light over the living room. Gas flames leapt on the hearth of a fireplace fronted with mustard and sea-green art deco tiles. Firelight flickered across the deep recesses of the ceiling beams and reflected in the glass doors of built-in bookcases.

What a beautiful, welcoming room. Was this where it had happened? Mabel's eyes instinctively went to a graceful upholstered couch against the end wall. Wasn't Walter Sauer, Sr. found lying on a sofa, in his own blood? Surely, this couldn't be the same one...? She supposed they might have had the upholstery cleaned.

Somebody cleared his throat, and Mabel looked away from the couch. The room was set up with three rows of chairs, most of them unoccupied. Mabel counted nine gray heads, not including Darwin's. Every head had turned as she walked in. There were three men and seven women.

Mabel froze as she looked to the front of the room. She recognized the skinny woman—who bore an unfortunate resemblance to Miss Gulch—now standing at the podium in what appeared to be blue-gray silk. Eyeglasses dangled from her neck on a chain, tangling in a pearl necklace.

Tentatively, Mabel took a backward step. Was it too late to flee?

Madam President slammed her gavel. "This meeting of the Medicine Spring Historical Society is now called to order."

She focused a sharp eye on Mabel and Darwin. "Will everyone please be seated." It wasn't a question.

Mabel was forced to slide in, leaving Darwin in the seat blocking the aisle. Now there'd be no escaping till the meeting was over. Her heart sank.

Chapter Four

WHY HADN'T SHE THOUGHT TO CHECK who ran the historical society? The president was that vindictive Elmira Gulch—Helen Thornwald, Mabel's vindictive backyard neighbor.

Helen, who looked to be in her mid-eighties, was thin and wiry. She still rode her robin-egg blue bike to the Sauer House in her Nordstrom dresses, massive Coach purse in the basket—and a bell that had scared the spit out of Mabel a time or two. She'd hated Grandma for decades and made it known she was prepared to report Mabel's overgrown yard and peeling paint and carry the feud into the next generation.

Saying Barnacle had "menaced" her was insanity. "And your little dog too," Mabel cackled under her breath.

"Hmm?" Darwin whispered, and the gavel banged again.

Mabel sealed her lips and shook her head.

The meeting proceeded through committee reports. The big issue confronting the group seemed to be the Sauer House, which the family had gifted to the society upon Sauer daughter Violet's death some twenty years before, but with limited funds for maintenance.

Darwin, the treasurer, presented the problem. "Winter is fast approaching," he warned, "and we need to prioritize repairs. The northwest corner bedroom, as well as furniture and other materials stored in the attic, are particularly vulnerable to damage."

Mabel sat through a long and doleful discussion of roof leaks, old wiring, raccoons in the attic, and a flood-prone basement. Any idiot, in her humble opinion, should realize this small group of golden agers could never manage to keep this place up on their own. A handful of paying visitors per year, a few donations from local businesses and the members themselves, a bake sale or a society cookbook weren't going to cut the mustard.

Mabel's hand inched upward. She coughed and looked around, as others turned and stared. "Um, if I might...?"

The gavel banged down. "Out of order. The business portion of this meeting is open to members only."

Mabel stood. "Excuse me. I'm Mabel Browne. My grandmother was also Mabel Browne. I have a suggestion."

Darwin gestured at Mabel. "Ms. Browne is interested in joining the society, Helen. Might I introduce her to the floor to offer her suggestion?"

"That is highly irregular."

To Mabel's surprise, a supportive murmur rose around her. She realized people's fondness for Grandma was in her favor.

"Let the girl speak," a deep female voice bellowed from the front row, and the gavel banged again.

"Cora Barkham, you're out of order."

"Oh, blow it out your nose." the deep voice snapped.

Bang.

Helen Thornwald fixed Mabel with a glare. "The chair recognizes *you*, Miss Browne." Her tone conveyed a clear warning.

Mabel shifted her feet. Why had she gotten herself into this? "Thank you. That is, I've been sitting here listening, and it's obvious you guys need a lot more money than you're able to bring in through the usual means."

All eyes were on her.

"Anyway, I'm thinking you're not taking full benefit of the resource you're sitting on. How many paid tours do you do in a year? A few walk-ins, a few groups, an annual school or Scout trip. What most people are interested in, though, are the ax murders. You need to play that up. Do a murder mystery event, a candlelight tour on the anniversary, maybe call in a ghost team..."

Mabel had been about to mention souvenirs, but her voice trailed off at the sound of several people sucking in their breath.

"Never." Helen's voice shook. "This is an historic jewel of American Craftsman architecture. This house was the residence of a leading businessman of the early twentieth century and his family. Cheap sensationalism has no place here."

"Now, Helen," Darwin cajoled. "I'm sure Mabel meant no harm. You know I've suggested a few things along that line, as well. The murders were tragic but a genuine part of our history."

"As long as I'm alive, my grandfather's name won't be dragged through the dirt merely to stick a few new shingles on the roof."

Mabel hadn't put it all together. Helen was a Sauer—her late mother had been Violet. Helen was the granddaughter of the ill-fated Walter Sauer, Sr.—the first ax murder victim. Her Aunt Edna had been tried for the murders.

"I'm so sorry," Mabel mumbled, sinking back into her chair.

The atmosphere had curdled again. It was clear others, while not as hostile as Helen, were shocked by Mabel's suggestion. She heard a few tongue clicks.

For the rest of the meeting, Mabel remained quiet, while Helen made much of an upcoming tour group. It seemed foolish, struggling to hold this money pit together and scrabbling for occasional tours, rather than tapping into the biggest resource they had.

They'd never let her join now. Maybe she didn't want to, either. If she wasn't welcome, she had a long list of other volunteer possibilities.

After the business meeting, a brisk, angular woman in a teal sweater set and gray slacks strode to the podium. She pushed back her salt-and-pepper bob and adjusted steel-rim glasses. While Darwin operated the projector, the woman offered a slide talk on local cemeteries.

This portion of the program, at least, offered a modicum of entertainment. Best of all, people focused on the screen and stopped staring at Mabel.

When the program concluded, Mabel joined in the smattering of applause. As the audience made a genteel stampede for the dining room, the cemetery lady waved and headed toward Mabel.

She stuck out a hand and shook with a surprising grip. "Nanette McKean—the membership committee chair. Glad you're thinking of joining us. We're like most local organizations these days—graying and dwindling." She ran a hand through her hair.

There was no graceful way for Mabel to say she was having second thoughts. She cleared her throat, darting a longing glance toward the refreshment table. "Um, yes, the thing is…"

Nanette clasped Mabel's hands, pressing them in a sort of over-friendly finger panini. She leaned in and whispered, "Don't pay attention to all that. Helen's always had a bee in her bonnet over the 'incident.' You aren't the first to suggest we be more open to presenting that aspect of the house's history. In a tasteful manner." She gave Mabel a significant look.

"Oh, of course," Mabel agreed.

"We do have a display in the parlor." Nanette nodded toward the second pocket door. "Your grandmother was instrumental in having that put together, along with Cora and Darwin. The room is kept locked at all times, however." She shook her head. "Helen deplores curiosity-seekers."

"Yes, I understand. Her grandfather and all that."

"Yes. Quite so." With a last squeeze, Nanette released her grip on Mabel's fingers. "Now, come right over here, and I'll give you a membership application."

She led the way to a small office set in the corner, sweeping Mabel along in her tail wind. Half the room was taken up with a desk and files, the other with racks of books and postcards and a tiny table with baskets of keychains and similar souvenirs.

"Used to be a butler's pantry," Nanette explained. "With pass-throughs from the kitchen to the dining room on one side and the living room on the other. One for serving meals and one for tea and the after-dinner drinks."

She rooted through a file drawer and pulled out two one-page forms. "I'm giving you an extra application for a friend—or in case something happens to the first one and you need a do-over. If you do it now, though, I can take that before we lock up tonight."

She jiggled Mabel's hand again. "We're so happy to have dear Mabel's granddaughter with us. She was well loved. Such an asset to the group, as I'm sure you will be."

Raised voices drifted from the dining room, drawing Nanette's attention and sparing Mabel a reply. It sounded as if Helen had gotten into a tangle with the booming-voiced woman.

"Oh, dear." Nanette ushered Mabel out and locked the office door. She hurried toward the squabble with Mabel trailing. "Helen and Cora have a few issues."

Mabel hoped there were still cream puffs on the table.

Chapter Five

AS NANETTE PLUNGED INTO THE MILLING cluster of gray heads, Mabel sidled to the table and loaded a plate with goodies. Though somewhat picked over, there were still plenty for her to fill the tiny plate to overflowing.

"I refuse to discuss it," Helen was saying. "Now, if you want to discuss family skeletons—"

"Why, you horse-faced, gossip-mongering—"

Helen's narrow mouth lifted in a tight smile. "Why, I'm sure I said nothing about *you*, Cora dear."

Cora, a formidable brick wall of a woman in a pink-and-lime Lilly Pulitzer dress, thrust her face right into Helen's. "It's ugly, no matter who you're talking about, Helen. Let me remind you my son-in-law is an attorney. There are still libel laws in this state."

Mabel raised her eyebrows. Casting a glance over her shoulder, she eased back against the built-in waist-high cabinet where the tea and coffee were located. She helped herself to a cup of coffee and set it down.

She sighed as she bit into a shortbread cookie with a sugar and crushed-hazelnut crust. She had a good view of the fight here. It was oddly reassuring to see Helen attacking somebody else. Maybe her burning dislike for Mabel wasn't personal. Maybe that was just the way she was.

Nanette pushed herself between the women, clucking like a mother hen. The rest of the crowd, Mabel noticed, seemed divided between dismay and nervous amusement.

Although Nanette succeeded in opening up space between them, Cora was breathing fire. Her mottled-red face and neck clashed with the

Lilly Pulitzer. "Believe me. I'm not afraid to sue."

Helen maintained her superior sneer. She raised her teacup to chin height, paused, and said, projecting enough for everyone to hear, "Truth is a defense." Then, she elevated her pinky and sipped.

It took Nanette and Darwin, combined, to hold Cora back. Finally, she shook them both off, the way a horse might flick away a couple of flies.

Setting her dessert down with a rattle, Cora turned and spat, "If your grandfather was anything like you, it's no wonder somebody bumped him off."

A gasp ran through the group, and Helen lunged at Cora, but Nanette and Darwin caught her as Cora flounced off toward the hall.

Mabel dusted powdered sugar from her lips and pulled out her steno pad. Apparently, there was more potential excitement in being a historical society volunteer than she'd anticipated. Feeling inspired, she began scribbling a few notes.

After a few seconds of tense silence, the general chatter resumed.

"Another sip of tea, Helen?" Nanette held out a cup.

Helen ran a hand over her forehead. "Thank you, dear. I have such a headache. That dreadful woman."

In that moment, Helen's eyes locked onto Mabel and she pointed a bony finger at her. "You brought this on."

Helen advanced, ignoring the proffered tea. "Well, well, missy. Aren't you moving right in where your grandmother left off?"

She cast a glance at Mabel's untouched sandwich cookies then turned with an audible sniff. "You've obviously inherited her skill in the kitchen…along with that hillbilly hideaway you call home."

Mabel's fists clenched. "My grandmother was sick," she choked out. "It wasn't her fault things got a bit run down. As I'm sure you already know."

Helen sniffed. "Not that it made any difference."

Nanette stepped between them as Mabel clenched her fists.

"Now, Helen, you don't mean that." Nanette patted Helen's hand.

"You've had a trying evening."

Helen peered around Nanette to stab Mabel with her eyes. "I've already told you, young lady, and I'm warning you again. I'm sure I'm getting all manner of rats and cockroaches and other vermin from your unkempt property, and that will stop. I've notified the township, and they will be sending an agent to inspect. If you want to avoid a condemnation order, you'd better start an immediate clean-up. And lock up that dangerous animal before they get there, or they'll be confiscating him, as well."

Mabel sputtered, but Nanette continued to block her, and Darwin placed a calming hand on her shoulder.

"You're lucky I'm a compassionate woman." Helen spat the words. "I should already have reported your dog. The next time he appears on my property, I will do so."

She turned to Darwin and handed him a key ring. "Would you be so kind as to warm up my car, dear? These cold evenings are so hard on my sciatica."

Darwin gave Mabel a wry smile and obediently headed outside. Helen swept past in his wake. "I'll go fetch my wrap and be waiting in the foyer, if you would please bring the car around to the front curb…?" Behind her, the group started breaking up, collecting plates and coats, and carrying the coffee and teapots into the kitchen.

"I'm so sorry." Nanette placed a gentle hand on Mabel's arm. "I must apologize for Helen. She wasn't herself tonight." She darted a quick glance around and whispered with a little giggle, "Or I suppose I should say she was a bit *excessively* herself."

"I'm wondering if it's going to be a big problem for her if I join the group."

"Oh, no. That's just Helen. She has her little hot buttons, but she loves the society, and she loves this house. She knows we need more members—particularly younger members—if we're going to survive."

After Cora's and Helen's departure, the tension in the air dropped the way a headache vanishes after the ibuprofen kicks in. Several people stopped to welcome Mabel and say nice things about Grandma Mabel.

Nanette convinced Mabel to sit back down and fill out the application. Nanette pointed at boxes to check for membership, tour guide, front desk and gift shop, and so on. "You can leave that section blank, unless you know now what you're interested in doing, volunteer-wise."

"Are you ladies about ready to lock up?" Darwin jingled keys.

Mabel picked up the plastic grocery bag, still full of chocolate-orange sandwich cookies. Maybe it was a bit embarrassing, but she wasn't all that sorry to have a good supply of one of her favorite cookies, all to herself.

"I'll give you a call in the next few days," Nanette told her, "and we'll set you up with a job. If it isn't to your liking, we can always try something else."

She handed Mabel a folder. "We haven't had a new member join in so long that I haven't had to make up packets in quite a while. This was the last one, so I guess I'll need to do up a couple more."

Darwin opened the front door. "How old is that packet?" He looked back at Nanette. "Does it have…?"

"Yes, it does." She turned to Mabel. "The account of the murders. Perhaps you'll find that interesting."

Mabel didn't want to read about the murders before bed. But next day, she typed up her notes about the meeting and pondered. Maybe she should try all the different jobs at the historical society, if she was going to write this book. She could talk to Nanette about that.

She was a bit worried by Helen's threats regarding the township. Her property wasn't that bad, was it?

Mabel looked around her. The clean-up was going to be a lot of work, though, and she hardly knew where to begin. The yard was beyond her. She made a mental note to call somebody—or at least, look for someone to call.

Starting the clean-up, however, didn't appeal at the moment. That afternoon, she took Barnacle for a walk then settled in to read the murder account. But for a few small details, the information tracked what Grandma Mabel had told her, though she did learn a few new things.

Despite its now being ancient history, the account still gave Mabel chills. The gruesome murders had happened right here in Medicine Spring, mere yards from where she now sat—alone, except for her animals.

She fell asleep on the couch at some point, and around three that afternoon, the ringing of her cellphone woke her. Barnacle lay across her legs, which felt paralyzed.

Mmpphh. She reached around for the phone, finally finding it wedged in the cushions under a purring Koi.

"H'lo," she mumbled.

"Mabel? Thank the Lord. This is Nanette."

Still sleep-muddled, Mabel searched her memory banks.

"From the historical society."

Mabel pulled herself upright. "Oh, yeah. Hi."

"This is an emergency."

"What? Are you all right?" She fumbled for her shoes.

"Yes. It isn't that. It's that bus group we have arriving at four. Helen was scheduled to lead the tour, but she hasn't shown up, and I haven't been able to reach her."

"Oh, dear." Mabel's thoughts raced. "Do you want me to go check her house?"

"We don't have time before the bus arrives. I've already asked Sally Godwin to run over and check on her, since Sally is too hard of hearing to lead the tour herself."

Mabel rubbed her eyes and yawned. "I hope she's all right. Is there something else you need me to do?"

"Yes." Nanette blew out an audible breath. "I need you to lead the tour."

Chapter Six

"YOU NEED ME TO WHAT?"

Nanette sighed. "I forgot to take that new member packet for copying last night, so I stopped to grab it a moment ago. Helen wasn't here and neither was her bike. I'm over here right now, but I have a doctor's appointment at 4:30. I've waited months to get in and I cannot reschedule. You and Darwin live the closest, but I haven't been able to reach him, either. He doesn't believe in cellphones, which makes it unbelievably inconvenient for the rest of us."

Mabel heard the stress in Nanette's voice, but at the moment, she was feeling an enormous amount of stress herself. "I can't. Couldn't somebody else get there by four? I don't know the first thing about the Sauers or their house, beyond what I read in the packet last night."

"I'm sorry. I know it's a lot to ask. But I can't keep calling and hoping. I need to know I have someone ready to do this. You're the closest and youngest. You don't need to know anything special. There's an information sheet you can read from. Please, Mabel."

It had been a long time since Mabel had felt this needed. Well, she had planned to try "all the jobs," and this was one of them. "What do I need to do?"

"Oh, thank you." Relief oozed over the line. "Please get here as soon as possible. I'll give you the basics and show you how to set the alarm and lock up when you leave."

Mabel scrambled to splash her face and brush her teeth and hair. What should she wear? She pulled out the black jeans again, thinking maybe that could be her new uniform.

Barnacle went to the back door and scratched. Koi sat by her dish and meowed.

"You guys," she muttered. "You're hours early and I'm in a rush here."

Nevertheless, she hustled Barnacle out then dumped food into the dishes. Taking care of the animals' afternoon expectations now was for the best anyway, in case the tour ran late.

She locked her door at 3:30 on the dot. Barnacle stood at the back door and barked, and Koi jumped onto the back of the couch to watch her leave.

When she got to the Sauer House, Nanette's car sat at the curb. Mabel found her pacing by the front door.

Nanette pulled her inside. "You're a lifesaver. Here, let me show you what you need to know."

"No news about Helen then?"

Nanette shook her head. "Frankly, I'm worried."

"I'm sure she's okay." Though Mabel felt obliged to try to reassure Nanette, she couldn't imagine what might have detained Helen this long. "Hopefully, the person you sent to check on her will let you know soon."

"I hope so too." Nanette gave herself a little shake. "Here." She thrust a laminated sheet at Mabel. "I'm sorry I don't have much time, but this should give you enough of the basics to get you through the tour."

Mabel scanned the sheet. Bullet points corresponding with various rooms and architectural features covered both sides.

"I know it seems awfully dry, but I usually share a few little anecdotes to help liven things up a bit." Nanette quickly ran through the stories and suggested some natural points in the tour for Mabel to work them in.

"And I know you'll be asked—go ahead and tell them the basics of the Sauer murders early on. Helen wouldn't approve, but she isn't here. This is a true crime club, and you might have a riot on your hands if you don't at least answer questions."

Thanks to Grandma—and the new-member packet—Mabel knew

a *lot* about the murders. She shivered.

The group had paid in advance, Nanette told her. All Mabel had to do was make a head count and keep track of them in the house.

"Don't let them touch anything, for goodness sake," Nanette emphasized. "Or wander off where they aren't permitted. There are alarms set to go off if anyone comes close to the off-limit areas."

Fifteen minutes later, Nanette was gone. Mabel was alone in the ax murder house.

The little creaks and groans, which probably happened all the time and went unnoticed when other people were there, sounded loud in the silence. Mabel jumped at a small click before taking a deep, calming breath.

The shadows were already lengthening, spreading from the corners like grasping arms.

"Stop it." Mabel stomped around, turning on every light in the first-floor public rooms.

Moving around helped a little, as did the light. This was a beautiful old house. The Sauer family had lived here in peace, for years after the murders. Nothing else bad had happened here ever since, right?

All the same, Mabel positioned herself in a chair near the front door. Just in case.

Though she was nervous, Mabel felt a certain relief when at last she heard the babble of voices outside. She wouldn't be alone in here anymore.

Mabel opened the door, fixing a smile on her face. "Welcome to Sauer House."

The group filed into the entryway, all smiles and excited conversation. They looked like retirees, apart from a late thirties/early forties ash blonde in a purple tunic, black tights and boots, and a balding man in a bus driver's uniform.

"I'm going to stay with the bus out there." The driver hiked a thumb. "Am I okay to sit at the curb?"

Mabel directed him around the side of the building, where there was parking space for the occasional tour bus. He left with a Styrofoam cup of scorched-smelling coffee from the pot in the kitchen, which somebody had no doubt brewed hours ago.

Mabel corralled her flock of chicks and ran through the ground rules, bearing down particularly on not touching anything. She did a quick head count and was relieved to find it matched the number Nanette had given her.

"If you'll come this way, please?" Mabel pointed through the open pocket door. "We'll step into the living room for a short introduction. Please sit on the folding chairs, rather than the antique furnishings."

As the group shuffled and jostled its way into the room, a few rubberneckers paused to take pictures, holding up others behind them. "Could we please keep moving so we can get started?" Mabel asked. "We'll have lots of time for that later."

Several people ignored her, as if they hadn't even heard her. Clustered around the couch, they chattered, pointed, and snapped more pictures.

"This is it, right?" A man pointed at the couch. "Where Walter, Sr. got killed?"

"What?" Mabel wove her way over to them and began tugging them away from the couch. It probably wasn't kosher tour-guide etiquette, but she had to get control of these nosy tourists. "No. The murders didn't occur in this room, people. Now sit down. I'm about to begin, and you don't want to miss anything."

"But it was on the couch, right?" A man in pants belted near his armpits leaned down to peer more closely, as if looking for telltale blood stains.

"There's another parlor." A blue-haired, round little woman in a lilac polyester pantsuit tapped his arm. "There's a floor plan in this book." She rummaged through a "Save the Whales" tote bag.

Mabel had already lost control of her tour. "If we'll all take a seat, I'll be happy to tell you a bit about the murders," she bellowed.

Blue Hair gave her a dirty look. "There's no need to shout, young woman."

"Is the couch still here?" the blonde asked. "I'm sure it was removed as evidence, but—"

Mabel had had enough. Pulling out her airhorn keychain, she sounded a short blast.

Everyone jumped, including Mabel. Somebody screamed. Too late, Mabel realized even a tiny airhorn wasn't appropriate for indoor use.

"Sit down." Mabel glared, blaming every one of them for the ringing in her ears. "Please."

Giving Mabel a variety of glowers, the group members who'd been milling around sat. "You'll have to speak up." High Pants fiddled with his ear. "I think you blew out my hearing aid."

"I'm sorry," Mabel told them. "I can't imagine why that went off like that."

"Maybe if you try real hard you can figure it out," Blue Hair said meanly.

Mabel flushed. "Welcome to the Sauer House," she repeated.

"What?" several people asked.

Oh, good grief. Now she'd deafened them and would have to shout the entire time. Mabel wished she had a lapel mike. Or a bullhorn.

"Welcome!" Her throat would be raw by the end of this tour if she had to keep projecting like this. "The Sauer House was constructed in 1913, by local dry-goods merchant Walter Sauer, Sr., for his bride Margarethe. It's built in a variant style considered to be part of the American Craftsman or Arts & Crafts movement, with Prairie influences."

Several hands went up. Mabel knew very little about architecture, and in fact, had never even heard of American Craftsman or Arts & Crafts style before reading her new member packet. All she knew about the Prairie school of architecture was Frank Lloyd Wright had more or less invented it—and that he hadn't designed the Sauer mansion, which was a sort of local concoction. She placed her information sheet on the podium and hoped the answers were somewhere on there.

"Yes." She pointed to a petite seventy-something Asian woman in a pink tracksuit, because she hadn't given Mabel trouble yet.

The woman stood. "The house is very nice. But I'm sure I speak for all of us when I say we're most interested in learning more about the tragic 1939 murders. Feel free to skip ahead."

All right, Mabel thought grimly. If that was what they wanted, she'd give them what they asked for. Nonetheless, they were going to get the rest of the tour she was responsible for, whether they wanted it or not. "Look. My job is to tell you about the house and the Sauer family. Does anybody here want to hear about those things?"

A few hands crept to shoulder height and drifted back down. Perhaps they were being polite.

"Let's do it this way. First, I'll give you the rundown on the ax murders, and then, we'll take the regular house tour. If you promise to behave and listen to the historic stuff, I promise to keep the house history brief. I'll also tell you something you might not know—about how the Prairie school of architecture and Frank Lloyd Wright himself relate to the horrific events that occurred here."

Chapter Seven

A GENERAL MURMURING WENT THROUGH THE tour group. Mabel frowned. If those fakers could hear each other whispering, they could surely understand what she was saying without her shouting. She began to have a bit of sympathy for her seventh-grade homeroom teacher, who'd needed to leave in the middle of the first semester.

"We agree to your terms," the tracksuit woman told her. "A few of us are new to the group and not as familiar with the basic events, so that might provide a good orientation for them. But we'll need to hear the new information about the Frank Lloyd Wright connection *before* the tour."

Mabel was about to refuse, but Tracksuit Lady added, "That will help us get the most out of the tour, I'm sure."

"Oh, all right. Can you all hear me?"

Every hand went up, including Hearing Aid Guy, who seemed to have experienced a miraculous recovery.

"We have a deal." Mabel referred to the laminated sheet Nanette had furnished. "Here's what happened. Walter and Margarethe Sauer married in 1912 and started their marriage in a Victorian house, which is still in the family and sits back there." She gestured toward the house now occupied by the insufferable Sauer granddaughter, Helen.

"In 1913, they moved into this house, which Walter had built for his bride. Their children, Walter, Jr., Edna, and Violet, were all born here. Margarethe's health was always fragile, and particularly after the birth of her children, she spent much time in her bedroom. Junior went into business with his father. Violet married in 1935 and had a three-year-old daughter Helen, at the time of the murders. Edna, the older Sauer daughter, didn't marry and lived here with her parents and brother.

"In October 1939, Edna made the bone-chilling discovery of her father's and brother's bodies, both brutally murdered with an ax-like implement. Walter, Sr. was found lying on the couch in the parlor." Mabel gestured at the locked door behind her.

"Like Andrew Borden." Blue Hair sat up. "The parallels with the Lizzie Borden case are inescapable."

Mabel cleared her throat. "Yes, anyway, Walter, Jr. was found on the floor near his father's body, with similar injuries, except with apparent defensive wounds."

"So Father was probably caught napping, but Junior fought back," High Pants said. He and Blue Hair exchanged nods. Mabel had their full attention now.

"Edna was suspected from the beginning." Mabel frowned. "She didn't have much of an explanation as to where she was when the murders occurred—only that she'd been out for a walk, though she was vague as to where. Margarethe was in the house but heard nothing from her room—possibly her pain medicine had knocked her out.

"In the spring of 1940, Edna was brought to trial, but the court of public opinion was already in full session. Newspapers back then could get away with inflammatory statements, more so than today."

Mabel scowled. "The Medicine Spring paper figured Edna for the murderer from day one. Basically, because she was older and unmarried and wouldn't put on a phony sweet face for the public. Just because she didn't fall apart the way her mother and sister did."

Mabel noticed a few sideways looks from the audience. As an older, unmarried sister herself, who could be ever so slightly blunt on occasion, maybe she *was* a tad biased in Edna's favor.

"But the city papers reserved judgment, and as the trial progressed, public opinion evened out a bit. Edna had the best defense lawyer from Pittsburgh. All the evidence against her was circumstantial. Her lawyer made a lot of hay with testimony from Margarethe, who was too ill to appear in court but gave her sworn deposition from her bed. She testified she'd seen a strange man lurking around the property in the weeks before the murders. Ultimately, there weren't enough votes to convict."

The blonde raised her hand. "Where does Frank Lloyd Wright come in?" She clicked her pen, poised above her steno pad.

"That's a terribly sad and seemingly little-known story." Mabel felt a twinge of guilt that she relished telling the group something compelling that they didn't know, even if it was something horrible.

"Frank Lloyd Wright was a married man when he fell in love with a client's wife, Mamah Borthwick. Their affair was a big national scandal, but when he built his Wisconsin home Taliesin, Mamah and her children moved in with him. Three years later, while Wright was away in Chicago, Mamah sent an urgent telegram, asking him to come home, because 'something terrible' had happened. What that was we'll never know. Did she even send the message herself?

"Later that day, while Mamah, her children, and six others—mostly employees—were eating lunch, a butler locked them in, poured gasoline around the dining room doors, and set fire to the building. He'd left one window unlocked, and when the frantic victims tried to escape, he was waiting to attack them with an ax. Only two survived—Mamah and her children did not."

Everyone began talking at once, and hands shot up all over the room. As flattering as their reaction was, they needed to get on with the tour. Mabel held up her hands. "That was nothing more than a curious and disturbing link between the Sauer mansion and a more famous Prairie house. You can find the rest of the story online or in the library, but right now, we need to continue the tour if we're going to finish on time."

Amid a bit of grumbling and a lot of chattering, Mabel got the group moving. They followed noisily, as she lectured about ceiling beams and colonnades as if she knew what she was talking about.

"Can we take pictures?" someone asked, though flashes had been going off pretty much constantly.

"Go for it."

She showed them the upstairs bedrooms. Margarethe's remained unchanged, but the group seemed more interested in Edna's room, and the victims'.

"Is the house haunted?" Blue Hair asked.

"I'm getting orbs in these photos." Tracksuit stared down at her camera.

Oh, please—she's got to be kidding. Mabel rolled her eyes but remembered to be diplomatic. "Not to my knowledge."

By the time Mabel fought her way back down to the first floor, several of the group had beaten her there. "Is this where the murders happened?" High Pants gestured at the closed pocket door.

"Oh, don't touch that." Mabel reached out as the blonde took the door pull. "We keep it locked."

But no alarm sounded, and the door slid back, smooth as a well-oiled zipper. The rest of the group stampeded for a look at the murder room. "Stop," Mabel ordered, even though she was the tiniest bit curious herself.

While she was still pushing her way to the door, somebody screamed.

A few of the women and High Pants came charging back at Mabel, but Blue Hair and Tracksuit shoved their way on into the parlor. Mabel fought her way in behind them.

The blonde had dropped her steno pad from a limp hand. She stared down at the period rug with its geometric pattern of cream, rust, and jade. A body lay there, blood spreading outward, staining the carpet.

Suddenly, Mabel knew why Helen hadn't shown up to lead the tour.

She lay face down, in a stunning pearl-gray crepe suit with matching pumps—one on, one off at this point. Her perfect coiffure, now bloodstained like the gray suit, rested matted on the rug.

Chapter Eight

MABEL SWALLOWED HARD AND TRIED TO take deep, calming breaths. Her heart pounded in her ears, and she felt sick and dizzy, looking down at Helen. They'd never let Mabel lead another tour.

Still, she was in charge right now, and Helen needed help. Mabel knelt and tentatively touched her wrist, planning to feel for a pulse. As soon as her fingers brushed that solid, cold flesh, however, she knew Helen was beyond CPR.

"Is she…?" The blonde, having scooped her steno pad back up, crept over for a better look.

Mabel tried to speak but could only nod.

Lights flashed. Mabel spun around. Blue Hair and Tracksuit were taking crime scene photos.

She scrambled to her feet. "What's wrong with you people? Get back."

Tracksuit took another quick shot then started backing up, sharp eyes scanning the room. "There's nothing wrong with us." Blue Hair lifted her chin. "We're trying to help, not being morbid."

"We study true crime." Hearing Aid inched into the room as the women backed out, still craning for a better look. "We might be able to help solve this."

"Oh, good grief." Mabel pushed forward. "Get out and let me lock this door till the police can get here."

She shoved the last two women out of the room. As she closed the door, she cast one last searching look around the room, trying to understand what on earth had happened. Had Helen fallen and hit her head? She knew head wounds could bleed profusely.

Mabel realized, as the door clicked shut, that in her state of shock and agitation, she'd forgotten all about fingerprints. Both she and the blonde had already touched the handle, so they'd probably messed up any possible prints. She thought of trying to secure the door, but it had an old-fashioned lock that required a key. A key she didn't have. Her hands shook so hard she had to clasp them together.

When she turned, the group was milling like a herd of agitated cattle. A few would-be crime scene investigators chattered, while others stood apart, quiet and green-looking. She realized she was missing people.

"Hey!" Mabel cupped her hands into a makeshift megaphone. "Everybody take a seat." She pointed to Blue Hair, sitting in the closest seat. "Start counting off, please."

Three people were missing. This was bad.

Hearing Aid started getting up.

"Whoa." Mabel caught his arm. "Where do you think you're going?"

"I have a bad prostate."

"You." She pointed at a somewhat younger, middle-aged man— one of the nervous, sick-looking people who'd been silently huddling. "Buddy system. Please accompany this gentleman to the facilities then come right back here."

For a split second, it looked like he was about to argue with her, but then, he seemed to decide he wasn't going to win this one. Heaving a sigh and shooting Mabel a resentful glance, he got up and gestured for Hearing Aid to lead the way.

Just then, a portly woman in "mom" jeans and sequined jack-o-lantern sweatshirt came in, shaking her hands as if to dry them. One runaway, apparently another potty-breaker, accounted for.

"The rest of you, please stay where you are." Mabel pulled out her phone and dialed 911, stepping into the entryway, away from her audience.

Within a couple of minutes, she'd managed to stammer her way through an account of what was going on. The dispatcher promised the closest available unit would be there in a few minutes.

The front door opened, and the blonde walked in.

Mabel grabbed her. "Please go sit back down while we wait for the police. Where were you?"

The blonde peered over a pair of tortoiseshell glasses. "I ran out to the bus for my tote." She jiggled the bag at Mabel. "I needed more batteries for my voice recorder."

Mabel gripped her arm and escorted the woman to her seat. "Exactly what are you recording?" she hissed in the blonde's ear.

"Why, your tour, of course." Her innocent smile looked more like a smirk.

"Interesting, since the tour is over."

"I thought since we have nothing to do but wait around, you might have more to say."

Mabel looked at her tour group. Even if she had more to say, she'd never regain control of this babbling crowd of would-be crime-solvers.

She drew a deep breath. Heaven help her, she was still responsible for them.

Someone cleared his throat. The bus driver hesitated in the doorway, twisting his hat. "Excuse me…?"

Heads turned.

"We're expected back at the garage, and we need to board now."

"I'm sorry, but you can't. There's been a d—an emergency. We have to wait for the police."

The driver began to protest. In the middle of the room, a hand went up. "Several of us do need to get home. We still have an hour-and-a-half drive, and people will be waiting to pick us up at the bus garage in Wilkie."

Someone else spoke, not bothering to raise a hand first. "We're supposed to eat at the Old Country Buffet by the turnpike ramp. I have diabetes. I need to eat."

This group was a regular barrel of monkeys. Mabel plowed a hand through her hair. "Look. You cannot leave. Nobody can leave. I'm an attorney."

A few suspicious looks flitted over her.

"Trust me. The police will be here any minute." She dug in her pocket and handed the diabetic a handful of her emergency fruit chews. "Here, take these. If you need more, I can get you a few crackers in a moment. I'm sure this won't take long."

Then, she focused on the driver. "You'd better radio your dispatcher or whatever you do in a situation like this."

"Ma'am, we don't generally have situations like this."

"Perfect. That means this is a special situation, right? Call in and explain."

"Explain what? What the heck happened in here?"

Mabel drew closer and whispered. "Here's the thing. We have a dead body back there, and—"

"We have a *what*?" The driver peered around her.

"A body." Mabel resisted the temptation to spell.

"It isn't one of mine, is it? What were you people doing in here, anyway? I'm going to catch so much trouble over this."

"No, no. It's one of ours. Mine, I mean. I mean nothing to do with you. You're good here."

"Then why can't we leave? I'm too old for this."

"It's a legal thing. Never mind. Go radio your people, okay?"

"We got cellphones now, lady."

"Whatever. That isn't the issue. Use whatever you've got—flares, ship-to-shore line, Pony Express. Please do as I ask, all right?"

He left, grumbling under his breath—to make that call, she hoped, rather than abandon the lot of these people to Mabel.

Mabel returned to the podium and held up a legal pad she'd pulled from her bag. "I'm going to pass this around and ask you each please write down your name and contact information for the police."

The blonde stood. "Meanwhile, I'll be coming around with my recorder. I'd like each of you to tell me where you were at the time the body was discovered and what you observed."

"No, you won't." Mabel gestured for her to sit. "That's a job for the police. And possibly me," she said, "since I'm a lawyer."

The blonde folded her arms. "You're a tour guide."

"Well, I'm both." Mabel squared her shoulders and glared back at her.

The doorbell screeched.

Mabel scowled at the group, giving the blonde a bit longer glare. "Please stay where you are. That must be the police."

Two officers stood at the door—a tall, skinny young man and a forty-ish woman with short red curls. "You reported a body, ma'am?" The redhead pulled an old-school pad and pen from her pocket.

"Yes, sir, ma'am." Mabel rolled her eyes. "Sorry. Yes, officer. Through here."

As they stepped into the living room, the excited buzz died down. Mabel heard the trailing fragments… "another ax murder," "well, all that blood." Above them all, rose one voice she couldn't pinpoint. "That's why she didn't want us to open that door."

Mabel turned her head, but she only knew the voice had been female. Surely, no one seriously suspected *her*?

"I took the liberty of having everyone write down their names and contact information," Mabel told the redhead, whose name patch read "Sizemore," and who appeared to be a lieutenant.

"Yes, well, let's see what we're dealing with first. Are you sure the individual is deceased?"

Mabel swallowed and nodded. "Yep."

"Did you lock the room?"

"No. I didn't have the key." Mabel slid the door back as the tour group rose to jockey for a better look. Exasperated, Mabel turned to bellow at them, but Sizemore cut in. "Sit." She nodded at the younger officer. "Jerry, would you babysit for a couple of minutes?"

Helen hadn't moved. The pool of blood seemed to have congealed and darkened since Mabel last saw her.

"Maybe she had a heart attack and hit her head on the way down."

Mabel peered at Sizemore with a glimmer of hope. "The corner of that display case looks like it could split your skull."

Sizemore gave Mabel a raised eyebrow and seemed to be trying to control a smirk. "I'm not ready to draw any conclusions here, but there's no blood on that corner that I can see. And from here, this looks to me like a huge neck wound."

She snapped on latex gloves. "Unless this lady managed to fall neck first onto an ax, I'd say we've got a homicide."

Chapter Nine

"LET'S TAKE YOUR NAME AND INFO first, and then, why don't you walk me through what happened?" Sizemore had called for additional backup before dragging in a couple of folding chairs and having Mabel sit for an interview.

Mabel explained about the tour. "They kept wanting to see the murder room, and I—"

"Wait a minute." Sizemore held up a hand. "Why would this tour group—which just arrived from..." She consulted her notes. "How would people who only now arrived from Wilkie know about a murder room?"

Mabel giggled without meaning to. "Not this murder. Not that it's necessarily a murder, you know. But they weren't talking about Helen. This is the Sauer ax murder house, and they wanted to see where the murders took place. In 1939. Not now," she reemphasized.

The proximity of Helen's dead body was unsettling. Mabel shifted in the creaking chair but still saw her in the corner of her eye.

When she'd finished fumbling through her explanation, Sizemore, staring over the top of her glasses, nodded. She made another note.

They had almost finished Mabel's interview by the time the crime scene techs descended.

"Is there something you'd like me to do to help out?" Mabel asked. "I can do interviews, if you like. I'm a lawyer." She strove for a modest smile.

Again, the look over the top of the eyeglasses. "Where do you work? Are you in criminal practice?"

Mabel flushed. "I guess some people thought my work was criminal," she said with a weak grin.

When Sizemore didn't crack a smile, Mabel swallowed. "Um, no."

"Thank you, but we'll handle the police work. You're a witness, and I think we're done with you for now."

Mabel craned her neck for a last look. She'd never gotten to see this room, and now she was being hustled right back out again. Not that she could focus on much else, anyway, with Helen's body right there on the rug, and techs scrambling over everything.

"Oh, one more thing." The officer held up an index finger, as Mabel turned to leave, still scanning as she went. "Are you familiar with what objects belong in this room, the condition, and so on?

Mabel wanted to say "yes" and be able to go over the room before leaving but had to shake her head.

"Do you know who else would be able to do that?"

Mabel gave her both Nanette's and Darwin's names. Then, after a moment's hesitation, she added Cora to the list. "Is it okay for me to call them?" she asked. "Nanette, at least. I was responsible for this tour, and she'll need to know."

Sizemore appeared to reflect for a moment. "Go ahead. But don't give out any more info than the basic 'she's dead,' 'we found her,' 'police called,' etc. Nothing about apparent cause of death, condition of the room, and so on. Understood? You'll compromise our investigation if you start spreading information we'd prefer to withhold for now. Got that? You'll regret it if you violate that, because we *will* find out."

Mabel resisted the impulse to salute. "Yes, ma'am."

She pushed her way back through the group in the outer room, now slumping in chairs under the watchful eye of additional police who seemed to be collecting their information. The young male officer—Jerry?—was in the office interviewing the blonde.

Mabel turned and went back into the murder parlor. She cleared her throat. "I thought you should know—a few people took pictures in here. You should also be aware the blonde in the purple tunic is packing a voice recorder."

Sizemore's eyes widened. "Thanks. We'll look into that. Have a good evening."

That had clearly been a dismissal, so Mabel left.

She waited until she got outside before calling Nanette. Her hands shook so badly by then—maybe due to the situation, and maybe the cold—she made two tries before managing to dial. The wind had picked up, and she wouldn't have been surprised to see a snowflake. She moved to the lee of the bus, now sitting in the pickup zone at the curb.

Mabel took several deep breaths as she waited for the call to ring through. She dreaded telling Nanette.

As soon as Nanette picked up, Mabel launched into her account. She'd barely gotten started, when

Nanette began wailing.

"*What*? Oh, Mabel, this is a disaster. What happened?"

"I don't know. The police put me under a gag order, anyway."

"How did you ever happen to find her?" Nanette asked. "That door is always kept locked."

"Well, the room was open tonight," Mabel told her. "I don't know why."

"Did you take them *in* there?" Tentative disappointment quivered in Nanette's voice.

"Oh, wait a minute—hold up. I don't even have a key. That group was impossible to control. They had an ax-murder bee in their bonnets, and I *told* them not to go near that door. But somebody tried it, and it popped right open. If there's supposed to be an alarm on that door, that sure didn't go off, either."

"That's impossible. No more than a handful of people have keys to that door."

"Maybe Helen opened it herself." The wheels started turning in Mabel's head.

"She wouldn't have gone in there. She'd have no reason to. She hated that room."

"When would she usually arrive when she was doing a tour?"

"Oh, I guess anywhere from twenty minutes to half an hour ahead. She's already done the tour so many times, it isn't like she needed time to prepare. She always wanted to get there early enough to make sure the heat was on, though, if it was a cold day. Drink a cup of tea. Chat with anybody else who was there."

"Hmm... When did you get here? Was anyone else scheduled this afternoon?"

"No, only Helen. In the morning, Darwin came in for a genealogy consultation. I don't know how long he was there. He said he might start taking the air conditioning units out of the windows, if he had enough time. Cora was doing a bit of cataloguing, I think. I got there maybe a quarter till, and they were both gone. I couldn't believe Helen wasn't there yet. Most days, she rides her bike over if the weather's fit, and I didn't see it or her car outside either."

"She got here somehow. Maybe she walked?"

"Maybe."

"Was the door locked?"

"Of course. Even if one of us is in there, we lock it if we're alone. It's a good security precaution. Anybody who wants a walk-in tour can ring the bell."

Hearing Aid came outside, along with the driver. Mabel guessed police were starting to release the witnesses. She moved away from the bus but watched as they approached.

"Hey, Nanette, I've got to go. I need to talk to someone."

"I'm so sorry you got caught up in this. Do you think...could it have been her heart?"

"I don't know for sure what killed her, and I'm not allowed to say more. I imagine the police will be calling you."

"Me?" Nanette's voice rose. "Why? I wasn't even there."

"Tracing her movements, for one thing, I'd guess. Or trying to. Finding out her routine when she was leading a tour. The usual procedures and stuff around here—like with the doors and locks. The room contents. I told them what I know, but that's not much."

Nanette sighed. "Poor Helen. I mean she wasn't always the kindest person, God rest her soul. It was because she was so high strung. So proud of her family. She would do anything to protect the family name and the house, and sometimes that made her a bit short with people."

Mabel stifled a laugh. If Helen was "a bit short," then Genghis Khan had been no more than unmannerly. "Oops." Mabel saw the bus doors open. "Gotta go. We can talk later."

She caught up to Hearing Aid as he was re-boarding. "Excuse me."

Hearing Aid turned, halfway up the steps. "You? I thought the cops sent you home."

"They, uh, did. But I had to stop and make a call, and then, I saw you come out."

He grunted, with a "So what?" kind of expression.

"Do you have any idea how much longer they're going to be in there?"

"I would guess a long time. They're dealing with a full-on dead body."

"That's true." As Mabel glanced back, the front doors of the house opened, and the blonde emerged. It would take a long time to question that many witnesses. She wished they had let her help…but maybe they considered her a suspect. She hoped not.

"How did it go?" Mabel asked the blonde.

Her cheeks were flushed, and her eyes snapped. "Fine. Not that it's any of your business." She took a couple of deep breaths and seemed to collect herself. "Sorry," she told Mabel. "It's been a rough night."

"Tell me about it." The blonde had only been a visitor. At least, she hadn't been responsible for the tour that ran aground on Homicide Reef…and on her maiden voyage, no less.

The blonde stuck out her hand. Mabel shook it.

"Devereaux Reid." As soon as Mabel released her hand, Devereaux dug inside her bag and pulled out a business card.

Mabel held the card beneath the light. Under her name, it read,

"Writer, Author, Speaker." Hmm…maybe Mabel should have cards made. The inscription looked pretty impressive. What should she put on hers?

Devereaux cleared her throat.

Mabel looked up. "Sorry. Nice card."

"I was saying I was shocked to see Mrs. Thornwald like that."

Mabel's eyebrows rose. "You recognized her?"

"I'm working on a true crime book about the Sauer ax murders, and naturally, I contacted the historical society here."

"She gave you an interview?" Mabel failed to keep the disbelief out of her voice.

Devereaux grimaced. "No. I even called ahead. But she was so rude."

Mabel grinned.

"She all but threw me out on my ear. I explained my story would be very respectful, and I wanted the input of a family member, so the account would be well balanced. You'd think, wouldn't you, that if someone's publishing a book about your family, you'd want it to be accurate? Right?"

"Yes, of course," Mabel agreed.

Devereaux leaned closer, as the next batch of witnesses emerged from the house. "She called me a 'cheap gossipmonger.'" Her impression of Helen's enraged screech was spot on, and despite the circumstances, Mabel couldn't hold back another grin.

"It wasn't so funny when she threatened to sue to prevent publication," Devereaux growled.

"Oh, she was going to sue everybody—join the club. But let her try. I mean, not that she can now. She would've been tossed out of court, though." Mabel hesitated. "Unless, of course, you said something defamatory about Helen personally. You didn't, did you?"

"Needless to say. The book isn't even written yet. Say, is that true, what you said? Are you really a lawyer?"

Mabel ignored the insulting question. Her thoughts were turning over what the blonde had said about writing a book on the Sauer case. Devereaux's project made Mabel's idea of writing about volunteer opportunities for seniors seem unimpressive. Plus, this sort of felt like Devereaux was horning in on Mabel's territory, since Mabel was the one who belonged to the historical society and lived right next door...and whose grandmother had lived through the murders.

"Is there money in true crime?"

Devereaux stared at her for a long and awkward moment. "Have you heard of Devil in the White City? In Cold Blood? The Stranger Beside Me?"

Mabel stared back.

"Mega bestsellers," Devereaux told her. "What do you think?"

"I'm also a writer, you know. I was sort of thinking about a book on the Sauer case myself."

At least, I am now.

Devereaux's eyes narrowed. "I thought you were a lawyer."

"A person can be both. Have you heard of John Grisham? William Carlos Williams?"

"I thought Williams was a doctor."

"You grasp my point." Mabel waved an airy hand. "A person can do two things. If you're smart and capable."

"Yes, if...." Devereaux gave her a tight smile. "Well, good luck in your endeavors. I see the last few stragglers coming, so I need to go."

As Mabel watched the last of the tour group boarding, a wave of exhaustion washed over her. She looked back at the house, all lit as if for a party. Emergency vehicles lined both sides of the block—local police cars, an ambulance, the coroner's van, and the county crime tech unit.

Across the street, lights blazed in all three houses, and dogs were barking. Mabel saw moving silhouettes in the windows. It appeared the neighbors were watching the show. She wondered if any of them had a police scanner. They'd know there was a death, anyway, if they could make out the lettering on the coroner's van.

It occurred to Mabel she was responsible for locking up and setting the house alarm. She hesitated, not wanting to incur the wrath of Sizemore, who'd pretty much thrown her out half an hour ago. All she wanted was to go home to her animals and her own sweet bed.

She couldn't afford one more slip-up tonight. It was her first full day as a historical society volunteer, and she'd already let the president die on her watch, failed to brook a tour-group insurrection, and was probably going to get the museum a bunch of bad reviews on Yelp.

Mabel turned reluctant feet back toward the steps. The younger officer who'd been first on the scene stopped her at the door. When she explained about locking up, he told her they'd be handling that, and she should go home to bed. "We'll call if we need you. Otherwise, you can come down tomorrow and sign your official statement."

"Oh, okay. Do you need the key?"

"No, thanks. We'll padlock it."

Mabel nodded. Weariness had settled into her bones. "Make sure the door's locked and the alarm is set, or there's going to be big trouble."

The young man grinned and leaned confidentially toward her. "I believe there already is, ma'am."

Chapter Ten

AS EXHAUSTED AS MABEL WAS, SHE struggled to sleep. The flashing lights in front of the Sauer House strobed across her bedroom curtains. She kept seeing Helen, lying there on the floor.

The image was horrible—all her childhood nightmares come to life. Poor Helen. As miserable as she had been to Mabel, she was nothing more than an unhappy old lady. She didn't deserve this. Nobody did.

Mabel's thoughts kept turning to Sizemore's questions. She supposed they were standard, nevertheless it did make her wonder if she considered Mabel a suspect. That was silly, of course. She'd barely known Helen. Though every time their paths had crossed, the encounter had seemed to end badly.

Mabel flipped her pillow to the cool side. Besides, Helen had always been threatening her—not the other way around. Mabel should be in the clear, right? She was the victim here—nobody could blame her for being Helen's target.

When she fell asleep at last, the nightmares returned. This time, she found herself in Oz. Helen's feet, clad in ruby slippers, protruded from under the Sauer house. Accusing voices surrounded and hammered at her.

She woke, screaming, about 8 AM, when her cell rang. Koi launched off her chest, digging in her claws for maximum lift-off. Mabel scrambled for the phone, but Barnacle was stretched across her legs, both of which were numb.

"Hello," she croaked.

"Cora Barkham here," a voice boomed. "What in heaven's name did you do over here last night? I got to the house this morning and there's police tape all over the place and a padlock on the door. Nanette says you killed Helen."

Had she awakened in Oz?

"Of course not. I'm not in jail, am I?" Mabel forced herself into a sitting position, making Barnacle grunt.

"Don't blame me. The call was breaking up." Cora huffed. "I thought she said you killed Helen. Is she or is she not dead?"

Mabel repressed the impulse to say, "She's really most sincerely dead." She swallowed a nervous giggle, a breath shy of hysteria. "Here's the thing. I was leading the tour around, and somebody opened the murder room door."

"Impossible," Cora barked. "That door is always locked."

"Well, it wasn't last night. And there she was, dead on the floor."

A snort and a sigh. "I warned her and warned her about her sodium intake, but no, she wouldn't listen. Feel bad, you know. We didn't always get along, but the good Lord knows I tried. This was so preventable. She should have cut back to no more than 1500 milligrams a day. That's what my doctor told me, and he's very good."

Mabel's head hurt, and Cora's alto profundo wasn't helping. What's more, Cora had nearly succeeded in convincing Mabel that Helen's sad demise was the result of a runaway salt habit. Maybe that gaping ax wound had nothing to do with it, after all.

The phone vibrated in Mabel's hand. "Cora, I'm so sorry, but I have another call coming in."

As soon as she extricated herself from Cora's dire warnings about her sodium consumption, she found herself on the line with a reporter from the local weekly, The *Medicine Spring Statesman*. She hadn't even gotten out of bed yet.

Mabel thought fast. As a witness, she was under a gag order from the police. More importantly, she wasn't authorized to speak for the historical society.

"You know what? Why don't you call one of these people?" Mabel rummaged around for her volunteer packet and found the contact list.

She read off numbers for Nanette, Darwin, and Cora.

When the reporter pressed her, Mabel cut her short. "No. I'm sorry. No comment."

"Perhaps you could at least tell us a little bit about the deceased...?"

"No," Mabel repeated, keeping her tone firm. That was one topic she was not touching. "Sorry, but I had a difficult night, and I just woke up. I need to go now." In more ways than one.

She managed to get off the phone and onto her feet, though her legs were still shooting pins and needles. She staggered down the hall with Barnacle jumping at her and Koi twining around her ankles.

Frost glittered on the grass when Mabel opened the back door to clip Barnacle to his run. She shivered and wrapped her arms around herself.

Koi had escalated from purring and ankle rubbing to full-on screeches, so Mabel dumped food in her bowl before starting the all-important pot of coffee. While it brewed, she ran for the bathroom.

She was expected at the police station this morning to sign her statement. Ugh.

Before returning to the kitchen, Mabel dug out ibuprofen for her now-raging headache. This, she thought, was the difference between a dead-end legal job and a glamorous writing career. Instead of sitting in a cramped office behind a desk piled with documents, she was now coming upon dead bodies and conferring with the police, like Jessica Fletcher. And, the grim thought intruded, there was no paycheck coming every two weeks, either.

When she opened the kitchen door, Barnacle bounded inside and drank with much noisy slurping, scattering water in every direction. When she set his food down, he did the same with that, shoving his snout into the bowl before she got it anywhere near the floor.

Mabel didn't worry about cleaning up the spill. He'd find every stray kibble within two minutes then polish the floor for her.

She poured a huge mug of coffee and thought about breakfast.

She'd have loved a plate of biscuits and gravy. But since the biscuit fairy didn't deliver, Mabel dumped shredded wheat into a bowl, sniffed the milk carton, shrugged, and added that.

She wished she had a newspaper subscription. The murder had happened early enough that the city daily should have at least initial coverage.

Would Lisa be up? Mabel sighed, looking at the time. Her lifelong best friend, Lisa Benedetti, now taught kindergarten in Medicine Spring, and she started her day obscenely early. Not only would Lisa be out of bed, she'd already be at work, supervising the before-school drop-offs she took care of for working parents.

Mabel texted her the barest details of her horrific night as a historical society volunteer, knowing Lisa would call back when she could. If only Mabel liked children…and didn't mind getting up early. Right now, being a kindergarten teacher seemed like a way better career path than her own had turned out to be.

Munching contentedly, Mabel checked headlines on her phone. She found an article on the daily's website, but it was sketchy and gave her no new information.

In fact, one glaring error was at once apparent. Somehow, they had taken her name down as Maybelle, like the late matriarch of the Carter country music dynasty.

The unauthorized name change hadn't fooled Mabel's family. Her phone vibrated in her hand, with Elvis singing "That's All Right, Mama." Her mother's ringtone.

She sighed.

"Hi, Mom. What's new?"

"You're asking me what's new?" Mom's voice rose. "We get the news here too, Mabel. I can't believe I need to read a newspaper to find out my daughter's involved in a murder."

"A murder *investigation*. There's a difference."

"Whatever. Are you all right? When were you planning to tell me?"

"Mom, I'm fine. I would've called, but the police interview ran long, and then, it was too late. This morning, the phone's been ringing nonstop." She shoved aside her soggy cereal and poured another mug of coffee.

"What on earth happened?"

Mabel wasn't sure whether the gag order applied to eighty-year-old mothers or not. She knew her own mother well enough, however, to realize she was a poor risk for sharing secrets with. She gave her the same short version she'd given Nanette and hoped for the best.

"Do you want us to come up there? Your father is at his Hooked-on Crochet class at the library till eleven, and then the guys go to lunch. We could be there by…oh, 4:30. I could bring you a couple of pies—maybe sweet potato and apple? Would you like that?"

Mabel would definitely love pies. She also loved her parents. But they would further complicate an already complicated situation. She wasn't at all ready to have them delving into her work situation—or see how little progress she'd made on clearing out Grandma's house.

"Mom, I'd love to see you, but right now isn't the best time. I'm fine for now, so don't worry. Maybe we can set something up for my birthday in a couple of weeks—how would that be?"

"Do you need a lawyer?"

"Mom. Of course not. I already know lawyers, remember? The guy I shared a secretary with at the firm used to work for the DA. If I need something, I'll give you a call. Don't worry."

After much persuasion, Mom agreed she and Dad would wait before descending on Mabel. But before she hung up, she whispered, "Will you need money? I know lawyers are awfully expensive…"

"Mother. Thank you, no. I'm fine."

After she hung up, Mabel collapsed. Now that she was unemployed, her mother appeared to think she was destitute. Could she sink much lower?

Chapter Eleven

BY THE TIME MABEL PARKED HER six-year-old Kia in the police visitor lot, it was late morning. Sizemore wasn't on duty. Another officer took her statement and told her they'd be in touch if they needed anything further.

Mabel's few bites of cereal seemed long ago. She checked the time—already past noon—and decided to treat herself to brunch at the Coffee Cup Diner, which served breakfast all day. Now she'd concluded her duties with the police, maybe she could concentrate this afternoon on cleaning out the house and start planning her first volunteer article.

But even as she thought that, she felt with a pang that it was going to be hard to write the peppy sort of fun article she'd envisioned. In the forty-eight hours or so she'd been a historical society volunteer, she'd gone to her first meeting and gotten herself publicly berated by the president, lost control of her first tour group, and discovered the same president's dead body. Making this sound upbeat was going to take a lot of creativity...maybe more than she had.

The diner sat in the middle of the main drag in Medicine Spring, between the High Tone barber shop and Barb's Gift & Candle Nook. The windows were ruffled with brown-and-white gingham curtains and painted with pumpkins and scarecrows.

The bell jingled as she opened the door to a rush of warm air, smelling of bacon and coffee. Laughter and conversation enveloped her.

The diner was crowded, so Mabel took a seat at the counter. Maybe something would open up by the time her breakfast arrived. She didn't have to look at a menu to know she'd be ordering the Farmhand—two eggs, bacon and sausage, one pancake (regular or buckwheat), home fries, and coffee. She realized she should be watching what she ate a little better, but today was not that day.

By the time her food arrived, Mabel was ravenous. Right as she was about to plow into her plates of food, she felt a gentle tap on her shoulder. The touch was so quick and light, a hummingbird might have grazed her shoulder.

"Mabel?"

She turned at the soft voice at her back.

Miss Birdie, an ancient girlhood friend of Grandma Mabel's, smiled at her. She was a wisp of a woman with wrinkled, nut-brown skin, a thin frizz of gray hair, and a tendency to wear the flowered cotton dresses of her youth.

"Miss Birdie. Sit down. Have you had your breakfast?"

"Oh, God bless you, baby." She hopped up onto the high stool, as spry as a sparrow. "I had my breakfast about six this morning, same as always." She grinned and shook her head at Mabel's breakfast plate. "You're so lucky to have a healthy young appetite. Most I ever manage to put away is my bran flakes and prune juice."

Miss Birdie ordered half a chicken salad sandwich on whole wheat, a cup of tomato soup, and iced tea. When she'd placed her order, she rested a dry, weightless hand on Mabel's. "Now, how you doing, baby girl? Missing your grandma, I'll bet."

"I sure am, Miss Birdie."

"Oh, how I miss her too. It's hard to get to my age and see all your friends go before you do." She took a sip of her tea and leaned in. "And now Helen has joined her, I saw in this morning's paper." She shook her head.

There would be no escaping this murder. Helen's final exit would follow Mabel wherever she went. "Yes, she has."

"I hear tell the old hatchet they keep in there's missing."

"Hatchet?"

"For display at the museum. It was in the case. I saw it years ago, when that back room was still open. They're saying it went missing."

"Who's saying?"

Miss Birdie looked around then lowered her already reedy voice, almost into the inaudible range. "I wanted to warn you, baby, people been talking to the police."

Mabel stabbed a potato with her fork. "I know that. I was there this morning, myself."

"I mean they been talking about you. About your little dust-up at the meeting the night before."

Great.

"They know how she threatened you. How the bad blood all went back to her and your grandma, God rest her soul."

How did she hear this stuff?

"That's fine with me." Mabel tried to convince herself. "If they want to gossip, they can go ahead. The disagreement amounted to nothing—just Helen being Helen, from what I hear."

"Be careful what you say, baby, and don't lose your temper. This town can be awful for spreading stuff around. I feel like you're an adopted grandbaby of mine, and those police can be so suspicious of the most innocent things."

Mabel squeezed Miss Birdie's hand. "Thank you for the warning. I'll be careful. Promise."

Miss Birdie whispered again. "You okay for money, puddin'?"

That afternoon, Mabel threw a ratty tennis ball for Barnacle, before settling in to sort Grandma's papers from the desk in her overcrowded living room. She managed to fill a couple of trash bags and set them near the back door, though when she looked around, she was discouraged to see the room looked pretty much the same.

Still, she felt she couldn't bear to do any more today. She decided to turn to her writing. If she was serious about her new career, she couldn't afford to let another day go by with little progress.

Although she'd cleared a lot of paper from the desk, Mabel still had no writing space, so she moved the remaining stacks of paper to the floor. Before she could set up her laptop and notes, Koi jumped onto the newly cleared surface.

Mabel hated to move her. Instead, she got the lemon furniture polish and wiped all around the cat. Then, she sat in the creaky desk chair and opened her computer in her lap.

For the next half hour, she concentrated on creating an outline, while Koi settled herself, purring, to watch with dreamy, slitted eyes. Most of that time went to figuring out how to do a header and page numbers. Once she had that in place, she figured she'd done enough for today. All this writing stuff was new to her, so she'd better ease in and not fire something off without knowing what she was doing.

Mabel wondered who'd been ratting her out to the police. She knew she shouldn't blame anybody for telling the truth—of course, she and Helen had been at odds. But Mabel could as easily have told them about Cora and Helen's catfight, and she hadn't. Mabel wasn't the only person in Medicine Spring who didn't get along with Helen.

Mabel's eyes narrowed. Was Cora the snitch? Having come right out and suggested Mabel was capable of killing Helen, she was not a fan of Mabel's. That much was clear. It would be like her to take glee in telling the police every detail of Helen's confrontation with Mabel.

Should she worry? How seriously were the police taking what people were telling them? Even unflappable Miss Birdie had seemed concerned.

Mabel got up and stretched. An SUV was parked at the curb in front of the Sauer house, and someone's arms stuck out the car window, taking a picture. Honestly, people. Mabel shook her head.

Should she take a picture, maybe? Her article ought to have a picture or two, she thought. But not while the house had that yellow tape all over it. Aarrgghh, this was all so hard...

Barnacle appeared at her side, looking hopeful. "Let's go," Mabel told him. "I think we both need to get out of the house."

The day had warmed up by a few degrees. Mabel took a deep whiff of leafy-smelling air. "I guess we go this way." She started toward the Sauer mansion. Being down at the dead end meant they pretty much had to pass the ax murder house to get to another street—unless they cut through the woods–and Helen's yard.

Helen wasn't around to yell at them anymore. Not to be callous, but that part of the tragedy, at least, was a relief.

Mabel turned and crossed the back yard. She hesitated where her field ended at the edge of the woods. She looked back and forth from the Sauer mansion to the narrow trail leading, more or less, to Helen's Victorian on the other side of the woods. She wondered if Helen's bicycle had turned up yet.

If Helen had walked, would she have taken the sidewalk around the block—or the short cut through here? The sidewalk was longer. Helen was off the deep end when it came to the woods, which despite the court's ruling in Grandma Mabel's favor, Helen still seemed to think belonged to her.

She squinted. Was that a game trail? Or had Helen herself used it regularly? She'd sure been quick enough to drive Mabel off when she'd approached the woods.

Mabel frowned. Knowing Helen, Mabel felt sure she knew what Helen had been up to. "Pretty smart old lady. I'll bet she was working on an adverse possession."

Though Helen had lost the case, she'd never accepted defeat. The only other way she could ever establish a legal right to the patch of woods would have been through squatter's rights.

Mentally, Mabel checked off the elements she remembered from law school. To establish a legal claim, Helen would've needed to use the property in open defiance of Grandma's—and Mabel's—rights. Using this path regularly, in full view of Grandma's back windows, might have been enough. Chasing her off the path, which Mabel owned now, would only have made Helen's case stronger, since one of the requirements was the claim must be hostile to the landowner's rights. Helen, God rest her soul, had been nothing if not hostile.

She pulled Barnacle away from sniffing the bushes. "Let's take a look."

She pushed aside trailing brambles, which had already lost most of their autumn purple leaves. Helen had been so skinny she'd have slipped right through. Mabel covered more territory, so to speak, and ran into brush on both sides of the narrow, but well-beaten path.

Feeling a tug at her hip, Mabel paused to detach herself from a thorny cane of multiflora roses. Darn—a snag in her most slimming pair of stretch denims.

Mabel chewed over what all this meant, if anything, in terms of Helen's homicide. Assuming it was a homicide…which it was, because as Lt. Sizemore had pointed out, who accidentally axes her own neck? Would this new twist on the property dispute make Mabel a more likely suspect?

Surely not. Nobody killed someone over an unused patch of woods and a lousy footpath, right? But even as the thought occurred, she realized how often neighbors killed neighbors over such seemingly trivial matters.

Before Mabel could emerge from the woods, she ran smack into a substantial potting shed, solidly on Mabel's side of the line but clearly belonging to Helen. She walked around for a better look.

The shed had an open side, facing on a well-worn footpath leading from Helen's driveway. Mabel didn't think she'd ever encountered a potting shed outside an Agatha Christie novel, but all the pots and bags of soil made the building's purpose obvious.

Barnacle was thrilled, which Mabel soon discovered was likely due to a smelly bag of fish meal—and maybe the dead mouse in a back corner. While Mabel peered around the small room, Barnacle continued exploring with his nose. "That's what I call teamwork," she told him, and then "Don't eat that," as he tried to grab the mouse.

Barnacle seemed unbothered by her scolding and overall poor

attitude about his taste for wild game. But all of a sudden, two things happened almost at once.

Somebody grabbed Mabel's shoulder, and Barnacle launched himself, growling viciously, at her attacker. She fumbled for her keychain airhorn, but her assailant clamped down on her wrist with a vise grip before she could get to it.

Chapter Twelve

MABEL WHIRLED AROUND, FIGHTING AND KICKING for her life. Barnacle hurled himself at the man who'd grabbed her. Mabel heard his sleeve rip.

"Oh, no, you didn't just rip my new jacket," the man yelled. "Call off your dog, lady, and I mean now."

"Let me go." Every true-crime TV episode she'd ever seen raced through Mabel's head—not to mention Agatha Christie's very proper British bodies in potting sheds. Mabel didn't want to be a body in the potting shed.

Barnacle seemed to share her viewpoint and continued growling, jumping, and snapping at the man's legs, even after he'd dropped Mabel's arm. "Call off your dog!"

Mabel looked wildly about. If she unleashed Barnacle, she might be able to slip past her attacker. Could she outrun him? Needless to say, she couldn't. If only she had her pepper spray.

Then, suddenly, Barnacle's furious attack stopped, and he dropped into an abrupt sit. "Good boy." The man dropped what looked like a wrapped bite-size candy bar into Barnacle's waiting mouth.

"Exactly what do you think you're doing?" Mabel demanded, pulling pieces of wrapper out of Barnacle's slobbery jaws.

"Saving my hide." The man grinned, eyes sparkling. Mabel couldn't help noticing they were the clear hazel color of a mossy spring.

"Dogs shouldn't eat chocolate." Not to mention it was a terrible waste of candy.

The corners of his eyes crinkled. "There's hardly any chocolate on those—they're mostly nougat with a bit of coating. Besides, your dog's a moose. It would probably take an entire Easter basket to bring him down."

He was about five-feet-ten—not much taller than Mabel and solid looking, though quite a bit trimmer. He appeared about her age. His head was shaved, which to her surprise, she found attractive...and resented it.

"John Bigelow." He extended his hand. "And you're...?"

She glared. "Mabel Browne." Reluctantly, she took his hand, which was strong and warm, and quickly pulled hers away.

"What a wonderful name. I love the old-fashioned names." The grin flashed again.

Barnacle grinned up at John and gave him a quick doggie wink. Though likely a tic, it seemed as if the two were sharing a little joke at her expense.

"What are you doing here?" they asked at the same moment.

"Walking my dog."

He raised his eyebrows. "In a potting shed?"

"I only now realized this is on my property," she told him with as much dignity as she could muster. "What are you doing here?"

"I'm a PI. Or was. My cousin Bennett asked me to look into what happened to his Aunt Helen."

It was Mabel's turn to raise her eyebrows. "You have ID, I assume."

John reached for his hip pocket then pulled his hand back. "Actually, no..." He reached back again and brought out his wallet. "Well, I do have ID. But I don't have my PI license with me."

Mabel waved away the proffered driver's license but took a surreptitious peek out of the corner of her eye. It seemed like he was who he said he was, anyway. "What are you looking for?"

He shrugged. "I'm not sure. I was trying to retrace her steps—figure out how she got over there." He tossed his head in the general direction of the Sauer mansion. "It's part of my method. Sometimes, I pick something up. Sometimes, the different perspective gives me new ideas."

Even if he was John Bigelow, that didn't mean he was either a Sauer relative or a private investigator. Nobody was around to hear her screams. Mabel tried to shove past him, out of the shed. "Excuse me."

He did step aside, to Mabel's relief. But as she debated whether to continue toward Helen's driveway or head home, he pointed. "You said this shed is on your property?"

"Yes." Mabel folded her arms.

"Back through that way?" He pointed. "That's your house?"

"Yep. It's time Barnacle and I head back to it, if you'll excuse us." Oh, no. Maybe she shouldn't have told him where she lived.

"Have coffee with me."

Mabel felt her color rise. "Excuse me?"

"You're the person who found Helen's body, right?"

"I was *one* of the people who found her." Mabel could hardly deny something that had already run in the paper. Not unless she could convince a hardboiled PI that Maybelle Browne was another person altogether. Belatedly, she remembered he was a cousin of the family and added, "I'm sorry for your loss."

"Thank you. I really didn't know her well. I'm related to her nephew, on his mother's side, and not through his father, who was Helen's brother, Edward."

Mabel let the names and relationships filter down through her brain layers.

"So please let me buy you a coffee, Miss Mabel Browne. Maybe a cruller?"

"I don't care for crullers."

"I will happily buy you a custard doughnut. Or a scone. Or a tuna salad sandwich. Whatever your heart desires. I also need to pick your exceedingly sharp brain. I'm pleading here."

She looked into his heart-melting hazel eyes. "Oh, all right. I guess I'm about ready for an afternoon snack or early supper, anyway. But I'll buy it myself. Don't expect much. I'm guessing I don't know any more than you do—and the police won't let me say much, anyway."

He grinned again, seeming unperturbed by her prickliness. "Bless you. May I drive?" He gestured toward Helen's back driveway.

"No, thanks. I have to take care of a couple of things first. See you at the diner in fifteen minutes?"

As she made her way back along the path, she thought about John Bigelow. She wasn't going to get into a strange man's car during a murder investigation. Nor did she want to feel as if they were going on a date.

But she was curious. She wanted to find out what he knew and about the family relationships. She also had to admit she sort of wanted to spend a little more time with John and his hazel eyes.

The Coffee Cup crowd had thinned by the time Mabel found a parking spot and made her way inside. John sat at the back booth. His face lit when he saw her.

He stood when she walked up, something Mabel secretly loved, despite her feminist sentiments. "I was afraid you might change your mind and not come." He arched a brow at her and smiled.

"I figured you wouldn't give up, and I'd better talk to you now and get it over with."

He laughed. "I'm flattered."

Mabel rolled her eyes. She wasn't going to take the bait.

"Beauty, confidence, and brains." John smiled. "And a half cup of sass."

"Um, thanks." Mabel dove behind the menu to cover her awkwardness. This guy was too much. He obviously thought he was going to weasel something out of her by being charming and complimentary. She steeled herself against the flood of charisma.

The waitress came by, and Mabel ordered a Rachel sandwich, thinking turkey was better for her than the corned beef she was craving. Silencing her conscience, she added an order of hand-cut fries. John asked for a salad plate with tuna, cottage cheese, and coleslaw. *Health nut. Probably jogs.*

Mabel leaned back once they'd ordered, and their coffees had arrived—his black, and hers a cinnamon latte with a drift of whipped cream. "Tell me about Helen's family."

"There's not much to it. My cousin, Bennett—Helen's nephew—has a son, but he was an only child. Helen had one child that died at birth, plus a daughter who ran off long ago, and nobody heard from till maybe a year or so ago. She has a son."

Having met Helen, Mabel thought she could understand why her daughter might have taken off.

"The daughter—Linnea—has been living in Pittsburgh. Since she connected with her mother again, I guess they've reestablished a relationship."

Though apparently not enough of a relationship for Linnea to be the one asking John to investigate Helen's death.

She took a sip of latte. John reached across and dabbed a smidge of whipped cream from her nose with his napkin. Mabel was humiliated to feel herself blushing again. What was she, fourteen? "What's Bennett hoping to prove?"

"I'm bound by client confidentiality, the same as an attorney. But Helen was the last of that generation. As they say, blood's thicker than water—what the law refers to as 'natural love and affection.'"

Mabel had been about to identify herself as a lawyer but thought better of it. The less he knew about her, the better. She was a writer now, anyway.

"Were they...close?" She'd hoped to keep the incredulity out of her voice but wasn't 100 percent successful.

John smiled and sat back. "They were. Helen was Bennett's godmother. With her own kids gone, I rather think she doted on him. In her own way."

Mabel pleated her napkin. "Sometimes, it's easier to love someone if they aren't under the same roof." Although of course, living a few yards away from Helen hadn't made her and Helen best friends, either.

"In this case I'm sure you're right. Bennett took care of a lot of things for her after she was widowed. I believe she always spent holidays with his family."

How to ask her next question delicately? "He'd have a key to the house, I presume?"

"Probably." John's raised eyebrow confirmed she hadn't been as subtle as she'd hoped. "She wasn't killed at home, as you know."

Yup. She'd stepped in it, all right. Mabel raised both hands in protest. "I wasn't suggesting anything. Just thinking about the relationship."

"It's okay. It's reasonable for you to wonder. And before you ask, I have no idea if he's in the will."

Time to change the subject...though she made a mental note to see if a will had been filed at the Register's Office.

"You said, 'I was' a PI—are you retired now?" He seemed awfully young for that—fifty, at most.

"Taking a break," he told her. "I'll be going back. By February, if things work out. For now, I'm teaching a couple of criminology and investigative techniques courses at the community college and subbing at the high school."

Mabel hadn't gotten many opportunities to cross-examine witnesses in her legal career, but John's story had noticeable holes. Why February? What needed to "work out?"

She cleared her throat. Now wasn't the time to press. "So, in essence, he wants to know who killed dear Aunt Helen...?"

His smile returned. Maybe he was just a cheerful person, or more likely, she amused him for some reason. "You might say that. Now, what can you tell me that might help Helen's family get closure?"

"Nothing, I'm afraid. What I do know—which isn't much—I'm not allowed to share."

He leaned back, coffee mug in hand. "Let me try and see how close I am. You don't have to tell me, but maybe you could say hot or cold?"

She felt herself flush. "You know that doesn't make it all right."

John shrugged. "Close enough. Here's how I see it. Helen was scheduled to lead this tour."

Mabel tried to look noncommittal, mentally zipping her lips.

"Let me state that as a fact," John said, "because Helen pretty much *always* led the tours. Especially since it was a true-crime group, from what I hear. No way Helen would ever have let anybody else take that one. She couldn't take the chance of a group dissection of the Sauer murders, with people trying to figure out whodunit."

He was so obviously right that Mabel found herself nodding, anyway.

"Thank you." His seemingly perpetual smile spread into a broad grin.

They both sat back as their lunches arrived. Mabel studied her plate. The sandwich was grilled to golden perfection, oozing strands of sauerkraut and globs of Russian dressing. The side of fries was mounded so high they were sliding off the plate, glistening with grease and sparkling salt crystals.

Mabel squeezed out a pool of ketchup. Why had she thought a Rachel was a good idea? They were impossible to eat neatly under the best of circumstances. Since she could eat a saltine and end up with a stain on her shirt and stuff stuck in her teeth, this meal was a guaranteed disaster.

The sandwich did smell good, though. She wasn't trying to impress John Bigelow, either. If he didn't like the way a normal woman ate, then he could take his charm someplace else.

Mabel was surprised how hungry she was, considering her big breakfast. But soon the bread was falling apart, and she had to keep wiping grease and Russian dressing off her hands and chin. The waitress dropped another stack of napkins on the table.

"I love these, but they're impossible to eat without ending up looking like the sandwich won the fight." She self-consciously picked sauerkraut off her chest.

"Worth the effort, though." John smiled.

"Want a fry?"

"No, thanks." He held up his hands, apparently to ward off the calories and cholesterol rising up from her plate.

John dabbed his mouth and cleared his throat. "So... Helen was scheduled but either never showed up, or she called off. Otherwise, you wouldn't have been leading the tour, especially as a newbie. Not to mention a newbie she'd already tangled with. How am I doing?"

Mabel focused on her plate, sturdily chewing her way through the second half of her sandwich.

"I'll presume—for the same reasons—that it wasn't a call-off. She'd have dragged herself off her deathbed to lead that tour herself, since she felt like she had to have that control."

They both seemed to realize the unfortunate wording at the same moment. Helen had come to lead the tour, all right, and she'd ended up on her deathbed.

John groaned and buried his face in his hands. "Tasteless gallows humor unintended."

"So stipulated." Now it was Mabel's turn to grin.

He looked up. "What are you—a lawyer?"

Oh, shoot. "Sort of."

Again, the raised eyebrows.

"I'm in a career transition at present, okay? Actually, I'm writing a book. It was time for a change." At least, that was what the law firm had told her.

"Wow, I'm impressed." He looked as if he meant that. "I may have a few law-type questions later on that maybe you could answer."

Ugh. Mabel, like most attorneys, disliked giving curbstone advice—an old expression that made her think of being buttonholed on the street, right as you were about to cross.

"But my bigger concern, for the moment, is trying to figure out what happened to Helen."

"We do have police, you know."

"Yes, but they don't have much experience with homicides. Medicine Spring hasn't seen a suspicious death in at least twenty years. In fact, the Sauer ax murders might have been the most recent ones prior to that."

"I hope they don't latch onto me," Mabel forced a laugh. "Since I was there when she was found, and she and I had had a teensy issue or two. The police seem so suspicious."

"See, this is what I mean." He leaned across the table. She had to struggle to focus on what he was saying, when he looked at her with those incredible eyes. "They don't know how to handle a homicide investigation, so they might tend to jump at the first suspect crossing their radar."

This wasn't comforting.

Chapter Thirteen

MABEL RUBBED HER HANDS TOGETHER AND swallowed. John's suggestion that the police might latch onto somebody convenient like her—because they were inexperienced with homicides—was unnerving.

"I'm thinking you and your group found Helen there at the house. In fact, we all know that." John leaned back, gazed up at the ceiling and then back at Mabel.

"How much can you tell me? Without violating any restrictions the police put on you, of course."

Darn it. She liked him. "How do I know you're who you say you are?"

John laughed again. He waved at the older waitress, working the counter.

"You need something, John?"

"No. But would you mind giving me a character reference for my charming, but suspicious, lunch companion?"

She shook her head, grinning, and wiped down the counter. "John can be endlessly aggravating, but he's a good boy at heart. What do you need to know?"

Mabel concentrated on not blushing again. "Nothing, thanks."

"Look," John said, "I know you haven't spent much time in Medicine Spring, but I grew up here. Pretty much all the older people, at least, can tell you anything you want to know about me, right down to and including the time I peed my pants in the first grade."

"Okaaay…here's the thing then. Yes, obviously, I was at the scene. One of those true-crimers with the single-track minds opened the parlor door."

John's eyes lit up. "Aahh, that's good. The door was unlocked? And she was in the parlor. Hmmm… History repeats itself."

He was quick. Grudgingly, Mabel admired that. She'd barely said anything, and she'd already given away more than she'd intended—or the police might have wanted her to.

Had the door been unlocked? To be accurate, as she'd have told a witness to be, she hadn't seen that for herself. She was taking the word of the tour group members.

It went without saying nobody on the tour was authorized to have a parlor key, but there was no guarantee they hadn't. Who'd been on that tour? They had all boarded the bus in Wilkie, but they could've come from anywhere. The police—and maybe the bus company—would have all the names and addresses. Neither Mabel nor the historical society did.

John snapped his fingers. "Where are you?"

"Sorry. I was considering one of the visitors might have had a key somehow. Not realistically—I know that. But we can't say for sure."

"Good thinking. Don't edit yourself when we're brainstorming." He made a note. "Now the crime scene?" He looked up with his pen still poised above the notepad.

"I think that's what I'm supposed to keep to myself."

"All right. Let's keep playing our guessing game then. Okay?"

She sipped her cooling latte. If she didn't say anything, she couldn't be accused of violating instructions, right?

He winked. "So who opened that door? One of your tourists?"

She didn't answer, but he nodded, anyway. She'd already said that. "Which one? Do you remember?"

Surely, there was no harm in telling him that. She wasn't giving away anything that could lead to catching the killer.

"It was this woman." She rummaged through her purse and came up with a handful of used tissues, an ATM receipt, and a few loose breath mints—somewhat worse for a coating of lint. Finally, she produced a business card, which she flipped across to John.

"Giselle's European Facial Waxing...?" He looked up. "Giselle?"

Dang it. Mabel's hand went automatically to her smooth upper lip. She grabbed back the card. "No, wait a sec."

More digging. Soon, she found what she was searching for and handed the correct card to John. "Her name is Devereaux Reid. She *says* she's a true-crime writer, and she's working on a book about the Sauer ax murders."

"May I?" He made a clicking gesture, as if to take a photo with his cellphone.

"Sure. Go ahead."

After he'd passed the card back, Mabel tapped the table. "I'm wondering now—not seriously, I guess, but wondering..."

"Don't edit yourself again. We're brainstorming here."

"I wondered if Helen's death might have any connection with the old ax murders."

That appreciative glint returned. "It is quite a coincidence--her body being found in the same place her grandfather and uncle were killed."

Mabel nodded. "I think so. I mean what are the odds?"

He sipped his coffee, made a face, and stood up. "Time for a refill. May I?" He reached for Mabel's cup.

"Maybe a glass of ice water, as long as you're up, thanks."

She watched as he walked to the counter. She wished his eyes weren't that lively shade of hazel, his ready smile so appealing, or his jeans so well fitted. She also seemed so in tune with him—and that was dangerous.

This felt good, having someone smart to bounce ideas off—and maybe help her investigate. But even if the waitresses knew him, Mabel wasn't sure he could be trusted. He was too complimentary, for one thing. Mabel had never received that many male compliments in her lifetime—let alone from a single man on a single day. Did he think she was a foolish middle-aged woman who'd tell him anything in exchange for a little flirtation?

He returned, carefully setting down her water glass along with a big chocolate chip cookie. "Do you like chocolate? I took a chance."

"Oh, no, thanks." She tried to avert her eyes from that seductive slab of goodness. "I mean, I like them, but I shouldn't be adding that to a grilled sandwich, fries, and a latte."

"I'd be happy to help with that." He broke the cookie into two pieces and held them up. "Why don't we be bad together?"

Mabel hadn't done so much blushing since she was fourteen. To cover her embarrassment, she snatched the smaller piece of cookie. "Thank you."

John paused to nibble a piece of cookie. "Now, where were we? Devereaux Reid. The ax murders. Since you referred to them as 'the old ax murders,' you're differentiating them from Helen's, right? Therefore, we can confirm hers was also an ax murder, I believe."

He didn't wait for a reaction from Mabel. "An interesting possible link." He shot her a glance. "Don't blame yourself for tipping anything. The rumors are already flying. In fact, the ax-murder angle was already on an online site by the time we sat down to eat."

Relief mingled with irritation. "Then you pretty much know more than I do at this point," Mabel told him.

"Not really." He wiped chocolate from his fingertips with a napkin. "After all, not everything online is true. I guess all I'm saying is you can't keep a lid on anything in this town. I don't think you're likely to tell me any critical details about the crime scene that aren't either common knowledge or I can't pick up elsewhere. I'm more interested in your personal impressions."

Mabel leaned back. She didn't want to let her guard down, but she couldn't deny a certain sense of relief.

He stroked his upper lip. "The deaths may not be linked, per se. Helen's murder might have been a crime of opportunity, for instance. Like maybe he—I'm going to say 'he' for convenience, but it could as well be 'she.' Don't want to be sexist here." He winked at her. "Like maybe he could just get to that ax at that moment, for instance. Or maybe Helen's death had nothing to do with the old murders, but somebody wanted to get rid of her and decided to copycat."

"Maybe."

"Tell me about Devereaux Reid. What's her deal?"

Mabel thought, trying to separate her instinctive reactions from facts.

"She was on the tour with the Wilkie true-crime group, but I got the impression she wasn't a member of the club or whatever that organization is. She said she was writing this true crime book about the 1939 murders, and she'd brought her notebook and a voice recorder and camera."

"All right."

"She tried to record interviews with the rest of the group before the cops got to them."

John's eyebrows shot up. "That's different."

"She claimed she was trying to 'help.'" Mabel made air quotes. She repressed the thought that maybe Devereaux's claim wasn't any more bizarre than Mabel's own offer to help. But then, Mabel was a lawyer. She'd been trained to ferret out the truth from slime balls trying to hide dirty secrets. The police should have let her assist.

"Mabel? You in there?"

"Sorry. I'm tired. I guess I'm drifting a bit, trying to wrap my head around everything that's happened the past couple of days."

"Back to Devereaux. She opened the door and found Helen's body?"

Mabel nodded. "I was telling her not to touch the door and bam. She did it, anyway, and then, the screaming started."

"Did she touch anything?"

Mabel shut her eyes and thought. "I didn't see anybody touch anything in the room. She and I both touched the door pull. I feel so stupid about that. I was in shock and not thinking. The others who forced their way in were too busy snapping pictures to touch anything. All I could think was I had to get everybody out of there and…and give

Helen her privacy."

"Wow." John's eyebrows lifted. "They snapped pictures of the body?"

"In their defense, they seemed to think they were helping. I wish I'd had the presence of mind not to touch anything, either."

He shrugged. "I'm guessing the handle had prints of more than one person from the historical society. I doubt they're dusting every day over there. Don't beat yourself up."

"The police weren't thrilled."

"Of course not. But they aren't the poor person who ran smack into the dead body of someone they knew."

"I wonder..." Mabel rubbed her forehead. "I've been assuming Devereaux first opened the door when I saw her doing it. Theoretically, though, she, or any one of several others, could've opened it earlier, while I was leading the tour upstairs. A few of them were trailing behind. Only for a couple of minutes, but..."

"I'm assuming you didn't hear any screams?"

"No. Not then. But the attack would've had to happen in seconds, and maybe Helen wasn't able to react. I mean if she'd been back there and conscious all along, she'd surely have come out to lead the tour. If she was able. But what if she'd been passed out or tied up and gagged back there or something?"

"Interesting, even if unlikely. That would open up a whole new field of suspects."

Chapter Fourteen

AFTER JOHN HAD ENJOYED A SECOND cup of coffee and they'd shared that chocolate chip cookie, Mabel gathered her things and called for checks.

John held up a finger. "One check, please. Right here."

"I told you I wanted to pay for my own."

"I know, but please give me the pleasure of treating you. Next time, I'll let you pay. Maybe."

Mabel bit down on her lip, mid-sputter. *Next time?* He'd only been picking her brain, but it sure sounded like he considered this some sort of date. Her clamoring common sense reminded her that unless she could use it to her advantage, flirting with a potential suspect was a bad idea. Since flirtation was not part of Mabel's skill set, she had to admit she was more likely to be duped than he was.

She raised her hands. "I'll pay the tip then."

As they headed to the parking lot, John turned. "Where now?"

"I need to make a quick run to the library then head home and feed my animals."

He smiled. "I've met your dear Barnacle. What other pets do you have? Or are you raising chickens?"

She smiled back. "No, just a cat named Koi."

He pulled out his phone. "Would you mind sharing your number? Maybe we can compare notes again soon."

Mabel hesitated. Not many people had her number—her former boss, her best friend Lisa, her family, the church prayer chain. But then, she thought, why not? I'm going to live for a change.

As she gave her number to him, John punched it in then read it back. "Got it."

Mabel's phone sat in the palm of her hand. "I might as well take yours while we're at it. In case I need some info or run across something you might be interested in, of course."

"Of course." Humor danced in his eyes. "For business reasons only."

John walked her to her car. "I'll give you a ring." He opened the driver door for her.

After he'd walked away, Mabel sat in her car and watched him get into an aqua-and-red muscle car. The red was primer.

Mabel returned his wave and backed onto the street. She checked her rearview till she turned at the next corner but didn't see John leave the diner lot.

When she reached the library, she took a minute to check her phone before getting out of her car. She'd had it silenced during lunch, and now saw she'd missed a text from Lisa.

Mabel redialed.

"Mabel!"

"Hi, are you okay to talk?"

"Only for a sec. I have one little boy, still waiting for pickup. He's playing with Legos right now, but Mom should be here soon. Tell me everything."

Mabel ran through the events of the night before but decided she wasn't ready to mention John Bigelow. She still needed time to digest her feelings where he was concerned.

"Wow. Who do you think did it?"

"I have no earthly idea, but I hope they soon find out. She and I had a not-so-good history, but this was awful. Plus, I feel like a suspect."

"Pfft. Don't be silly. Hey, you should investigate—I'll help."

"This isn't TV, and we're not detectives." Mabel sighed. "But in the unlikely event I need backup, I'll keep you in mind."

"Oh, hey—got to go. Be safe, okay?"

"I'll try."

Half an hour later, Mabel was home. She slid her purse onto the bench in the front hall and dumped her library bag next to it.

Once she'd fed her pets and brewed herself a pot of pumpkin-spice chai, Mabel grabbed her library bag, locked the doors, and headed upstairs. With the early darkness and her exhaustion from the night before, reading in bed seemed like a fine idea.

Her bedroom was so cold. These high ceilings and lack of insulation meant she'd be freezing all winter, unless she spent a fortune on heating bills. With a sigh, she inched up the heat and changed into her flannel granny gown and fuzzy slipper socks. Then, she added an extra quilt from the cedar chest at the foot of the bed.

Barnacle circled three times and settled himself on the creaking floor with a sigh. Koi, with an air of superiority, leapt onto the bed and began kneading and purring. Mabel plumped up her pillows and cracked open her library book, *Fatal Blow: The Story of the Sauer Ax Murders*. The copyright page said 1959—the twentieth anniversary of the murders.

Mabel wondered if Devereaux Reid planned on delivering any bombshells in the book she claimed to be writing. A new book would have to offer something fresh, or what would be the point?

As she read, the inky shadows cast by her reading lamp seemed creepier and more ominous. Mabel thought again how isolated she was here, in this old house at the dead end.

It seemed Margarethe's health had always been somewhat fragile. But after the birth of Edna, barely nine months after Walter, Jr., she spent much of her life as a reclusive near-invalid, something Walter seemed to blame Edna for. This struck Mabel as unreasonable, particularly given Violet's subsequent birth.

Walter, Sr. had a reputation as a sharp and even unscrupulous businessman, with a bad temper. Margarethe, on the other hand, was reputed to be a saintly woman who managed to keep the family together and softened his worst behavior in the community. Somehow, she even managed to convince him to make a generous donation to the library and local light opera as well as help fund the town's first hospital.

1939 was eventful and turbulent for the Sauers. Walter, Jr. joined his father's business in 1934 and in 1939 was promoted to vice president. This enraged Paul Gregory, a long-time plodder who'd given his life to the company, only to be bypassed by the twenty-six-year-old. Walter, Sr. had reportedly tried to force Edna into marrying a much older man, whose business he coveted, but she refused. The man subsequently married Edna's younger and more pliable sister, Violet—Helen's mother.

By 1939, Violet's husband and Walter, Sr. had merged their companies and driven a rival's dry-goods business into the ground. Their competitor, Heinrich Weber, died by suicide a year after the Sauer murders, leaving a destitute family.

Rumors circulating at the time said Edna was bitter and resentful. Her less-talented brother got the education and a good job, and all she got was her father's attempt to force her into a marriage alliance to benefit his business. Darker 1939 gossip also said Walter, Sr. was a nasty and even violent drunk, and that Edna had become his repeated target.

Mabel sniffed. She identified with Edna's battles—the plus-size, less conventionally attractive sister, with intelligence and talent going unnoticed and unappreciated. "I get you, Edna," she said out loud.

She'd drunk too much coffee. Helen's murder had left her agitated. So had John Bigelow. She should sleep, but her brain was wide awake, and she kept reading.

After two AM, she closed the book, stopping before the ax murders. She'd heard about them from Grandma Mabel her entire life and could wait till tomorrow to find out how closely her version tracked the one in this book.

But the back story had been interesting. Although suspicion had fallen at once on Edna, Mabel could already see where the destroyed business rival should've been at least equally suspect. And the disgruntled employee, Paul Gregory, whose promotion Walter, Jr. had grabbed. The last part of the book covered the investigation such as it was, as well as Edna's trial. She wanted to read that too, but that part of the story could wait.

Mabel slept in fits, dreaming, waking, straining at small sounds and wondering if someone was trying her doors or making his way upstairs. But Barnacle snored away—either nobody was there, or he was simply such a sound sleeper she might as well forget relying on him for protection.

The sun was already high when the pounding started at the back door. Koi launched off Mabel's blanketed form and shot under the bed. Barnacle lumbered to his feet and stood half on the bed and half on her stomach, barking wildly.

Mabel struggled out of a sleep fog and shoved Barnacle off her bladder. She made her way to the window but couldn't see who was there.

Throwing on her bathrobe, Mabel grabbed the baseball bat she'd kept by the bed for protection since finding Helen's body. As soon as she opened her bedroom door, Barnacle flew downstairs, barking and snarling.

He skidded around the foot of the stairs and into the hallway, legs flying, and raced for the back.

As Mabel edged into the kitchen, she let out the breath she'd been unconsciously holding. Her younger sister, Jennifer, stood hunched at the back door in a crayon-red wool jacket, arms wrapped around herself.

Mabel fumbled with the lock, then as she clipped the dog to his tie-out by the door, Jen hustled past him. Barnacle switched from snarling to his happy bark, jumping and fawning over her. Jen bent to pet him, her shiny cap of blonde hair falling forward over adorable, rosy apple cheeks.

Mabel shoved her excited dog outside and shut the door. "Thank goodness." Jen unwound her scarf. "I thought you'd been murdered and Barnacle along with you. I've been knocking forever." She cupped her hands over her mouth and red nose and puffed into them.

Mabel rolled her eyes. "You couldn't have been waiting more than five minutes. I can't teleport, y'know." She yawned. "It was a rough night and a short one, Coffee?"

At her nod, Mabel set out two mugs and started the coffeemaker.

Jen removed a stack of papers from one of the kitchen chairs and sat down. "Good grief, it's freezing in here. Isn't your furnace working?"

"I haven't turned the heat on yet. Hang on." She squinted at the thermostat and nudged the dial up a bit. "Would you like coffeecake? I have one in the freezer."

"Maybe a smidge."

Mabel, back turned as she pulled the carton from the freezer, rolled her eyes. Jen was five inches shorter and at least seventy pounds lighter than she was.

Jen looked around the kitchen. "Love what you've done with the place."

"Ha-ha." Mabel didn't need the reminder.

"Seriously, Mabes, if you want me to come help you haul junk out of here, I will. It's been six months already. You ought to rent a Dumpster and grab a shovel. Grandma Mabel wouldn't want you to live with all her mess like this."

"I *have* had a few other things on my plate, you know."

"I understand. But if you'd get a plan in place for dealing with this, that would go a long way."

Mabel gritted her teeth. "Did Mom send you?"

"No, not really." Jen's face gave her away. "You know Mom. She doesn't like the idea of your living next door to a murder house. The fact you were there in the room with the body and got yourself involved has her freaked out."

"I'm not all that thrilled about it myself." Mabel pulled sour-cream coffeecake from the microwave and cut a piece for Jen. "But the police are on the case, and I don't think I'm in any danger here."

"Mom thought you might like to come home for a while. At least till they arrest someone?"

Mabel let Barnacle inside. She poured the coffee and sat down across from Jen. "See, here's the thing. The police haven't told me not to leave town, but—"

Jen's jaw dropped. "Are you a suspect?"

Mabel wiggle-waggled her hand. "I don't think so—I mean not so much. Sort of. A little bit."

Jen stared.

"It isn't a big deal." Mabel took a bite of coffeecake and washed it down. "Helen—the person who got killed—was Grandma's neighbor to the back. She and Grandma had a dispute over the property line way back when. Then, she went nuts on me about Barnacle 'menacing' her when he wandered back there—Barnacle!" She nodded at the dog in question, currently beached out on his back, all four legs in the air. "I mean really?"

Jen grinned. "That does seem like a pretty flimsy motive for murder."

"Well…"

"There's more?"

Mabel sighed. She didn't want to get into this right now and add more fuel to Jen's crusade to get Mabel to toss most of what was left in Grandma's house. But there was no hiding the truth. "She said she was reporting me to the township, and I'd lose the property if I didn't get it cleaned up."

Jen leaned over the table. "Omigosh. Do you think she followed through?"

Mabel shook her head then shrugged. "I don't know. The property isn't *that* bad. I haven't seen anybody from the township or gotten any notices."

"I guess that might be a motive, though. For some people."

This wasn't news to Mabel, but still her stomach flipped. "I know. But not a strong one."

"People kill for nothing."

Chapter Fifteen

JENNIFER HAD BEEN LESS THAN COMFORTING. Mabel tried to tell herself there was no way she was a serious suspect, but now she could clearly grasp that some people might see her that way.

Barnacle rolled over and shook himself. He pawed Jen's leg. She reached down and petted his perky ears, but from the way his nose was working, Mabel knew he was in fact after the coffeecake.

Jen's phone started playing a blues riff. "Oops. That's my alarm—gotta pick up Taylor for her doctor's appointment."

Before heading back outside, she put her hand on Mabel's shoulder. "Mom wants you to come for dinner Sunday. I'd do what she wants—let her and Dad see you're all right and calm her down."

Calm Mom down and agitate Mabel for days afterward.

"Maybe. I'll call later. Hey, how are Betsy and Josh? I haven't had a chance to call them in a while." Jennifer's son Josh was a freshman at Ohio State, hours distant. His twin Betsy attended Bartles Grove College, only ten miles away, where Mabel had grown up, and where Jen and her parents still lived. Mabel had always been close to them—particularly Betsy, who was her goddaughter. Maybe she should stop in at The Grind, where Betsy worked, and say hi.

Jen grinned. "They're good. Josh is still adjusting to being on his own. I think Betsy may have a new boyfriend, but you know how private she is."

Mabel walked Jen out. Now—how to spend her day? She should work on her writing. Or even order that Dumpster Jen had suggested. But Helen's murder—and her own implication in it—made it hard to focus on anything else.

"Let's take our walk, Barnacle. Clear our brains."

Half an hour later, after walking down to the lake at the edge of town and back, Mabel felt clearer. She refilled the pets' water dish and grabbed her purse and keys. She'd forget Helen's murder for a while and put together a couple of boxes of goodies for Betsy and Josh.

She drove out to the mall, where there were a lot of fun shops to distract her from all the stress waiting back home. For a couple of hours, she wandered from store to store, picking up candy, crackers, chips, packets of cocoa and tea bags, USB drives shaped like animals, paperbacks, and magazines. Mabel finished her shopping spree with comfort food—tomato soup and grilled cheese at the Panhandle Family Restaurant.

Her phone vibrated as she finished paying.

"Mabel? John Bigelow. How're you doing today?"

"Oh, hi." She felt absurdly pleased he'd called. "Fine, thanks. What's up?"

"Not much. I found out a few little things."

"Yeah? Like what?"

"Like I said, nothing earth-shaking this early on. Just a daily status report, you might say. But I was hoping I could come by and we could do a sort of check-in."

Mabel couldn't see why they'd need to discuss stuff in person. She wasn't about to stop him from coming, though. "Um, sure. I'm at the mall right now. And I thought I might swing by the historical society afterward, if they're open."

"When you think you'll be home? I could bring dinner."

"Maybe five or so?"

"Around 6:30 work for you?"

Mabel wasn't sure about letting him see her mess. She wasn't sure it was wise, either, having somebody she'd just met come to the house. Not with an ax murderer on the loose. But Barnacle would undoubtedly protect her.

"Mabel? Did you hear me? You're always disappearing on me."

"Okay, but I'm warning you my grandmother had dementia, and

she let the place go a bit." Mabel wouldn't mention she'd already lived there for six months, with no appreciable change for the better.

"Perfect. No problem. See you then."

Mabel checked the time. Still early. She should have plenty of time to run to the Sauer house before heading home and tidying up a bit—both the house and herself.

Making a quick decision, she called Lisa.

"Hey, Mabel. I was going to call you later. I've had parent meetings all afternoon."

"I wondered if you might do me a small favor…?"

"Not knowing what it is, I guess so. Are you all right?"

"Yeah. The whole episode has been sort of overwhelming."

"What do you need? Are you safe over there right now? Want me to come stay with you for a few days?"

Mabel laughed. "Which question do you want me to answer first? Yeah, I'm fine, but that's sort of why I called. I have someone coming over at 6:30, and it's like when you sell something online. Not a good idea to meet them alone, you know."

"Are you finally starting to sell off your grandma's stuff?"

"Not yet." It seemed like everybody she knew was pushing her to clean out the house. "It's actually a new friend, but I thought it might be good to have someone there when he arrives, you know? Just long enough to let him know you can ID him and you'll be checking up later."

"A new friend, huh? A he… I was about to see if you wanted to come kayaking with our church singles."

"Wow, thanks, but I already have plans." Not to mention she'd capsize for sure. If there was an eligible man there at all, she would take him down with the ship.

Lisa laughed. "I haven't even told you when we're going kayaking yet. But maybe your 'plans' are more long term…?" She hummed the wedding march, just loud enough for Mabel to hear.

Mabel ignored the teasing. "Can you make it? I'd like to see you, anyway."

"I can be there in half an hour, if you want."

"Could you give me an hour? I have one more stop."

"Can do. See you soon."

Since Lisa was a compact, brown-eyed beauty with a tangle of dark curls and a gorgeous smile, maybe inviting her hadn't been a bright move. But Lisa had tentative marriage plans with a shy cabinetmaker from her singles group. Not to mention Lisa was the most loyal person in the universe. Mabel had promised to be her maid of honor, though she knew she'd tower over the bride and possibly also the groom—at least if she had to wear heels, which she tried to avoid at all costs.

Lisa was forever trying to fix Mabel up with one "interesting" guy or another. Once before, she'd succeeded in dragging Mabel to her singles group. The women had outnumbered the men by half, and there were even fewer men in Mabel's age and size categories. There was no way she was going back there, only to feel like a wallflower at the seventh-grade dance.

The yellow tape had disappeared from the front steps when Mabel pulled in front of the historical society. The door, to her surprise, was unlocked.

A sign taped to the hall desk read *Please Wait. Back Soon.* But before she decided what to do, Darwin emerged from the far end of the hallway. "Hi. I saw you drive up."

She peered around the corner. Tape still closed off the murder room. "I wasn't sure the building would be open."

"All except the back parlor." He nodded that way. "But we scarcely needed to have anyone on duty. There hasn't been a soul here all afternoon. I didn't even bother locking after lunch. I doubt anybody even realizes we've reopened. By tomorrow or the next day, when the word gets around that the building's back open for visitors, the curiosity seekers will descend." He grimaced.

"I came to see you, if you have time?"

He smiled. "My pleasure." He gestured toward the office.

Mabel took a seat and refused the coffee Darwin offered. "I still can't believe Helen's dead. Let alone—you know—murdered."

He shook his head. "I can't, either. She wasn't always the easiest person, but she *was* this house. She was devoted to it and its history. Nobody knows what she knew about this place and the Sauer family."

"I hope you know enough to answer a few questions for me."

He frowned. "I can try. What do you want to know? If I can't help you, maybe Cora could. She's been here longer than I have."

Privately, Mabel thought talking to Cora would be a last resort, since she seemed to harbor a distaste for Mabel second only to Helen's. "I was interested in the Sauer genealogy and history—and any documents you might have in the archives."

Darwin tilted his head. "I have quite a few things. Is there a particular aspect you're interested in?"

"I guess the Sauer family and the descendants, if you have a family tree, or something like that. I'd be interested in what happened with the survivors too, after the murders occurred."

"Hold on. Let me see what I can dig out for you." He made his way to the file cabinets, stretching to step around an air-conditioning unit, which took up a significant chunk of floor space in the tiny, crowded office. He rooted around, coming up with a stack of folders, and shoved the drawer back into place with his hip.

"You could start with these," he told her then grunted. "That AC unit's out to kill me." Darwin dumped folders onto the desk in front of Mabel. He rubbed his shin and examined a nick in the threadbare knee of his pantleg. "I had to wrestle four of these out of the windows the other day. I ripped up my hands and strained my back, and now the sharp corner on that thing got my leg too."

"Are you okay?"

Darwin waved a dismissive hand. "Just got my pantleg. Go ahead."

Mabel spread out the documents. There weren't a lot of Sauers. Walter, Jr., obviously, had been killed when he was young and unmarried.

The only Sauer grandchildren, Helen and Edward, came by way of Violet, who'd married Walter, Sr.'s business associate. Helen, in turn, had given birth to two children—a son who'd died in infancy and the daughter who'd run away as a teenager and only recently returned.

"There's something off about the daughter." Darwin tapped her name on the family tree. "Gone all those years, broke Helen's heart. Then, all of a sudden, she's back fawning all over her. Accusing the nephew of trying to ingratiate himself where he didn't belong. He's the only one who gave a hoot about Helen."

Mabel filed this bit of family intrigue away in a corner of her brain. To be honest, it rather sounded as if Helen's daughter was a chip off the old block.

Helen's late brother Edward was the father of John's cousin, Bennett, an only child who was now the father of another only child, Christopher. Christopher and Helen's daughter, Linnea's son, Michael, were the solitary living heirs in the present generation.

"Edna never married." *Of course.*

Darwin didn't reply. He was trying—without much success—to maneuver the offending air-conditioning unit to a less dangerous location, off to the side of the room. "If Helen had been a little bit flexible, maybe we could've had central air in here by now, and I wouldn't need to do this twice a year."

"Edna never married?" Mabel repeated.

"Oh, sorry." He nursed his bandaged hand as he abandoned the air conditioner. "I'd love to take a sledgehammer to that thing. No, Edna didn't marry. In fact, Paul Gregory—he was the older Sauer employee who got bypassed when Walter, Jr. got his promotion—did you know about that? In fact, he was a suspect himself. Anyway, Gregory actually proposed to Edna—in the dock, as it were, while the trial was still going on. She turned him down cold."

"I wonder if he was still trying to move up in the company."

"Doing that didn't help."

Mabel thought. "Would Cora have known the family?"

"Sure. She's almost ten years younger than Helen, though, so she wouldn't know anything firsthand from that time. Helen was only a toddler herself. Once, they were pretty close, but that fell apart a while ago."

"Yeah. I saw that." Mabel rolled her eyes. "Any idea what happened?"

Darwin leaned back and looked at the ceiling. "I don't like to gossip."

Mabel made her eyes as large and innocent as she could.

Darwin gave her a sharp glance. "Are you all right? You look a little odd."

Mabel cleared her throat. "Um, sure. Please don't think I'm looking for gossip. I want to understand."

Apparently feeling he'd discharged his obligation to be discreet, Darwin continued. "They were still friendly, but extremely competitive, when I first joined the society. Helen was a pillar of the DAR, and Cora pretty much ran the local Colonial Dames chapter. They'd both held about every office in the historical society, and both were president more than once. But the most recent election for president was very close, and things got a bit ugly. Anyway, Helen won by the skin of her teeth and—I hate to say this, but it's the truth—maybe a few threats."

Chapter Sixteen

HELEN HAD MADE THREATS DURING THE most recent historical society election. Mabel was unsurprised, based on their brief acquaintanceship. She wondered if Helen had struck the last nerve. "So that was her and Cora's final rift?"

Darwin smiled. "There was a bit more to it than that. When results were announced, Cora blew up and started making public accusations. Like vote buying, bribery, and bullying."

"Whew."

He nodded. "But things got worse." Although there was no one else there, he lowered his voice. "I realize you didn't grow up here, so you may not have heard the rumors. About Cora's husband?"

She had. "When I was visiting my grandma, the other kids used to say she…uh…bumped him off. That she buried him under that row of holly she put in at the back of her property." Mabel laughed nervously. "Kid talk."

"That's the story, all right. It was well known at the time that Cora's husband was a cheater. But at some point, he disappeared under 'mysterious circumstances.'" Darwin made air quotes. "Rumors were flying hot and heavy. The kids would've picked that story up from their parents."

"Where does Helen come in?"

"When Cora started making accusations about the election, Helen made a veiled reference to 'knowing where the bodies are buried, and the smoking gun is stashed.' Cora, needless to say, threatened to kill her. And then Helen smirked and said, 'It wouldn't be the first time.'"

Mabel's jaw dropped.

Darwin laughed. "We had an uncomfortable evening. But to be

fair, the 'death threats'"—more air quotes—"went both ways. I've heard Helen say essentially the same thing to Cora more than once. That was all part of how they related to each other."

Mabel reflected. "Do you think Cora would be willing to talk about the old murders?"

Darwin tilted his head. "Do you have a particular interest in them?"

She wasn't sure what to say. "That tour group had a lot of questions about the murders, and I'm sure—no matter what Helen wanted to think—they're a big reason people are interested in the house at all. I want to be better informed, for one thing."

His expression was shrewd. "For another …?"

She made a decision. Darwin had been kind to her since the beginning. She appreciated having someone at the society who wouldn't judge her over something she couldn't have helped. "I'm also a writer, and I may be able to use the research at a later point. Mainly, I just need to know what happened to Helen."

He raised his eyebrows.

Mabel leaned forward. "Don't you think it's a bit of a coincidence that there were two ax murders in this house, and then, all these years later, the granddaughter also happens to die the same way? That isn't the most common means of doing someone in, nowadays."

"No, I guess not. But do we know this really was an ax murder?"

She was startled. "I think so. She had a blow to her neck. The first officer on the scene said something about her falling neck first into an ax."

"How is that possible?"

"I think she was implying it wasn't possible. That someone had swung the ax. And she did say ax."

"Was a weapon found? I understand the display hatchet is no longer there."

"Umm." Mabel hadn't even stopped to think about anything else at the scene, which might've been used as a weapon. "I don't know. I didn't notice one, and naturally, the police weren't going to tell me anything."

"How ghastly, though. You think the crimes were somehow related? After all these years?"

"Yeah. I guess I do. Coincidence is a bit much."

"Well, no point in our playing Hardy Boys—or in your case—" He smiled and nodded at her. "Nancy Drew. I'm sure the police will solve the case in due time. I wouldn't be surprised if they had a suspect or two by now."

"That's the problem." Mabel's heart sank. "One of them, at least, seems to be me."

Lisa's car was already sitting at Mabel's curb when she pulled into the driveway. Inside the house, Barnacle barked nonstop. She hoped he hadn't used the kitchen floor for his potty needs.

"Hey, Lisa. Were you waiting long?"

"Nope. Just landed five minutes ago."

"Come in. Can I get you a drink?"

Lisa brought out a gallon jug from her back seat. "I thought I could make mulled cider if you have the spices—and there's enough time before your date arrives."

Mabel huffed. "He isn't my date. We're comparing notes about this murder."

Lisa grinned. "Whatever you say. Do you have cinnamon and cloves?"

"I think so. Grandma left a ton of stuff in the cabinet."

Lisa wrinkled her nose. "I hope what's left is still fresh enough."

Barnacle burst through the door as soon as Mabel opened it. He raced for the back corner of the yard and began the process of sniffing bushes, which always preceded his selection of the ideal potty spot.

"The pans are under there." Mabel pointed. "I think the spices are up there. You might have to dig around a little bit. Barnacle got away before I could clip him to the tie-out cable, so I have to go grab him."

By the time Mabel came back inside, the kitchen smelled of apples and cinnamon. The table had been cleared and covered with a vintage tablecloth bordered with grape clusters. "I found the cloth in the cabinet over there. I figured I might as well dress up your table for your—um—visitor."

Mabel stared. "Wow. That looks nice. Thanks."

"I went ahead and made the whole gallon, so there will be plenty for your—company."

"Stop! I told you he's just looking into the murder, and that's all. You're still wonderful for helping, though." She blew Lisa a kiss. "Now, let me change real quick."

"Take your time." Lisa pulled a small bottle from her purse. "Here. Would you like to borrow my cologne? It's a real man magnet."

Mabel blushed. "Stop." Lisa was probably only teasing, but Mabel was going to feel like a fool when Lisa was still asking about John after he'd gone on his merry way, and nothing personal ever came of the relationship.

Mabel changed into clean jeans and a pink pullover that brought out the roses in her cheeks and hid her hips. Most important, she felt comfy. By the time she returned to the kitchen, Lisa had fed the animals, poured two mugs of cider, and set out a cheese plate.

"I think you need to come live with me," Mabel said—at the same time Lisa asked, "Is that what you're wearing?"

Mabel glanced down. "Appears so, doesn't it?"

Lisa opened her mouth, shut it again, and then took a bracing sip of cider. "Tell me about your guy quick, before he walks in."

"He isn't 'my guy.'" Mabel selected a chunk of cheese and sandwiched it between two crackers. She took her time, chewing, while Lisa watched over her cup rim, amusement dancing in her eyes.

"He's a private investigator." Mabel was finally unable to resist sharing that tidbit.

"Ooh…a PI." Lisa almost bounced out of her seat. She leaned forward. "Eye color? Hair?"

"Hazel. None."

"He's bald?"

"Shaved. Cop-like."

"Cool." Lisa reached over and patted Mabel's hand. "Sounds dreamy."

Mabel sniffed. "He's looking into this murder for a Sauer relative, so we're more or less on the same mission. I wouldn't care if he was a three-eyed bridge troll—as long as he can help me figure out who killed Helen Thornwald before I go to jail."

The glee went out of Lisa's eyes. "You don't seriously think that'll happen?"

"I hope not. I understand why they might suspect me, but they're a long way from being able to prove anything."

"Like means, motive, and opportunity?"

Mabel smiled. "Someone's been watching Law & Order. Yeah, it helps if they can show all that, and it's tough to convict someone if you don't have evidence. But I do sort of have a motive. The 'means'…I don't know. If they can come up with a murder weapon, and it turns out I might have had access to that in the critical space of time…"

Lisa's forehead creased with concern. "For real?"

Mabel waved a hand, attempting to be airy. "All circumstantial. Besides, there may be a half-dozen people who meet the same criteria. The bottom line is whether the prosecutor thinks she can prove one of us killed her—beyond a reasonable doubt. That's a pretty big burden of proof," she said, as much to convince herself as Lisa.

For almost an hour, they talked about the murder, Mabel's career issues, and Lisa's hopeful wedding plans. Mabel looked at the time. John was due in a half hour. And the cheese was almost gone. Oh, well. He'd said he was bringing dinner.

"Hey, I was going to try to start watching a DVD before John gets here." Mabel fished in her tote bag "I have to return it in three days and figured I'd better not wait till the last minute."

"Anything good?"

"Part of my murder research. Want to watch with me?"

"Now I'm curious." Lisa studied the box and shook her head. "You've got to be kidding."

"Nope." Mabel popped the DVD into the player. "I figure these guys always do extensive historical research on the properties they investigate, so maybe I'll pick something up."

"Ghost Diggers? Really?"

"They're archaeologists of the paranormal," Mabel said with dignity.

"Betting that came from a promo spot."

Mabel patted the couch. "Have a seat."

Barnacle jumped up, and Mabel pushed him down. "Come on, Lisa."

"Oh, all right. The things I subject myself to for you."

Mabel set her mug down, clicked the remote to scan the Season One DVD for the Sauer episode then picked up her steno pad and pen. The show started with an atmospheric shot of the Medicine Spring cemetery in a heavy fog, which she suspected came from a machine. The voiceover explained this was the Sauer family's final resting place—including Edna Sauer, who "though acquitted by a jury of her peers, is still thought by many to be guilty of the murder of her own father and brother."

The narrator—a man about thirty, with a chiseled face and shoulder-length dark hair—stepped into frame. "The lone survivor of this tragic family"—*that would be Helen*— "has requested we don't film at the house itself. Out of respect for her wishes"— *Abject fear of Helen's wrath,* Mabel translated— "we've elected to perform our investigation at the Medicine Spring Cemetery, where local residents claim to have seen shadowy figures and unexplained lights in the vicinity of the Sauer graves."

They got about a third of the way throug
arrived, carrying a pizza box. Lisa had spent
up with a running critique of the Ghost
"archeology of the paranormal."

Mabel, however, had filled a couple of p
It might have been a lot of hooey, however, the team's historical
investigator had done tons of research that provided a reasonable
background on the family and the tragic events that destroyed it.

Barnacle went nuts when John appeared, jumping, snarling, and
barking. But he stopped carrying on as soon as Mabel opened the door
and John spoke to him. He'd never done that with anyone before, but
maybe he remembered John from when they'd met outside. Or maybe
he was responding to the smell of pizza.

"Why, hello there." Surprise washed over his face when Lisa
appeared in the living room doorway.

"Hello to you." She beamed at John. "I'm Mabel's friend, Lisa.
We've known each other since kindergarten."

He smiled back, and Mabel felt a rush of irritation for her own
flash of jealousy over that smile.

He stuck out his hand. "John—Mabel's partner in investigation.
We're going to figure out who killed Helen and keep Mabel out of the
slammer."

"I'm glad to hear that." Lisa giggled. "That's been my job the past
forty-some years. I'll be happy to hand her off."

Mabel's jaw dropped.

John winked and laughed.

"Hey, I've got to get going. I'll call around eleven to see how you
made out. Oops." Lisa laughed again and dropped a big stage wink. "I
mean see if you figured anything out, of course."

Mabel fought a furious blush that surged up from her neck and
washed over her cheeks. "You want a hot cider?" she asked John.

ned.

e bent to fill his mug, Lisa made all sorts of hand motions and ned something to Mabel. With a big smile, she gave Mabel two numbs up behind his back.

After Lisa had gone, John gestured toward the paused DVD. "What on earth are you watching?"

"A documentary. Here, let's find some plates and napkins."

He narrowed his eyes at the screen. "Is this one of those ghost reality shows? If you call that 'reality.'"

"Yep." Mabel settled herself back on the couch with two slices of deluxe pizza and a wad of napkins. When she hit "play," the Ghost Diggers squad sprang into action.

They were attempting to take electronic recordings of voices inaudible to the human ear, by directing a series of questions at Walter, Sr.'s grave. "Are you here with us, Mr. Sauer? Did you know the person who killed you?"

When they played the recording a moment later, the team started exclaiming. "Oh, man." "Did you hear that?" "That was clear as a bell." "He said, 'Yes.'"

Mabel frowned. All she'd heard was static. She leaned in and shut her eyes for their replay. It still only sounded like static.

John snorted.

The scene cut away to a meeting with Devereaux Reid, back at Ghost Diggers headquarters. The caption read, "True Crime Writer and Sauer Ax Murder Authority."

Mabel jumped up and froze the screen. "That's her." She pointed. "The blonde from the tour group I was telling you about."

John leaned forward as Mabel returned to her seat. This time, she snorted, reading the caption. Start writing a book and suddenly you were an expert. She wondered whether, if she were to write a book about the ax murders, she might be asked to appear on TV.

John cleared his throat.

"Sorry." She clicked "play" again.

"I've done extensive research on the Sauers, as well as the horrific murders." Devereaux looked grave. "From the beginning, this was a family marked for tragedy." She projected sadness. "But my exhaustive research has finally led me to a definitive answer to the age-old question—who killed Mr. Sauer and his son?"

Chapter Seventeen

MABEL STARED AT THE TV. SHE clicked her pen, wishing, if Devereaux knew who killed the Sauers, she'd spit it out.

The Ghost Digger who'd been interviewing her leaned forward. "Are you prepared to say, based upon your research, that Edna Sauer— the chief suspect at the time, and in fact, still to this day the *acquitted* suspect—was indeed guilty as charged?"

Mabel gasped, and Koi, who'd been snoozing in her lap, rocketed off the couch. Mabel hit pause. "What sort of evidence could she have at this point?"

"I can't imagine," John said.

Mabel lifted her chin. "Edna wasn't guilty." As she said it, she realized she should be keeping an open mind. After all, what evidence did *she* have, either?

"What makes you say that? The verdict?"

Mabel was forced to concede she had no real evidence. "Just a feeling." Though, if she were being honest with herself, she'd have to admit her opinion was based in part on this vague sense of sisterhood with the disrespected second-class sister.

"Who do *you* think was responsible?" he asked.

"I don't know. The evidence was circumstantial. Edna happened to be there that day." Mabel started ticking things off on her fingers. "Her father was overbearing and reputedly abusive. Their relationship was strained over his trying to force her to marry his creepy old business partner. She had blood on her clothes. Nobody knew where the ax disappeared to."

"It was never found, either."

Mabel made a note. "It wasn't?" She dimly remembered seeing an ax in the display case photos but hadn't yet gotten that far in the Sauer murder book.

"Kind of like what happened in the Lizzie Borden case, what they've been displaying is an unrelated hatchet found in the cellar after the deaths. We learned all about the Sauer murders as kids."

"Ohhh...well, I guess that's gone now, too. Hmm...it would be a pretty big deal if someone were to find the original ax, wouldn't it?"

John nodded. "I'd think so."

"I wonder if they could get any evidence from the ax today, with modern forensic techniques."

"Doubtful, after eighty years."

Mabel restarted the show. Could Devereaux have found the missing ax, after all these years?

Devereaux had little more to say on the subject, however, beyond teasing her new book for the answers. She suggested a few questions for the Ghost Diggers to try asking at the graves. "The family knows." She looked straight into the camera. "I believe the family always knew. And so does someone else."

"When did this run?"

Mabel checked. "Last spring." Her thoughts tumbled. "What on earth could she be talking about? She has to be making stuff up to sell books."

He grimaced. "She will sell books. Everybody in Medicine Spring will be standing in line. Probably across the country too. The Sauer ax murders are almost as famous as Lizzie Borden or Villisca. New evidence? That's huge, if true. Especially if she does solve the case. Can you imagine?"

"Is that likely?"

He shook his head. "I have to agree with you. Not when this much time has passed, short of a signed confession that can be authenticated."

Although they went back to the show, it never returned to Devereaux or her assertions. When the credits started rolling, Mabel popped out the DVD. She yawned. Her restless night was starting to catch up with her.

Now that the show was over, and she and John sat together on the couch and staring at each other, Mabel was at a loss for what to say. She glanced away and started gathering plates, mugs, and napkins. As a pizza crust slid, she made a grab, but Barnacle was quicker. Koi, who had been snoozing across the back of the couch, stretched to her full length and yawned. Pizza without chicken or anchovies bored her.

"Yeah, well, I had a short night last night," she said. "I think I'd better try to get to bed early."

John picked up the empty pizza box and tipped his head toward the TV. "Did that give you any new thoughts?"

Mabel walked back into the kitchen and deposited her armload onto the counter. She opened the pantry door so John could dispose of the fragrant pizza box. Barnacle's taste for garbage had necessitated her keeping the trash receptacle behind a closed door.

"A few. That show made me wonder more about the original murders and any connection to Helen's. She said, 'The family knows' and 'So does someone else.'"

John tilted his head. "*If* there's any truth to that, and we could find out what she meant, it would be a major break."

"If."

Barnacle stood at the back door, her signal to let him out. Who had trained whom?

Mabel watched from the doorway as the dog sniffed around the yard. "I learned something else new today." She told John what Darwin had said about Cora.

"You've been a busy girl."

The cold poured in through the open door and all the heat was going out, so Mabel closed it. "Did you learn anything today?"

"I did call in a favor from a friend on the force, so I got updated on at least a bit of what's going on in their investigation."

"You can do that?"

John puffed up his chest. "Leave that assignment to me, partner."

She leaned back against the edge of the counter. "What did you hear?"

"Not a lot at this stage. They're still waiting for the autopsy results. But the fingerprints have all been processed—for what they're worth."

"Not much?" she guessed.

He shook his head. "They sorted out yours and a couple from the tour group. Also Helen's, as you'd expect, and a few others from the historical society. Not all were in the key areas, but a lot were. Naturally, some prints couldn't even be made out because of overlapping and smudging."

"Phooey."

He shrugged. "None of this is surprising."

"Did they find any they can't identify?"

"Apparently, not yet. But if someone from outside came to commit a crime, he—or she—might have worn gloves, anyway."

Mabel nodded.

"The autopsy should narrow down the dimensions and characteristics of the wound. Depending on how distinctive those are, it could point to the weapon."

"It's probably the missing hatchet, right?"

John shrugged. "That it was discovered missing right after Helen's murder sure points that direction, but we can't assume. She might've removed it herself some time ago. Nobody else, from what I understand, ever goes in there much.

"Do you know who has keys?" he asked.

"I'm sure the police checked into that. As far as I know, at least all the board members—Helen, Cora, Darwin, Nanette, and whoever else. I don't know a lot yet. I was only there for one meeting, so far, and the cursed tour."

Her phone rang. Lisa's face popped up on caller ID.

"Your bodyguard?"

"What?" Mabel felt herself flush.

"I assume your friend Lisa's making sure you're okay—I like that.

She made sure I knew she'd be checking up afterward, and that I would be suspect number one."

Mabel picked up.

"I'll let myself out," he whispered, his warm breath disturbing Mabel's hair, as well as her heart rate. He held up his hand in a phone gesture, mouthing, "I'll call tomorrow."

A moment later, Barnacle bounded in as the back door opened, and he thrust a cold, wet nose into Mabel's free hand. She petted his cool, rough fur. John must have dragged him over, cutting short Barnacle's usual nasal inspection of the shrubbery.

"He left a minute ago," she told Lisa.

"Are you sure? Better look outside. Make sure you lock your doors." Lisa was a true-crime aficionado and ran any situation she encountered through every familiar murder scenario.

"Yes, Mom." Mabel obligingly peered out the window. John was getting into his car. He grinned and blew her a kiss.

Mabel darted out of sight, leaning back against the kitchen wall. "He saw me checking on him!"

"Good. Is he driving away?"

"I don't know, because I'm in deep hiding. I'm dying of embarrassment here."

"Better to die of embarrassment than a date gone bad."

Mabel groaned but didn't bother correcting her.

"Now, lock those doors."

When Mabel eased back into the square of window, John's taillights were cruising up the block. She reached over to flip the lock then drew her hand back. "Huh."

"What?"

"John already locked my door."

"I like that, Mabel. He's being solicitous."

Mabel felt a peculiar sensation in her chest. She'd never had anybody protective of her before, other than her family and Lisa.

"How did it go? Tell me everything," Lisa demanded.

Mabel checked the front door. "There isn't anything to tell. We finished watching Ghost Diggers, ate pizza, and compared a few notes about the murder investigation. Then, he left."

"Did he give out any signals?"

"Like what?"

"A lingering glance. A compliment. A casual touch. You know."

Mabel realized she didn't know. Flirting had never been part of her repertoire. "Of course not. I told you we were just comparing notes on Helen's murder."

"He's got potential. I'm happy to finally see you with someone who can appreciate you. It wouldn't hurt to send a few signals of your own. But subtle, you know?"

"Um-hmm." Mabel was totally clueless, not that it mattered.

She continued to deflect Lisa's suggestions on her nonexistent love life while dispensing bedtime snacks and finally heading upstairs. When they'd said good night, and she'd nestled down into the quilts, she cracked open the Sauer book and picked up where she'd left off. Soon, she was once again caught up in the story and kept turning pages long after she had intended to shut off the lights.

Chapter Eighteen

M ABEL WOKE WITH THE S AUER BOOK on her chest, pages crumpled under Barnacle's snoring bulk. Koi lay across her forehead, tail tickling Mabel's nose.

Mabel sneezed and sat up, dislodging Barnacle, who gave a huge yawn and stretched. Koi leapt to the headboard and glared at her, tail flicking.

Mabel was stumbling down the hall when her cell rang. She shuffled back and fumbled to answer it.

"Good morning, dear. I didn't wake you, did I?"

"Hi, Nanette. No, I was up." More or less.

Nanette paused. "I feel a bit to blame for your awful experience, since I asked you to fill in."

"You couldn't possibly have known."

"Have you heard anything from…?" Nanette hesitated. "The police?"

"Not since I signed my statement."

"Did they say if they have any…?"

"Suspects? No, they didn't." Mabel didn't want to get into the suspicious way they looked at her.

"I hope they can soon find out who did this. For Helen's sake, of course, but to be honest, I don't feel safe at the house since this happened, either. We don't even know a motive. What if there's a crazy person who wants to murder everyone connected with the Sauer house?"

"Oh, I'm sure that isn't true. After all, she was in the back parlor, so I'm guessing whoever killed her had a key."

The long pause told Mabel this perhaps wasn't the most

comforting perspective. Instead of a random crazy stranger, hadn't she suggested the murderer was likely someone right in their own organization? Maybe one of Nanette's friends?

"Of course," Mabel hastily added, "the parlor might've already been unlocked. Maybe Helen had unlocked it and left it open while she worked."

"Frankly, I don't like any of the options. But I find it hard to imagine her having left that door unlocked. She was so protective of her family—that's why the door was kept locked. If a visitor had walked in, she wouldn't have wanted the room on full display."

"I suppose that's right. What do you think Helen was doing in there, if she hated the murder room so much?"

"I've wondered that, myself. It appeared she might have been rearranging the display case. I'm sure you know it was not her favorite room."

After another brief hesitation, Nanette cleared her throat and continued. "Cora asked if I'd heard you were…investigating Helen's death."

"Where would she have gotten that idea? All I want is to make sure the police don't decide to pin this on me, merely because I was there."

"Of course you do, dear, and I don't blame you a bit. I wouldn't worry about the police, though."

They chatted a few minutes, and then, as Mabel was excusing herself, Nanette cut in. "Oh, I almost forgot to make sure you knew Cora called a meeting tonight." Her tart voice conveyed her feelings regarding last-minute scheduling.

Mabel sighed. The very last thing she wanted to do right now was attend another society meeting. Maybe she ought to see it as an opportunity to pick up some sort of clue, though.

Mabel moved through her morning routine while still mulling over the conversation. The back parlor was always kept locked. Helen hated the parlor and its reminder of her grandfather's and uncle's brutal murders and the ensuing scandal. The murders must have been quite scarring for Helen's mother Violet, and Helen herself had grown up under their shadow.

So why had the parlor been unlocked? What had caused Helen to go back there? Nanette's suggestions were rather hard to accept. Why would Helen care about cleaning or rearranging a display nobody was ever supposed to see?

Mabel kept turning over everything she knew. What if Helen hadn't gone back there willingly? What if she'd been moved postmortem? The coroner should know. Forensic people—on TV, at least—always seemed to be able to tell if a body had been moved after death. Something to do with the way the blood pooled.

But what about the display case? Why would Nanette say she might have been rearranging the display? Had she seen it? Was the display different from when Nanette last saw it? What if it hadn't been Helen, but somebody else, who'd moved things around, maybe in connection with a robbery? What if Helen had been forced into the back in order to unlock the case?

Mabel shook her head. In a house full of antiques—including a lot of small, portable items—why would somebody be so anxious to burglarize the back parlor?

Mabel cast through what she'd seen of the room. There didn't seem to be anything of special value there—old furniture, photos, a bloodstained scrap of fabric, newspaper articles. At least, nothing worth more than what was available for the taking in the front rooms.

No, not a burglary gone wrong. Too many pieces didn't fit.

When she'd finished breakfast and taken Barnacle for his constitutional, Mabel decided to ship the goodie boxes to her niece and nephew and maybe pick up something a little classier for the refreshment table.

Then, she needed to stop at the courthouse. She'd been dragging her feet over Grandma Mabel's estate filings and suspected she was close to receiving a stern notice from the Register of Wills. While there, she might as well stop at the Clerk of Courts and see if she could get a copy of the Edna Sauer trial transcript. She hoped such a thing was still on file and available for copying.

Mabel rushed to refill the animals' water dish, then located supplies to ship the packages. Luckily, in this instance, Grandma Mabel had never thrown anything away, and she had several containers to choose from. She filled two boxes with the treats she'd selected, stuffed crumpled newspaper in the spaces, sealed them with packing tape, and plastered on hastily scrawled labels.

Then, she ferreted out her estate file—a tote bag from Drapers' Funeral Home, which she'd been using to corral the original packet from the Register of Wills, receipts, her middle-of-the-night notes, estate checkbook, and other odds and ends. She'd been feeling bad about herself for not being on top of this, but she'd never done estate work before.

Under all of that, though, was the simple fact that working on the estate meant Grandma Mabel was dead. It meant it was all real, and the one person who'd ever truly understood her—and loved her anyway— was gone forever. At least, until she saw her again in heaven. Which, as much as she missed her, Mabel was in no hurry to do.

Mabel had finally—belatedly—posted notices to the newspapers and the other beneficiaries of the estate. According to the checklist, it looked like all she had to do right now was file the record of that at the courthouse. She pulled out the correct forms and slipped them into her handbag.

"Be good," she told her animals.

The post office—miraculously—wasn't crowded. Mabel shipped her parcels and bought a sheet of stamps. Afterward, she slipped into the European bakery next door and splurged on a box of glazed fruit tarts for the meeting and a Napoleon for herself. She figured she deserved a treat, not only for taking care of the dreaded estate filing but also to comfort herself for discovering a murder and ending up on the suspect list.

She took a cup of rich, dark coffee with two creams and sat at a wrought-iron ice cream table in the window to eat her pastry before carrying her coffee back to the car. Her next stop was Bartles Grove, the county seat.

Fall was lingering this year. Despite many already-bare trees, there were still bright splashes of red and gold. With the sun shining and a Napoleon resting comfortingly in her tummy, Mabel felt herself begin to relax. Teaming up with John had helped too, she realized. Surely, a PI would figure out this murder eventually, with or without her input.

But could she trust him? The Napoleon made a restless movement in the pit of her stomach.

The parking spots near the courthouse were all taken. Mabel circled the grassy square with its Civil War monument, and mature oaks, still clinging to their rusty leaves. She saw an SUV pull out of a space on the far side. Mabel hurried to block the spot. Parallel parking had never been her greatest skill, but she nailed it on the second try, fed the meter, and took the footpath across the square.

As soon as she'd cleared the metal detector, Mabel decided to get the Register of Wills out of the way. As Mabel approached the high counter, she felt a familiar attack of fear and trembling.

Mabel's years at the law firm had prepared her to draft pleadings and memoranda, to write letters threatening bad landlords with rent withholding. The rules of Pennsylvania Estate Law were but a dim bar exam memory at this point, though. And the Register of Wills might as well have been an obscure government office in Fiji, presided over by functionaries waiting to sanction Mabel for some murky violation.

Today, the clerk gave a casual glance at her papers before stamping and tossing them into an in-basket.

"Do I owe anything?" she asked, not believing her good fortune.

"Nope, you're good to go. Have a nice day."

"You too." Mabel rewarded the clerk with a big smile and ran for the door.

She hadn't gotten very far when she realized she'd forgotten something. The clerk had already wandered into the file area, so while she waited for her return, she dug a scrap of paper from her tote and printed Helen's name on it.

The clerk reemerged. "Was there something else you needed?"

"I'm sorry. Would you be able to check whether a will has been filed for this decedent?"

"Time for bifocals." The clerk chuckled, pushed her glasses onto the top of her graying curls, and squinted. "Oh, that poor woman—what a tragedy. I'm pretty sure we don't have anything yet but let me look."

Moments later, she reappeared and shook her head. "You might try back in a couple weeks."

"Thanks for checking."

Oh, well. Nothing ventured, nothing gained.

The Clerk of Courts was much busier than the Register's office, and attorneys waited ahead of her, begging for lenience and various favors. Finally, she arrived at the counter and discovered the Sauer trial transcript was still on file.

"We did a copy of the whole thing for someone else last year." The clerk, a slender young man in geeky glasses and bow tie, leaned in to convey what passed for exciting news at the Clerk's office. "The lady was a writer. She's doing a book about the murders. Pretty cool, huh?"

"Extremely." Mabel leaned an elbow on the counter. "I'm a writer myself, you know."

"Really?" He gave her what could only be called a dubious look.

"Really," Mabel snapped then collected herself. She supposed the general public expected writers to look a certain way. Like Devereaux, maybe? Men could be all Hemingway macho, or Stephen King intense. Women authors should get the same leeway.

While the clerk made her copy, Mabel thought about her image. She ought to get a pair of decent boots. Maybe an uptown haircut.

When the clerk returned, she paid the fee and collected a thick envelope of pages. "Was she a blonde?"

"What?"

"The writer you made the other copy for. Was she a blonde?"

He grinned. "Sure was. She promised to sign a copy for me when the book comes out."

Mabel gritted her teeth. "How lovely."

It was near dusk by the time Mabel got home. She'd thought of stopping at The Grind, to see if Betsy might be working, but knew she couldn't spare a minute. If she went straight home, she had time for a quick dinner and nap before the meeting. That is, if she didn't change her clothing and put on fresh makeup. Since she'd been missing so much sleep the past few days, she decided that was more important than trying to impress anybody at the society with her grooming.

But when she stretched out on the couch and closed her eyes, her mind still raced. John hadn't called all day. If he'd learned anything new, surely he'd call, wouldn't he?

She also found the simple and familiar action of lying down on the couch now made her think about Walter Sauer, Sr.'s murder. He had been lying down, just like this, when death came for him.

Her eyes flew open. She'd half expected to see a descending ax. Breathing fast, she looked around the shadowed room. Barnacle would make a racket if anyone came in. She needn't worry about being ambushed.

But thoughts of Walter, Sr.'s murder led to thinking about the afternoon of the tour. She had come to the Sauer mansion, talked to Nanette and then waited. She had waited, alone in the house, for her tour group to arrive.

Or had she been alone?

For the first time, the thought struck Mabel that she might have been alone in the house with Helen's killer, as well as her dead body.

Chapter Nineteen

MABEL NEVER DID FALL ASLEEP THAT afternoon, so she was one of the earlier arrivals for the society meeting. This time, she set out her refreshment contribution with a little burst of pride. She'd transferred the tarts to one of Grandma's vintage plates. Not that she would pretend she'd made them herself, if anyone asked, but they did look good this way. Maybe people would assume she'd made them.

She took a seat near the back, hoping to keep a low profile. Nanette, seated near the front, saw her and waved.

"Hello there." Darwin smiled and gestured at the chair next to her. "Is this seat taken?"

"Help yourself."

"How are you doing?" He gave her a look of concern. "Still holding together?"

"I'm okay." Mabel knew nobody wanted the truth when they asked how you were—at least, not casual acquaintances who were being no more than polite.

"I'm sorry you've had such an awful introduction to our group."

"Thanks. That wasn't your fault."

Darwin's hand went to his pocket. He pulled out his phone and glanced at it. "Excuse me. I have to take this."

Mabel set her bag on his chair. The least she could do was hold his seat.

Cora stood at the podium, her oak-like frame draped in a Lilly Pulitzer wrap splashed with blue, pink, and yellow shells and seahorses. It might be October outside, but in here, looking at Cora, and with the heat cranked up, it felt like July. It looked as if Cora had had her steel-gray hair freshly cut and highlighted with subtle silver streaks. Unlike the last time Mabel had seen her, Cora was all but glowing.

Mabel didn't want to answer questions, so she slithered down in her seat and pretended to be too absorbed in her paperwork to chat. In fact, she was starting to make her way through the trial transcript. As she went, she slashed with her yellow highlighter and made notes in the margins. She felt odd, reading this in the murder house—reading the testimony now, right after the murder of Edna's niece.

Her sense of Edna's presence was strong this evening. She glanced up at Edna's portrait, hanging on the wall where she could hover over Mabel's shoulder as she read.

The rap of the gavel silenced the chitchat. "Thank you all for making the effort to come out for this special meeting." Cora folded her hands on the lectern. "I know we all are still in shock over the horrible tragedy here this week."

Amid the general murmur, heads turned Mabel's way. Darwin returned and slid in next to her.

"Police are telling us the parlor will be cleared for us shortly to get in and clean," Cora said. "We opened for visitors as soon as the main part of the building was cleared. However, we soon realized we'd be overrun by curiosity seekers, and that didn't seem appropriate. The board has decided to lock down and defer public reopening until after Helen's funeral, which the family hopes may be as early as next week, if the coroner releases the body." She dabbed at her right eye with a tissue.

"As vice president, I have assumed the presidency. The nominating committee will be contacting candidates, so we can elect a new vice president to take over my previous duties."

Cora had gotten the hotly contested presidency, after all. Well, well, well.

"Now, the other thing I hoped we might go over tonight relates to the gala being held to celebrate Margarethe Sauer's life and benefit the fund for the new Community Hospital Mothers' and Children's wing, which will bear her name. The board believes, given Helen's justifiable pride in her family, this will be the best way to remember and honor her, as well."

Mabel leaned close to Darwin's ear. "Where is this gala, and what does she expect us to do?"

"The Country Club ballroom," he whispered back. "It's less than two weeks away at this point. We all have tickets to sell, and we're supposed to come up with ideas for the silent auction."

That didn't sound overwhelming, Mabel thought with relief. Normally in these situations, Mabel would buy a few tickets herself. Or she could probably get Lisa, and some of her family members, to take one. "How much are tickets?" she whispered.

"$100 a plate," Darwin whispered back, nearly giving Mabel a coronary.

"I don't have to sell any, do I?" she hissed.

"I wouldn't think so, since you're new. But that's Cora's department, so I don't know."

At that moment, Mabel became aware Cora had stopped talking. When Mabel glanced up, she saw Cora giving her and Darwin the evil eye. "Sorry," she whispered, more at Darwin than Cora, for getting him in trouble. She made a zipping motion across her lips for Cora's benefit, causing another glare.

Cora adjusted her eyeglasses and continued through the rest of her new-business items. Discussion was subdued, as might have been expected under the shocking circumstances. Cora ran a tight business meeting, banged the gavel, and they were adjourned.

At that point, a couple of people closed in on Cora, and another contingent moved toward the refreshments, but the rest turned toward Mabel. A woman whose figure resembled a Russian nesting doll clasped both Mabel's hands. "You poor thing. We feel terrible you were caught up in this awful tragedy."

Mabel murmured her standard reply, that her involvement wasn't the woman's fault, and that she was doing all right. She tugged gently at her hands, trying to break away without making an obvious escape attempt. But the woman teared up in sympathy, released Mabel's hands, and wrapped her arms around Mabel's shoulders. "You're so brave, dear. In your place, I'd have keeled right over on top of the body." The lady put a trembling hand over her lips. "I'm sorry—I shouldn't have said that."

Then, she brightened. "You'll have to come to dinner one evening soon. I have a son who collects salt-and-pepper shakers. I think you two would hit it off. Do you care for salt-and-pepper shakers at all, dear?"

Mabel opened her mouth, but no sound came out. She had nothing to contribute on the topic of salt-and-pepper shakers.

Two other women closed in from either side like synchronized dancers. "How did she look, Marlene?" one asked, while the other hissed, "Her name is Mabel—you know, she's Mabel Browne's granddaughter. Oh, that's right—you missed that meeting. I should introduce you."

The nesting doll lady cleared her throat. "Allow me." She maintained her sturdy grip on Mabel's shoulders. "Mabel, this is Regina Simon, and over here is Betty Rominski." Mabel had the uncomfortable feeling this woman was staking a claim on her...perhaps as a future daughter-in-law, if Mabel and the nesting doll lady's salt-and-pepper-shaker-fancying son made a love connection.

"I'm so sorry, Mabel," Mrs. Simon corrected herself. "Might I ask how dear Helen looked? I don't want to be prurient, but do you think she went quickly? I do hope she didn't suffer."

"Eh, if she's dead, she's dead." Mrs. Rominski raised a shoulder. "I wouldn't wish ill of her or anyone else, but she wasn't the nicest woman I've met. May God rest her soul." She crossed herself piously.

"Um...." As Mabel cast about for something appropriate to say, Darwin tapped her shoulder.

"Excuse us, ladies, but I need Mabel for a moment. Good to see you back, Regina. That sciatica is awful, isn't it?"

Mrs. Simon shrugged. "I'm still suffering, but what can you do? Life goes on."

Mabel smiled a faint apology. "Thank you," she murmured as Darwin pulled her toward the office.

He smiled. "I know what it's like, when those three get you trapped." He ushered her into the office, leaving the door ajar. After seeming to reflect, he closed it the rest of the way. "Nosy parkers." He tilted his head. "Do you mind? Do you have a moment to sit?"

"I—uh—yeah, I guess so." Mabel glanced back at the refreshment table.

"I won't keep you," he promised. "By the way, did you bring those tarts? They're wonderful."

"Thank you." Mabel felt no need to disclaim having made them, since he hadn't asked. She wished she'd saved a kiwi one for herself.

Darwin shuffled the papers on his desk. "At the risk of sounding like Regina and Betty, I wondered whether you'd learned anything new since we talked earlier."

"No. I wish. Maybe when the autopsy's done, we'll know more."

He frowned. "Do you think we should be worried here? In the house, I mean?"

"I don't know. The attack might have been directed at her, personally, rather than anything to do with the house or the society. But I don't think it was a random break-in, because nothing was taken."

"Hmm…" Darwin stroked his upper lip.

Mabel's ears perked up. "What? Did you hear something? Is something missing?"

"Nanette inspected the room pretty thoroughly for the police, and she could say better than I. But I think a crazy person might be responsible—you know, someone obsessed with the old ax murders, acting out the old crime."

Now why would he think that? Mabel's brows rose. "Why so? Do you think they would've killed anybody they found here that day? Or was Helen targeted because she was a Sauer?"

"I have no earthly idea, and I don't want to upset you, because I realize you *were* here that day. I'm only speculating."

To be fair, he had done more than speculate. He'd stated it as his belief but offered no evidence to support his theory. Her glance flitted away from his. Probably just playing armchair detective, but could Darwin be pushing this farfetched scenario for reasons of his own? Like what? Misdirection from the true culprit? Away from him, perhaps.

Of course, Darwin had no motive she could see. But could one of her true-crimers from the Wilkie tour bus be the perpetrator? A deranged murder fan? Surely not. When they'd arrived from an hour and a half away, Mabel was alone in the house. Right? Helen had failed to show up for the tour and was presumably dead in the back parlor before the bus arrived.

Still, her thoughts returned to Devereaux Reid, who'd had issues with Helen over the publication of her true-crime book. Devereaux had been thwarted by Helen once already and stood to lose the benefit of all her research, as well as the publishing opportunity she'd been counting on.

A chill ran along Mabel's arms. A modern-day ax murder of a Sauer descendant, right here in the murder house, would almost definitely sell a lot of books. How ambitious was Devereaux Reid? How angry at Helen?

She shook her head. Devereaux had arrived along with everybody else on the tour. She might've had enough time, by lagging behind, to slip into the back parlor and kill Helen. But by that time, Helen had to have already been dead. Mabel needed to see that autopsy report.

"Excuse me—are you all right?"

"I'm sorry." Mabel rubbed her eyes. "I was woolgathering."

He stood. "No, I'm sorry for holding you up. I hope you'll continue with the society after all this. We need people with fresh ideas." His face brightened. "The board has been talking. We plan to get a new alarm system. No need to feel unsafe here."

She gave him a weak smile. In her heart of hearts, Mabel knew she would never have any need to feel unsafe in the Sauer house, anyway, because she would never be here alone again.

Chapter Twenty

MABEL'S HOUSE WAS DARK WHEN SHE returned. She fumbled for the key and used her phone's flashlight app to find the lock.

Once inside, she switched on lights. "Barnacle?" She'd wait and relock after his last trip outside.

It was odd, his not being underfoot the moment she'd opened the door. In fact, he was usually barking by the time she stepped out of her car.

"Barnacle."

Mabel's heart pounded in her throat, squeezing off her breath. This wasn't normal. If he'd been shut in somewhere, he'd be barking by now. "Barnacle!"

And where was Koi? "Here, kitty."

Neither animal appeared. The house was silent. Much too silent.

Not bothering to take off her jacket or put down her bag, she hurried toward the front hallway. But before she could reach that light switch, she stumbled over him.

Barnacle lay in the dining room doorway, still and limp. His tongue lolled onto the carpet.

"Wake up!" she shrieked. This couldn't be happening.

She stooped to touch him, but her knees buckled, and she fell onto them. She grabbed his fur and shook. "Barnacle."

He was still warm. His body was limp, not stiff. *Please, let him be alive.*

She put her hand by his nose, feeling for breath.

At that moment, she sensed movement behind her. Before she could turn, someone touched her.

By sheer instinct, she swung her purse around and started kicking as hard as she could. She screamed and scrambled away into the shadows of the front hall, fumbling for her phone.

Not finding it, she came up with her keychain airhorn and blasted it above her own screams.

A man's voice cut through her panic. "Stop. It's me."

Mabel's scream turned into a sob. "Stay away from me."

"Mabel." John Bigelow stepped over Barnacle's body and flipped on the light. "It's me."

Mabel's breathing came hard and ragged.

Ignoring her for the moment, John dropped to his knees and ran his hands over the dog's face and limp body. "What happened?"

"I found him like this. Is he...?"

John scooped him up as easily as if he were as small as Koi. "He's alive. Who's your vet?"

"I d-don't know. I've only had Barnacle for six months."

"Then, I'd say the emergency clinic at this hour. Come on. I'll drive you."

"K-Koi...."

He paused at the back door. "Your cat? Is she all right?"

"I don't know. She's missing."

"Shh, it'll be all right. She'll be hiding. It's what cats do. We need to get this guy to the vet right now. We don't have time to look. Okay?"

Mabel nodded and followed him out, locking the door with trembling hands.

John eased Barnacle down across the back seat.

"You don't have a seat cover. He's sh-shedding."

"That's the least of my worries. Get in."

Mabel slid in next to Barnacle. Her hands buried in his fur, she prayed silently and desperately. "Please, Lord. He's a good dog. Please. Please let him be okay."

John already had the engine running. As soon as she was inside, he threw the car into reverse and squealed out of her driveway. "Tell me what happened," he demanded.

"I don't know." Mabel laid her head against Barnacle's side. She thought she could feel him breathing. "Come on, don't do this to me. Hang in there."

The car screeched around the corner by the Sauer mansion.

"I came home a few minutes ago. He didn't meet me like he always does and didn't come when I called. When I went searching, I found him there on the floor."

"I had office hours today," John said, "and decided to stop by on my way home. But you didn't answer when I knocked and called."

"I never even heard you. I was so worried about Barnacle."

"He's going to be all right."

"I hope so. I don't know what happened...if he got into something, or.... He'll eat anything."

"Now don't get excited, but is there any chance somebody could've harmed him?"

Mabel's jaw dropped. "Both doors were locked. I think."

"Was your back door locked for sure when you came in?"

"I never checked. I used my key, though. It felt like the lock turned."

"Is there another way in?"

"The front door." A thought struck. "Or there's a basement door. I don't use it at all."

John's brow creased. "Locked?"

"I think so. It should be."

"I hope you're right."

Mabel tried to envision the basement door. She simply hadn't thought much about it. Could it be? Her skin crawled at the thought of someone coming into her basement and creeping up the steps.

John blew out a heavy breath. "I'm so sorry this happened."

"Why would anybody want to hurt poor Barnacle?"

"I don't know. If someone broke in, would he have tried to defend the house?"

"Ye-e-es. At least, I'm sure he'd confront someone coming in. But

126

if they were nice to him, he'd probably settle down."

The sign in front of the North Ridge Clinic glowed red and blue, with EMERGENCY in red, over the side entrance. John's car skidded into the parking lot. Before Mabel could get out, he was opening the other door and lifting Barnacle.

Mabel scrambled out and ran to the emergency entrance. She tugged at the door, but it was locked. Then, she noticed a small sign tacked to the side—*Ring bell for admittance after posted hours.*

She punched the button several times in succession, till a bearded young technician in blue scrubs opened the door and grabbed a cart parked in the entryway. John pushed through from behind her and laid Barnacle down.

While he took a seat in the lobby, Mabel trailed the cart to an exam room. After having explained to John what had happened, it only took moments for Mabel to convey the basic information a second time. The vet, a young black woman with a crown of braids, ran efficient hands over Barnacle. She looked in his mouth and shone a light in his eyes.

The vet smiled encouragement at Mabel and laid her warm hand over Mabel's cold one. "We're going to take your boy for some bloodwork now. Please try not to worry before we know what we're dealing with. His vital signs are actually quite strong. This will take a few moments. You can either wait in here, or there are coffee and magazines in the waiting room."

Mabel didn't want coffee or magazines, but she couldn't sit in this tiny pea-green exam room, either. She went back out to the lobby, where John waited. He rose when he saw her, eyes questioning.

"They're doing tests."

"Look, I've been thinking. I didn't want to lose time getting your dog here. But I should've checked your house."

"You don't think someone was still in there, do you?"

"I doubt it. But I should've checked."

Mabel put her hand on his arm. "You can't be in two places at once. As long as Koi and Barnacle are all right, I don't care if somebody's hauling everything out of that house this minute. In fact, if someone else did that for me it would be a huge help."

He grinned and sat back down. "It's good to hear you joking. I hope he's all right."

"He was my Grandma Mabel's dog, so he's a connection to her. But I love him too, you know." She cleared her throat.

"You were named after your grandma?"

"Yep. I'm happy her name wasn't Bertha."

"You dodged a bullet." He grinned again. "You're taking care of clearing out the house and handling the estate?"

She nodded. "But I'm also going to be living there. She left me the house, along with a little money to help maintain it."

"You were close?"

"Very. But I think she worried about me, and that was partly why she left it to me."

His eyebrows went up. "Worried about you? If you hadn't finally recognized me back at the house there, I might be a dead man right now."

She managed a smile. "Grandma's attitude might've been her generation. You know—a woman on her own and all that." She frowned. Her whole family, and even her best friend, seemed to worry about her.

"It's wonderful she left you the house. Living there must be a special connection with her every day of your life now."

She nodded, but her eyes drifted toward the lab hallway where they'd taken Barnacle.

She couldn't let herself worry. "Please," she prayed silently.

"This thing with your dog might've been a warning." John frowned.

"A what? Why?"

"You've been stirring the pot. Somebody killed Helen. That person isn't going to want a busybody figuring it out."

Mabel bristled at being called a busybody, then shivered as what he'd said sank in. An ax murderer might have it in for her? They always said killing got easier after the first time. Now John was saying this person might have been *in her house.*

"Miss Browne?" The tech stood silhouetted against the hall lights.

Mabel jumped up, dumping her purse to the floor and spilling pens, wallet, and breath mints John began scooping everything back inside.

"You can come see your pup now." The tech smiled, and Mabel's knees went wobbly.

"Oh, thank God." She started shaking. "Will he...is he...?"

"Dr. Collins will fill you in."

Barnacle still lay on the cart, looking much the same as when she'd left him. Mabel rested her hand on him and burrowed her fingers into his fur, appreciating the warmth, and the rise and fall of his side. John set her purse on the padded bench and sat down beside it.

Dr. Collins entered with a smile. "Your boy's enjoying a good rest. He's just heavily sedated from whatever he ingested and should pretty much sleep it off overnight."

Mabel smiled her gratitude, and shamelessly buried her face in his ruff, which smelled pretty doggy.

"Do you have any idea what he got into?"

"No. I came home and found him like this. I don't have medications around the house, unless it was something of my late grandmother's. I'm living in her house now, but I don't think there's anything like that."

"We may never know. Possibly a visitor dropped a pill. But the outcome could have been much worse. Your fella should be fine in the morning."

"Can we take him?"

Dr. Collins nodded. "His bloodwork is good, and the dose of sedative he got isn't much above therapeutic levels. He doesn't require professional observation, especially considering what it would cost to hospitalize him overnight. But you might want to check him a couple of times for your own peace of mind. Please do call if you notice anything unusual. But you shouldn't." She handed Mabel a printed list of things to watch for.

When they returned to Mabel's house, the lights they'd left on in their rush to get to the vet were still burning. Fog blanketed the overgrown bushes.

She couldn't help seeing the house differently. She'd come home after the meeting to the familiar "Grandma's house" that had been a safe, comfortable haven for her entire life. Now, this was the place where earlier this evening, somebody had possibly broken in and poisoned her dog.

"Would you get the door, please?" John hoisted the now snoring dog from the back seat.

She hurried to unlock and fling the door wide. Koi emerged from the front hallway, gracefully rubbing her body against the doorframe. Thank God for her second miracle of the night.

"Hey, sweetie. You scared me. Did you see the bad person? That must have been scary for you too." She rubbed Koi's head, relief flooding her body.

The cat yawned and blinked, as if to say, "The idiot dog ate the food. I had sense enough to go hide."

"Where should I put him?" John staggered through the back door with sixty pounds of dead dog weight. Apparently that impressive first rush of adrenaline had subsided.

"I guess on his bed." Mabel nodded toward the kitchen corner as she scooped out cat food.

John laid Barnacle down as tenderly as a newborn baby. He watched him for a moment. "I'm glad he's going to be okay."

"So am I. Would you like coffee? Or a cup of tea or cocoa?"

"That would be nice. Whichever you want. While you make that— if you don't mind—I'm going to check the house."

Mabel was, in fact, relieved he was checking the house. Very relieved.

She began heating milk for the cocoa. Had a murderer stood right here in her kitchen earlier today? Had Barnacle wagged at him? Or her? She wondered if the intruder had put the sedative into some kind of food.

How had the poisoner come in? Mabel cast a nervous eye toward the door to the basement. With a shiver, she threw the lock.

The cocoa was ready by the time John returned. She filled two mugs and handed him one.

"Did you find anything?" Mabel rubbed damp hands over her pantlegs.

He shook his head. "But I didn't check the basement yet."

Mabel cleared a spot for her mug by moving still another stack of papers. Something was written on the envelope on top of the stack. Mabel had a bad habit of writing herself notes on random scraps of paper and then losing them.

She squinted at the scribble. Grandma's thrifty habit of buying low-wattage bulbs for every fixture in the house would ruin Mabel's eyesight if she didn't soon get around to replacing them.

Abruptly, she dropped the envelope as if she'd singed her fingers. Block printing read:

CONSIDER THIS A FRIENDLY WARNING. YOU ONLY GET ONE.

"What?" John read over her shoulder. His lips compressed. He put out a hand. "Don't touch it again."

"I don't intend to."

"I guess we have our answer. Our ax murderer was here."

Mabel hugged herself, as an icy sensation ran over her body. She was having trouble breathing.

"Would you like to call the police about this? Or would you rather I do it?"

"I will. In the morning, though. I'm exhausted. I doubt I'll sleep, but I can't deal with one more thing tonight."

She looked at the wall clock, an Atomic Age sunburst, and

groaned. "No wonder. It's after one in the morning."

"Let me check your basement before you call it a night. Hang on." She watched as he flipped the door lock and turned on the light over the steps. "Was this locked while you were out?"

Mabel shook her head no. "Be careful," she called as he headed downstairs. An acute sense of violation still vibrated along her nerve endings. Someone had come into her house with evil intent. The echo of that presence lingered in the very air.

She laid her head on her arms, thinking she could fall asleep like this. In fact, maybe she'd bring her sleeping bag down here, so she could check on Barnacle in the night. He sure wasn't going upstairs tonight, and she felt like they needed to be together.

John reemerged, peeling a cobweb off his shoulder. "That outside door wasn't just unlocked—it was ajar."

Mabel stared. "I wouldn't leave a door ajar, especially this time of year. Besides, that door's so warped, I never open it to begin with."

"I managed to close and lock it. And I checked all over the basement and didn't find anything. I think you're safe for now. Whoever did this has delivered their message—I doubt they'll do anything more tonight. You'll be safely locked in. Plus, I'll be here with you."

"Oh, no, no," Mabel protested. "There's no need for that, as you pointed out."

"There may be no need, but I'm kind of a belt-and-suspenders guy when it comes to personal safety. Especially a woman alone. Don't worry—I'll be occupying the couch."

"You will be occupying your own warm, comfy bed at home, and that's final. Please. We'll talk in the morning."

He gave her an exasperated look. "I disagree, but you're the boss. Let it never be said I tried to push a woman into anything."

"Thanks." Mabel felt an odd mix of relief and disappointment that he hadn't tried a little harder to protect her. And somewhere, deep in the recesses of her brain, a faint, niggling doubt flickered. After all, what did she really know about John himself? She had taken his word about where he'd been coming from, when he popped up in her house earlier.

"I'm going to check outside a bit before I go anywhere," he said, "so if you see a flashlight moving around, don't worry."

After he left, Mabel relocked her back door then went around, obsessively checking other doors and windows. As John had warned, she could see the glow of his flashlight moving around the yard and bushes.

He had to be a good guy, she thought as she changed into sweats, washed her face, and brushed her teeth. He'd taken care of Barnacle, right? But wouldn't that be a brilliant cover for the ax murderer/dog poisoner?

Aarrgghh. She hated feeling suspicious of everyone who crossed her path.

When she came back downstairs, toting an LED flashlight, the Sauer murder book, and her copy of the transcript, she paused to peer out the leaded glass panel in the front door. John's car was gone. She was alone. And her watch dog was all but unconscious.

Chapter Twenty-One

MABEL SPREAD HER SLEEPING BAG NEXT to Barnacle. "You're lucky to be the one with the bed." He answered with a snore.

She ran back upstairs and grabbed pillows, then snagged the old granny-square afghan from the couch in the living room on her way through. After arranging as comfortable a nook as possible on the hard floor, she plugged in her reading lamp. She drew the curtains, turned off the kitchen light, crawled into the sleeping bag, and propped herself up against the wall. Koi settled herself on Mabel's feet and started her bedtime ritual of kneading and purring.

She'd planned to continue reading the Sauer book—but since she'd gotten to the part about Edna's trial, Mabel figured she might as well read from the transcript. Deciphering the fuzzy type took a while, but gradually she got used to it.

After a while, she got the idea of flipping back and forth between the transcript and book, using the author's research to fill in what was going on around the trial and what people were saying outside the courtroom.

A creaking sound on the basement stairs made Mabel freeze. She concentrated, trying to listen over the chugging of her own heart in her ears. The noise didn't repeat, and though she stared at the door, the knob didn't move or rattle. At that moment, she thought how nice it would be to have John a few paces away on her couch. But after a few quiet minutes, she settled back down.

Edna hadn't been popular. The newspapers had been hard on her, pointing out how quickly she'd seized control of her father's company and started buying new clothing and household furnishings. From what she'd already read, Walter, Sr. had been a domineering tightwad, and reportedly outright abusive. Mabel couldn't blame Edna, though she understood why she aroused suspicion.

Violet, accompanied by her adoring and well-off, but unpolished older husband, stood by Edna, coming to court every day and speaking on Edna's behalf. Margarethe had given a statement soon after the murders, but always fragile, she didn't survive the combined stress of her losses and Edna's trial. She died early in the summer of 1940, before the jury acquitted Edna for lack of evidence beyond a reasonable doubt.

Mabel found Margarethe's statement interesting. She had told police that in the week leading up to the murders, she'd twice noticed a tall stranger lurking near their house and back woodshed. The police had treated this as unsubstantiated at best. The man hadn't been spotted since, and Margarethe was considered an unreliable witness, due to her emotional state and various medications she was taking. There was also speculation she was merely trying to create doubt to protect Edna.

But what if Margarethe's report had been true? Might the killer have been no more than a surprised burglar who'd been casing the house earlier?

Nobody else had ever been prosecuted, once Edna was released. She had taken over as sole mistress of the Sauers' haunted mansion without delay, living alone with the ghosts of what their lives once were, attended by a couple of day employees. Her sister, Violet— perhaps feeling sorry for her, and also comfortably provided for by her own husband—had deeded the house over to Edna.

Now free of interference, Edna redecorated tastefully and expensively, though not lavishly. She ran the business as ably as her father had, if not better. Profits remained stable, and she inspired strong employee loyalty. Mabel, having spent many years as a disgruntled employee, guessed Edna's human relations secret lay in respecting her employees' abilities and showing them appropriate appreciation.

Except for Paul Gregory, Walter, Sr.'s faithful employee, who'd lost his expected reward to nepotism. Maybe if he had kept his head down and done his work, he might still have gotten that promotion. But after Edna had rejected his over-eager marriage proposal, he had quit in humiliation and gone to work for the Weber Company, the Sauer firm's competitor. That business, however, soon went under, and he wasn't heard from again.

Mabel felt sorry for him. She had experienced some of those feelings herself. But she didn't blame Edna for refusing to marry her own employee—a much older man, whom she hardly knew. His motives would be suspect. Romance was unlikely, given the lack of any prior relationship, not to mention Edna's admitted lack of glamour.

Edna had died in her mid-sixties, a few years before Violet's husband. This left Violet—Helen's mother—as the sole survivor of the tragic Sauer family.

Mabel wished she'd picked lighter bedtime reading. Try as she might, she saw no obvious link between the old murder case and Helen's. Still her instincts told her a clue lay somewhere in the 1939 killings.

She turned out her lamp and punched down her pillow. The basic template matched. Both the 1939 victims and Helen were members of the same family. All three murders occurred in the same room in the same house. A similar weapon seemed to have been used for all the murders. In both 1939 and in Helen's murder, the weapon seemed to have disappeared.

Viewed that way, there had to be a connection. Maybe a link with one of the original parties? Heinrich Weber, the business competitor, was dead, having killed himself after his business failed. Gregory, the disgruntled employee, had disappeared. He might be someone to try tracing, though he'd be ancient at this point. At Mabel's former law firm, they had detectives to handle this sort of thing. John would be able to do that, she thought.

Mabel didn't believe Edna had killed her father and brother.

But maybe the murderer was someone else entirely. Maybe somebody the police had never even questioned. Maybe a crazy person, like the ax-wielding Taliesin murderer. Maybe another family member, though there were few to choose from, and unlikely, at that. Besides, they were all gone. Could a child or grandchild still bear a grudge? Or hope to gain something by bumping Helen off?

Like what? she asked herself. And why now? Again, she wondered about the will.

Mabel flipped her pillow and punched it down again. She'd never sleep tonight at this rate.

She turned her flashlight on and checked Barnacle. He was still sleeping like a sweet baby angel. Koi opened slitted eyes, stretched, and yawned, showing tiny white teeth.

Mabel decided she'd write down all her scattered thoughts and come back to them tomorrow when she was fresher.

Mabel woke next morning, disoriented. She was stiff all over and wrapped up like a human burrito. Barnacle's icy nose snuffled over her face.

"Get down." She flailed at the covers before realizing she was zipped up like a mummy on the floor. There was no place for Barnacle to get down to.

She sat up and rumpled his ears. "How you feel this morning, old boy?"

He wagged, yawned, and stretched. Koi, disturbed and scowling, stalked off to use the litter box. When she first got up, the cat could be like an irritable, one-foot-tall woman who'd snap your head off if you tried to wish her good morning before her first cup of coffee. Though in Koi's case, her morning mood elevator was a bowl of premium kibble.

Mabel disentangled herself and went to let Barnacle outside. He bounded off with a happy bark, chasing after a rabbit that hopped into the bushes.

Almost immediately, he tangled his cable in the brush. Groaning, and holding the legs of her sweatpants up above her ankles, Mabel picked her way through the frosty grass to get him loose.

A dense layer of fog isolated the house from its neighbors. Despite the fog, Mabel could see a car parked back in the pull-off in the patch of woods at the end of the street, mere yards from her house.

She froze, heart thudding, and gripped Barnacle's collar. He seemed to notice the car at the same moment and began barking and growling.

"Come on," she told him, wanting to get inside the house and lock up.

But at that moment, the car door opened.

Chapter Twenty-Two

MABEL TUGGED, BUT BARNACLE REMAINED LASER-FOCUSED on the strange car.

"Morning, Mabel." John stretched and shut his door.

She stared. "Were you sitting out here all night?"

"I told you I didn't feel comfortable leaving you alone overnight, after what happened to your dog."

Barnacle, seemingly appreciative, smiled and wagged.

John strolled over and rumpled the dog's ears. "I'm glad to see you so chipper this morning, buddy."

"I wish I felt as good as he seems to." Mabel cast a fond glance on the frisking dog.

"Rough night?"

"The floor isn't that comfy. And I had a lot to think about."

"Try sleeping in your car when the temp's in the thirties." John turned up his collar and hunched his shoulders.

"I haven't made coffee yet, but I could rustle us up a pot."

"That would be great, but I was thinking of treating us to breakfast out."

Mabel felt herself weaken. She loved eating out—particularly breakfast.

"Tell you what." John gestured toward the kitchen door. "If I can freshen up a bit while you make coffee and whatever else you need to do, I'll take us to the diner."

"Okay," Mabel heard herself say.

"While we're eating, you can tell me what sort of deductions you came to overnight." He grinned.

When it was time to leave for The Coffee Cup, Mabel started having second thoughts. "What if the poisoner comes back?"

"Well, this time everything's locked up and the note said you'd gotten your warning. For now, whoever did this should be waiting to see if you do what you're told. They could've done worse but didn't."

"I'm bringing them," Mabel announced. "That's the safest."

"Really?"

"Yes, really. The weather isn't too hot or cold, and Barnacle loves riding in the car."

He looked skeptical. "Does your cat like to ride in the car?"

"Not that much. But I'm doing it for her safety."

"You know you can't take those animals everywhere you go."

"Maybe not. But I can at least take them to breakfast."

She handed John the leash. "Could you please put him in my car?" While he did that, she crept back inside and pounced on the unsuspecting Koi. She stroked her head and called her pretty kitty then stuffed her into the carrier before Koi could brace her claws on the opening. "I'm sorry. This is for your own good."

"You can ride with us if you want." Mabel gestured at the front passenger seat. Barnacle was currently hanging over the back, dripping drool.

John peered into her car, grinned, and mouthed over Koi's outraged squalling, "That's okay. I'll see you there."

The Coffee Cup was packed when they arrived. "This doesn't look promising." But then Mabel noticed Miss Birdie at a corner table, waving.

"I'm about to get up, baby," Miss Birdie said as they joined her. "I got here early for my blueberry muffin and hot tea, and by the time I finished working my crossword puzzle the place was like this." She gave John a coy smile. "How you doing, young man?"

"I'm doing quite well, ma'am. Yourself?"

She inclined her head, still smiling.

"Miss Birdie, this is John Bigelow. My, um, friend."

"Miss Birdie and I are acquainted." John smiled at the elderly lady.

"I keep forgetting you grew up here."

"Miss Birdie was my Sunday School teacher when I was in the

nursery."

"Have a seat, you two." Miss Birdie patted the chair next to her. "I'm going to take care of my check, and I'll be leaving you two lovebirds alone."

Mabel felt a rush of mortification. "Miss Birdie…" Having her mother and Lisa always pushing her to find a man was bad enough. She really didn't need the senior citizens of Medicine Spring chiming in.

John grinned. "I'm not sure how Miss Mabel feels about that."

Miss Birdie eyed her and nodded. "Oh, I suspect I can tell how she feels about it."

"It's been good to see you." Mabel pointed. "Isn't that your friend, Ms. Katherine Ann, peeking in?"

Miss Birdie looked up and waved. "Oh, my, yes, it is. We're taking our daily power walk around the square. Goodbye, youngsters."

Mabel blessed Ms. Katherine Ann for her timely arrival. And John, for not teasing. He handed her a menu with a smile and ordered two coffees.

Lack of sleep always made Mabel crave sweets and starches. She hoped they could solve this murder before she had to bump up a jeans size.

She needed her strength for today in any event—and since John had ordered her a regular coffee, she guessed she'd be skipping the butterscotch drizzle latte. That meant she could afford the Rib Sticker— oatmeal with apple-crumble topping, two eggs with sausage and choice of biscuits, toast, or one pancake. Though she did want potatoes. Maybe she could get a side order.

But…she didn't want to appear excessive, especially on John Bigelow's dime. Maybe she'd substitute potatoes for the bread.

When the waitress returned, she placed her order, feeling virtuous. John ordered the Popeye—two poached eggs on a bed of spinach, with a whole-grain English muffin. His selection sounded healthy—and more than a little bit skimpy.

"So…" He ran a finger around the rim of his mug. "What insights came to you in the night? If you're willing to share."

Mabel looked around. The back table was isolated. The waitresses' coffee station stuck out on that end of the counter and made the walk-through too narrow for another table.

"I already checked around us. Not a soul in earshot."

Mabel spread out her notes then leaned closer and lowered her voice. "There are too many coincidences and similarities for all these murders to be unrelated. There's a link somewhere, in my opinion."

John nodded. "I agree. The only other possibility I see is someone using the pattern of the old killings. Either symbolically or as a smokescreen."

"I'm assuming you know the basics of the old murders and the case against Edna…?"

He nodded. "Every child who ever grew up in this town does. Or, at least, some version of them."

"I tend to agree with the jury. The case against her was circumstantial, at best. She discovered the bodies. She had an unsubstantiated alibi about being on a walk. There was blood on her clothes. She didn't get along with her father, who was reportedly abusive. Hardly an open-and-shut case."

"Could've been her. Could've been someone else. We may never know after all these years. The people who might've known are all gone."

"There were other good suspects," Mabel told him. "Maybe even likelier than Edna." She ran down the list of possibilities. "Then, there was Margarethe's account of a lurking stranger—who could have been any of those men—or even a fabrication."

"I'm not seeing any obvious connections with Helen," John said. "Let's look at things from the other direction. Leaving aside the old murders, who are your suspects for Helen's murder?"

Mabel thought. "Most people who knew her seem to have had some sort of conflict with her." Then, she remembered John was related to her. "I'm sorry. I didn't mean—"

He waved his hand. "If you're worried I might take offense, forget it. I'm a shirttail relation, at best. I knew Helen only in the most casual way. For the record, it's true. She could be a pill."

"I guess two spring to mind, then. Cora, who was Helen's rival, and Devereaux, who was determined to blow the lid off the old murders in her book, pretty much over Helen's dead body." Surely, she could eliminate Nanette and Darwin? Neither had a motive she could see.

And John? Mabel bit her lip. She might not see motives for any of these people, but that didn't mean they weren't there. Mabel considered mentioning Linnea, but that would naturally lead to questions about Bennett or John himself. She and John might've teamed up to investigate, but it wouldn't be smart to let her guard down entirely, given his family connections.

He sat back to allow their waitress to set down their food.

As soon as she left, he picked up the thread again. "How would you see Cora as having killed her?"

Mabel shrugged, spooning up a creamy, crumbly mouthful of oatmeal. She chewed, swallowed, and dabbed her lips. "You've heard the rumors about Cora's husband, I presume?"

At John's nod, she continued. "I heard Helen and Cora got into a bit of a public catfight after a meeting. Helen referred to knowing 'where the bodies are buried' and the existence of a 'smoking gun.'"

He paused in the smashing of his eggs into the bed of spinach. "I'd think the police would find that interesting."

Mabel grimaced. "I'm afraid they'll just try to pin the murder on me."

"It's way too early to worry about that. They'll be looking at everybody with motive and opportunity right now. You're probably way down on their list."

John's words should have been comforting, but all Mabel focused on were the words "on their list." She did not want to be on their list. At all.

"Do you really think Cora …?" He made a slitting motion across his throat.

"Oh, I don't know. I just met her. But she is a big, strong woman, even at her age, which was about ten years younger than Helen. And assertive to the extreme, like Helen was. She might've been capable of killing either her husband or Helen, I guess."

"How would the murder have happened?"

"Maybe they'd planned to meet—to have it out. Or maybe Helen wanted Cora to pay her off."

"Blackmail?" John's face was dubious.

"Not necessarily for money. The motive could've been control of the historical society or something similarly ridiculous. Or maybe Cora had discovered the same thing Devereaux had dug up about Helen's family knowing more about the murders than they pretended to. Maybe she threatened to reveal the details. Anyway, they get into a tussle, one of them grabs, say, the hatchet from the display case, and Helen ends up dead. Cora and the hatchet disappear." She hesitated.

"Though how she'd have gotten here to poison Barnacle I don't know, since she was already at the podium by the time I arrived, minutes after leaving here."

John shrugged. "Unless she has a helper. Like a grandchild or someone like that. What about Devereaux?"

"Hang on." Mabel moved on to her eggs, potatoes, and sausages for a couple of bites.

"I'm sorry. I'm not giving you a chance to eat."

"No problem. Sort of the same deal. Possibly prearranged, but since Helen had driven her off once before, I'd say she might've surprised her. An argument, and maybe Helen threatened or attacked her."

"With an ax?"

"I'd guess the display hatchet. She might have been holding it—or grabbed it to brandish, and their shoving match turned fatal."

"Since she came in on that bus, from a town over an hour away, isn't that an issue?"

"Depends when the coroner pegs time of death. She could have killed Helen, driven to Wilkie, and hopped on that bus to return as the innocent tour member who finds the body."

John smiled. "You paint an intriguing picture."

"Thank you." She took another bite of breakfast, feeling absurdly pleased. She ignored the little voice in her head that whispered, *Hasn't he been picking your brain and giving very little back?*

Chapter Twenty-Three

JOHN COUNTED OUT BILLS FOR THEIR meals plus what looked like a generous tip. "Tell you what. Let me sniff around and see if I can find anybody who can place Devereaux in the area earlier that day."

"That would be great." Mabel had to admit she sort of wanted Devereaux to be the guilty party and promised herself to try to be more objective. "Oh, hey, before I forget. Do you know who Paul Gregory is? Or was?"

"Of course. He lost his promotion to Walter, Jr. then tried to get Edna to marry him. What about him?"

"It might not amount to anything, but he was a suspect back in the day, and I wondered if he might still be alive. Is that something you could find out?"

"Sure. If so, he'd be ancient at this point."

"Yeah." Mabel sighed. "There's probably nothing there. But maybe he still has younger family in the area."

John smiled and pushed up from the table. "I'll see what I can do."

"Thanks for breakfast. I won't be needing lunch today." She scanned her phone and saw a missed call. "I'm going to call Nanette back. She may have heard whether Helen's body's been released, so they can arrange a funeral."

"I meant to tell you they have released the body. The autopsy report should be available soon."

When she stared at him, he said, "Sorry. My cousin just told me. That's something else I can follow up with my friends in the department." John pulled out a tiny notebook and pencil stub, scribbled, then ripped out and handed the sheet to Mabel.

She squinted at it. "What's this?"

"Please call this guy about a security system for your house, okay? And say I recommended him. He'll work with your budget." Before she could reply, he added, "I think you'll sleep better...I know I will."

Mabel thought about the poisoner, creeping into her house to harm her dog. About the long, dark hours of the night. She nodded. Yes, she thought she would sleep better.

Mabel could see her car, still undisturbed, with Barnacle sitting in the driver's seat. "I need to get going. Thank you again."

"Entirely my pleasure."

As soon as she'd said goodbye and gotten into her car—which took a bit of time, as it involved shoving the resistant dog into the back seat—she dialed Nanette.

"Hello?" Nanette's voice reflected puzzlement.

Mabel raised her voice over Koi's caterwauling. "This is Mabel. Sorry. I have my cat in the car with me, and she's unhappy."

Nanette said something, but her voice was so soft, Mabel had to shout, "What?"

Eventually, she made out that Nanette was inviting her to her house. She managed to take down an address, over aggrieved cat noises, and figured her GPS could handle the rest. "I have to make one stop," Mabel shouted. "I can be there in about half an hour."

Then, for the second time in recent days, Mabel headed for the police station. She handed over the warning note and signed a statement, but the officer's skepticism was obvious. Clearly, he suspected she was trying to divert suspicion. "You can check with the vet," she told him, wondering if he thought she'd drug her own dog, simply to prop up her story.

Nanette lived in a perfect fairytale cottage down on Creekside Lane, a narrow street bordering Bartles Creek. The only thing missing was roof thatching. Mabel parked at the curb, and after giving her pets strict orders to stay put and be good, she opened the creaking gate in the white picket fence, ducking under an arched trellis that still bore a vine with remnants of brown, crepe-like flowers she didn't recognize.

Steppingstones marked a curved path through the tiny yard to the front door. A few plants still bloomed—purple and lilac asters, golden and garnet mums, and some mounded peach-colored things she couldn't identify. The cottage with its garden was Mabel's vision of Miss Marple's St. Mary Mead.

The front door opened. "I'm glad you could make it. Welcome to my home."

"Your place is charming."

"Thank you. Come on in. I have both tea and coffee. I wasn't sure which you prefer."

"Either, thanks."

"Here. Sit, sit." Nanette guided Mabel to an overstuffed, chintzy couch. Gazing around in wonder, Mabel thought Nanette might have been the inspiration for Shabby Chic. A weathered wringer washer with chipped yellow paint had been converted into a stand for a miniature jungle of glossy green plants. Gleaming barrister bookcases with glass fronts crowded two sides of the small sitting room, barely leaving space for the couch, two armchairs and a steamer trunk repurposed as a coffee table. Ceramic fairy faces peeked from the corners, and a glimpse of Nanette's bedroom was all rosebuds and acres of frothy ivory voile.

"Let's do tea, shall we?" Nanette smiled as she poured two fragrant cups and pushed one toward Mabel.

"Mmm...what is this?"

"Ordinary blackberry sage tea bags, but I love them." Nanette held out a bowl. "Sugar?"

Mabel pounced. The crystal bowl held real sugar cubes, which she dearly loved, but hadn't seen since Grandma Mabel's passing. She spooned up three, put two in her teacup and pressed one to the roof of her mouth, till she felt the hard edges soften and crumble.

"Cookie?"

Mabel was beyond stuffed, following that epic breakfast, but didn't want to appear rude. She selected a toasty golden sand tart, glazed and crowned with a flower design of slivered red and green candied cherries. It was almost as thin as a business card, she told herself. How many calories could a thing like that possibly have?

"Was there a particular reason you wanted to see me today?" Mabel popped a chip of cookie in her mouth and let it melt.

Nanette leaned back, cradling her teacup. She smiled. "No, not really. Just feeling terrible about your joining us only to fall right into this whole mess with Helen. Do you like the tarts?"

"They're incredible."

"I'd be happy to give you the recipe."

"Thanks, but I can't bake. I'm happy eating yours."

"How are you feeling since your horrible experience?"

"I'm stiff from sleeping on the floor, and my muscles feel like I've been moving pianos, but as long as Barnacle's all right, I guess I have no complaints."

At Nanette's blank expression, Mabel remembered she knew nothing about Mabel's most recent "horrible experience."

"Oh, sorry. Barnacle's my dog. He had a medical episode overnight, and I had to take him to the emergency vet. But he seems fine now." Mabel decided not to mention the poisoning. Although Nanette seemed friendly, Mabel was no longer sure whom to trust. If nothing else, Nanette might share the story with the wrong person in all innocence, especially—for instance—if Cora was involved.

"Oh, I'm so sorry. They're like family, aren't they?"

"Yes, they are."

"I was referring to your stumbling upon Helen the way you did. That's the stuff of nightmares, as they say."

"It was unnerving," Mabel admitted. She set her cup down and frowned at the steam rising from the pale, rosy brew. Perhaps she shouldn't be ingesting anything offered by members of the historical society right now. Nanette had been quick to point out that she hadn't been at the house when the body was discovered—but she had certainly been alone in the house when Mabel first arrived to lead the tour. Alone with Helen's body.

Looking up to see Nanette nibbling a cookie, Mabel reassured herself. They were both eating and drinking the same thing. She was being silly, suspecting a gentle soul like Nanette.

"Have the police been bothering you?"

Mabel jerked in her seat. "Sorry. My nerves are still a bit jangled. They haven't contacted me since I gave my statement. I'm taking that as a good sign. Though it hasn't been all that long."

"At least the coroner released poor Helen's body." Nanette sighed. "The family will be planning a funeral, I'm sure. Linnea called to say they'd be coming home over the next couple of days to talk to Drapers'."

Drapers' Funeral Home had handled Grandma Mabel's funeral, as well. They'd been in business for four generations. Mabel presumed they'd also handled Walter, Sr. and Jr's funerals.

"We'll order an arrangement from the society, of course." Nanette sipped her tea. "However, I discussed with Linnea about our accepting donations in lieu of flowers—either to the society or the Margarethe Sauer Hospital Wing fund."

"That sounds lovely." Mabel wondered if she should have a second cookie. They were so thin as to be almost nothing.

She slipped another cookie onto the bone china plate. "How's Helen's daughter holding up?"

A grimace flickered across Nanette's face. "She'll be fine, I think, as soon as the shock of the way it happened wears off. You realize they were estranged for years?"

Mabel nodded, mouth full of cookie.

"They loved each other, I'm sure." Nanette frowned. "At least, I presume so. I was never blessed with children, but I can't imagine one stops loving over a disagreement."

Which had spanned decades at this point... Mabel took another sip of tea and zipped her lip.

"I think they might have reconciled, had Helen lived. Linnea had recently started coming back around, you know."

Mabel nodded, mouth full of cookie.

"I think Helen was delighted, though she'd never let on. Have you ever seen Linnea? Here..."

Without waiting for a reply, Nanette got up and fetched an album from the shelf beneath one of the end tables. She spread it open across their laps and pointed at what appeared to be a high school senior portrait of a sharp-faced but handsome girl with short, slick brown hair. "This was how she looked when she left home. I haven't seen her since."

"Who's this?" Mabel indicated an attractive young man with a full head of blond hair and trim beard a shade darker. He wore a graduation gown and what appeared to be a doctoral hood. Helen stood beside him, his arm resting across her shoulders. Both were smiling.

Mabel stared. She'd never seen Helen smile. Here, in fact, she was beaming.

"Oh!" Nanette wore a smile of her own. "That's the nephew, Bennett. He was such a blessing to Helen. Just a godsend. She'd have done anything for that boy."

Mabel looked back at Linnea, then again at Bennett. John's cousin. *The estranged heir...and the usurper?*

What had brought Linnea back after all these years...and so shortly before Helen's sudden, unnatural death? Was it another case of natural love and affection? Had absence made the heart grow fonder—or more regretful of youthful impulses?

Mabel wondered about Linnea's finances. If Helen had died intestate, Linnea would have been her sole heir.

"Have you heard anything yet about cause of death?" Mabel ventured.

Nanette took a dainty sip. "Yes. Linnea said it was her heart."

Mabel's head came up so abruptly her tea sloshed. She dabbed at her lap, relieved she had splashed herself and not the upholstery. "Her...heart?"

Chapter Twenty-Four

MABEL STARED AT NANETTE, SLACK JAWED. "HELEN died of...a heart attack?"

"That's what Linnea said. Though she did have that...wound. Whatever occurred may well have precipitated the heart issue."

"Indeed." Mabel gently set her cup down, trying to imagine a scenario that would have resulted in an ax-like wound and a heart attack. "Does that mean the police aren't treating Helen's death as a homicide?"

"That, I haven't heard, one way or another. But one would presume...."

What Nanette would presume, Mabel didn't know. She herself would presume that an ax wound meant homicide. Even if the ax blow turned out not to be the closest proximate cause of Helen's death, that injury would, as Nanette said, surely have precipitated it. However inexperienced the Medicine Spring PD might be with homicides, that much should be a no-brainer.

"Nanette, excuse my asking. I've been puzzling over this since the night I found her. I didn't have a chance to examine the room. Even if I had, I didn't know the room's contents, so I wouldn't have known if anything was missing or out of place."

"You're wondering what I observed when the police called me in to look at the parlor?"

Mabel nodded, grateful not to have to ask.

"That was interesting. Even though Helen hated that room, and never wanted it opened, she was in there. The display case had been opened."

"Unlocked?" Mabel asked.

Nanette nodded again. "As opposed to broken into. And the hatchet was missing, so I'd think that's the presumed weapon?"

This was what Mabel had believed all along.

"There's a back door in the corner. Have you seen it? It leads into the garden. I don't think it's been used in years."

Mabel shook her head. Having only been inside the room once, she hadn't had a chance to notice much more than the body on the carpet.

"Maybe the killer left the case open and ran out that way," Nanette said. "I'm sure if I had bumped someone off, and people came into the building, I'd bolt."

"Same here." Mabel grinned, hearing Nanette talk about bumping people off.

"Was there anything else?"

Nanette slowly shook her head. "I told the police everything looked about the same, except for the missing hatchet. A few pieces in the case appeared to have been moved a bit. It appeared as if Helen had been dusting. There was a microfiber cloth on the floor under her."

"Did it look like there was a struggle?"

Nanette shrugged. "A chair was out of place—it might have been jarred. A rug was crumpled. But nothing knocked over, or anything like that."

"That's all I saw, in my quick glance. But enough, wouldn't you think, to say the scene suggested some sort of struggle? Given Helen's orderly nature?"

Nanette rubbed her chin. "Well…yes. But it could have been a result of her reeling about."

Mabel glanced at the time. "I'd better get going. I have my animals with me, and I need to get them home. Thank you for the tea."

"Thank you for coming. I hope you'll continue with the society. We'll never survive without younger members like yourself. If I hear anything more about funeral arrangements, I'll let you know."

As she drove home, Mabel's mind churned. She wondered about the missing hatchet. It was interesting that it and the original ax had both vanished. Either could be anywhere at this point. Though the more she thought about the murders—especially Helen's—the more a quick disposal somewhere in the vicinity seemed probable.

She tried to put herself in the murderer's mind. Maybe there had been a struggle, as she'd imagined. Not planned. A weapon of opportunity, maybe even picked up in self-defense. An elderly woman in a high state of anxiety and stress, further heightened after the wound had been inflicted, collapsing with a fatal heart attack.

Did the killer even stop to check whether Helen was still breathing?

Mabel's cell rang as she pulled into her driveway. She tucked the phone under her chin as she lifted out Koi's carrier and collected the leash with her other hand.

"It's John. Am I interrupting anything?"

"No, I just got back from Nanette's."

"I won't hold you. More than to let you know I talked to the neighbors across from the Sauer house."

"Oh, yeah?"

"I got a description that sounded a lot like Devereaux Reid, from somebody who saw her around the house earlier in the day. Needless to say, we can't prove the person was her, but...." Mabel unlocked the back door and set the carrier down. "What time of day was that?"

"The neighbor couldn't remember exactly but said midday. She saw a blonde going up the steps, carrying a portfolio or computer bag of some kind."

"Did she see her come out again?"

"She wasn't paying particular attention. But she noticed her go in and happened to remember, because there isn't a lot of traffic over there on a typical weekday. Not unless they get a school group or something."

"That's all, then? No suspicious prowling, or anything like that?"

"Only what I told you."

"It would be interesting to know whether she was signed up for that tour ahead of time."

"And whether she was expected earlier that day, or was a drop in." John cleared his throat. "But I'm guessing if she had an appointment, only she and Helen knew about it."

Mabel considered. "Darwin was there earlier, taking out air conditioners. Maybe he saw her or knows whether she had an appointment. I should ask."

The day of Helen's funeral came at last. As a historical society member, Mabel had felt an unwelcome duty to attend. Lisa, after shameful cajoling on Mabel's part, had agreed to accompany her. Mabel made a mental note to get Lisa something extra nice for Christmas.

The old stone church sat but a few feet from the sidewalk. Mabel imagined elegant buggies drawn by matched teams of gleaming bay horses pulling up to deposit well-heeled worshippers on a Sunday morning.

She parked in a corner of the lot that had been added in the 1930s and waited for Lisa before walking in. "I hate funerals," Lisa grumbled. "And I had to get a sub, to do this."

"You're a true friend, and I owe you."

"Believe me. I'm planning to collect."

The hearse sat alongside the building. Two men in dark suits stood next to it. The older man walked over, carrying a handful of small white flags on magnetic bases. "Will you be going to the cemetery?"

"Good grief, no." Mabel coughed. "Are we okay to park over there?"

"Yes, ma'am. When the service is over, please wait until the other cars exit before pulling out."

In the dim narthex, Mabel accepted a bulletin and paused to let her eyes adjust. As she'd noticed at Grandma's funeral, older folks' services could be sparsely attended—one presumed because so many of their peers had already predeceased them. Miss Birdie and Ms. Katherine Ann, both in black, sat together on an outside aisle.

As usual, even with so many empty seats, the back couple of pews were already filled. "I see Nanette and Darwin." Mabel pointed halfway up the aisle. "Let's sit with them."

The organist was already droning a mournful prelude as Mabel motioned Lisa ahead and they clambered over knees.

"Hi," Mabel whispered, and both greeted her, their smiles including Lisa. "This is my friend," she hissed.

"I'm glad you came." Nanette, in the aisle seat, reached across Darwin and squeezed their hands.

The room smelled of candle wax and chrysanthemums. It was still too soon after Grandma Mabel's death for Mabel not to feel anxious at a funeral, even when she hadn't been close to the deceased.

Nanette leaned over Darwin again. "That's Linnea, the son-in-law, and the grandson."

Helen's daughter sat straight-backed, her husband's arm around her shoulders. The grandson, who appeared to be in his early twenties, sat about a foot apart, staring down.

Probably fiddling with his cellphone. Why people couldn't even put those things away at a funeral, Mabel couldn't imagine—let alone for one's grandmother.

She considered Linnea's rigid back. Would she be in her fifties now? If she'd left home on bad terms in her teens, and only started coming around more recently, the rift must have been enormous. Mabel wondered if anyone knew what had caused it...or what had brought Linnea back.

"Excuse me." Darwin maneuvered over Nanette and stepped into the aisle.

"Isn't that your guy?" Lisa hissed. She pointed at the man now angling past Darwin on his way up the aisle, as Darwin turned toward the back of the church.

"I don't have a guy," Mabel said automatically, then added, "Hey,

157

it is him."

John slipped into the second row, which Mabel knew was customarily reserved for family. It figured he'd be here, she realized, since he was related.

But John didn't sit. He reached over and tapped the grandson's shoulder. After a whispered exchange, the young man followed John back up the aisle.

As they passed, Mabel's eye caught John's and he winked.

Lisa bumped shoulders with her and grinned. "Look at you, girl—flirting at a funeral."

Chapter Twenty-Five

As the organist struck up Pachelbel's Canon, people turned, including Mabel. The pallbearers wheeled Helen down the aisle, guided by the older man from the parking lot, no doubt the funeral director. John and the grandson both served as pallbearers, as did Darwin and a fourth man roughly John's age. He no longer had the beard she'd seen in the graduation photo at Nanette's house, but this must be Cousin Bennett. Muscular, with a bit of gray at the temple, this fourth pallbearer also had the square jaw of a movie hero. At the moment, that jaw was set in a way suggesting tight control over some strong emotion.

She hadn't liked Helen. And there was no denying Helen hadn't liked her. But seeing her grandchild and beloved nephew escort her coffin into the church made Mabel sad for Helen's death and the awful way it had happened.

When the pallbearers had been reseated, the pastor, a slender young man who looked to be still in his thirties, stepped to the lectern, black vestments swirling. As he read the familiar words of the funeral rite from the Book of Romans, Mabel's thoughts wandered back to Grandma Mabel.

The promised resurrection was comforting and in fact, joyful. But thinking of Grandma and now Helen, rising up to heaven, brought stinging tears. Mabel blinked hard.

Lisa patted Mabel's hand and slipped her a tissue. Mabel blew, honking faintly like a forlorn goose.

The service wasn't overlong. The minister delivered a fine sermon, with appropriate references to Helen's regular church attendance and community service, and conversations they'd had regarding the Scriptures. Still, Mabel wondered if their discussions might've consisted more of Helen's instructing the young man as to where he was off track.

Stop it. Just because the woman had taken a dislike to Mabel and made her life difficult didn't necessarily mean she hadn't been precious to other people in her life.

Still, the portion of the service devoted to eulogies was briefer than customary. Linnea talked about her mother's cloudlike coconut cakes and what a bottomless fount of advice she'd been.

I'll bet. The thought popped into her head before she could rein it in. Mabel squirmed in her seat, feeling—as Grandma Mabel used to warn her—that she'd given the stained-glass Jesus above the altar a tear in His eye.

After chastising herself, Mabel settled back into an attentive posture, only to find her thoughts drifting to coconut cake. She was hungry and could already smell the food being set up in the downstairs social hall.

Cora, resplendent in purple-and-gold Lilly Pulitzer butterflies, also offered a few words. "Surprised she isn't struck by lightning," muttered someone behind Mabel, echoing her own thoughts.

But Cora's grief seemed genuine. Maybe she was remembering their youthful friendship and regretting their later animosity. Or maybe she had a lot more than that to regret.

Mabel studied Cora's powerful shoulders and remembered how thin Helen had been. She couldn't have weighed half what Cora did.

Mabel forced her thoughts back to the eulogy, which Cora was just ending with a dab at her eyes.

As if in response to Cora's seemingly heartfelt words, Darwin's breathing became ragged, and he also accepted a tissue from Nanette. He pulled himself together, however, in time to line up with the other pallbearers.

When the service concluded, and the coffin had departed, Mabel got to her feet. The organist was throwing himself into a stirring postlude, which made conversation difficult.

160

"Are you going to the cemetery?" Nanette dabbed at her eyes.

Mabel shook her head.

"I'm not either." Nanette gestured toward the steps to the social hall. "You are staying for the luncheon, aren't you?"

The food smelled divine. The last thing Mabel wanted, however, was to make conversation with bereaved family members. Or the police.

Lt. Sizemore, in a tasteful dark suit, leaned against a pillar, watching the mourners. Even out of uniform, she looked like a cop—maybe because of her devotion to navy blue.

Lisa stuck out her hand to Nanette. "Hi, again. I'm starving. Let's go down."

Nanette smiled and shook her hand.

"Were you close?" Lisa politely asked.

Nanette thought, chewing at her lower lip. "I wouldn't say 'close.' But goodness, I've known Helen all my life. She could be difficult—she was a strong personality. But she had a warmer side, as well. The society relied on her. She knew everything about the Sauer family and the house. And she was a born leader. She knew what had to be done and made sure it was."

No matter what her minions had to go through to make it happen, Mabel thought. She trailed after Lisa and Nanette. A peek revealed Lt. Sizemore, watching them go.

Quite a few people milled around downstairs. The scene reminded Mabel of a wedding reception, when restless, hungry guests wander about while the bridal party finishes having its pictures taken.

A drink station was set up at one end of the social hall, underneath the kitchen pass-through window. Tables along the wall held desserts and finger foods.

They chatted a while longer, and then Nanette stuck her head through the kitchen window. "Need any help?" The women in the kitchen were strangers to Mabel, but several smiled and greeted Nanette by name.

"Sure." A big-bosomed older lady, in a black dress covered by a yellow apron emblazoned with I'm Cooking For Christ, indicated trays of veggies, cheese, and crackers. "These need to go over there. These," indicating rows of salt and pepper shakers, "go two sets to a table."

"Would you mind taking the trays?" Nanette rubbed her wrist. "I've been having trouble with my carpal tunnel."

"No problem." Mabel and Lisa grabbed a couple of trays and headed for the tables by the wall.

Mabel was shoving things around to make room when she saw Devereaux Reid, through the window above the appetizer table, heading across the parking lot toward a small red car.

In books and made-for-TV mystery movies, the perpetrator always showed up at the funeral. Odds were the killer had been there among the mourners, and that, of course, was why the police were there.

When there was nothing left for them to do, Mabel collected a paper plate, a few veggies, and dip. Nanette had already disappeared into the kitchen, likely to help or gossip.

"Let's sit. My feet are killing me." Mabel took a seat on one of the folding chairs along the wall, and Lisa plopped down next to her with her own plate of appetizers.

"Do you know any of these people?" Lisa gestured with a baby carrot before popping it into her mouth.

"Not really. I've met a couple of them at the society, but I don't remember names." Mabel hunched down and turned her head away from the cluster of gray heads around the crudités. "The one in the black hat with the droopy feather wants me to marry her son, though."

Lisa giggled. "Aren't you getting popular these days?"

When the ladies had moved safely out of range, Mabel resumed people watching. Maybe the murderer was here right now, and she hadn't even met him or her yet. What did a killer look like?

As she and Lisa continued to talk and nibble, Mabel lost track of time. She jumped when Nanette called. "Could you please come over here?"

Mabel hustled back across the room. Cora and Darwin, returned from the graveside service in the tiny burial ground a few blocks away, huddled with Nanette beside the drinks.

Of the three, Darwin seemed most haggard, the lines in his face looking deeper and older.

Nanette's composure surprised Mabel a bit. Even from that first phone call when Mabel reported Helen's death, Nanette hadn't reacted with noticeable grief. Maybe simple pragmatism was behind her lack of overt displays of mourning. Evidently, Darwin was more sensitive— or maybe he'd just been closer to Helen.

Cora, it went without saying, had been at odds with Helen right up to the end. At the moment, she appeared to be beaming directly at Mabel, which Mabel found decidedly unsettling.

"We have a question for you, dear," Cora bellowed at her.

Nanette made a useless shushing gesture.

Darwin faced Mabel. "With Helen gone, we wondered if you might step in and assist with our end of the hospital gala."

Mabel frowned. "Doing what? Helen was a Sauer granddaughter. I don't know the first thing about Margarethe, and I'm no good at planning things."

"Don't worry," Cora stage-whispered, as if concerned people in the parking lot might miss what she was saying. "I'm quite capable of taking over Helen's duties. But that will create a vacuum elsewhere in the committee, you understand."

"Phone calls and mailings," Nanette said. "For instance."

"We still need donations for the silent auction." Darwin watched platters of food go out to the serving tables as if he was having trouble focusing.

"I can furnish you with a checklist," Cora told her. "All you have to do is work your way down the list."

"Any of us will be happy to answer questions, if you need us." Nanette patted Mabel's arm. "We need more hands, though. It seems more important than ever right now, somehow like a memorial to Helen.

This was so important to her."

Mabel squirmed. Why did Nanette have to put the request that way? Would she appear callous if she begged off? Darwin met Nanette's eyes, then looked at Mabel, who was frowning at the thought of having to make phone calls for donations.

Darwin touched her arm. "It occurs to me there's another significant job Helen left unfinished—the biographical booklet about Margarethe's life and all her good works. Helen had already compiled a lot of information, but since you're a writer..."

Mabel perked up. "I might be able to pull something together." She attempted to appear modest but confident. "But I don't know if I can manage that, plus making phone calls. After all, I do have my own writing project—a *book*. Plus, I still have my grandmother's estate to deal with, and her house to clean out."

"I suppose I *could* work on the booklet myself," Darwin said.

That wasn't at all what Mabel had in mind. "Never mind. I agree that sort of thing would benefit from a professional writer's touch. Maybe you'd be willing to handle the calls?"

Darwin narrowed his eyes. "Maybe."

"Do I need to do more research on Margarethe?"

"Oh, Helen had all that in her file." Nanette's tone was airy. "All you need do is perform your writerly magic and whip it into shape."

"That's all, huh?" Mabel tried to imagine using her writerly magic, but her imagination didn't extend that far. She wondered if writerly magic was something one could develop—she hoped so.

"I'd be honored to do whatever I can." It also occurred to Mabel her new assignment would give her entrée to Helen's files.

"Wonderful." Cora clasped Mabel's hand, crushing fingers. "Could you stop by sometime tomorrow?"

"We're getting extremely close to the event at this point." Nanette's expression was apologetic.

"Around ten, maybe?" Mabel asked. The sooner the better, in her opinion, and ten was practically the crack of dawn.

The minister entered the social hall at that point and raised a hand for the blessing. Most people had gravitated to their seats by now, and it appeared Darwin had saved a seat with a few other historical society members. Only one spot remained at Darwin's table. Mabel made a polite gesture for Nanette to take it, then scanned the room, biting her lip.

Where was she going to sit? John was nowhere in sight. And where was Lisa?

Oh, there she was at the next table, in the clutches of the mother of the salt-and-pepper collector. Mabel didn't know whether she should feel amused or offended at being so easily replaced. All the same, and despite a pang of guilt, she pretended not to notice Lisa's desperate look in her direction.

The family, as was customary, had reserved seats near the front. As soon as the amen had been said, they were called up to the buffet line.

Seeing an empty space at the head table, Mabel shrugged. What better opportunity to snoop on Helen's relatives?

Chapter Twenty-Six

MABEL SLIPPED IN BEHIND HELEN'S SURLY-LOOKING grandson, still glancing down at his phone as he waited for the food line to move. Nobody seemed to notice her joining the family, as they focused on ham, Jell-O, and potato salad. She considered introducing herself but thought better of it. Better to stay under the radar for now and not speak up till it counted.

As she reached the salads, John passed with a loaded plate. He did a doubletake and backed up.

"Mabel?"

She averted her eyes while scooping pasta salad.

He leaned closer. "Where are you sitting?"

"Uh, every place seemed taken except for that one at the family table."

He grinned and shook his head. "This is my beat, Nancy Drew."

Mabel huffed. "What? I'm just eating."

John snorted. "Whatever. We'll compare notes later."

Mabel wrinkled her nose at his departing back.

When she got to the table, she caught several raised eyebrows, not only from Helen's next of kin, but also Lisa, Cora, and Darwin. She gave them a waggle wave, then slipped into the last open seat, next to a fifty-something man with a caved-in chest and a wispy mustache that matched his wispy gray-blond comb-over.

Mabel stuck out her hand. "Hi, there. My name's Mabel."

He looked down at her hand and then up at her face. Finally, as Mabel was about to withdraw her hand, he gave it a low-energy shake. He squinted into her eyes. "I'm sorry. Do I know you?"

"Nope." Mabel spread her napkin across her knees. "You are?"

The man drew back a bit as if startled. "Duane. I'm Duane." He gestured to his other side. "Linnea's husband."

Linnea leaned back for a gander at Mabel, who found herself staring back at a sharp-featured, younger version of Helen. "Hi." Mabel reached behind Duane for a handshake, which never developed. "You must be Helen's daughter. I'm sorry for your loss."

Linnea's squint was more scowl. "Forgive my asking, but how are you related?"

Mabel laughed uneasily. "I'm not. But all the other seats were taken."

Before Linnea could respond, inspiration struck. "My—er—boyfriend is related by marriage?" Mabel made a vague gesture in John's direction.

An uncomfortable pause followed, during which Mabel busied herself with slicing ham.

"I see." Linnea's tone suggested maybe she did, in fact, see.

Mabel swallowed a mouthful of ham and mashed potatoes. "Again, I'm so sorry. I'm—er—*was* your mother's backdoor neighbor."

Linnea placed her knife and fork at either side of her plate with great deliberation. She turned to face Mabel, though this was complicated by Duane's leaning forward, concentrating on his plate, in a seeming attempt to dial himself out of a brewing confrontation.

"Why are you really here?" Linnea hissed. She pulled a crumpled tissue from her sleeve and pressed it against her eyes. "First, your grandmother spent years tormenting poor Mother. Now, you step in where she left off. Haven't you had enough? Why can't you let this feud go?"

As Linnea's voice rose, others turned to look.

Mabel's mouth opened and closed, but nothing came out.

Linnea drew a sobbing breath. "I hope you're happy."

"But—"

"Mother is *dead*, and isn't it the world's biggest coincidence you're the one who took over her tour? That you happened to find her? Please leave."

Mabel's hands shook as she picked up her place setting. "Look. I tried to be a good neighbor to your mother and so did my Grandma. It wasn't our fault she didn't want to get along—with us or anybody else. I darn well had nothing to do with her untimely ax murder. God rest her soul."

John appeared at her elbow. "Hi, ladies. Is everything all right down here?"

"John Bigelow." Linnea's voice was like ice. "Would you kindly show your girlfriend the way out?"

A smile quivered at the corner of his mouth. "Of course, Linnea. I do believe we're about ready to go."

Mabel slid her purse strap over her shoulder, juggling her still-full foam plate. She pushed out her chair with an audible screech and stood. "I'm sorry for your loss," she repeated, chin up.

As they worked their way toward the door, she felt all the eyes following her. Nanette's registered mild distress. Darwin's expression wavered between shock and glimmering amusement. Lisa, whose table had yet to be called up to the buffet, hastily grabbed her sweater and purse.

Lt. Sizemore lounged in a corner, eyeing them over her coffee cup as they left.

Mabel made a sharp turn toward the kitchen. She pulled out a sheet of aluminum foil and covered her plate. She might be wrongfully accused and publicly humiliated, but there was no way she was wasting all that beautiful food.

As Mabel turned into her driveway, a movement on the seldom-used front door caught her eye. Someone must have tried to make a delivery while she was out.

Barnacle was already barking by the time she got out, balancing her plate of food. His commotion followed her from the back of the house toward the front porch.

A green sheet of paper fluttered from a strip of adhesive on the door. Her heart jerked. The document looked official.

Mabel ripped the slip down and carried it to the edge of the porch, where the light was better. A carbonized Township form spelled out several violations.

Ordinance 483 (C): Lawn areas—grass height not to exceed 6 inches.

Ordinance 483 (D): Private recreational areas—grass and/or weed height not to exceed 12 inches.

Ordinance 487 (A) (2): Standing water—areas where water stands or accumulates and is allowed to become stagnant shall be drained or tightly covered.

Ten days. Mabel's heart sank. Even if she could cut the grass and brush, how on earth was she supposed to eliminate low spots on the property in that amount of time? Besides which, this was October, for goodness' sake—mosquito season was already over.

She crumpled the paper and stomped her foot. Helen Thornwald was still harassing her from beyond the grave.

Chapter Twenty-Seven

BY THE NEXT DAY, THE FUNERAL luncheon ordeal had faded. At least, Lisa had refrained from saying, "I told you so," and John had merely smirked and told her to forget it. Mabel had been offering sympathy, like a decent neighbor, and even helped with the luncheon set-up, with never a thank-you. She comforted herself with these facts—and her reheated plate of ham and potatoes.

She'd also formulated a plan for dealing with the township complaint. First, she'd make sure where her property lines were, so she knew where her responsibilities began and ended. Then, she'd file an appeal as spelled out on the back of the form and try to buy a little additional time, at least for the standing water issue.

That settled, Mabel fed her animals, locked her doors, and set her new alarm system, before heading to her first meeting of the Gala Committee. With luck, she'd be out of there by noon.

When she arrived at the Sauer house, Cora, Darwin, and Nanette already sat around the living room, files spread out and travel mugs in hand. A box of bakery scones sat in the center of the coffee table, and Mabel helped herself. She'd already had breakfast but could always squeeze in a scone. She thought that might have something to do with the traditional wedge shape.

"Mabel. Glad to see you," Cora's voice boomed as she shoved a bulging file at her. "This is what Helen collected for the tribute booklet. I'm sure you'll make Margarethe's biography sing."

Mabel sighed and set down her scone. She tried to stuff leaking photos, clippings, and papers back inside the folder. "Do you maybe have a bigger folder? Or even a plastic bag?"

"Of course." Darwin disappeared into the office, reemerging with an expanding file.

Nanette patted her hand. "I'm sorry Linnea was so dreadful yesterday. It must have been the strain she's been under."

"Undoubtedly." Mabel repressed an eye roll.

"Do you have a good idea of what we need for the biography?" Darwin asked, then answered himself in the next breath. "Of course you don't. I'm sorry. How could you? Well, the concept is simple."

He pulled out a stack of booklets from a drawer in one of the built-in bookcases and handed it to Mabel. One covered early local history, another the maple industry, and several featured bios of local figures. "Something about this length." He pointed to one of the bios. "Nothing major. Showcasing Margarethe's exemplary character, naturally, and her many contributions to the community, which continue to this day."

Mabel opened the Walter, Sr. bio, bearing the society's copyright from almost twenty years ago. The text followed a chronological format until mid-adulthood, when it shifted to thematic chapter headings, like "Business," "Family," "Faith and Philosophy." She flipped to the back. His death rated a bare mention—simply a date and that his passing resulted from an unsolved homicide, along with that of his son and namesake.

"Helen wrote that one." Nanette's smile flickered. "We used to offer it in the gift shop but ran out of copies a year or so ago."

"Bought most of 'em herself as gifts." Cora sniffed, and nobody commented.

The bio was no longer than many a summary judgment brief Mabel had written over the years. She knew she could do this. The booklet would be her first publication as a professional author.

"We should do a book-signing at the event." She envisioned herself at a table with flowers and stacks of books and a crowd of eager fans lined up for her autograph.

After a brief silence, Nanette agreed. "Perhaps. That would be lovely."

The meeting ended soon after the scones were gone. Mabel gathered her materials and escaped into the crisp October air.

Someone was burning leaves. She loved the smell and thanked the Lord Medicine Spring didn't have a burning ordinance.

Twenty minutes later, wearing jeans and boots, Mabel set out through the high weeds at the back of her lot, toward the Sauer boundary. A few goldenrod and asters still bloomed, releasing a spicy scent as they swished against her legs.

Barnacle darted forward, seemingly intent on flushing out birds and insects. Mabel wished she could enjoy the afternoon like he did.

She consulted the copy of the deed she'd pulled from her hip pocket. The front south-westerly property corner was simple enough. A boulder sat there, and she'd known about the pin driven into it since she was a child.

She hadn't brought a measuring tape but figured she could eyeball things pretty well since she only needed to find the corners right now, based on the landmarks identified in the deed. The approximate line ran along the Sauer property, and their overgrown boxwood hedge straddled well to either side. She'd start searching the woods along the back edge. She hoped the old oak mentioned in the deed was still standing.

The hedge turned a corner to enclose the Sauer back yard. The line was less obvious here, but as Mabel's boots squished through a big wet area all but hidden by grass and weeds, she regretfully concluded the marsh was on her side of the line. Maybe the inspectors wouldn't come back this far.

Ultimately, a wall of wild raspberry brambles cut her off from the woods. Mabel was inclined to forget searching for any more surveying stakes back there. The Health Department notice hadn't mentioned anything about the woods. Maybe she'd locate that point another day.

But Barnacle pulled at her arm, intent on snuffling along the ground.

"Aw, buddy, I know I owe you a better walk. But let's go a different way, huh?"

Mabel peered into the shadowy woods. She didn't see an old oak tree, but it did look like there was a huge, rotting stump in more or less the right area.

Curious now, she dragged Barnacle out of the raspberry bushes. "I'm not going through brambles. This way."

Scrambling over rocks and downed branches, Mabel made her way into the woods. As she was climbing over an uprooted sapling, Barnacle lunged, jerking the leash.

Mabel felt it slip from her grasp, burning her hand. She lost her balance and crashed awkwardly onto her left hip, leaving her nearly upside down, legs caught in the tangle of fallen tree limbs.

A broken branch jabbed her side, ripping her shirt. Mabel kicked at the air, but her feet didn't touch the ground through the springy bed of fallen tree branches.

"Barnacle?" What if he ran off after a deer or something? If his leash caught in the brush, he might choke—or stay trapped in the woods and starve.

There he was. She could see him, still nearby and busy snuffling. Mabel was relieved he was sticking around, whether through loyalty or lack of imagination. Finally, she struggled, elbows first, to the ground. She crawled out of the entangling web of branches and fumbled to her feet.

In a flash, she'd planted her foot on the trailing leash. "Gotcha."

Barnacle, oblivious to his own near escape, kept following his nose.

"Hey." She could see the Sauer back yard through the trees. It was as big as Mabel's field. A shed and small barn sat near the tree line in back, vestiges of the era of carriage horses and chickens. Now, most of the space was taken up with perennial beds and shrubs. A sundial marked the center of one planting, and another featured a fountain that no longer spat droplets into the air.

The woodshed would have been there, where Margarethe had reported seeing a prowler. Mabel looked up. Those must be the windows of Margarethe's bed-sitting room.

As Barnacle snooped through the leaf litter, she pondered. Had the police searched the outbuildings for the ax? *Axes*, she corrected. She imagined they must have.

She wondered if anyone had dug around the back yard in 1939. She hadn't read anything about that. Maybe she should try a metal detector.

Then, Barnacle barked. One deep *wuff*, probably directed at a bird or squirrel, but the sound made her turn her head.

A glint of something metallic caught her eye. Inch by inch, she panned back.

She saw the gleam again. Part of an old junkpile, or so she guessed, but now she was curious.

Mabel tugged Barnacle closer to what appeared to be a heap of old, rotted prunings. The brush pile sat near the Sauer back yard, but without a worn path leading to it from the house. Small broken branches marked the way from the yard, as if somebody had recently shoved his way through the brush to get to that old dump. Why?

When they got near enough, Mabel pulled back a few branches. She could see clearly now. There was that flash of metallic trim—she'd found Helen's missing robin-egg blue bicycle.

Chapter Twenty-Eight

"JOHN?" MABEL MADE HERSELF RELAX HER death grip on her cellphone.

"Hi." There was a smile in his voice. "To what do I owe the pleasure?"

"We found Helen's bike. Barnacle and I. In the woods behind the mansion."

"Her bicycle was missing?"

"I don't know whether it was officially missing. But she usually rode it when she worked over there, and it wasn't there the day she was killed."

"A change in her routine."

"I figured she might've walked. Since it's getting dark early, it might've been easier. Here it is, though."

"Are you in the woods right now?"

"Staring right at it."

"Hey, look, I just got done teaching. I'm talking to one of my students. It'll take me around twenty minutes to get over there. You want me to call the cops, or do you want to?"

Mabel didn't want the cops at all. That was—she realized—one reason she'd called him instead. "I guess you ought to do it, so we have time to get out of here. I'm worried they already think I bumped her off, and I'd rather avoid the third degree."

"I'll call. But you have to stay put. For one thing, you need to mark the spot. For another, you know very well you're going to look way more suspicious if you split before they get there."

Blast.

Mabel blew a huff of air up through her sweaty bangs. "All right.

But hurry. I don't want to deal with Sizemore without backup."

"Your hero is on his way. Try not to worry."

Easy for him to say. He wasn't under a cloud of suspicion. Mabel searched around for someplace to sit. A fallen tree rested on brush, a couple of feet above the ground, but it didn't present the most comfortable-looking perch. She looped the leash over a handy branch and eased her posterior onto the least bumpy section of trunk.

She stared at the bicycle, its once-perky white basket rimmed with blue silk flowers now dented. Helen had most definitely not ditched her bike here. Neither had anyone else with a good motive.

Was someone keeping an eye on the bike, wondering if and when it would be found? She squirmed on her hard seat. There wasn't enough room for her plus-size rump.

Who had shoved that bike out of the way back here? And why?

As Barnacle poked through the fallen leaves, she heard a metallic clink. Could his tags have hit the bicycle bell? Mabel could clearly see the bell was no longer attached to the bike. Helen had once rung that bell when she'd sneaked right up behind Mabel, scaring the spit out of her. It might easily have gotten knocked off the handlebars as the bike was being rammed through the underbrush.

Somebody had been in a hurry. Helen's killer in a panic lest the murder be discovered right away?

If Nanette had arrived and seen Helen's bicycle in its usual spot at the back door, she'd instantly have realized something was wrong. Knowing Nanette, she'd have started searching for her.

Barnacle barked and wagged his tail.

"Yo," called a female voice from the Sauer back yard. "Mabel Browne, are you in there?"

"Between the barn and the shed—straight back. You'll see broken brush."

Moments later, Sizemore appeared, fighting her way through the briars and bushes. She paused a couple of times to unsnag her uniform shirt, swearing creatively. A younger, male officer trailed her.

Sizemore stopped when she reached the bicycle. She stared at it a few seconds, and then up at Mabel. "How did you get back in there?"

"I came from over there." Mabel gestured. "And saw the sun hit the bike, so I wanted to check it out."

Sizemore raised her eyebrows. "How odd. Convenient—your prowling back here in the brush like this, huh?"

"Yeah, I guess so." Mabel knew sarcasm when she heard it. She'd heard a lot. "Whoever ditched the bike probably figured nobody would check back here anytime soon."

Sizemore slipped her sunglasses into her shirt pocket and smiled. "And along you came."

"Along I came."

"May I ask what brought you back here, Ms. Browne?"

Mabel eased off her tree-limb seat. Predictably, she managed to hook the elastic of her underwear on a snag, giving herself a near-fatal wedgie. Barnacle jumped on her, assisting in his own way.

Sizemore laughed. "You need help over there?"

"No, thank you." Mabel shoved at Barnacle and tried to work her way back onto the limb, hoping to relieve her predicament.

"Mabel?" John's voice called from the back yard.

Hurrying to extricate herself before another witness arrived, Mabel felt the fabric rip. She didn't care—she was free. Mopping sweat, she dropped to the ground, right as John popped up next to the police.

The three shook hands, and Mabel supposed he was introducing himself, while she scrambled to rearrange her wardrobe malfunction.

"I was asking Ms. Browne what brought her to this unlikely location."

Barnacle wriggled his way over to welcome John, dragging Mabel with him. He'd have continued into the barricade of underbrush if she hadn't planted her feet and fought back.

Sizemore folded her arms and watched Mabel's struggles. Having her as an audience made Mabel feel even more awkward and flustered.

Finally, Barnacle gave up. He lay down with his chin on his front paws, refusing to look at her when she told him, "Good boy." *Et tu, Barnacle?*

"Still waiting." Sizemore's tone gave the impression she thought Mabel was stalling long enough to concoct a story.

"I'm here because I inherited my grandmother's property."

"Sorry for your loss, but—"

"Thanks. I inherited my grandma's property, and she had—"

Sizemore twirled her finger in a classic "cut to the chase" gesture. John smirked.

"She had dementia, and the property got kind of rundown. Next thing I knew, I got this notice. It gave me so many days to cut the grass and get rid of brush and so on."

"Mm-hm."

"I wasn't even sure where my back property line went or what was here." Mabel pulled the folded deed from her hip pocket. "I thought I'd try to figure that out first."

"Because...?"

"I don't know," Mabel snapped, horrified to realize tears were prickling at the back of her eyelids. "It's all too much, and it's so hard, and I don't even know where to start."

John started working his way around the brush in her direction. Sizemore raised her eyebrows and waited.

"I'm doing the best I can, you know. It's not like I wouldn't have gotten around to cleaning up the property. But she had to go and report me, just because she hated Grandma."

A trace of a smile flickered at the corner of Sizemore's mouth. "Who did?"

Mabel clamped down hard on her lips. Sizemore obviously already knew "who."

John reached her. He grazed her hand with a quick feather touch and almost imperceptibly shook his head, warning her to shut up.

"She was a real pain in the butt, wasn't she?" Sizemore pulled a sympathetic face.

"Look, I'd never have hurt her. Never. It's…I've been through a lot. Grandma. My job."

"And she was the last straw."

Mabel started to nod. Nodding was a bad habit she'd picked up while listening to her old boss, the managing partner at the law firm. She stopped herself. "No." Her voice sounded louder than she'd intended. "I mean, yes, she was a pain in a lot of butts. But nothing any of us would've killed for, myself included."

Sizemore kept right on staring at her, not saying another word. *Cop trick.* Mabel knew Sizemore was hoping she'd get nervous and start blurting things out. But it was also a lawyer trick, and Mabel wasn't falling for it. She stared right back until Sizemore shrugged and pulled out a pair of crime-scene gloves.

"Okay. I'll take things from here."

"I can go?" Mabel asked warily.

Sizemore smiled. "We know where you live." Then, almost as an afterthought, she asked, "Is this some kind of shortcut for you back here?"

"Are you kidding? No, this would be way far out of my way."

"You're saying you'd only go this way in case of emergency? Like if you had to avoid being seen, maybe?"

"Like I'd never go this way, period. I've never been back here in my life."

Even as she said it, Mabel remembered. "Well, not since I was a little kid, maybe, and playing in the woods." *Just shut up.*

Sizemore grinned.

"I can't stand that woman." Mabel fumed as she and John walked back across the field.

"She's only doing her job."

"I know, but I hate that smirk, every time she thinks she's scored some kind of point."

John kept his eyes down, seeming to watch the tall weeds part with each step. "You hate that she goads you into saying things you don't want to say…or not being careful how you say them."

Mabel came close to snapping but stopped herself. Maybe he was right. Probably, she admitted. "Why would I have reported that bike if I was guilty? What did I have to gain?"

He shook his head. "Nothing I can see. She's fishing right now. I doubt she suspects you more than anyone else. You just give her more to work with."

Mabel groaned so loudly Barnacle glanced back to check on her. "I like to think I'm usually sharper. This hasn't been the greatest time of my life."

"I know."

They walked in silence a moment, then John cleared his throat. "You could hire a landscaper to do all this." He waved a hand. "To bring you into compliance in a hurry."

"You're right. I don't have time for it, and I hate outside work. Grandma used to love yardwork. She had a beautiful garden. To me, it's backbreaking labor, a lot of sweat, and then you turn around and have to start over."

"I bet they'd waive the citation on this field. After all, you're on a cul-de-sac, and it's an actual field. It's not like you're in the middle of town."

"I intend to try. I want to get a delay, at least, on the wet areas. That would only leave cutting the grass and cleaning up weedy flowerbeds."

"If that's all that needs to be done, I could give you a hand. Do you have a mower?"

Mabel frowned. "I imagine it needs a tune-up."

"Let's check on that first. I can't lend you a mower, unfortunately. I have a front yard I can do with a weed-trimmer, and the back is naturalized."

"You don't have to cut my grass."

"Maybe I want to help you."

She opened her mouth to argue, then came to her senses. "Thank you."

He tilted his head, smiling. Too late, she wondered, was he going to expect something in return?

Back at the house, John dragged the mower from Mabel's shed, while she made tea. When they sat down to drink it, he shook his head. "I didn't see a gas can anywhere. Also, from the looks of that mower, you may be better off buying a new one."

More money. "Maybe I can have someone check it out, and then decide."

"I know a guy who's supposed to be pretty good. Honest, anyway. If you want, I'll drop it off for you. But I need to retrieve my car from next door."

"That would be great. I'll need to work on the appeal."

She got up and found the rest of the sandwich cremes. "Have a cookie."

John took one and twisted it apart the way she always did. But to her horror, he used the top cookie to scrape orange icing into her wastebasket. Barnacle hovered, drooling.

Mabel groaned as she watched the pumpkin-colored, sugary slab disappear under old food wrappers like the Titanic slipping beneath the waves. "Any four-year-old kid knows that's the best part."

He mimed a shudder and complacently ate his denuded chocolate cookie.

She yanked Barnacle's snout out of the garbage. "Get out of there."

"How do you think that bike ended up where it did?" he asked.

"It wasn't on any logical route Helen would've taken from her house."

"I doubt Helen would've run her bike in there herself, even if she'd wanted to hide it. She was too proud of it to bang it up that way." He took another slurp of tea. Despite his physical appeal, he was an uncouth tea drinker. Silently, she gave him one demerit. Well, maybe a half demerit. "In all likelihood, the killer hid the thing."

"Yup." She took another cookie. "I think he—or she—panicked after the murder and wanted to eliminate that bit of evidence as fast as possible."

"The whole thing seems unplanned, doesn't it?" John scraped another cookie.

Koi leapt onto John's knees, walked around a bit, then settled her purring bulk. He popped his cookie into his mouth, dusted crumbs from his hands, and petted her back. Koi sniffed his leg and licked. She was almost as bad as Barnacle when it came to snuffling for crumbs. Mabel smiled, glad John wasn't one of those macho types who claimed to hate cats and only seemed to appreciate an oversized dog.

"Let's think about the day of the murder." John scratched Koi's head, and the cat flirted shamelessly, rubbing her chin on his hand. "From all appearances, Helen was attacked where you found her, right?"

Mabel nodded.

"It would appear the killer either came up on her from outside, or he—or she—was already there in the building, right?"

It was unimaginable anyone from the society would've attacked Helen. *Except Cora*, a little voice whispered in Mabel's ear. Cora, who might already have killed before. Whom Helen had taunted with exposure. "Helen would've had to unlock the door for anyone coming in."

"I assume there's a visitor book?"

"Yeah. But not everyone's going to sign. Like a murderer, for instance."

He grinned. "That would be too easy, wouldn't it? Is there a separate head count of some kind?"

"There's a legal pad on the office desk. You make checkmarks for visitors. They use the numbers for planning and, I assume, grant applications." She stopped, thinking back. Her tour group had been such a disaster. Had she marked the legal pad? She was pretty sure she had.

Maybe she should have counted the police and crime techs.

"If Helen let somebody in, there should be an extra person in the count then."

"Unless she was attacked before she could do that."

He shook his head. "We have no way of knowing who the checkmarks are. I'm sure the police are questioning anyone else who worked that day."

Mabel dug out a junk-mail envelope from the pile on the table and started a list. *File appeal. Check visitor book? Find landscaper.* She sighed and chewed her lower lip. *Work on writing volunteer article.*

Ugh. None of it sounded like much fun. In a burst of defiance, she added *Start writing true-crime book.*

Koi jumped down and began batting a pen cap around the floor. Barnacle, who had been dozing, raised his head and strolled over to watch.

"Hey." She looked at John, "Did you get a chance to look up Paul Gregory?"

"Oh, yeah. I meant to tell you. You're practically neighbors."

"What?"

He laid a hand on her arm. "Easy. I mean he's buried up there in Beulah Meeting Cemetery."

Mabel eased back in her seat. "Does he have any family still around these parts?"

"Nope. After Edna turned him down, he never did marry. If there is anyone, it would be a pretty remote cousin."

"I guess that's that, then."

John got up and carried his cup to the sink. "I'd better get going. I'll be right back for that mower."

Mabel rose and followed him to the door. "Hey, John?"

He paused, hand on the doorknob.

"I was wondering. Have you searched through Helen's stuff at the house?"

He shook his head. "I imagine the police have, but Bennett gave me a key."

Mabel wasn't sure how to frame a polite request to dig through her dead neighbor's belongings for clues.

John laughed. "Your face is like a Times Square billboard. Your thoughts scroll right across your forehead."

Mabel put a hand to her forehead, then sheepishly lowered it with a scowl.

He tweaked her nose. "If you're a good girl and do all your chores tomorrow, maybe I'll bring you with me."

Chapter Twenty-Nine

MABEL CONSIDERED HER WARDROBE FOR SEARCHING Helen's house. She might not have completed her to-do list, but after what she'd been through, she deserved an outing.

The black jeans. They were slimming—and straddled that line between artsy writer and sexy private investigator. Mabel wasn't so much going for Jessica Fletcher as the heroine of one of those made-for-TV mystery movies. The female leads were always beautiful and had at least two hunky men vying over their affections.

Thinking of hunky men reminded her uncomfortably of John. She'd told him she'd checked off every item on her to-do list for the day, which was true. But she'd been able to cross them off by deciding to move a few to tomorrow.

Yesterday had wiped Mabel out, and she'd overslept. But she had managed to complete her appeal form and stick it in an envelope for the next day's mail. After treating herself to a mushroom pizza delivery for lunch, she'd needed a short nap. All the stress and nights of sleep deprivation were catching up.

Finding a landscaper, or even a kid with a weed trimmer, would have to wait a day. She couldn't face going to the Sauer house to examine visitor records, either. She didn't want to talk to anybody, and to be honest, she didn't like being in that building anymore.

She'd finished her afternoon with cold pizza and her laptop, trying to figure out how to write an article about volunteering. Should she start with a general article? Something like "volunteering is good for the community, and good for you." But then, she supposed she'd have to say *why* it was good.

Maybe she should do a list of tips. Wouldn't that be simpler?

Already, Mabel had enough experience to warn readers what not to do. *Don't make suggestions at the first meeting, no matter how good they are. Don't let anybody push you into doing a hard job on your very first day. Don't antagonize the president before you even start. Don't find any bodies that died under mysterious circumstances (especially the president). In fact, don't find ANY bodies. And don't bring the luscious, seasonally appropriate, orange-filled sandwich cookies.*

After wracking her brain awhile, she'd ended up typing a title, Volunteering: Good for the Community and Good for You. She studied it a moment, then added an exclamation point. But was it too long?

Disgusted, she'd decided to call it a day. She could do this. The writing would go better when she was fresh.

Since John wasn't free till 9 PM, Mabel busied herself with cleaning out the supply cabinet beneath the staircase. This was a frustrating job, with rusty cans of long-outdated cleaning products crammed cheek-to-jowl next to musty boxes of old photos. Koi and Barnacle rendered aid by squeezing into the cramped space to sniff around. Their explorations revealed a massive mouse nest in a hatbox, along with the sad remains of what might have been Mabel's great-grandmother's church hat.

When she'd finished all she could bear for one session, she fed the animals and herself, and showered. Now, she needed to figure out the rest of her wardrobe for the evening. Short black boots, despite the impractical kitten heels. Maybe the long, silky red tunic, with black leggings. She knew it wasn't the most sensible ensemble for investigative work on a chilly evening. But it was so flattering.

Turning slowly in front of the mirror, she saw herself in a made-for-TV mystery movie promo. She'd be wearing this outfit, leaning forward in a Nancy Drew crouch with a flashlight in hand.

Barnacle grinned up at her. She was pretty sure he was laughing. "Oh, shut up. I feed you, you know."

Grabbing keys, coat, and a flashlight, she headed out to her car.

In a couple of minutes, Mabel arrived at Helen's driveway. Helen had planted the postage-stamp yard with a Victorian sense of excess. Most of the perennials had died back and been trimmed to the ground, but a few asters and chrysanthemums still bloomed in a palette of whites and purples amid severely pruned boxwood and holly.

John leaned over the curlicued white railing enclosing the broad front porch. He hailed her with a wave and a shout. Mabel waved back.

She parked behind John's car. Despite the crisp evening, she left her coat on the seat.

"Come on in," he called down. "The heat's off, I'm afraid."

"No problem." She tried not to shiver. It had to be at least a bit warmer inside. "Sorry I'm late."

"I just got here." John opened the door for her. "I usually work clockwise around each room, floor by floor. I don't know that we'll find much. I expect the police already took anything of interest."

"Maybe something will jump out at us that wouldn't mean as much to them."

"Not likely, but possible."

Mabel was looking around the shadowy entryway, wondering where they ought to begin, when John tapped her arm. "Hey, Mabel…"

"What?" His face had assumed an expression composed of equal parts discomfort and indecision. "Yes?" she prompted.

"Look. I can tell you right now one thing the cops did find. A copy of Helen's will. Her lawyer confirmed it was up to date."

"And?"

He let out a breath. "Bennett's the executor. He's also inheriting the bulk of her money. Linnea gets the house, along with a small annuity for upkeep—and some snark about maybe learning to appreciate her heritage."

"Did they know about that? Bennett and Linnea?"

He shook his head. "Bennett says he didn't. He just heard this afternoon. Who knows about Linnea? She's been gone for years."

Mabel frowned. She didn't know Bennett, so his word was open to question, as far as she was concerned. And although Linnea might have been away for years, she'd certainly been back and reconnected with Helen more recently.

"Don't make more of this than it's worth, okay?"

Mabel didn't meet his eyes. Here were the lurking family motives she'd wondered about from the beginning. Did Bennett need money? Was Linnea furious and vengeful...or hoping for an inheritance she desperately needed?

And what about John? For all she knew, he was only telling her about the will now, in case it was about to become public.

Mabel gave herself a mental shake. She was here for a reason, and she needed to repress her suspicions for now and concentrate on the job at hand. "Okay. Do you want to divide up the search?"

He hesitated, and Mabel was sure he didn't trust her to do a good job. "Sure," he said after a moment. "You want to go through the kitchen while I do the basement?"

"All right." She doubted there was much to see in the kitchen, but she wanted no part of Helen's basement, which if true to period, was dank, cobwebby dirt and stone.

John ducked his head as he started down the cramped steps.

Mabel shivered and rubbed her arms. Not one word about how nice she looked or even an admiring glance. Right down to business. Sometimes he said flattering things to her, but it had become increasingly clear his real goal was information.

She'd never stepped inside Helen's house, even as a child. Grandma must have been here often, before the land dispute had come between them. Had they sat right at this table, drinking coffee and complaining about their husbands? Mabel laid her hand on the surface, as if she could pick up those long-ago vibes. Cora must also have visited once upon a time.

If Cora had been complaining about her husband, she'd eventually eliminated that problem. If one believed the gossip.

Helen sure had a knack for antagonizing the people in her life. Looking at it like that, Mabel was way far down on the enemy list.

The house felt cold. Not only because the heat was off, but because the heart that gave it life had stopped beating.

Giving herself a shake, she gazed around the pristine kitchen. There was even a fresh, retro-style embroidered dish towel with a sunbonnet baby and the word "Wednesday." The very day she'd passed. No wonder Mabel's mess had freaked Helen out.

Mabel reached for the nearest drawer pull, then gasped and drew back her hand. Prints. She was already a suspect. What if the police came back and dusted everything?

"John," she called down the steps. The musty smell of ancient cellar rose to meet her.

"Did you find something?"

"No. I'm afraid of leaving prints."

He laughed. "The police already released the house. But if you're worried, wait for me."

Darn it. She wasn't going to trail after him and lose her chance to investigate on her own. Slipping the hem of her tunic over her hand, she opened the drawer. Twist ties, openers, and other catch-all kitchen junk.

The next drawer was more fruitful. She found a box of sandwich baggies—or as Mabel christened them—crime-scene gloves.

It was clumsy work, trying to keep the bags on while rifling through drawers. But Mabel persisted. She was headfirst into the freezer when John came up behind her. "Mabel?"

She jumped, hitting her head.

"Looking for fish sticks?"

She rubbed the bump and glared at him. "Sometimes people hide things in freezers. My grandma used to keep rolls of twenties in hers."

"What on earth do you have on your hands?"

"I'm improvising."

"Did you find anything?"

She shook her head. "You?"

"Nope." He gestured at the cabinets. "Did you check these?"

"Go for it."

Mabel started to peel off her plastic-bag gloves, then thought better of it. She still didn't want her fingerprints anywhere in this house.

They worked their way through the kitchen and moved on to the living room. Helen's feminine, cream-colored desk sat in the corner. John stared at Mabel's bagged hands. "Allow me."

While John started leafing through papers, Mabel hovered. She was nosy enough to wonder what was there. Anything about herself, for instance.

"They'll have gone through all this for sure," he told her. "We're not going to find a smoking gun."

"Or a bloody ax."

Watching John thumb through beauty shop receipts and electric bills soon made Mabel queasy. Nobody wanted other people going through their personal papers. Helen would despise Mabel's doing it, above anyone else.

"I'm going to keep browsing," she told him. "Upstairs," she added, and he nodded absently.

At the top of the steps, Mabel hesitated. She might've ventured a peek inside Helen's medicine cabinet but still felt that uncomfortable, voyeuristic sensation that had struck her at the desk. Mabel could almost feel Helen hovering at her elbow, pursing her lips in disapproval.

"Hey, I'm trying to help here." She spoke aloud. "Well, help myself, of course, but also help you rest in peace. Give your family closure."

Her uneasiness persisted as she crept across the hall to an open bedroom door, 100-year-old floorboards creaking at each step. "Come on, Helen. Can't we bury the hatchet?"

As soon as the unfortunate choice of words left her lips, Mabel grimaced. No, tact wasn't part of her skill set.

The charming bedroom reflected shades of the cottage garden. Lilac and pale green predominated in the linens and wallpaper, against a cream-colored backdrop of wainscoting and ruffled curtains. The sleigh bed could have belonged to Marmee in *Little Women*.

Mabel crossed to the nightstand. An empty glass stood next to a lilac-and-green-shaded lamp, a purse-size bottle of ibuprofen, and a large milk of magnesia. A historical romance in a library jacket held a bookmark at about the two-thirds point. Mabel was glad Helen had been reading that instead of a mystery. After all, you pretty much knew true love was going to triumph in these things, so Helen wouldn't have been left hanging, when she met her demise.

The drawer contained a denture cup, tissue packet, and reading glasses in a case. The Bible was a newer, large-print edition, so it didn't have any family information written in front.

A small closet had been built out into the room. Mabel eyed it but was drawn instead to the simple oak table under a back window. Small wicker file cabinets sat to one side, and stacks of books and notebooks on the tabletop. It appeared Helen had a second office up here.

When she came close enough for a better view, Mabel realized nothing appeared current. There was no apparent correspondence. The books all seemed to be local or U.S. histories, or explorations of Victorian and American Craftsman architectural styles. The notebooks she flipped through all seemed to contain annotated tidbits about the Sauer family, the Sauer houses, or historical context for the family's unique timeline.

Helen had been working on a family history, Mabel recalled, in addition to the Margarethe Sauer biography. But Mabel already had the Margarethe file back home. This heap of paper seemed to be Helen's central workstation for the larger project.

Mabel switched on the desk lamp and immediately heaved a sigh of exasperation. Helen, like Grandma, seemed to have favored low-wattage bulbs. Mabel flicked on her flashlight and thanked made-for-TV mystery movies and Nancy Drew for her PI savvy.

The far corner of the desk held a variety of books, most appearing to be from Helen's own collection, or at least privately borrowed. Mabel wondered if Linnea realized there were also library books that needed to go back. She flipped through them but didn't see anything stuck between the pages. This was disappointing. Her fictional heroines would have turned up a deed or letter that broke the case open.

In the nearest corner sat Helen's notebooks. She seemed to favor 5x8 spiral bound. There were so many.

Mabel would be here all night if she tried to check every page. She might be here a month if she tried to *read* every page. As a compromise for now, she decided to turn them over and shake to see if anything fell out.

This was a clumsy operation, particularly in plastic-bag gloves. But nothing much fell out, anyway, apart from a few loose perforated pages. She did inspect each of those, but they told her little beyond such tidbits as conventions of Victorian décor, or household expenditures for coal and kerosene.

Stacks of legal pads occupied the right side of the desk. It appeared Helen had been handwriting chapters of her book, although Mabel saw what appeared to be an old-fashioned typewriter case sitting nearby on the floor.

Discouraged, she reached down and worked one of the two-drawer file cabinets forward. She shone her flashlight into the top drawer. Genealogy charts, family records, and similar Sauer stuff, it seemed like. The lower drawer was more of the same.

Mabel shoved the cabinet back again and pulled the second one forward. It appeared filled with Helen's work on her Walter, Sr. biography, as well as bound copies of the 100-page-or-so booklet.

Hello. A large mailing envelope sat wedged at the back. Mabel had to lay her flashlight down in order to dig her fingers in and pull the envelope out.

The return address label read, Devereaux Reid, with an address in Coffeyville, a town less than halfway between Medicine Spring and Wilkie, the point of departure for the true-crimers.

The envelope was too big to be a letter. On the other hand, it wasn't thick enough for a book manuscript. Mabel fumbled to extract the contents.

She sat down to read. Devereaux's cover letter was dated about a month ago. This packet appeared to be her original approach to Helen and didn't reveal much.

Besides identifying herself, and listing her credentials—business writer, true-crime researcher—Devereaux said she'd had a lifelong fascination with the Sauer ax murders and a desire to see them finally solved, "to provide justice to the victims." She alluded to extensive previous research but considered access to family memories and records vital to giving a complete and truthful picture of the tragic incident in her upcoming book. Devereaux promised to steer clear of sensationalism and treat the Sauer name with the utmost respect.

"I have developed a working theory of the murders and believe your aunt, Miss Edna Sauer, innocent of all charges wrongfully leveled against her. I'm sure you'll be interested in what I've learned and hope you'll see your way clear to lend your assistance to this important project. You will, rest assured, receive full attribution for your valuable contributions."

Mabel had to admit that didn't sound all that bad but was sure Helen hadn't seen things that way. At the very least, wouldn't Helen want to see this book before it was published and have a chance to correct the record? Wouldn't she want to hear Devereaux's theory?

Devereaux had included her resume. Mabel scanned it and sniffed. It wasn't as if Devereaux was a published true-crime writer. Or a historian. Or even a journalist—or involved with law enforcement. By the most generous reading, Devereaux was a public relations staff writer—not even an account exec. Her only publications had all appeared in trade magazines and company newsletters.

If Devereaux was qualified to write a book about the Sauer ax murders, then so was Mabel. Mabel pondered her own resume. "Mabel Browne spent her entire childhood a stone's throw from the notorious Sauer house. Decades of legal experience. Well-versed in criminal law. Many years of writing experience."

It sounded good, and Mabel couldn't help feeling a small surge of excitement. True, her criminal law background consisted of a couple of courses in law school, plus the bar-review class. And her writing experience so far had consisted of legal memos about contract law and landlord-tenant disputes. But she could build on that as well. Ms. Reid seemed to be building on far less impressive expertise.

"Mabel?" John's voice drifted up the staircase.

"Here."

She skimmed the rest of the packet. Presumably, the letter and the other contents had all arrived in the same envelope. Devereaux had enclosed what appeared to be the opening pages of her proposed true-crime book.

John emerged from the hallway's shadows with a yawn and stretch.

"Find anything?" they asked each other in unison, and both laughed.

"You first," Mabel said.

He sat on the bed, sinking into the puffy, flowered coverlet. "Not much. But I didn't expect to. Real-life investigations aren't like the Hardy Boys, you know. In the real world, you don't always know what's a clue and what's regular...stuff."

Mabel sniffed. Her entire legal career had consisted of sorting out and trying to make sense of minutiae. Maybe she was better suited to investigative work than these big-picture cops and PIs. "What time do you have? I'm a little concerned about my animals."

John consulted his cell, yawning again. "Almost midnight. They'll be fine, now you have that security system." He nodded toward the desk. "What you got?"

Mabel gave him a quick rundown. "If Devereaux had reason to kill Helen, there might be a clue in this packet."

"Did you read any of her manuscript yet?"

"I was about to. Want me to read aloud?"

"Sure. Read me a bedtime story." He grinned, put his arms behind his head, and lay back against the mound of pillows.

Mabel cleared her throat, adjusted the lampshade, and began.

"For the better part of a century, many have attempted to solve one of the most compelling cold cases in U.S. history—the brutal ax murders of Walter Sauer, Sr., and his son, Walter Sauer, Jr. Theories abound, but all are problematic. With all key players and witnesses now deceased, it's been widely believed the case would remain an enduring mystery.

"Recent research into this long-ago crime, however, has led me in new directions. At this point, it is my strong belief that elder daughter, Edna Sauer, did *not*, as popularly supposed, murder her own father and brother. I here propose a new—and I think compelling—theory as to who wielded the fatal blows on that brisk October afternoon. I will demonstrate that while Edna Sauer may not have been guilty of that crime, she—and others in the Sauer household, in fact—well knew who was guilty. For reasons I now intend to make public for the first time, they carried that knowledge to the grave. Let's step back in time...

"October 5, 1939 seemed an ordinary morning in the sleepy town of Medicine Spring, Pennsylvania. Although Germany had invaded Poland the month before, the United States still clung to its stance of neutrality, trying to pretend the world had not just changed.

"Walter Sauer, Sr., a well-to-do local merchant, came home from his dry-goods store to eat lunch. Although nobody in that house knew it, their world was about to change, as well."

Mabel looked up at John. "We need to talk to Devereaux."

Chapter Thirty

JOHN SAT UP ON THE EDGE of Helen's frilly bed and reached for the manuscript pages. "She doesn't say who she thinks killed the Sauers, does she?"

Mabel jerked the papers away. "Speaking as a writer myself, I doubt she would. This is only the teaser, to get you hooked on reading more." But to be sure, she flipped to the end of what looked like the first chapter.

"You figure that's her real name? If so, I might be able to get a lead on her."

Mabel shrugged. "Sounds fake."

Should she get a pen name? The idea was attractive, but maybe it would be more satisfying to let everybody know without a doubt that she, Mabel Browne, had written that bestseller...

John snapped his fingers. "Mabel."

"Sorry."

"This makes me wonder what her information was. Is there a postmark?"

Mabel squinted at the faint date stamp, then passed it over to John. "September...something? Can you tell?"

He held it under the lamp. "I get September...maybe fifteenth or eighteenth? Or sixteenth? A few weeks before the murder, anyway."

"Helen must have gone ballistic."

He nodded. "This almost reads like an accusation of complicity. By the family, at least."

"Which, in Helen's universe, was personal. No surprise she wouldn't cooperate."

"Agreed."

"I'm trying to remember what Devereaux said in that Ghost Diggers episode. Something like, 'The family always knew, and so did someone else.' I have it in my notes."

"You thinking current generation?"

"I hadn't gotten that far, but wouldn't that be something? If Helen *knew*?"

"Given those assumptions, it's not too far of a leap to blackmail, is it?"

Mabel stared at John, his face half in shadow. "You think Devereaux found this out and tried blackmailing Helen?"

He shook his head. "I'm brainstorming, not opining. But maybe she's doing her research. In the process, she figures out a likely scenario for the murders, one implicating the family. That in itself should be enough to sell books."

"But then Devereaux contacts Helen and sees her reaction. She realizes there's quicker, easier money to be made."

"Not saying it happened, but it could have."

"I see that. But then, wouldn't Helen be trying to kill Devereaux—not the other way around? You don't want to kill your cash cow, do you?"

John shrugged again. "Let's close up shop for tonight. I'm teaching tomorrow."

Mabel held onto the manuscript, but John shook his head. "I don't think we need that. I'd put it back for now."

"Could you? I had enough trouble getting it out with my baggies."

He snorted. "Sure."

As they headed downstairs, Mabel's thoughts returned to the intriguing topic of blackmail. The more she thought, the more plausible it seemed.

"Hey, John. If Devereaux was trying to blackmail Helen, why would she kill her?"

"Oh, any of a bunch of reasons. Maybe Helen refused and threatened to call the police Or, say Helen lost her cool and attacked

Devereaux. It couldn't have taken a lot of effort for someone that much younger and fitter to turn the tables."

"We need to talk to her." Mabel paused at the kitchen door. "But she won't want to say much."

"Maybe not. With the right cover story, we might learn something useful, anyway."

Mabel felt as if she was wearing concrete boots. Despite the stimulating effect of the unheated house, she yawned. "Can we come back to check Helen's bedroom closet? And the attic?"

"Sure. But neither of us is in any condition to do that right now. Maybe over the weekend, okay?"

They left through the kitchen door, and John locked up.

The security light over the door had come on as they stepped outside. He waited for Mabel to unlock her car.

"Good night." She shivered as a gust of wind swirled leaves across the driveway.

"Good night. Go home and get warm. Be sure you lock up and set the alarm." In two long steps, he came and opened her car door for her, then straightened up, inches from her face. He whispered in her ear, disturbing her hair with his warm breath. "I'm going to dream about you in that red top."

Sleep that night was elusive. Thoughts of blackmail tumbled through Mabel's head, along with John's words, "I'm going to dream about you." Along with them came questions—had Devereaux solved the Sauer murders—or was she bluffing? What had she claimed the family knew? Who was the "somebody else" who supposedly knew what had happened? Just the family? Or others? What was John Bigelow's angle?

Her head felt like a dryer on fluff cycle—her thoughts were like red boxer shorts tumbling past the window, chased by a white tank top, followed by purple socks. On and on, without any pattern, until hours later, she dropped into a deep, exhausted sleep.

Mabel woke with the sun in her eyes and Koi chewing on her hair. Since John was teaching, she didn't expect to hear from him until evening, if at all.

She'd better call around for a landscaper first and have that over with. Then, she needed to get to work on the Margarethe biography.

The first item on her to-do list proved easier than she'd feared. After staring at listings for landscapers she didn't know the first thing about, she gave up and called Nanette. That was one good thing, she realized, that had come from volunteering—she now had a few contacts for questions like this.

Nanette suggested Acey Davis. "He's not what I'd call a landscaping service, exactly. But he does all sorts of handiwork for me and a lot of other local people. He isn't going to overcharge you."

Mabel breathed a sigh of relief and wrote down his number.

"Now, I should warn you. He can be a tad independent. If he takes a notion to go hunting or something, he'll up and go without any warning. He does a good job, though. Eventually."

That might not be the most helpful work ethic for somebody on a rush job. Mabel explained her predicament.

"That still gives him two weeks to finish a not-very-big job. I should think you'll be all right. But be sure and tell him you've got that deadline."

"Should I offer him a bonus if he finishes early?" Mabel swallowed hard on the idea of paying extra.

Nanette considered. "Couldn't hurt. Might not help, but then again, if his truck needs work, or he has his eye on a new TV or something, that might motivate him."

Within half an hour, Acey Davis had agreed to come out and size up the job, when he "had a minute." Mabel impressed on him the urgency of the township notice, and that seemed to inspire him more than the idea of extra money.

"That blasted township. Always up in a man's business. What's it to them what you do with your own personal property?"

"Well, there's a health code that—"

"Load'a bull. I can pretty much guarantee it ain't a health problem. Nosy neighbor turn you in?"

"Yeah, she did. But she's dead now, and—"

"Oh, hey, now. There's no call for violence."

"I didn't… Never mind. She just died, all right? Nothing to do with me. But I've still got this notice, and—"

He chuckled. "I sure am glad to hear that. It was the way you first put it, you know? Don't you worry, missy. I'll be out and size 'er up. We'll get that interferin' township off your back."

Mabel thanked him effusively, choosing to forgive his suspecting her of murder. Now she could spend the rest of the day concentrating on that bio. Studying her calendar, she realized how little time she had to digest all the information Helen had accumulated, let alone write a biography that would make Mabel's reputation as an author.

She cleared space on the kitchen table and dumped the papers out. Helen had already organized some of her research material into folders. Maybe there was an outline.

Koi, with her instinct for inserting herself into anything Mabel was trying to accomplish, jumped up, pushing an envelope of photos to the floor.

Thank goodness, the floor wasn't wet or particularly dirty. Mabel gathered the scattered pictures and spread them across the table.

These had to be family photos. Mabel hoped they were labeled. Although Helen might have known who all these folks were, she certainly did not.

Family groups. A mother and a baby. A group of children. A little boy with a wagon. Someone in a WWI doughboy uniform. Most—Mabel realized with gratitude—seemed to be identified. Enough photos of Margarethe were labeled for Mabel to start recognizing her without flipping the picture.

She'd been a beautiful woman, slender and fine-featured. Violet took after her mother. Edna, on the other hand, had inherited a strange combination of each parent's features. She had her father's large, boxlike shape and low brow, along with her mother's narrow nose and full lips. The features that seemed so delicate and appealing on Margarethe simply looked out of place on Edna. It was as if the baby factory had run out of the correct features when assembling Edna, and filled in as best they could, with parts at hand.

But Edna's eyes, overshadowed as they were by that low brow and an unruly mane of dark waves, were truly beautiful. At least, Mabel thought so. They reflected intelligence and boldness, almost challenging the viewer to underestimate her. "I get you, Edna. They all underrate us, don't they?"

She arranged photos by approximate time period. There was but one baby photo of Margarethe, a fuzzy shot in a white christening gown. Another showed her as a little girl with corkscrew curls, sitting in a tiny cart hitched to a long-horned goat.

Margarethe had been a lovely bride. Given the time period, Mabel had expected a simpler dress than the high-necked Edwardian extravagance that seemed to have swallowed her, in the single image from her wedding day. Probably a family dress. There was so much going on—acres of satin and sheer stuff, tucking and ruching, lacy insets and beading. Mabel shook her head at those leg-of-mutton sleeves.

Margarethe's small-featured face looked stiff...maybe from the sheer magnitude of what, at age eighteen, she'd gotten herself into. Walter, Sr., some fifteen years older than his bride, wasn't very handsome, Mabel thought. Heavy-featured, and excessive mustache. Not that appearance was everything—Mabel knew that better than most. But they did seem an odd match.

She shuddered. Thank the good Lord Margarethe hadn't been able to see their future.

Or, studying that rigid little face, Mabel wondered. Maybe she'd had an idea life wasn't going to be all sunshine and orange blossoms.

Two hours later, Mabel had done a preliminary sort through Helen's files and made an outline. She'd divided the work into sections and set a schedule to finish in plenty of time—if all went well, which it so often did not. This wasn't so different from what she'd done at the law firm, when she'd had to write a big brief for one of the partners.

She wished she'd had a chance to read through all of Helen's notes but planned to do that as she wrote. She didn't have time for much else.

Mabel glanced at the clock. Lunch was overdue.

As she shoved her chair back, she glanced down. Barnacle was dancing between her and the back door, but a dropped photo caught her eye. She'd missed it when she picked up the others, undoubtedly because Koi was sitting with her fluffy tail partly covering it. The cat blinked up at her with a single silent meow.

"What have you got there?" Mabel slid the picture toward her.

"Huh." The photograph looked as if it dated to around the time of the murders, when Margarethe was largely confined to her bedroom. She reclined on a lounge, wearing a simple, long dressing gown and slippers. A book lay in her lap.

Still beautiful in her mid-forties, she was thinner than on her wedding day. Her cheekbones were sharper and her eyes hollow. Her faint smile didn't reach her eyes.

Mabel took all this in, but what held her frozen was Margarethe's flowered dressing gown. She held the old picture close to her nose, trying to decide if she was seeing what she thought she was.

It had to be. She knew that pattern. Those pansies—they'd be purple and yellow on a peach background. Her heart started to chug. It seemed impossible. But in a burst, Mabel felt as if a window had opened, and she could see things she hadn't been able to see before. Could it be? Was this the secret the Sauers had so carefully hidden for more than eighty years?

Had Devereaux seen a copy of this picture? Somehow, Mabel felt sure the writer had come to the same realization she had. She needed to call John, and they had to get to Devereaux before this day was over.

Chapter Thirty-One

BARNACLE WHINED, PULLING MABEL BACK FROM her churning thoughts. While letting him out, she dialed the phone with her other hand.

The call went to voicemail. "John? Mabel. Call as soon as you get this, okay? I think I have something."

Then, she paced. Why hadn't she thought to ask what John's schedule was today? She had to start writing, if she was to meet her deadline. But how could she concentrate on anything but that photograph?

Mabel checked again, in case she'd missed John's call back. Nothing.

She pulled out a frozen potpie and stuck it in the oven. Then, she grabbed a spoonful of peanut butter to tide her over till it was ready.

She plopped down and picked up the photo again. The picture might mean nothing. If she was right, though, this was a bombshell. Mabel couldn't begin to imagine what Helen would have done to keep the lid on the scandal.

She pushed the photo aside and began typing. *Concentrate.* The first section—an overview of Margarethe Sauer's remarkable accomplishments, despite the infirmity of her last years—didn't take much thought. Helen had already written a lot of it. Raising an accomplished family. Writing two books of poetry, published by the local university press. Becoming perhaps the greatest philanthropist in the entire county, if not the tri-county area, despite her husband's hardheaded, frugal reputation.

Mabel rolled her eyes. How long had Helen struggled to come up with a nice way of saying Walter, Sr. had been a ruthless businessman and self-centered cheapskate? Every non-family source she'd seen had been pretty blunt about what a hard man he was.

Still, that frail-looking woman on the fainting couch had convinced him to launch a drive for a new firetruck with a big donation. The couple had been sustaining members of their church. Margarethe had spearheaded creation of the Medicine Spring Wind Symphony, and the Sauers had been among the largest donors. The list went on and was impressive.

She checked her phone again. Maybe she'd inadvertently muted it. But no, the volume was up all the way.

Sighing, Mabel went back to work. *Focus.*

It didn't take long to work through the portion Helen had already roughed out. "Wish you'd pushed a bit harder, Helen," Mabel muttered. By then, the timer had dinged, and she took a break to remove her potpie from the oven and poke holes in the crust to cool it enough to eat. Barnacle and Koi moved in as the broken crust released the chicken scent.

"Beat it, guys." She shoved at them, but they crowded back in.

Keeping one eye on her circling animals, Mabel arranged some of Helen's notes and photocopies to use for the next section. As she did, a clipping from the *Tri-County Shopper*—a weekly carrying features, school sports, and community events—jumped out at her. It was dated a couple months earlier and written by Devereaux.

Absently forking potpie into her mouth, she read. Had Helen come upon this article herself, or was this part of the packet Devereaux had sent?

Rather in the spirit of O.J. Simpson's infamous *If I Did It,* the piece was written as a hypothetical. As she read, Mabel alternated between disgust and admiration for Devereaux's clever method of stirring up interest in her upcoming book. Anybody could concoct a wild theory and throw it out there in place of facts.

Had Devereaux been paid for this drivel? Maybe the *Tri-County Shopper* was so hungry for copy they'd pay Mabel. Maybe she should try submitting something to drum up interest for her book.

Shaking herself, she returned to the story. Devereaux set up the opening like a mystery—much like the book excerpt they'd found in Helen's file drawer. Tension built as the unsuspecting Walter Sauer napped. He woke abruptly to see his attacker but was caught off guard. The attack came as a horrific shock—he knew and had trusted his assailant.

He moved to escape but caught flat on his back, was at a disadvantage. A single ax blow ended his life.

Walter, Jr., entered the room, perhaps to speak to his father. Though younger, stronger, and more agile, he was caught unprepared, as well, for the brutal onslaught. A few blows brought him down.

That's where the article ended, of course. Devereaux wouldn't simply be giving away the shocking resolution to one of the country's great unsolved true crimes. The governing principle was the same as in a fifth-grade book report. "If you want to know how this story ends, read the book."

Devereaux had figured out who the Sauer ax murderer was—or claimed she had. She'd also told Helen she not only knew this, but that the Sauer family had always known. But instead of reporting her conclusions—and evidence, if any—to the police like a decent citizen, she'd gone to Helen and teased the public with innuendo.

John still hadn't returned her call. Mabel glanced at the kitchen clock. She ought to keep writing but felt a sudden need for some form of action. Grabbing her cell, she dialed the historical society.

Darwin answered.

"Hi. Are you going to be at the house a bit longer? Could I come over for a few minutes?"

"I'm here till five." Although he sounded puzzled, Mabel didn't bother to enlighten him.

Barnacle rose from his spot under her chair, looking hopeful. She started to tell him "no," then relented. "All right, buddy. I'm going to have to tie you outside for a moment when we get there, though. No dogs allowed. The historical society is prejudiced."

From his accusing expression, he seemed to understand what she was talking about. But at the sight of his leash, he brightened and started wagging his tail. Koi leapt gracefully onto the nearest chair and sat with her tail wrapped around her tidy front feet, watching them.

Mabel paused to rub her chin. "I owe you, sweetie."

Koi squeezed her eyes shut and slowly opened them to meet Mabel's with an intense, steady gaze. The message was clear. "Ham it is." Mabel picked up a furry paw to shake on it. "Hope you never develop a taste for caviar."

Darwin's was the only car parked beside the house when they arrived. Mabel decided the original hitching post by the front steps was a good spot for Barnacle. If they were lucky, he wouldn't scare away any prospective visitors. "You be a good boy," she told him. "I'll be right back."

As she lifted her hand to ring the bell, the door opened. "I saw you coming." Darwin ushered her inside. "I must say, I was thrilled you called. I've been going crazy here by myself. We had a rush of curiosity seekers early on." He grimaced. "But now, we're back to normal. Not a single visitor."

Mabel started to tell him they ought to schedule an ax murder mystery night, but then, clamped her mouth shut. This was obviously too soon after Helen's unfortunate death to be in good taste.

"I can't stay but I wondered if I could take a glance at the visitors' book."

He raised his eyebrows but gestured toward the hall table. "Of course. Would you like to carry it into the other room where you can sit?"

"No...well, maybe."

Darwin carried the heavy book into the living room and offered her coffee. "Oh, no, thanks." She could smell the overheated sludge from the hall and thought the fumes alone might be loosening the bond on her tooth fillings.

She settled herself in a folding chair, since even society members weren't allowed to make themselves at home on the vintage furniture. Darwin placed the book in her lap.

Mabel had hoped he'd go about his business, but it seemed he was too thrilled to have company to let her go. "Are you looking for something in particular?"

She paged back. "Um…well, I wanted to have a glance at the day of my tour."

Darwin's face fell. "Don't take those comments personally. They'd had a dreadful shock, and then, as you know, the police detained them."

Mabel's jaw dropped. Remembering Grandma Mabel's warning she'd catch flies if she wasn't careful, she snapped it shut. He thought she was checking her reviews, did he? And it appeared they weren't great.

Stoically, Mabel squinted her eyes and tried to skim past the true-crime group's comments. Ignoring them was easier said than done, with words like "unprofessional," "argumentative," and "short-tempered" jumping right out at her. *Humph.* Wouldn't they have a rude awakening if she reviewed *them*?

There was Devereaux. Mabel's finger stopped tracing down the page. The town listed was the same as on the address label stuck to the packet she'd sent Helen. "Lovely house, yet the sadness is palpable. Visit my website for information re: my upcoming book on the 1939 Sauer ax murders."

Darwin was still sitting a few feet away.

She pointed at the book. "Do you know about this woman? It appears she's writing a book about the murders. Claims she's solved the case."

Darwin's lips twitched. "A lifetime later and all those investigators, she steps in and figures out one of the country's great unsolved mysteries. Good for her." He grinned. "She only wants to sell books."

"Maybe. Do you know her?"

"I've met her, anyway. Before this." He tapped the book. "She stopped in to ask about the family and the murders."

"She didn't tell you she thought she'd solved them?"

"She was looking for info. If she had any theories, she didn't share them with me."

"Did you show her anything here?"

Darwin's eyes flickered. He leaned toward Mabel. "I showed her the display," he whispered, as if Helen were about to appear behind him and smack him on the head.

Mabel gasped. "You didn't."

"She was so persuasive. Darn it, I understand not sensationalizing what happened, but that room should be open."

"Weren't you afraid of it getting back to Helen?"

He laughed but shifted in his seat. "I regretted it afterward."

"Have you seen this woman since that day?"

He shook his head.

Mabel glanced at her phone. Blast. "Sorry. I missed an important call." She stood and handed the book back to Darwin. "Thanks for letting me see this."

Mabel hurried outside and down the leaf-strewn front steps. Barnacle got to his feet and barked a greeting.

She released him from the hitching post and redialed John.

"Mabel. What's up?"

"I can't explain right now. Can we get together somewhere?"

"Let's do this. I confirmed the contact info for Devereaux Reid. Why don't you call and see if we can stop by and get some information for that biography? Flatter her a bit. If we're lucky, maybe she'll invite you over tonight. Meanwhile, I'll fix an early dinner at my place, since you hosted me last time."

"Dinner?"

He laughed. "Yeah. It's an evening meal. Often shared by friends, family, and lovers."

"I mean...yeah, I know. I mean your place? You don't need to. We can go out somewhere and eat."

"You can trust me, Little Red Riding Hood. Didn't we have a nice evening when we ate at your house?"

Mabel felt herself flush and was glad only colorblind Barnacle was there to see. "I didn't mean that."

"Let me give you my address." She heard the grin in his voice. "I want to cook for you."

Mabel told herself she needed to start thinking like a modern, grownup woman. "Can I bring dessert?"

He did laugh out loud at that, and she wondered if he expected orange sandwich cremes. "No, thanks. You're my guest. Let me treat you."

Mabel hung up after John promised to text his address and Devereaux's phone number. "This is something new," she told Barnacle.

Mabel crept along, squinting as she drove, looking for house numbers that for the most part weren't there. Hickory Hollow Road led out of Medicine Spring into the countryside. John had said his house was a yellow '30s bungalow. At the edge of town, she spotted his address. The porch light was on. As it turned out, she didn't need the house number, since she recognized his car.

Mabel parked, then sat for a few moments, not quite ready to go inside. She checked her reflection. Her hair was wilder than usual, but that couldn't be helped. She shoved renegade strands into place and, with a sense of hopelessness, told them to stay.

She'd decided to go with buttercup yellow—a V-necked pullover and stretchy, dark-wash jeans. She adjusted the top. It was a modest V, but she didn't want to give John the wrong idea.

The front door opened, and he waved. "Coming in?"

She waved back, then gathered her purse and the packet of Sauer photos. As she joined John on the porch, she drew a deep breath. "What a nice house."

It *was* an attractive little house, and well-maintained, unlike Mabel's Victorian. The paint appeared fresh, the uncluttered porch held a pair of wicker chairs, a small table, and an old-fashioned porch swing. The grass was trimmed, and the red geraniums along the walk didn't compete with a single weed that she could see.

"Thanks. I've been here a year now, and it's starting to feel like home."

A wonderful garlic aroma drifted through the front door. "Smells good."

"Thanks again." He motioned for her to precede him inside. "I should've asked if you like eggplant. I made eggplant parmesan, but it's healthy—not breaded."

Mabel loved breading but supposed healthy was a good idea.

"You want to follow me to the kitchen? We can talk while I finish up," He glanced back over his shoulder. "I talked to my friend on the force earlier today. Helen's bike was wiped clean."

Mabel sighed. "No surprise there."

Old black-and-white photos lined the short hallway. Mabel squinted in the dim light but couldn't make out much.

"Did you reach Devereaux?"

Mabel spoke to his back. "You were right. She jumped on my asking for help with the bio. She said just to come over after dinner."

"Drink?"

That would at least give her something to hold. "Sure. Whatever you're having."

Mabel trailed him to the kitchen, gawking at the comfy-looking living room with its gray-and-yellow color scheme. The tiny TV was old and boxy. Bookcases occupied a lot of wall space and seemed to run to history, paperback mysteries, and suspense. As she passed the battered desk under the window nearest the kitchen, she couldn't help noticing the orderly stack of sorting trays—and the holster hanging over the chair back.

"You want to bring that in here?" John pointed to the envelope. "We can talk while I finish the garlic bread and toss the salad."

"Sure."

"Have a seat at the table, if you want. Most meals, I eat right here. Or pull up a stool to the counter."

The kitchen was cheerful in red and white. Why couldn't Mabel's house be appealing like this? He must think she was a slob.

"Give me a hand?" he asked. "You can spread garlic butter while we talk. Or do you need to show me something?"

She set the envelope on the table. "This can wait. But I'd better wash my hands first."

As soon as she'd done that, Mabel sat at the counter. John's sleeves were rolled up, and he was ripping lettuce into a wooden bowl. The eggplant was cooling on the stovetop. A long loaf of crusty bread, already split, waited on a baking sheet. She started slathering the cut side with butter.

John had set out a glass of water. Mabel realized it was hers. She should've asked what he was drinking before telling him to give her the same. She had rather hoped for an icy Coke or Pepsi, or even a sweet tea.

"I'm dying of suspense over here. Tell me how you cracked the case."

He didn't sound as if he was dying of suspense—interested, but perhaps still more than a little skeptical. Well, maybe she wasn't a PI like he was, but she still knew how to analyze a case. He was about to get a shock.

"Earlier today, I was going through photos Helen had collected for the booklet. When I came to a certain picture of Margarethe, I knew. She killed them herself. The saintly Margarethe Sauer was an ax murderer."

Chapter Thirty-Two

"WHAT DID YOU SAY?" JOHN WAS no longer ripping lettuce. In fact, he'd plopped down on the barstool facing her.

"I know it's crazy. But it all fits."

"Shoot. Tell me what you've got."

"The garlic bread's ready."

John stuck the loaf in the oven and set the timer. He returned to the barstool, still ignoring the half-made salad. "Come on, woman—give. You can't drop a bombshell like that and then dilly-dally."

"You may or may not know the historical society has several artifacts from the ax murders, which were always kept in that back parlor, where the attack occurred. There was a hatchet, but that wasn't the real murder weapon. That disappeared the day of the crime and was never seen again."

"Yes, I know." His voice was threaded with impatience. "And?"

Mabel refused to be rushed. Jessica Fletcher never rushed her big reveal. Neither did any of the made-for-TV mystery movie heroines. "Another thing in the display case is a fragment of cloth with blood on it. From what I've read, police found the fabric caught on an exposed nail on the staircase turn, which the Sauers used to anchor Christmas garland."

She absently picked up her water, looked at it, and set it down.

"I guess I shouldn't have taken you literally. Would you like something else?"

"This is fine."

He grinned. "It's no problem. What would you like?" He rummaged in the fridge. "I've got orange juice. Fizzy water with cherry juice."

"OJ would be great, thanks."

"There. Now, back to the artifacts." He set a full glass in front of her then slipped back onto his barstool.

Mabel took a sip. "The fabric—purple and yellow pansies on a peach-colored background— matched an apron of Edna's, which disappeared after the murders. Both she and her sister Violet admitted this, but Edna said she hadn't had the apron in a while—that she'd donated it to someone collecting rags door-to-door."

"The fabric's significant?"

"It was evidence the prosecutor used to tie Edna to the murders. She did have spots of blood on her clothing, which she could've picked up when she discovered the bodies. But this fragment is soaked in blood—and Edna couldn't produce the apron it came from."

"And...?"

"It seems police weren't immediately called. Edna called her sister first, which she attributed to shock. Obviously, this gave her time to hide or destroy evidence."

"How does this point to Margarethe?"

"I'm getting there." Mabel inhaled, appreciating the garlic scent rising on the air. "Police found charred bits of this same cloth in the burn barrel behind the house within the first twenty-four hours. They speculated Edna had burned the evidence without realizing police had already found another fragment of the same fabric caught in the staircase railing."

"So?" John twirled a hand for Mabel to spit it out.

"This." Mabel rummaged through the envelope and handed him the photo of Margarethe in her flowered dressing gown. "This is the same fabric. I'd swear to it in court."

"Whoa. Big leap there. You're a lawyer—you know as well as I do—all this proves is there were two items made of the same cloth. Edna couldn't account for hers, but wouldn't police have checked Margarethe's gown?"

"Not if her daughters closed ranks and never told anybody the dressing gown ever existed. Not if they burned it. Margarethe, the invalid, was never a suspect. They questioned her very gently on stuff like whether she'd seen or heard anything, and that was all.

"Police—which in all likelihood would've been men in that time period—never considered there might've been more than one piece of clothing with that particular fabric in the same house. I imagine when Margarethe sewed that gown, she had fabric left over and used the scraps for Edna's apron."

The timer dinged, and John jumped up. "To be continued." He scrambled to remove the bread and finish the salad.

Once they were seated, Mabel focused on eating. Everything smelled and tasted delicious—even the eggplant. Who knew you could make healthy food taste this good?

But John was back to business. "I guess you're saying Edna and Violet got together and decided to protect their mother at all costs. Yeah, I could see that happening. *But...*" He took a forkful of eggplant, chewed, and swallowed. "There are obvious problems with your theory. One, Margarethe was bedridden. Two, what possible motive could she have had?"

"One." Mabel leaned forward. "She was *not* bedridden. That's a popular misconception. She was in fragile health and confined to her room most of the time. But she did walk around up there and come out on occasion."

"But killing two grown men with an ax is going to take considerably more than walking a few steps."

"Not if you catch one in his sleep and the other by complete surprise."

"I don't buy it." John shook his head. "Her husband, maybe. I understand he was an uncommonly hard man and even known to be abusive with the kids. In fact, that came out at trial as a motive for Edna. Why on earth would she kill her own son?"

He'd hit the snag in Mabel's theory. "I don't know. But that only means we have to figure that out. It doesn't mean I'm not right."

"There's no 'only' about it. You're making a huge leap."

"Not necessarily impossible, however. Let's assume I'm right, and Margarethe killed both men. What if her daughters made a pact to protect her, even to the extent of Edna's taking the rap?"

He motioned at her plate. "Eat your food before it gets cold. I'll wait."

"Thanks." When she'd cleared half her plate, she continued. "Darwin admitted today he let Devereaux into the murder room against Helen's orders to keep the public out. You know how proud Helen was of the family. If Devereaux figured out the same thing I did, can you imagine Helen's reaction? She'd never want anything to tarnish the family name, especially Margarethe's. And practically on the eve of the big gala?"

"Then what? Attack Devereaux, who's taller, younger, and heavier? Threaten to sue her to block publication?"

"Knowing Helen, she might've threatened to sue. But she'd have no cause of action. Plus everything would come out in court, anyway. I do think she might've physically attacked Devereaux if she was mad enough, though. I watched her and Cora acting like roller derby competitors the other night."

"You think Devereaux turned on her? Shouldn't she have been able to disarm an eighty-something woman without killing her?"

"She might've *wanted* to kill her. Maybe once Devereaux realized the value of this piece of historical info, she decided she could make more money blackmailing Helen than by publishing the story. But then, maybe Helen told her to take her dirty business elsewhere, because she was reporting her to the police."

"That's exactly what Helen would say, all right." John frowned. "I hate to admit it, but you're starting to make sense."

Mabel repressed the urge to throw her garlic bread at him.

As if sensing her desire to attack, he rested his palm on the back of her hand holding the garlic bread. "Your theory does make some sense. You've got a sharp eye, to catch this."

Mabel wanted to eat her garlic bread, but with John's hand on hers, and his eyes meeting hers, she couldn't move.

"There are still a few holes in your hypothesis. We don't get to gloss over them and pretend they're not there. It's highly unlikely Margarethe deliberately killed her own son. What possible motive could there be? You might shoot a gun in sudden fear and kill the wrong person. But face to face with an ax, she'd know exactly who she was swinging at and surely pull back."

"Because we don't see the motive doesn't mean it doesn't exist. For instance, what if Margarethe's 'fragile health' was really psychosis? She wouldn't have been the first mentally-ill person kept sequestered by her family."

Mabel cast a longing glance at her garlic bread, still trapped beneath their hands. Ah, well, she told herself, she could always have garlic bread. It wasn't every day someone held her hand.

That thought reminded her. "Hey, John. Would you maybe like to go to the Margarethe Sauer Gala with me?"

Chapter Thirty-Three

THEY DROVE ACROSS THE BRIDGE BEYOND the other side of town, following Mabel's GPS to Devereaux's address. After leaving behind the older section of Medicine Spring, with its Victorians, bungalows, and four-squares, they passed the shopping strip, consisting of a bakery, hardware, and other shops, then picked up the highway for several miles. John took the Coffeyville Exit onto a state route, past former farms, now converted to raw-looking new housing developments.

It was dark and had begun to rain. John's wipers swiped at a light-but-steady sprinkle. Mailboxes, trees, and at one point, a possum scuttling across the wet pavement appeared in the headlight beam.

"The address is 111A Shropshire Lane." Mabel squinted at her cellphone. "There should be a left in about a quarter mile, onto Crowmarsh Road."

He darted her a wry glance. "I take it she lives in a nouveau-olde-English village?"

"I'm guessing. Oh." Mabel gestured. "There it is."

A faux-weathered sign, reading "Village of Birchby Green" and featuring a silhouette of a raven-like bird on a branch, swayed in the wind. "Great night for a murder," John muttered.

"A great place for it, don't you think? Miss Marple would feel right at home."

"Perhaps the vicar has met his demise," he suggested, and she laughed. He'd said he'd be honored to accompany her to the gala. To her relief, he'd insisted on paying for both their tickets, though she'd gone through the motions of protesting. Mabel couldn't help a giddy surge of self-satisfaction.

The houses carried through the English village theme, with

imitation half-timbering on their facades. "Now, after the street makes a sharp bend to the left up here, you'll want the next right."

John made the turn into a cul-de-sac, boxed around by garden-style townhouses, each consisting of two units, with their own attached garages. "That must be the place."

They pulled into the end space, under a scraggly, dripping pine. Before opening the door, John turned to her. "Let's make sure we have our story straight. You're here to get her input for the biography. In exchange, she gets a credit in the booklet, as well as the gala program, plugging her book. You'll be taking notes, right?"

Mabel nodded. Given the rain, she decided to stick her notepad and pen in a pocket and leave her purse in the car.

"Good. Now, once you get a few of her 'insights,' I'll casually lead her into theories about the murders."

"I thought I was doing that," Mabel said. "It's my theory we're working on. And I *am* a lawyer. I know how to ask subtle questions."

John rolled his eyes, then caught himself, but it was too late.

"What's that supposed to mean? You don't think I can be trusted to interrogate a witness?"

"Of course not. I mean of course you can. But your experience is all stuff like contract disputes and wills. I think if Devereaux killed someone, it might be better if somebody with actual criminal-investigative experience did the questioning."

Mabel opened her mouth, then closed it. Maybe he was right. She'd never confronted a murderer. If John had experience with that, maybe he should take the lead this time. Although she'd been feeling excited, she'd perhaps been too casual about this interview, knowing she didn't have to face Devereaux alone.

Before they'd left the bungalow, John had taken time to strap on his holster. It was an uncomfortable reminder that sometimes killers found homicide easier the second time around.

"Let's go." Mabel pulled her jacket collar as far as it would go over the back of her head, but as it only covered her ears, it was a poor substitute for an umbrella. Why hadn't she checked the forecast?

Ducking into the wind, she aimed for Devereaux's unit. The light was on, as promised, though the adjoining unit was dark.

John tapped her arm. "You told her I was coming?"

"Yep."

"Good. We don't want her to freak out. But here, let me stand between you and the door."

Mabel stared at him, big-eyed. It hadn't occurred to her Devereaux might be lying in wait for them. Now she realized the possibility of ambush had occurred to John. She stepped back as he rang the doorbell.

The peal reverberated inside the townhouse. Mabel hunched under her increasingly damp jacket. Wet leaves blew across the sidewalk, slapping at her ankles. The wind was cold. It wouldn't be long before there were snowflakes in the air.

"Where is she?"

He rang the bell again. "Have you noticed there don't seem to be any lights inside? Maybe she decided to blow us off."

"She could be in the back. Mabel tucked cold hands into her pockets and stamped her feet.

He swiped droplets from his face. "The rain's picking up."

"I guess I should've called again when we left, but she said it didn't matter when we got here, since she planned to be in all evening."

Mabel scooted over as John turned around. "She's got to be in there somewhere," she insisted. "Maybe we should check around back. It's windy enough she might not be hearing the doorbell."

"Maybe not a knock, but she ought to hear a doorbell anywhere in a small place like this."

Mabel hesitated. She'd hoped John would check the back. She didn't have her flashlight and hated the thought of creeping around behind the darkened building. In this rain, she couldn't use her cell's flashlight app, either. The phone wasn't even paid off yet and she didn't want it getting wet.

Since he still didn't leave the top step, Mabel sighed. All right, she'd go. Maybe once she started moving, he'd be shamed into going around the back himself.

Mabel crossed in front of the attached garage, hugging the building, hoping the narrow overhang would offer a bit of protection. Then, she heard it.

"There's a car running in here."

Mabel pounded on the garage door. "Devereaux."

John nudged her aside.

"Hey."

He stretched to see through the top windows but was a couple of inches short. "Step into my hands." He crouched down and leaned a shoulder against the door.

Mabel stared. She clearly outweighed him.

"Right now, Mabel. If she's in there, the carbon monoxide will kill her."

That sent a jolt of fear through her, and she gingerly placed a dirty, wet boot into John's interlaced fingers.

"Step off, step off!" he yelled as she tipped him off balance and nearly collapsed them both.

"I'm sorry, I— Do you want to step into my hands?"

"No. Sorry. It was just an awkward position." He knelt and arranged himself on his hands and knees on the wet pavement. "Hurry, though. Stand on my back."

She finally had a date for a fancy event, and maybe a boyfriend. Now, she was going to stand on him and kill him. Life was unfair.

"Put your feet here and here." He gestured at his back. "When you get up there, lay your phone against the glass and turn on the flashlight, got it?"

Again, she planted her foot. As she let her weight down, she felt him wince, but brought her other foot up next to it.

"Hurry," he gasped.

Mabel placed her phone against the glass. In the small arc of white light, she could see a compact, silver sedan. "Somebody's in there."

"Okay," he wheezed. "Get down."

As soon as Mabel's boots hit the driveway, John staggered to his feet. He tried the door, but it didn't budge. "Grab a big rock, if you can find one," he told her. "Smash out any windows you can find on that side or in back."

As Mabel searched the plantings for stones, John picked one up from beside the steps, and threw it full-force against the garage-door window. The pane broke.

Mabel pounced on a rock as big as a bread loaf.

"Huh. Fake." She swooped down and picked up a key. "Let's go through the house."

"Be careful—" John's warning was cut off by the shriek of Devereaux's alarm system.

Mabel stared at the panel on the entry wall in front of her. A red light flashed over and over.

John pushed past her. He grimaced. "That's one way to call the cops. Leave the door wide open and see if you can get some windows open too. It's probably okay in here, but since CO's odorless, I'd rather be sure."

Mabel threw on lights and ran into the living room. She fumbled with the nearest window latch and shoved the bottom pane upward. Cold air and a spatter of rain blew into the room. She ran to the next.

She'd opened all but one window on the first floor by the time John returned from the garage, shaking his head. "She's dead."

Chapter Thirty-Four

TWO POLICE UNITS PULLED INTO THE cul-de-sac, lights flashing, and skidding on the wet pavement. John stood, silhouetted in the front door, hands up. Of course. The police were responding to the alarm, and not a call from John and her. They'd be expecting a possible break-in. John obviously realized that.

Mabel's knees wouldn't support her, so she slumped on the couch, watching in disbelief. In but a few weeks, she'd found two bodies. Even she was having trouble believing that coincidence.

At least, carbon monoxide would be accidental, right? Or at worst, suicide?

John stepped all the way outside now, and Mabel heard the buzz of voices and crackle of police radios in the driveway.

A wave of dizziness washed over her. Mabel had never fainted but suspected that was what this was. She fought the closing darkness, putting her head between her knees and trying to pull in deep breaths.

Abruptly, she remembered. *Carbon monoxide*. Mabel's eyes flew open and she held her breath.

Someone grabbed her and stuck an oxygen mask over her face.

While the young black male EMT monitored Mabel's oxygen and pulse, another dashed into the garage. Mabel watched, round-eyed. Where was John? She didn't have long to wonder, as the police came in along with him. "Have a seat, sir."

John sank into the chair indicated and focused on Mabel. "Are you okay? What's wrong with her?" he asked the EMT. "The carbon monoxide?"

The EMT shrugged. "Don't think so. She was having a lightheaded episode. Possibly shock."

Mabel tugged at the mask. Nobody looks good in a full oxygen mask, and she already felt better.

"Whoa there, miss. Let me check your oxygen first." He slipped a monitor clip over her finger.

The officer standing beside John shifted his feet and cleared his throat. "Is she all right for questioning?"

The EMT checked and nodded. "She seems better now. Easy does it." He put a steadying hand on Mabel's arm as she got up.

"You good to walk?" The officer gave her a sideways glance. "You aren't going to keel over on me, are you?"

She started to shake her head and felt the dizziness creep back in. "No. I'm fine."

"All right. Let's step out to the cruiser for your statement."

Mabel shot a helpless look at John. We're already getting your boyfriend's statement, ma'am. Tell us the truth, and you've got nothing to worry about. Right?"

What was that supposed to mean? Mabel's mind raced back twenty-three years, to her bar review course and her Miranda rights. She'd only gotten a C in criminal procedure. Maybe she shouldn't say anything. Should she contact a lawyer? Who should she call? Only one person in her old firm did criminal work, and she couldn't bring herself to call him.

The officer helped her into the back seat of the squad car, putting his hand on her head, like on TV. "This doesn't mean anything," he told her. "We just want you to give your statements separately, without influencing each other."

Mabel felt herself sweating, even though the evening was cold. Good grief, she was already acting guilty.

"All right now, ma'am. Could you please tell us what happened here tonight, as best you can? Starting with what brought you here."

A faint urine smell made her want to choke. Obviously, someone had literally peed himself on this seat, and the dampness was bringing the lingering odor back up. It wasn't her, was it? Of course not. She'd definitely know if she'd had an accident. She just wasn't thinking straight right now.

"Ma'am!" The officer's voice was sharp. "I asked you a question. Did you hear me?"

"I decline to answer on the basis that it might tend to incriminate me."

"You're claiming the Fifth?" The officer stared hard at her, his eyebrows elevated almost to his low-hanging hairline.

Mabel nodded. "Yes."

"You're not a suspect at this point, ma'am." His eyes added the word "yet." "We're only trying to figure out what happened here. I haven't even Mirandized you yet. This isn't one of your TV cop shows."

Mabel drew herself up and squared her shoulders. "I'm not some TV-watching idiot. I'm a lawyer."

"Hoo-boy. This night's going from bad to worse." He fixed her with a dark glare. "All right. You want to play it like this? We know this is the second body you've been involved with in the last couple of weeks. Maybe you have a good explanation for that. But if you aren't interested in sharing your story, we'll have to figure that out on our own. Get out."

Mabel hesitated.

"You have something to say?"

She shook her head.

He came around and opened her door. "Out. We'll be in touch."

Mabel shivered. The rain had let up, but she was already damp, and the wind was rising. She couldn't leave without John, who still hadn't come out of the townhouse.

Nor could she go back in there. She suspected this would be a long wait.

Chapter Thirty-Five

MABEL WRESTLED A BOX ONTO THE front passenger seat. "Right here," she told the print-shop employee, who waited behind her, arms laden with three more boxes.

They were here. Mabel couldn't help feeling a little rush of pride. The Margarethe Sauer biography was not only finished but bound in the sage and old-gold colors of the Sauer living room décor. She'd already seen the proof copy, so she resisted the temptation to dig into the cartons right now. So what if a lot of the content was Helen's? She'd taken pains to credit her. Ultimately, the finished product was Mabel's. She was now a published author.

And not even a self-published author, she reminded herself. The historical society had paid for the printing.

Tonight was the gala, and she had to admit she was as nervous as she was excited. The committee had already seen and signed off on the proof, but the Margarethe Sauer biography hadn't been made public yet. Plus, she had a date with John—one calling for a new dress.

Mabel drove straight to Medicine Spring Country Club to drop the books off. The committee had already been setting up that afternoon, and Mabel recognized Nanette's car. She pulled into the last space in that row and picked up half the boxes.

The ballroom had been decorated with sage and gold cloths alternating on each table. Glass bowls, wrapped with wide sage ribbons threaded with gilt, held what looked like bay leaves and gold and white mums, with fat cream-colored beeswax candles rising out of the bunch at staggered heights.

"Hi, Mabel." Darwin hurried to relieve her of the boxes. "Is this it?"

"I've got a couple more in the car, but I can handle them."

"I'll get them." He plunked the boxes on the end of the registration table.

"If you're sure. Thanks." She walked over to where Nanette was arranging place cards at each table setting. "The room is beautiful," Mabel told her.

"I'm a nervous wreck. This is so hard without Helen. For fifty years, she told us what to do. I'm afraid my own brain shut off somewhere along the line."

"Don't be silly. You're doing fine. Don't forget we have all these people on the committee with perfectly good brains too. It's not healthy to let one person run everything."

"Truer words never spoken," a voice trumpeted at her elbow. Mabel jumped like the victim of an unwanted surprise party.

"Community organizations shouldn't be run like dictatorships," Cora barked. "This group may not be a democracy, but we all have something to contribute. Even you, Mabel."

Mabel tried to smile and scowl at the same time. It didn't work.

Nanette giggled and made a fluttery gesture with her hands. "Oh, Cora. I'm sure you didn't mean that the way it sounded. She means you're our newest and youngest member, Mabel. Look how much you've already contributed."

Cora snorted. "Quite." She narrowed her eyes at Mabel. "Why don't you come sit down and tell us exactly what happened with that dead writer woman who's been all over the news the past week."

Mabel swallowed. She didn't want to discuss Devereaux tonight. According to John, a toxicology screen had revealed a high level of sleep medication in her system, as well as the carbon monoxide. Of course, Devereaux might have done that herself. But why bother, if you were going to use carbon monoxide, which as far as she understood, just put you to sleep anyway? And why would she kill herself the very evening she knew John and Mabel were coming over?

He was convinced she'd been murdered—and had told her the police were investigating along those lines. "It looked like she had some bruising," he'd said. "Somebody could have drugged her to get her into that car."

Nanette's voice jarred Mabel back to the conversation. "Darwin says she was at the Sauer house more than once. Writing a book about the murders." She rubbed her forehead. "All these murders. Helen would about die."

As if she'd just realized what she'd said, Nanette looked stricken. She burst into tears.

Cora sighed impatiently, shifting her pink-flamingoed and palm-treed butt in the chair. "I think what Nanette is trying to say is, did you kill her?"

"What? Of course not." Mabel sprang up. "I didn't even know her."

"You were at her house when the police arrived, weren't you?" Cora narrowed her eyes on Mabel. "Which, I believe you'll agree, might raise some questions."

At a loss for words, Mabel stammered.

"And you were on the scene when poor Helen's body was discovered," Cora added. "I'm not accusing you, you understand. I was devoted to your dear grandmother. You must realize your involvement in these murders has created a bad impression. That in itself sheds a poor light on the organization."

Mabel sat. "You know, I'm another victim here. I never asked for all these dead bodies, let alone to be blamed for them."

Nanette collected herself sufficiently to pat Mabel's hand. "No one's blaming you. At least, we aren't." She gave Cora a stern frown. "These deaths have been so upsetting."

"And all on the brink of the gala," Cora brayed. "Couldn't be worse."

Darwin dropped the boxes next to the others and handed Mabel her key. "I couldn't help overhearing." He touched her shoulder. "I'm so sorry for everything you've been going through."

Cora leaned across the table. "Why *were* you at that woman's house?"

Mabel wanted to scream. Cora was worse than the cops. "I already

227

told you and we told the police. She was writing a book about the Sauers. We went to get more background for the biography."

Cora sniffed. "Writing about the murders, you mean. Cheap sensationalism was all she had to offer."

"To be fair," Mabel said, "she'd also done a lot of general research. Besides, the murders are part of our history and solving them is important."

Darwin chuckled. "I don't think anyone—let alone someone off the street—is likely to solve a crime that's been stone cold for over eighty years."

Nanette sighed. "I have to agree. Sadly, too much time has gone by." She got up. "Let's finish up, Cora dear. I still need to get my hair done, or I'll break the cameras tonight."

Mabel watched as Nanette drifted off. She still needed to get ready for her big night, as well. But the conversation had taken away some of the luster. The finger pointing had made Mabel extremely irritable.

"Well, I disagree." She frowned. "I believe those old cases can be solved. In fact, I'm sure Devereaux did solve them."

Darwin started. "Are you serious?"

Mabel nodded. "If it turns out Helen was murdered, that might be why. At this point, I think she knew everything."

He dropped into a chair and gestured for her to sit. "Wait a minute. You can't drop a bombshell like that, then leave us hanging."

Cora turned laser eyes on her. "Certainly not. Explain please." She leaned back and folded her arms, as if prepared to sit there as long as it took.

"Sorry. I do have to run. And I need to think about the evidence more." Mabel gave them what she hoped was a mysterious smile. "But let's say I may have the murders figured out too. You'll just have to wait."

Chapter Thirty-Six

MABEL TURNED, SQUINTING TO SEE HER reflection in the old, flaked full-length mirror on the bathroom door. She shoved her seldom-worn glasses onto her nose and circled again. The spruce-green cocktail dress clung to her hips and ended in a swirl at the hem.

Now, the big issue. Kicking off battered moccasins, she stepped into the like-new, ten-year-old heels. She only wobbled a tiny bit as she made another turn. The shoes made a big difference, and her legs looked amazing…well, slimmer, anyway. But her toes were screaming.

Aarrgghh. She flung the pumps off and rubbed her unhappy feet. Amazing legs weren't worth it.

Barnacle barked and pounced, grabbing the nearest shoe for a shake.

"Give that back. It's not a toy."

He shook the shoe hard, grinning around his mouthful of Italian leather.

Mabel had no time for this tomfoolery. "Come on. Give."

Thinking she was joining his merry game, he romped off to a safe distance. Dropping into a play bow, he wagged his tail.

Mabel groaned. There was only one thing to do. She went the other way, trying to ignore what was happening in Barnacle's mouth at that moment. Marching into the kitchen, she opened the cabinet where she kept Barnacle's "good boy" treats.

At the first squeak of the hinges, he barreled down the steps and around the corner, legs skidding out from under him. Koi, hearing treat sounds, leapt from the top of the Hoosier cupboard. Holding the treat bags out of reach, Mabel trotted back and grabbed her shoes. Barnacle, focused on his treats and drooling uncontrollably, danced around her.

After she'd put the shoes away and rewarded Barnacle's cooperation and Koi's good hearing, she dug out her broken-in black dress flats and slipped them on. Ahh...better.

Her hair was already as good as it was going to get. For her entire life, it had been as if a storm had swept over her head and turned into hair. At least, her locks were clean, shiny, and abundant.

Mabel had nearly finished her face when the doorbell rang. Unfortunately, she still had one eye left to go. Koi hid under the claw-footed tub, and Barnacle raced downstairs, barking as if a home invasion were in progress.

Clapping one hand over her naked eye, she pattered after the dog. John stood at the front door, as Barnacle flung his body against it.

A wave of shyness rocked her knees. This must be how the other girls in her class had felt when their dates for the eighth-grade formal arrived at the door. She was only about thirty-five years behind schedule.

"You look beautiful."

"So do you." He'd worn a classic black tuxedo, and she was finding it hard to breathe.

"I brought you this." John pulled a clear plastic box from behind his back. Two white orchids gathered with gold ribbon nestled in the bottom.

"Oh." Mabel brought her free hand to her mouth.

"Is there something wrong with your eye?"

"Um, no, it's nothing. Have a seat and I'll be right down."

She flew back upstairs and attacked her eye with concealer, eyeshadow, and mascara. She ended up with a smear she had to scrub with a damp cotton swab. *Good enough.*

John sat at the kitchen table, checking his phone. He got up when she walked in, which flustered her still further.

"Do you want to wear your flowers on your dress or wrist?"

"Um, maybe my dress."

"Here." He removed her flowers from the box with gentle hands, then leaned in to pin them to her shoulder. Mabel's heart lurched.

She stopped his hand. "Wait. I think I'll wear it on my wrist."

He grinned into her eyes and she froze, her hand still over his.

He touched her cheek. "You have a bruise by your eye."

She felt herself flush. "That's only mascara."

"Are you ready?"

She nodded and slipped the flowers over her wrist. "Let me grab my coat."

The ride to the gala felt different from other times Mabel had gone places with John. She was hyper-aware of his clean, soapy smell and their being alone together. He wore that tuxedo like Humphrey Bogart.

"Do you have a plan for tonight?" he asked.

"Plan?"

He shot her a sidelong glance. "We're working, aren't we? Devereaux was our best suspect, but now she's off the table."

"We don't know she didn't kill Helen. I think my theory's still good. The security alarm was set, after all. Devereaux's death could've been an accident—"

"Highly unlikely. It would have been an easy diversion for a murderer familiar with that system to hit the button and arm it, then slip out during the countdown."

Mabel frowned. "Or a suicide. Maybe she couldn't face the consequences of what she'd done."

"Or maybe Helen's murderer is still out there and had to get rid of the person who'd figured that out."

A chill passed over the back of Mabel's neck and down both arms. "Somebody already threatened me. What if they think I know more than I do?"

"Nobody's going to hurt you if I have anything to say about it."

"I hope you do have something to say about it. But you're not with me 24/7."

She saw his frown in the flash of passing headlights. "No, I'm not.

Which is why you do need to be careful. I'm still willing to stay with you."

"No, I'm fine," she said hastily. "I've got my alarm system. But somebody could rig my car, or—"

"And this is why we need to figure out who came after Devereaux."

Mabel thought hard. They were pulling into the country club's long, wooded drive. She could see Bennett or even Linnea—perhaps with the help of her husband or son—as capable of killing Devereaux. She still couldn't come right out and voice those suspicions about the family to John, though. At least, she could be grateful there was no way he himself had harmed Devereaux since he had been with Mabel. She pushed down the intrusive thought, however, that he might easily have been complicit.

"I'm still suspicious of Cora. If you believe the old stories, Helen wasn't her first victim. Plus, no one from the society but Cora gave me grief about Devereaux. It's like she wants to keep the focus on me."

"She's old, Mabel."

"Once again, you're being ageist. Just because somebody's getting a bit older doesn't mean they aren't in good shape. Have you met Cora? She's a rampaging rhino of a woman."

John laughed.

He pulled into a parking space at the edge of the crowded lot. Mabel opened her door.

"Now, wait a minute. You have to let me play the perfect gentleman this evening."

The formality seemed a bit silly. Mabel's arms obviously worked. But John's gesture was still rather sweet.

As she waited for him to come around, she continued to pick at the possibilities. If not Cora, who?

John opened her door and reached to help her out.

She took his hand, still thinking. "We haven't talked about the family. If I'm right about Margarethe, maybe Helen wasn't the only member of the family who'd go to extremes to protect her memory.

"If Devereaux was trying blackmail, that would up the ante. She might've turned around and put the screws to somebody else."

"They'd laugh in her face." John turned from locking the car. "Nobody in this generation cares."

"The motive could be revenge," Mabel suggested. "For killing Helen."

John groaned as they strolled toward the entrance. "How would they know she'd done it? Even you don't know that. And why wouldn't they do the conventional—legal—thing, and report their suspicions to the police? No offense, but you're getting pretty far in left field."

Mabel wanted to sniff and pull her hand away, but it felt so nice where it was. "I'm brainstorming," she muttered. As she said that, her dark thoughts crept back in. One reason John never talked about suspects within the family was obvious. He was a member of the family. He might act like he was on her team, but he was working for them.

Who turned out to be the murderer in so many TV mysteries? The least likely person, that's who. Though she hated to admit it to herself, John fit that role a little too neatly. For someone she'd bumped into out of the blue, he'd already wormed himself into her confidence in a matter of days. What better way for him to keep a close eye on what she was finding out? What better way to distract her than with flattery and suggestions he could help her?

As they approached the entrance, Mabel slid a sidelong glance at her handsome escort. Did he already know who the murderer was? Or worse. Could he himself be Helen's killer and she'd been blind to it all along?

Chapter Thirty-Seven

THE COUNTRY CLUB LOBBY SWIRLED WITH well-dressed donors. Mabel and John threaded their way through the crowd. Seeing several floor-length gowns and quite a bit of sparkle, Mabel wondered uncomfortably if she was underdressed.

John, she was gratified to realize, fit right in. She squelched the pang of suspicion she'd felt earlier and tried to enjoy the moment. Her stint with the historical society might have started off on the wrong foot, but this, at last, was her night to shine.

She'd completed her first writing assignment. She'd been selected to be part of the committee for Medicine Spring's biggest fundraising event of the year, if not the decade. Tonight, she was here as a VIP, on the arm of this attractive man, who seemed to like her.

While he checked her coat, Mabel scanned for familiar faces. At first, she saw nobody she knew, but then Nanette caught her arm. "Mabel, you look lovely."

"Thanks. So do you." Nanette wore a soft purple, floor-length satin dress with matching slippers and bolero jacket. "Our committee is sitting together near the main table, if you'd like to join us?"

As John rejoined her, stuffing the claim check in his pocket, Mabel made a gesture of introduction. "This is John Bigelow. He's related to the Sauers."

"Oh, how interesting. I believe I saw you at the funeral. I'm so sorry for your loss."

Nanette and John made polite conversation on the way into the ballroom. Mabel trailed them, beginning to relax. A chamber orchestra in the corner played Mozart. She had zero responsibility for anything this evening, which felt good.

The committee table was easy to spot. Cora, resplendent in great flowing swirls of chiffon in Lilly Pulitzer turquoise and lime towered above it like a blinding beacon.

Darwin wore one of his shabby, "professor" suits in charcoal gray. "Everybody's raving about your booklet, Mabel."

She attempted to appear modest but couldn't help thinking her writing career was taking off. "Oh, it was nothing—a little thing like that."

"That's true," Cora boomed. "Considering Helen did ninety percent of the work."

Nanette tittered. "Oh, Cora. She's only teasing." She patted Mabel's hand. "We all appreciate your contributing so much talent and effort to make the biography a success."

Mabel, a little stiffly, made introductions around the table. No one else had brought a date. Cora's husband was dead, of course, and so was Nanette's. Darwin, she believed, had never married.

She found herself seated between the men, with an empty chair on John's other side. Nanette sat between Darwin and Cora.

Cora, directly across the table, filled Mabel's field of vision. Replying to a question from Darwin, Mabel glanced her way and found Cora staring back.

Startled, Mabel looked away. John had gotten up to fetch drinks. She tried to concentrate on what Darwin was saying about the shadow cast over the event by Helen's death but still felt those eyes on her.

"Have you heard anything more from the police?" he asked.

"Not since we found Devereaux."

"No theories?"

She risked a peek. Cora's eyes met hers, and Mabel looked away.

John returned with their drinks, weaving between tables. He caught her eye and smiled. The orchestra had finished their piece and was changing the music on their stands. In the sudden silence, Darwin spoke again.

"I'm sorry." Mabel refocused. "What?"

He smiled as John handed her a ginger ale and sat back down. "Oh, nothing. Just wondering if you'd heard any theories."

She mouthed, "Thank you," at John and shook her head at Darwin. "No. Not from the police." She leaned in close, not wanting Cora to hear, and whispered, "I sort of have an idea of my own...? But it's—let's say I don't quite want to believe it."

"Excuse me, miss." The server slipped Mabel's salad between them.

Darwin started to speak at the same time John asked, "Do you like hot peppers?"

"Pardon me," she told Darwin. She realized, she shouldn't be whispering about the murders here, let alone her suspicions.

"No," she told John. "You want mine?"

After that, Nanette pulled Darwin into another conversation, and Mabel was happy to relax, eat, and talk to John. She wished she didn't like him so much. It was hard to keep her guard up, the way she knew she should.

Mabel enjoyed her meal. The entree might've been banquet salmon, but the pecan crust kept it moist and delicious. With the salad, garlic mashed potatoes, sugar snap peas, and two excellent dinner rolls, dessert was going to be a challenge. She gave silent thanks for the gift of spandex.

Mabel excused herself before the cherry pie à la mode and coffee.

"Oh, I'll go with you." Nanette started to rise, but someone from the hospital committee called her back.

The women's lounge was deserted. When Mabel emerged from the stall moments later, she found herself facing Cora, instead of Nanette. She was leaning back against the sinks, arms folded.

"Hi." Mabel eased past the monument in swirling chiffon. "Good dinner, huh?"

Cora narrowed her eyes. "Is something bothering you tonight?"

Mabel gave a feeble chuckle while pretending to concentrate on rinsing her hands. "What would be bothering me?"

"I know quite well when someone is staring at me all evening. If you have an issue, I suggest you state it."

Cora still hadn't budged, and Mabel had to circle around her, hands dripping, to reach the dryers. "Don't be silly. You're straight across from me. I can't avoid looking at who's in front of me, can I?"

Cora glared. "I didn't ask for your back chat. I've dealt with gossips before, and we will get along much better if you stop making trouble, young lady."

Mabel focused on the blast of warm air rippling over her fingers. She fought the urge to spin around and tell Cora exactly what she thought of her.

Cora had been the one staring at *her*. She was also the one who had pursued Mabel into the restroom. Because of a guilty conscience?

Mabel was too smart to escalate this further. And Cora *had* referred to her as "young lady," which was worth something.

She turned around, wiping the last water drops onto her skirt. "I'm sorry I upset you. That wasn't my intention."

Cora launched herself off the row of sinks and loomed over Mabel. "I accept your apology. But know this—you are not the first person to think they could push me. They are no longer here. I am. Remember that."

The rest of the evening was a bizarre combination of boredom, pleasure, and anxiety. The after-dinner speeches were dry as usual, except for the moment when Cora acknowledged Mabel as the biography author, though she had to spoil the moment by saying most of the groundwork had been Helen's. She asked Mabel to stand, and the applause was satisfying.

A slideshow on Margarethe's life and legacy followed. For several minutes, a male voiceover praised her gentle, compassionate character and generosity to the community. Mabel enjoyed the pictures of the old library and hospital, both of which Margarethe had been instrumental in modernizing or replacing.

She tried to keep her eyes to herself. But when the photo of Margarethe in the flowered dressing gown appeared, Mabel couldn't keep her gaze from drifting to Cora.

It was impossible in the near darkness to see whether she reacted or not. As far as she could tell, Cora maintained her stoic expression through the entire screening.

The best part of the evening—even better than being applauded—came when the orchestra struck up dance music. Mabel had never learned to dance much beyond the elementary school introduction, but John persisted. "Come on, Mabel. The guy does the heavy lifting. All you need to do is follow."

Mabel protested. But he smiled and continued to hold out his hand.

She took her time getting up. "You'll be sorry. I'll crush your toes. You'll never dance again."

"I'll take the chance. It's worth it, just to hold you in my arms."

Mabel laid her hand in his. If he was only using her to get info, maybe the trade-off was worth it to her too—just to have him hold her in his arms.

The orchestra was playing "Begin the Beguine." Many older couples were on the floor, and Darwin had already glided past them with Nanette.

"Have you ever learned the basic box step?"

"Not really."

He was still holding her hand as he demonstrated. "You could count, but it'll probably work better if you don't even think about it. Relax and let me lead."

She frowned in concentration, watching his feet.

John laughed again. He stretched out a finger and smoothed her creased brow. "That's not relaxed."

He pulled her close. Mabel's knees wobbled.

"I may be the one stepping on your toes, you know," he whispered in her ear. "I was the worst one in my sixth-grade dance class."

Mabel tried to copy Nanette's position, placing her left hand on John's tuxedoed shoulder.

"As I start to step forward, move your corresponding foot back."

"What do you mean by corresponding?"

He chuckled. He did that a lot around Mabel. "Forget I said that. Do what comes naturally. Let the squished toes fall where they may."

They fumbled the moment John led off. "Don't look down. Just...feel it."

That made no sense, but Mabel shut her eyes. He smelled so good.

They stepped off again, and surprisingly, relaxing did work better. She let herself fall into John's rhythm, gliding in time with the music. She only crunched his toes two or three times.

"You having fun?"

"Mm-hmm," she murmured into his shoulder.

"So am I. You're the only one I'd put on this monkey suit for."

"Hey, John."

"Hmm...?"

"Can we go back to Helen's house? As soon as possible. I'd like to check the attic."

A heartbeat later, he sighed. "I've never in my life met a woman so resistant to romance. Can't you pretend to like me? You only have another hour or so to hold it together."

Mabel started to argue, then realized she should be happy. Someone who was just trying to figure out what she knew wouldn't be discouraging her from spilling her theories, in favor of a bit of romance.

"Sorry," she mumbled. They were so close to the same height, she had to hunch down a bit to nestle her head on his shoulder, but despite the slight crick in her neck, the moment felt like heaven.

He's for real, Mabel, said the voice in her head. *Don't mess this up.*

She argued with the inner voice–*he's playing with you, Mabel. Don't be a fool.*

When "Begin the Beguine" ended, and the orchestra struck up "Moonlight in Vermont," John smiled and pulled her into his arms again. No sooner had they begun to dance than he stopped. Mabel's eyes flew open.

Darwin had tapped him on the shoulder. "May I cut in?"

John stepped aside. She had nothing against Darwin. In fact, she liked him. He'd been one of her two true friends at the society. Still, Mabel felt a surge of irritation. Over his shoulder, she saw John ask Cora to dance. Her eyes widened.

Darwin held her at a very correct distance, much like a proper gentleman in an eighteenth-century painting. "Are you enjoying yourself?"

"It's been fun. I'm not a very good dancer."

He smiled. "Neither am I."

Like John, he seemed to be exaggerating. She couldn't help noticing all the fumbles and stumbles were hers. "I'm so sorry. Is your foot all right?"

"It's fine," Darwin assured her, though his face looked a bit tight. "If I were a better dancer, like your friend John, I'm sure you'd have no trouble following."

Mabel was concentrating on trying not to inflict any more damage on Darwin's feet, and she had to ask him to repeat his next comment.

"I said it will be a relief to have this event out of the way."

"It will." Mabel sighed. "I'd say it'll be nice to get back to normal. But I'm not sure what that is…or if it's even possible anymore."

He peered into her face, his eyes clouded. "You did join us at an inauspicious time. And you're right—normal will change. It has already. There's no going back."

"Were you and Helen…close?"

Darwin's face tightened again. He chuckled, but there was no humor in the sound. "Helen was hard to be close to. But she was part of my life forever. She even babysat me once, many years ago."

Mabel processed this amazing piece of information, trying to imagine Darwin as…what? A baby? Helen must've been a teenager. Mabel found that even harder to envision.

"She loved the society. And the house. She helped sustain us financially. I find myself wondering if she remembered us in her will. Do you know?"

"What?" The question startled Mabel. But she realized her friendship with John must make it seem like she had some connection to the Sauer family herself. "No, I don't know."

"For all her money, she wasn't excessively generous. She could've defrayed a lot of our maintenance problems. But she always said her family hadn't donated the house to the society, just so the Sauers could continue to carry the entire financial burden."

"In fairness, I guess that's valid." Nevertheless, Mabel had to agree Helen was not the most giving person she'd ever met.

The song ended. Mabel stepped back, happy to stop abusing Darwin's toes.

"Shall we continue?" he asked, as the orchestra struck up "Sentimental Journey."

Her heart sank. "Um…" She cast a wild look around for John.

"You said earlier you have a theory. I have to admit I'm curious. Was your idea about Helen's…death? Or the other murders?"

Mabel squirmed. Naturally, he'd be curious. But something about his persistence made her uneasy. "You know, I'd rather not have that conversation right now."

At that moment, to her infinite relief, John tapped Darwin's shoulder. For a microsecond, Darwin held on. But gentleman that he was, he bowed over her hand, then passed it off to John.

There was something vaguely feudal in this whole dancing etiquette. Men lead. They get to cut in. Men hand women over as if they're returning a borrowed hedge clipper.

Mabel scowled at the thought but couldn't help melting when John folded her into his arms. She nestled against his shoulder. "What took you so long?"

Chapter Thirty-Eight

THE MORNING AFTER THE GALA, MABEL felt like Cinderella after the ball. Her shimmery green dress lay crumpled across a chair, her feet hurt, and her coach had turned back into a pumpkin.

At least, now she could go back to concentrating on the property clean-up and her writing career. And solving a murder. Four murders.

As hot water cascaded over her head, Mabel turned the crimes over in her head. All of them. Walter, Sr. Walter, Jr. Helen. Devereaux.

There must be a connection. When she found that connection, it would unravel the whole mess.

Later, at her kitchen table, trying to write about the benefits of volunteering, Mabel faced another issue. She might be able to interview a few volunteers and put together a magazine article. She needed a lot more personal experience, however, if she was going to write a book. Everything online suggested she needed some special expertise before a publisher would even talk to her.

Her sole volunteer experience thus far had been an unqualified disaster. She wasn't sure how many more she could tolerate.

Besides, writing a true-crime book seemed way more attractive right now. She was certain to get TV appearances—at least, locally. Her former law-school classmate—the one who'd fired her—might enjoy a big, fat slice of crow pie.

She knew she shouldn't think of the book like that. But she was so tired of making a mess of everything she touched. What if she could write a bestseller? How much money would she make?

Because, let's face it—how far would her inheritance and the settlement from the law firm stretch? The house was going to need a lot of work. Insulation. Probably a French drain for the basement. New siding. Higher-watt lightbulbs.

The bell rang, and Barnacle raced, barking, for the front door. Koi dissolved under the Hoosier cupboard.

Hanging onto Barnacle's collar, she opened the door.

The human string bean on Mabel's front porch threw his hands up. "Whoa there."

"Sorry. You activated my security system."

"Beg pardon?"

"My dog. He's my security system."

"Oh, he-he. I get it. That's a good one." He stretched out a tentative hand. "Good boy, buddy. You wanna dial it back a notch?"

Barnacle stopped rioting and began to sniff. As he started wagging, Mabel let go of his collar.

After ruffling the dog's ears, the man stuck out a hand with noticeable dirt under the fingernails, and Mabel shook it. "Acey Davis, ma'am. I come to eyeball your yardwork job."

"Oh, great."

Barnacle, seeming to realize Acey presented no immediate threat, concentrated on an intense inspection of his feet and pantlegs. Acey, unperturbed, pulled a cigarette paper and battered packet of tobacco from his shirt pocket and started rolling a smoke. Bits of tobacco sifted down onto the porch boards.

"Hey." Mabel frowned. "I'm sorry, but I'd rather you not smoke here."

He gave her a bemused look. "I ain't in the house."

"I know, and that's great. But, um, you are on the porch, and I'd rather you do that outside. Maybe on the driveway, where the stones are. Fire hazard, you know?"

"Women." He shook his head. "You're the boss. Mind if I finish rollin'?"

"That's fine." Mabel managed an encouraging smile as she jerked Barnacle back from his examination of the scattered tobacco. "Let me get you an ashtray, and I'll be right out to show you the job."

Twenty minutes later, she'd provided him with a coffee tin for his smoldering butts and pointed out the areas needing work. Ten minutes after that, he'd pulled out an envelope addressed to him from the electric company—stamped "past due"—and scrawled an estimate on the back.

Mabel grimaced when she saw the total. Though the charges might be reasonable, they were still more than she'd hoped. It was a little weeding and brush cutting, at least if they were able to ignore the swampy area out back. But with nobody else seeming to have the remotest interest in the job, she figured she'd better lock him down while she could. For now, she'd repress any concerns about that past-due envelope he was using for his official estimate.

"Would you please add a finish date, and sign and date this?" she asked.

"Oh, I reckon I can get 'er wrapped up in less than a week. No need to go all formal on it, is there?"

"Humor me, Mr. Davis." She pushed the envelope at him. "I'll give you twenty-five percent in advance, to get you started."

"Oh, all right." He scrawled his signature and tried to hand the envelope back.

"Don't forget a finish date—and today's date."

"Used to be a handshake was a man's bond. Feels like you don't trust me." Though he grumbled all the while, Mabel noticed he was filling in the dates she'd asked for, so she kept her lips firmly sealed.

Once his truck had rattled off down the block again, Mabel sighed and threw the back-of-the-envelope contract onto the kitchen table and her checkbook back into her purse. "Come on, Barnacle, let's take a walk."

The afternoon sun rode low between the trees, a thin glimmer in a sulky gray sky. As Barnacle snuffled and left his mark on the bushes, Mabel's thoughts circled.

Could Cora have killed Helen? Yeah, probably. In fact, she could easily imagine that scenario. But killing Devereaux? That was harder to picture.

What if she'd had help, though?

Mabel tugged to get Barnacle moving again. Cora would also have needed an accomplice to break into Mabel's house and drug Barnacle. Even if Mabel could visualize Cora in her Lilly Pulitzer creeping in through the narrow, cobwebby basement door, there seemed no way she could've slipped away from the meeting to do the deed, let alone hotfoot it back before anyone noticed.

Who else did that leave?

John's name pushed its way into her head, and she shoved it back. Mabel refused to believe him capable of murder. Besides, his only apparent motive was for Devereaux's murder...if she'd been threatening blackmail or to expose the Sauer family secret. Then, as he'd told her, he was a shirttail relation, at most.

But what if a relative had killed Helen for money?

What about John's cousin Bennett? Or Helen's snippy daughter? Either of them might have had financial motive for killing Helen. Then Bennett, at least, could have pulled John in on his scheme. And any of the Sauer dynasty might have had reason to kill Devereaux, if they thought she had found out one of them had murdered Helen.

No. John was not a murderer. If anyone in the family had done it, surely it hadn't been John.

There was Michael, Helen's sullen grandson. Maybe he was on drugs or had a gambling problem and had hoped to get money from Helen. Or he might've served as muscle on behalf of his mother. Mabel heaved a sigh. From all accounts, he wasn't even local. That didn't mean he couldn't have done it, of course, but it would have complicated things.

Who else was left? Darwin? Nanette? Mabel snickered, startling Barnacle. Maybe Nanette harbored a secret ambition to be society president. Maybe she was scheming to displace Cora next, by framing her for Helen's murder. Or perhaps Darwin was determined to remove the obstacle Helen presented to his dreams of offering murder mystery events so he could finance a new roof for the Sauer house.

Mabel circled back to Cora. But if Cora had offed Helen that didn't necessarily mean she'd also killed Devereaux. The method had been altogether different. That might've been a simple matter of convenience. Or it might mean a different murderer. Cora and an accomplice?

Maybe Darwin or Nanette had a deeper ulterior motive? It wasn't as if Mabel really knew either of them beyond historical society chit-chat. After all, she'd just met them a couple weeks ago. As far as she knew, they'd both spent a lifetime here in Medicine Spring, unlike her—plenty of time to develop a grudge against Helen. And Darwin, at least, had been the person who'd pointed her toward the old gossip about Cora, and her increasingly hostile relationship with Helen.

Maybe there had been more to it than the desire to share a juicy story. Had Darwin *wanted* her to focus on Cora for darker reasons of his own?

"Who drugged you, Barnacle?"

Not for the first time, Mabel wished he could talk.

They'd circled behind the overgrown field separating her house and the mansion. A couple of cars sat parked near the back. One, she thought, was Cora's.

Thunder rumbled, and Barnacle's head popped up from deep within the Sauer hedges. He skittered closer to Mabel, and she ran a soothing hand down along the shaggy length of his back.

"Just a bit of thunder, buddy. It won't hurt you." But the wind had picked up, tossing the treetops and sending fading leaves swirling through the air. Lightning flashed, illuminating the ridges of the Sauer roof, and the first fat raindrops fell.

"I guess that lightning could, though," she admitted, turning for home. Barnacle needed no encouragement. With the next thunder crack, she had to hustle to keep up.

Cold rain pelted her shoulders. Mabel lowered her head and

shoved against the wind. She was glad they hadn't walked farther.

She and Barnacle clattered up the wet, leaf-strewn front steps, out of the rain. She collapsed, gasping, onto the creaking porch swing. From her spot deep in the shadows, she watched the rain pelting down and gushing from the downspout.

As in a creeping nightmare scenario, her front door opened.

Chapter Thirty-Nine

WITH A GUTTURAL YELP, MABEL SCRAMBLED off the swing and away from the front door, backing up against the porch railing. She fumbled behind her for the opening.

"Hey." The voice was John's. "Sorry. Did I startle you?"

Barnacle, wagging, lumbered over and planted a big, wet paw on John's pantleg.

"Yes, you startled me," Mabel hissed. She shoved at his chest. "What's the idea of strolling right into my house when I'm not home?"

He grinned, nice white teeth gleaming, and caught her arms. "In my defense, I didn't know you weren't home."

He did smell so good.

Mabel steeled her wobbly knees and pushed herself away from his manly chest. "Of course, I wasn't home."

"I saw your car." He gestured at the driveway. "But when I knocked, nobody answered, and I was getting soaked. So I opened the door and started hollering."

Mabel folded her arms across her damp chest. "I was right out there in the field. You must've seen me."

He shook his head. "No, I didn't. My mind was elsewhere."

"We were right there." Mabel pointed.

"Did you see me drive up? Or, for that matter, notice my car over there?"

"Um, no. We were all the way back along the Sauer hedges, and I wasn't paying attention. And we were trying to beat the rain—I never even glanced at the driveway."

John spread his hands. "There you go."

He had a point. Embarrassment and residual adrenaline mingled with an impulse to throw herself on his chest again.

"Come on, May—after what happened to your dog, I was worried when you didn't answer the door."

"Don't call me May. And hey—how did you get inside without setting off my alarm?"

"Come sit." He pulled her to the porch swing. "I wanted to talk to you about that. You know you have to turn the system on when you leave, right?"

"Doggone it." She surged back to her feet, setting off a round of barking from Barnacle. "I forgot. I was only right out there."

"I know. You mentioned that. Put yourself in my shoes. There's a storm, your alarm's turned off, and there's no sign of you or the dog. How was I to know I wouldn't be finding *you* out cold on the floor this time? Or worse."

Thunder boomed and rumbled again, and Barnacle kept barking. He stood at the top of the porch steps, as if ready to challenge the weather.

"Would you like to come back inside?"

John wrapped his arms around her in a casual hug, setting off another tremor in her knees. "I wish I could. I only stopped to tell you I have to go see my cousin this evening. But I wanted to do this again."

Darn, he was good at this. How many women had he wrapped those arms around? *There's no fool like an old fool,* Mabel told herself. She forced herself to stiffen.

John sighed into her hair, and his warm breath made her quiver again. "I thought we were making progress. But I see I'm back to square one." He stepped away and gave her a wry smile. "Is it the buzz cut?" He ran a hand over his head. "I'll grow it out if you want."

Mabel found a grin creeping over her face, and she bit her lip. "Don't be silly. I'm not a fool, you know."

"Who said you were a fool?" He pretended to think about it. "I said you were beautiful. I recall saying you were smart. Why would you think I believe you're a fool?"

"Never mind." The conversation, not to mention his being three feet away from her, was interfering with Mabel's ability to think. "I'm glad you stopped. No time for a cup of tea?"

He shook his head, looking regretful. "No, I honestly do have to get going. I'm meeting Bennett for dinner in Bartles Grove. Let me check the house first. Then make sure you lock your doors and set the alarm—got it?"

John's sweep of the house didn't take long. Soon, he was at the back door, ready to leave. The dim ceiling fixture left much of the room in shadow.

"Thanks again. Don't get wet."

John considered the rain streaming off the overhang and laughed. "I'll call or stop by after dinner."

The wind yanked at the door as Mabel tried to close it behind him. When she finally shut it, her clothes were spattered, and a puddle lay across the floor. She watched through the sheet of rain coursing down the pane as John slid into the driver's seat and reversed out of the driveway.

Irrationally, Mabel felt out of sorts. She poured food into the animals' dishes, brooding over John's presuming to walk into her house when she wasn't home. Also over his turning right around and leaving, once he was here.

He'd taken her in his arms, which had—for the moment—made her feel he cared about her. Maybe. But he'd left without even trying to kiss her.

If he'd tried, would she have kissed him back—or slapped him?

"Stop looking at me like that," she muttered to Barnacle, who'd inhaled his food and was now sitting and mopping his entire face with his big tongue. "You're right. Why would he try to kiss me, even if he wanted to? Even I don't know whether he'd be welcome."

After a dinner of leftovers, she tried to settle herself to work on her writing. Cracks and rumbles of thunder kept making her jump, and Barnacle paced and yelped. The room was already dark, and twice, the lights flickered.

Mabel set up an outline for a volunteer article and wrote the first line. Then, she deleted what she'd written. She tried again. Maybe she needed to let the outline mellow awhile.

Opening a new document, she started a rough outline for a Sauer true-crime book. Now that Devereaux wouldn't be writing hers, the field was wide open.

That fleeting thought shamed Mabel. She didn't want to be a bone-picker. When Devereaux was alive, the thought of writing a book about the murders had been exciting and gave her a competitive thrill. Was she a horrible person even to think about writing the book now?

No, she decided. After all, she'd already come up with this idea before Devereaux's death.

Barnacle's brown eyes watched her.

Glancing away, she felt a strong sense of Grandma Mabel's presence and averted her face from the print of Jesus on the wall. Things were bad, when both her dog and her dead grandmother started criticizing her at the same time.

"It's my story," she said out loud. "I grew up with that story. Your story," she reminded Grandma. "I simply didn't happen to be the first person to think of writing a book."

Maybe she should come up with a different approach. Maybe from the viewpoint of Grandma and the other people who grew up with the tragedy. She wondered if Cora was still at the house. *I could start by interviewing her.* That way she could work on her writing without ...having to write.

While she was at it, maybe she could pick up something tying Cora to Helen's murder. One thing Mabel had learned in her years as a lawyer—mostly by watching others—was how to ferret damning admissions out of someone without their realizing until it was too late.

Mabel squinted into the wet darkness. It looked like a light was burning in the mansion, but she couldn't tell if somebody was still working, or it was a security light.

Mabel dialed the Sauer house number. She didn't even hear the phone ring before a booming voice answered. "Medicine Spring Historical Society and Sauer Mansion. May I help you?" Mabel moved the phone away from her ear.

"Cora?" Mabel didn't know why she even asked. The voice was unmistakable.

"Yes. Whom am I addressing, please?"

"Mabel Browne. I'm glad I caught you."

Cora seemed to feel no need to fill in awkward conversational gaps. The silence on her end of the line ticked by.

Mabel cleared her throat. "I was wondering if I could drop by and chat for a few minutes about the murders."

"Why on earth?" Cora's voice rivaled the thunder outside.

"Well, because you know more about them than almost anybody."

"How dare you? Is that an accusation?"

"Oh, no. Hey, I wasn't talking about right now. It's about the 1939 murders."

"I was a small child when those occurred."

"I realize that. But they must've been one of the biggest things to happen here while you were growing up. Your parents must've talked about them."

"I'm sure your grandmother did, as well."

"She did. But she was only a little girl like you, and she's gone now. I never got to talk to her parents, either."

"Why all this interest in the old murders?"

"I'm thinking of writing a book."

Cora snorted like a spirited horse. "If you can get over here in the next few minutes, I might be free to talk for a moment. But I know very little that would be new to you. Nor can I dilly dally—my parakeet Buster is waiting, along with half an anchovy pizza."

Koi, sitting at Mabel's feet, looked up, ears perked. Could she possibly have heard the word "anchovy?" The way Cora talked, speakerphone was hardly necessary.

Mabel shuddered. She did not share her cat's fondness for salty, bony little fish.

"Thanks. I'll be right over."

As soon as she hung up, Mabel checked her phone battery. She still had around seventy-five percent. If Cora agreed, she'd record their interview. To be safe, she grabbed a pocket notebook and extra pens. She tugged on her yellow slicker.

Koi sat beside the Hoosier cupboard, tail coiled around her front paws, watching Mabel's departure with narrowed eyes. Her disapproving expression made Mabel vaguely uneasy.

"I'll be back soon," Mabel promised.

The words had barely left her mouth before the cat vaulted to the top of the cupboard in two fluid leaps. As Koi landed, her shoulder struck a glass jar, toppling it over the edge. The jar seemed to fall in slow motion, turning in the air, hitting the pull-out shelf below, just as Mabel made a desperate, hopeless grab to catch it.

The jar shattered, spraying fragments of glass, along with a thick, gooey liquid, over everything within range, Mabel included. Barnacle fled to the hallway, where he cowered, growling. Koi looked down from her perch and began washing her paws.

A foul smell, suggestive of rotting food mingled with fermentation, rose on the air.

Barnacle crept back into the room, sniffing the spillage. "No!"

Mabel dragged him away and shoved him into the basement, then shut the door. She had to clean this up right now. Whatever this goop might be, it was sure to harden if she left it here...if Barnacle didn't eat it first.

Mabel called the historical society number, but nobody picked up. She felt sure Cora would still be there, and hopefully, she'd get the voice mail saying Mabel would be a few minutes late.

Grabbing rags from Grandma's stockpile and a bucket of warm water, Mabel set to work. She had to be careful to get up all the broken glass, as well as the gluey, moldy ooze. A faded paper label amid the wreckage identified this stuff as sourdough starter.

She glared at her cat. "You did this on purpose."

Koi turned her back and lay down.

When the spill had been cleaned up, Mabel released Barnacle and ran upstairs, peeling off spattered clothing as she went. She changed in seconds and hustled back downstairs.

Barnacle followed her to the door.

"Sorry, Buddy. You've got to stay and guard the castle. I won't be long."

As she locked the door behind her, he jumped up with his big paws on the door pane, looking tragic. "Sorry," she mouthed.

An intense blue-white lightning bolt lit the yard, accompanied by another tooth-rattling thunder crack. Barnacle howled like a paid mourner and his claws scrabbled at the door, making her wince.

Without looking back, she ran for the car. Wind slapped rain gusts against her body. Her jeans, sticking out beneath the hem of the slicker, were getting soaked. She slid behind the wheel and slammed the door.

Why was she always so impulsive? She should've waited.

Cora was at the house right now, though, and Mabel felt as if she'd burst out of her skin if she didn't get some answers.

You're not made of sugar. You won't melt. Grandma's voice was in her head again. Apparently, this was going to be an ongoing special feature of living in her house.

Mabel's windshield wipers beat away the rain with little noticeable effect. She squinted, grateful the house was only a long block away.

Mabel parked at the front curb. She checked the time. A quarter till seven, but already dark as night. The streetlamps had come on.

John was probably eating by now. She didn't really expect him to stop by afterward, not in this weather, but he'd said he might. Just in case, and in the also unlikely event her meeting with Cora ran long, she decided to send a text.

Went to interview Cora at Sauer house. Probably home by 8. If we don't connect, talk to you tomorrow.

Wind caught the car door and Mabel threw her body against it to get it latched. She ran, gasping at the wet gusts. Her boots skidded on the porch boards and she caught herself.

The doorbell faintly resounded through the old house.

When nobody appeared, Mabel wondered if Cora had stood her up and gone home, after all.

She rang again. Through the beveled glass, she saw a dark figure approaching. Her view through the glass was so distorted, it was hard to make out who was coming, but it wasn't Cora.

The door swung open.

Chapter Forty

A LIGHTNING BURST ILLUMINATED THE SAUER entryway, accompanied by a massive roll of thunder that shook the windows. Darwin dragged her inside. "Come on in. It's not a fit night out for man nor beast."

Mabel laughed and wriggled out of her slicker, shaking off the water. With a belated pang, she realized she shouldn't have done that on the William Morris entry rug.

Darwin hung the slicker on the coat tree, which sat on a drip mat. "Don't worry." He leaned close and stage whispered. "The rug's a fake."

"I don't know why I decided to come out in this."

"I wish we'd had this rain last summer," Darwin told her. "My garden could've used it."

"My weeds did fine without rain. I shudder to imagine what they'd be if they'd been watered."

"What does bring you out on a night like this?"

"I have an appointment with Cora. Is she available?"

Darwin made a sympathetic face. "Sorry, she left a moment ago."

"Are you kidding? I just talked to her."

"She said something about her parakeet, and to please give you her apologies."

Mabel was acutely aware of her soggy feet and cold, clinging pantlegs. Conditions weren't suited to combustion, but she was smoldering. "She could have told *me* that. Before I left my nice, dry house. She knew I was coming."

"She did wait, but she thought maybe the rain discouraged you. She said you knew she had to get home."

"I called. Didn't you hear it ring?"

Darwin quirked his mouth in a look of apology. "I'm so sorry—I never heard a thing. We must have been upstairs, setting buckets under the leaks.

He brightened. "She said maybe I could help."

Mabel fought to control her temper. She *had* been held up longer than she'd expected. But she'd explained to Cora exactly what she wanted. How could she conceivably think Darwin, who was at least a decade younger, could help? Of course, that wasn't his fault. Maybe in fact it was a pretty good indicator Cora was guilty—and realized Mabel was onto her.

"Blast."

He gestured toward the back. "Why don't you try me? At least, come have a cup of tea. We can't afford to turn the furnace on yet, but I have a space heater that should help dry your feet."

The downpour still rattled on the roof tiles. If she waited a bit, the rain had to let up.

"Oh, all right." She smiled an apology. "Sorry. That's nice of you. Not your fault I'm wet and out of sorts."

He smiled. "I understand. Ladies first."

Mabel headed down the shadowy hallway but stopped two steps later. "But listen. I'm not thinking straight. You must want to get home by now."

He gave her a gentle nudge. "Not with the rain coming down like this. I'd be waiting it out, anyway."

"Well, in that case."

The cluttered office was lit by the desk lamp and one low-wattage ceiling fixture. A stench of musty paper and stale coffee scented the air. "Have a seat." Darwin whisked away a stack of Smithsonian magazines to make room for her backside.

He aimed a small electric heater at her and plugged it in. A grating sound accompanied a feeble breath of warmish air.

"Sorry, I don't have much choice here." Darwin rummaged through a basket on top of the bookcase behind him. "I already dumped the dregs of the coffee. Green tea okay?"

"Um, sure." In Mabel's experience, green tea tended to be bitter. But she didn't want to be rude.

As Darwin busied himself with heating water and pulling out tea bags, Mabel shoved a few stacks of paper aside, making room for her notebook. "I guess as long as I'm here, we might as well talk. I've got a theory about the murders."

He spun around. "What?"

She smiled, flattered that he seemed to take her seriously. "It's a bombshell."

Darwin turned to rinse out a couple of mugs. Mabel winced, noticing he wasn't actually washing them. Oh, well, hot water should kill germs, right?

"Cora knows about this?"

Mabel thought. "Well… the events all started back when Cora was a toddler, but yes, I think she might. The thing is, I'm pretty darn sure I know. And I can say the truth will shock a lot of people."

Darwin swore. "Sorry. Scalded myself." He held his hand under the running water.

"Hey, let me pour."

"No, it's already poured. Some of it, unfortunately, on me. Sit back. The tea needs to steep yet."

The lights flickered and died. Thunder again shook the windows. Mabel gasped as the room fell into absolute darkness.

Two beats later, the lights came back on.

"That's been happening all afternoon. I assume you want sweetener?"

"Yeah. What do you have?"

Darwin read off a couple of artificial sweeteners. "Sugar, if you're old-fashioned."

Mabel couldn't abide artificial sweetener. "I'm an old-fashioned girl." She held up three fingers.

He fiddled with the cups and brought them over. As he set Mabel's mug next to her notebook, she couldn't help noticing the angry red splotch across his hand, and the slight tremor.

"That looks pretty ugly. Maybe you ought to put something on it."

He shook his head. "It's fine. You were saying about the murders?"

Mabel took a cautious sip and set her tea back down with a grimace. It was scalding hot, not to mention almost as bitter as losing her job after twenty-three years' faithful service.

"Sorry." Darwin ducked his head. "Tea's not a skill of mine."

"It's perfect," she lied.

"The murders?"

Mabel tried another sip. After Darwin had perhaps scarred his hand for life, she felt obliged to drink his tea, no matter how hideous.

"I don't know that I have a complete theory tying all four murders together, but at this point I think I have a pretty good start."

He waited, swirling a wooden stirring stick around his tea.

"I'm sorry. Do you have more sugar?"

"No—I mean, of course. I'm sorry, that's my fault." Darwin jumped up and returned with a whole handful of packets.

Desperate, Mabel ripped them all open and dumped them in. "Sweet tooth." She offered an apologetic smile. After a tentative sip, she took a bigger swallow. Much better.

"So...you were saying?"

"Yes, sorry. Okay, here's the thing. I'm going to tell you my theory, and you tell me if it makes sense, all right? I haven't shared this with another soul, so at this point it's for your ears only."

As she said that, it occurred to her she had, in fact, told John pretty much all of it. For the purpose of what she was telling Darwin, though, what she'd said was true enough. What she wanted to impress on him was that he needed to keep all this to himself, until her book came out.

She didn't think she dared say what she suspected about Cora. That was entering slander territory, and Darwin might feel loyal enough to take it straight to Cora, despite any promises he'd made to Mabel.

"Do you understand what I'm saying?"

His face was grim. "I think I do."

Finally, Mabel had someone besides John to bounce her theory off. Darwin seemed prepared to take her seriously, which was a good start. She sipped more of her cooling tea. It went down a bit easier since she'd dumped half a bowl of sugar in it.

"Here's what I'm going to do." She set her cup down. "I'll tell you what I think, and you can help me decide where we go from here. What I have is only a theory, and I don't want to smear anyone's good name, you know?"

The lights wavered and went out, just as lightning washed the adjoining living room, and another thunderclap shook the windows.

Mabel waited. The lights didn't come back on.

She fumbled in her purse and came up with her phone. "Hang on." Her fingers seemed clumsy, and Mabel had trouble finding the flashlight app.

"There we go." The point of light shot Darwin in the eye. "Oops, sorry." She moved the beam out of his face.

Darwin blinked rapidly. "It's fine. You were saying?"

"It doesn't seem like they're coming back on. I should go."

"Finish your tea. They'll be back." Darwin shoved a bag of store-bought cookies across the desk to her. They reminded her of her contribution to the refreshment table at that first meeting. It seemed Darwin wasn't snooty about his cookies, either.

"Thanks." Mabel took a big bite, stuffing her mouth with soft cookie and raspberry jam. The sweetness helped clear the taste of that awful tea.

"I need to check something out front. I'll be right back," he said. "Help yourself."

Mabel had already helped herself to two but took a third. She chewed slowly and worked on swallowing. She realized she wasn't feeling all that well. She took another sip of tea, washing the cookie down, hoping to calm her stomach. But the bitterness made her feel all the worse.

As soon as Darwin's footsteps disappeared down the hallway, she got up, staggering a bit, and steadied herself with one hand on the corner of the desk. This was the perfect opportunity to dump the rest of that vile-tasting tea and get a drink of water before Darwin returned and noticed she'd barely drunk half of it.

Mabel dumped the dregs into the sink and flushed them away. It looked like the sugar hadn't all dissolved. No wonder the brew still tasted so bitter. She rinsed out the cup, ran cold water into it, and drank.

There was no point in sticking around. The lights were still out, and Cora had stood her up. Not to mention, she felt on the verge of collapse. Was she coming down with the flu? The last thing she wanted was to literally barf her cookies all over Darwin's office.

Mabel made her way back to her chair. Her head felt almost detached, as if she was drunk, and she felt worse by the moment. This had come on fast. She hoped she hadn't infected John or Darwin.

Mabel lurched into the sharp corner of the desk. She gasped with pain and felt her way along the edge till she could grab her chair. She sank with a thud.

Mabel put a hand to her head. She wasn't feverish or nauseated. But something was wrong. Maybe she should leave her car and walk home. Was it still pouring? In this interior room, she couldn't be sure, but it sounded like it.

Mabel felt around for her bag, then pushed herself to her feet. This abrupt, massive exhaustion was surely flu.

She dragged her feet, trailing one hand along the furniture and chair railing, on her way to the front hall. *Air.* She needed fresh air. Needed the lash of rain on her face to wake her up enough to drive home.

When Mabel stepped into the hallway, she nearly collided with Darwin, who was returning to the office. The lantern in his hand cast wavering, elongated shadows on the walls and ceiling.

She staggered. "Easy." Darwin caught her arm in a firm grip. "The transformer out front was shooting sparks but looks now like it went dead. I'll need to call the power company."

"Hey, I'm sorry." She heard her words slur. "I think I'm really sick. I might not be able to drive. Do you think—?"

Both phones rang, one on the table in the entryway and the other in the back office. Loud and grating, the ringers were obviously set for older people with impaired hearing.

Mabel and Darwin both jerked, and his grip loosened.

"Go ahead and get it. It might be the power company. Thanks for the tea and the heater. I need to get home and lie down."

"Wait. I'll take you."

The phone shrilled.

"No. You need to deal with the electric company. I'll be okay when I get some air."

Mabel reached the door and fumbled with the latch. Darwin reached over, probably to help, but at another shriek from the phones, he held up his hand. "Just hang on."

He stepped aside to pick up the nearest handset. "Sauer House."

Mabel gave the latch another twist, and the door opened. A blast of cold, wet air struck her full in the face.

She stumbled over the doorstep, caught herself, and shut the door behind her. The porch roof offered some protection from the wind and rain, but she had to keep moving.

The rain came steadily, but no longer fell in sheets. The houses at this end of the block sat dark, except for flickers that must have been the inhabitants' flashlights and candles. Her own sweet house, which didn't share the same transformer, beckoned her home, the kitchen light she'd left on for the animals still burning. She could drive that far.

Mabel made her way down the rain-slicked steps, fighting gusts of wind and clutching her leather bag to her chest. She hoped it wouldn't be ruined but was beyond much caring.

The raindrops had substance, icy and biting as they struck her face. They bounced and rattled around her feet.

Mabel dragged her leaden body weight inside her car and yanked the door shut against the tug of the wind. When she started the engine, her lights came on and the wipers swept away the raindrops and sleet.

She made an awkward turn in the side driveway, backing over a couple limp, frostbitten mums, and narrowly missing the near post of the port cochere. As she pulled onto the street, the front door of the house opened, and Darwin waved an arm.

Mabel cracked her window. "I'll replace them," she called. "Sorry."

He yelled something indiscernible over the wind.

Mabel had to get home and into bed. She offered what she hoped would be received as an apologetic wave and drove off.

In seconds, she'd reached her driveway. The car ended up angled toward the back door, its right front tire resting in the soggy grass.

She didn't care. She'd fix it tomorrow.

Inside, claws scrabbled at the kitchen door. Barnacle had accelerated from his usual mad barking to a mournful, keening howl.

The moment Mabel opened the door, he jumped her. She lurched against the edge of the counter.

"Okay. Hold on."

Dumping her bag to the floor, she shoved at the door with one hand and Barnacle with the other. As soon as she heard the latch click, she locked the door and turned to rearm the security system.

Barnacle wouldn't go out in the storm, even if she wanted him to. Mabel spread newspaper on the floor. Good enough for one evening.

The stairs looked daunting. Better sleep down here tonight.

She pulled off her wet shoes and clothing and tossed them toward the utility room, then found a sweatshirt and leggings in the basket of clean laundry she'd never gotten around to putting away. Barnacle pawed at her legs, whining and telling her his troubles, while Koi watched from atop the cabinets.

In moments, Mabel lay semi-comfortably on the couch, covered in two of Grandma's afghans and her own college fleece. She knew her makeshift bedding was unlikely to stay in place overnight, but she didn't care. She just needed to sleep.

For a moment, she lay still, willing herself to drift off. Her head hurt. It felt as if Michelangelo were attempting to chisel a latter-day masterpiece out of her skull.

Mumbling her irritation and misery, Mabel got back up. She staggered to the kitchen, where a big bottle of acetaminophen sat on the windowsill.

Flashing yellow lights drew her attention to the power company truck parked in front of the Sauer house. That had been quick. The outage must've extended beyond Carteret—the only thing that would bring a prompt response like this.

She took her pills and lay back down. The last images she saw before falling asleep were her pets. Barnacle sat with his chin resting on the edge of the couch, a look of concern in his brown eyes. Koi perched on the sofa back, tail tip flicking disapproval as she stared down at Mabel. Bedtime, her expression said, was for bed.

She'd call Darwin tomorrow and apologize for running out. If she felt better.

Chapter Forty-One

WHEN MABEL WOKE, HER CELL PHONE showed almost noon. The sky was blue, and every rain-washed surface gleamed in the sun.

She started to sit up, but the movement sent shards of stabbing pain through her brain. She had obviously slept well over twelve hours, yet all she wanted was more sleep.

Barnacle whined and pawed at her arm. She'd never made him wait this long to go out before.

Barefoot, she padded to the back door with him dancing around her feet. Koi sat by her dish, her theatrical meows growing weaker. As soon as she'd clipped the dog to his cable and filled the pet bowls, she started coffee, then waited mug in hand for enough to drip through to begin uploading caffeine.

When she was cradling her first warm mugful at last, she stood at the window, watching Barnacle explore the wet bushes. What a weird evening that had been.

At least, she felt a bit better today. Whatever she'd caught must be only a twenty-four-hour virus.

She glanced at her phone. Darwin had called earlier. She dimly recalled turning off the ringer. Mabel listened to his message, just checking on her and hoping she was feeling better.

She'd also missed a call from John around ten PM, which she couldn't even remember hearing in her drugged stupor. He had left a voice mail, saying he'd try her again sometime today.

Drugged stupor.

Now, why had she thought that? Because, of course, she'd had one of those sleeps that was so deep it was like she'd been drugged.

It was ridiculous to imagine for one moment that it had been anything more than that. She'd felt the same sudden, overwhelming exhaustion that always came with the flu. Had the same shattering headache.

And the County Health Department was already reporting the first flu cases of the season. When she'd seen that headline on a newspaper at the market recently, it had reminded her she still needed to get her shot.

Mabel yawned. She didn't feel like eating—another indication she'd picked up a bug.

She let Barnacle in. He came bounding, wet paws skidding on the floor, and plowed his face into his bowl. Kibble scattered, and Koi leapt into action, batting it around until Barnacle finished cleaning his bowl and warned her off with a growl.

The cat narrowed her eyes at him and began a thorough grooming. It seemed to be her way of announcing she was done playing, anyhow.

Mabel was still groggy. She dropped into a chair.

Koi leapt onto the table next to her and resumed her leisurely grooming session. Mabel didn't have the energy to shove her off. Maybe she ought to just lay her head down for a few minutes.

As she folded her arms on the table and began lowering her head, she met Koi's eyes. The cat had interrupted her paw-washing to fix Mabel with an intense stare.

"What? Could you please mind your own business for a minute?"

She rested her cheek on her arms. Her muscles didn't ache. When she'd had the flu, her muscles always ached. *Could* this be a drug?

That vile-tasting tea…

Not Darwin. He was her friend. Why would mild-mannered Darwin be going around drugging people? The only imaginable motive for Darwin to try to kill Mabel was…what? Had he killed Helen?

The very thought was ludicrous. He'd worked with Helen for years, and without the animosity Cora—and even Linnea—had exhibited. But if he had—and if he thought Mabel had figured that out…

Mabel opened her eyes. Koi was sitting upright, her neat, gold-tipped front paws together, still staring at Mabel.

What should she do? Lisa was at work. John probably would be too. She couldn't just call the police on Darwin with no more evidence than her feeling drugged. Not with other, more reasonable suspects out there. Even she could hardly conceive of his taking an ax to the octogenarian society president.

Blood test. A blood test should confirm whether she had something in her system that shouldn't be there, like the vet had done for Barnacle.

The dog padded over when she looked at him. Barnacle had been drugged. Devereaux had been drugged. If Mabel had been drugged, that fit the pattern.

A sick feeling rose in her chest. Would she be dead right now, if she hadn't managed to dump that tea while Darwin was out of the room?

She didn't have a doctor in Medicine Spring yet and wasn't at all sure she was up to a drive to the ER in Bartles Grove. Would her insurance cover a drug test?

The residue of whatever Darwin had given her…if that's what it was…wasn't improving her brain function. What had she told him last night? She rubbed her head. What had he said?

The previous afternoon was fuzzy. She'd told him she thought she knew who had killed the Sauers. Hadn't she? Or maybe that hadn't been clear. There were too many murders.

If Darwin had killed Helen—whatever his reason—might he think Mabel was telling him she knew *that?* Her heart lurched. He'd asked something about Cora. What had Mabel told him?

She grabbed her hair with both hands. If she could only shake her head clear.

Just on the off-chance Darwin really was trying to kill her, the first thing she needed to do was lock her door. Yawning, Mabel shuffled to the door.

Just as she reached for the lock, the door burst open, slamming into her. Mabel tried to push back, but Barnacle shoved out through the opening, wagging his tail.

"Here you go." Darwin flung a packet wrapped in stained butcher paper into the yard. Barnacle chased after it, out into the yard.

Too late, Mabel grabbed for him. Comprehension dawned. "You drugged my dog." Though she threw her weight against the door, Darwin's leg was firmly wedged inside.

"Good boy." He laughed as he slipped through and slammed the door behind Barnacle.

Mabel was already running. She pivoted for the basement door, but he was right there.

Darwin grabbed at her as she spun again toward the front hallway. He caught the back of her sweatshirt but lost his grip as she lunged away, shoving a kitchen chair in his path.

Koi, hissing, oozed beneath the table.

Darwin swore as his shin connected with the old solid-oak chair.

"What's wrong with you?" Her voice came out in a sob. "What have I ever done to you?"

She hesitated in the hallway less than a heartbeat. She might be able to get the front door open and escape outside, but she'd never outrun him. Her legs still felt about as agile as tree trunks.

Grabbing the banister, Mabel scrambled upstairs. She had to get to the bathroom, where she could lock herself in.

Downstairs, her phone rang. Right where she'd left it. On the kitchen table.

She heard his feet hit the stairs.

On the last step, Mabel stumbled. She cracked her knee against the edge of the stair—hard.

Blinding tears of pain flooded her eyes. She wanted to collapse and rock back and forth, but she had to run.

Limping, she sprinted and stumbled across the upstairs hall and threw herself inside the bathroom. She slammed the door. The old knob had no lock. There was only a flimsy hook screwed into the doorframe, which. Mabel jammed into the eye attached to the door. Bracing her feet on the base of the sink pedestal, she shoved all her weight back against the door.

Darwin crashed against the other side. The door shuddered. Mabel felt it give, then bang shut.

She swiped tears. "Darwin, why? I never did anything to you."

The door rammed into her again, as Darwin thudded against the other side. This time, she saw the base of the hook move.

"Stop acting so clueless," he raged. "You think you're going to talk me out of this, don't you?"

"But I don't know anything. Not about you. All I know…I think…is that Margarethe killed her husband and son, and the family knew it."

The door jumped with another loud bang as Darwin hit it. He swore and mumbled about his toe. Apparently, he'd kicked it.

He shook the knob and the whole door rattled. "Seriously? Are you kidding me? You know 'all about it,' do you? You don't even have that much right."

"What?" Mabel's head hurt, and she strained to hold the door shut.

"You ruined my life. And for what? I don't want to kill you. I never wanted to kill you. All I ever did was try to defend myself. You understand that, don't you?"

Self-defense…really? "Um, I guess so. Can you tell me about it? I really want to know."

"Look. I don't have all day. We have to end this, and I need to get out of here. Yes. Margarethe killed Walter. But she didn't kill her son. So much for your investigative prowess."

"Well, then…?"

"These blasted old houses and their blasted solid doors." Darwin rammed the door again. Once more, Mabel saw the hook give. It was coming loose.

"My grandfather killed Junior, all right? But it wasn't his fault."

Mabel saw a pattern emerging. Darwin and his family killed people. And it wasn't their fault.

She heard her faraway cell ring again. She needed to calm Darwin down somehow. Keep him occupied till he gave up, or someone came to see why she wasn't answering her phone. "How so? I mean, I'm sure it wasn't, but…?"

He panted as if gasping for breath. "Old Walter was a greedy, heartless old devil. He cheated my granddad out of everything he had on a real estate deal. The country was still coming out of the Depression. Granddad was desperate."

"Of course, he was."

"Granddad knew the old man always came home for lunch, so he figured he'd catch him in private. Plead with him—one family man to another—to make things right."

"Then, when he saw him lying there, he lost his temper?"

The door shook with another loud bang, as Darwin rammed it. "No," he growled. "You already told me Margarethe did it."

"But—"

"He was abusive…attacked Edna…planned to throw her out on the street, people said. I guess Margarethe had had enough. She was stark-raving nuts, you know. All that Greta Garbo, 'death scene of Camille' business is romantic bunk."

"But your grandfather—"

"Granddad ducked behind the drapes when he saw her and ended up seeing the murder right in front of him. He was shocked, of course. He knew he had to get out of there before he ended up getting blamed.

"He watched Margarethe leave, waited a while, then started running, right as young Walter came in and caught him. Junior attacked him—Granddad had to defend himself."

Darwin had stopped pushing. Mabel slumped to the floor, still leaning against the door, but easing her tired muscles. "Of course, he did," Mabel agreed. "But Edna was tried for both murders. I always heard the investigation died out after she was acquitted. I don't understand why you had to kill Helen."

"You do know." Darwin threw his weight against the door. "Liar."

Mabel, caught off guard, tried too late to brace herself. The wood splintered with a sharp crack. The hook clattered to the floor beside her, and she was thrown onto her elbow, sending shockwaves up her now useless left arm. Mabel struggled to sit upright, jamming her feet against the sink pedestal as she leaned her weight into the damaged door again.

Darwin's shoulder burst through the shattered door, washing the room with a pale film of light from the hall fixture. Seizing his advantage, he jammed the door into Mabel until he'd forced a big enough space to reach down and grab her.

Chapter Forty-Two

MABEL CRINGED, THROWING UP HER ARMS in a vain attempt to protect herself. She had nowhere left to run. No place to hide.

She had to remember she was still bigger than Darwin—and younger. Mabel rolled away from his grasping hands.

"Don't make this harder. Please." Darwin's breathing was ragged, and he sounded sincerely regretful.

"You're going to have to work for it, buddy." Mabel fumbled behind her, knocking toiletries off the old oak washstand. They clattered to the tiles. She came up with a can of deodorant and turned the jet full into Darwin's face.

He gasped and swiped at his eyes but didn't loosen his choking grip on Mabel's collar, as a feminine, summery fragrance filled the air. Darn. That stuff was gentle. Why couldn't it have been hairspray?

Still squirming on the floor, Mabel kicked at his shins. "Better run. People are coming to check on me, and I already heard the phone."

He struck back at her legs, landing a sharp kick on her right knee. Mabel saw stars.

Darwin was sobbing now, and so was she.

"Go," she gasped. "You can't make this one look like an accident. Get away while you still can."

"Oh, it's no accident. You just couldn't live with yourself after what you did to poor Helen."

Darwin caught her jaw, trying to force it open. "Come on, dear. It'll be easier if you just help out here." Sweat glazed his face. "Take your pills and you'll go to sleep, nice and peaceful."

Mabel tossed her head, fighting him. Though she continued to flail around, all she could reach was the plunger.

She swung as hard as she could with her left arm and smacked it across his temple.

He laughed as the rubber cup bounced off his head, stirring up the sweet wildflower scent of deodorant.

Tears stung Mabel's eyes. She wasn't even going to get to die with dignity.

Her size was all she had left to fight with. Although Darwin was freakishly strong, she outweighed him. If only she could manage to pin him down.

Suddenly, someone pounded at the back door. They both startled, and in the moment's hesitation, Mabel threw herself on Darwin.

Now, he was the one struggling to free himself.

The banging on the kitchen door increased.

Please let it be John.

Mabel drew a deep breath and screamed. "Up here!"

The back door opened. "Mabel Browne! Where are you? I need to speak with you right this minute."

Mabel knew that voice. Linnea had arrived.

Darwin's eyes widened. Seizing the momentary distraction, he shoved Mabel off balance. Feeling her control slipping, she fought to pin his arms. "Help!"

"Miss Browne." The strident female voice now came from the front hall. "Are you aware your animal has been running amok?"

Claws scrabbled on the stairs and Linnea shrieked.

Barnacle burst into the room, romping back and forth between Mabel and Darwin and frantically licking them both. Linnea followed, her face contorted with rage.

"So there you are. While you've been enjoying your amorous interlude, this dog has been amusing himself by digging up Mother's garden and relieving himself on the bushes."

Darwin kicked himself free of Mabel's grasp and lurched for the shattered door, shoving Linnea aside. "How dare you?" she hissed at him, then seemed to notice the damage for the first time.

She scowled at Mabel. "How can you live like this? Mother should have had the health inspectors in here long ago."

"Excuse me." Mabel scrambled past her. She had to get to her phone. Barnacle, his snout and paws covered in mud, frolicked around her feet.

"Just where do you think you're going?" Linnea called after her.

"Mabel!"

"John!" Mabel's knees went weak with relief at the familiar voice downstairs.

"How many men are you carrying on with? Your grandmother would be appalled."

Mabel made it to the stair railing, trailed by Linnea, who continued to yammer about Barnacle, the condition of the house, and Mabel's perceived loose morals. Barnacle barked, joining in the commotion.

Mabel peered over the banister. John was planted in the lower hallway with his back to the kitchen, gun drawn on Darwin. He must've come in through the back door, just in time to interrupt Darwin's escape.

"Are you all right?" he called up.

"I'm okay." She heard the quiver in her voice.

Darwin, wild-eyed and breathing hard, shifted his weight.

"Don't move, buddy," John snapped. "I wouldn't mind killing you, but that's up to you."

"Drop your weapon," boomed a woman's voice from behind him. Lt. Sizemore and a uniformed officer loomed in the kitchen entry, both armed.

John let out a long sigh as he set his gun on the floor and raised his hands.

A familiar scream came from the back door. "Mabel!"

"Lisa, I'm okay," Mabel yelled back. "Stay there."

"Wow." The male officer sniffed the flower-scented air still wafting around Darwin. "Smells good in here."

Though the evening was still young, Mabel didn't fall into bed until long after her body—and the better part of her brain—had checked out for the day. When at last she did, Koi nestled above her on the pillow, her tail curled like a fluffy new fringe of bangs over Mabel's forehead. Lisa had parked herself at her bedside to make sure Mabel stayed there. "You scared ten years off my life."

"I'm sorry." Mabel had said those words over and over. She'd said them to John, to the police, to Jen and Lisa—and even to Darwin, as he was being led away, bruised, crying, and smelling of flowers.

Lisa squeezed her hand. "You did a good job. Who knows when they'd have figured any of this out, without you?"

Mabel turned her face toward the wall. She didn't feel any satisfaction. Helen and Devereaux were still dead, and even poor, pitiful Darwin's life was as good as over.

"I blundered into the answer. I missed more than I got right. Nancy Drew has no worries about the competition."

"You're selling yourself short again." Lisa smiled. "You were incredibly brave, fighting off Darwin like that."

"I didn't do a thing anybody else wouldn't do. Didn't someone say facing death 'concentrates the mind?'"

"Samuel Johnson. More or less. I'm still proud of you."

Mabel glanced back at her best friend, beautiful as always, in the circle of lamplight, and still dressed in her teacher clothes "Thanks for checking on me."

"When all that time went by and you didn't answer your phone, I panicked. Your mom would kill me if anything happened to you on my watch, after all these years."

"John said the same thing. I mean, about my not picking up."

"And he brought the cavalry."

"It had been too long—he'd already tried me last night, and then a couple times today. So he came to check on me. When he heard all the yelling and crashing, he called 911."

"I'm ready to retire as your keeper. He's a good one, Mabel."

Again, Mabel turned her head toward the shadows on the wall. "Yeah."

Mabel was wearing her writer/girl detective best when John picked her up the next evening. She didn't have the figure for slinky, but the clingy, midcalf, black-lace skirt looked good, topped with a creamy cowl-neck sweater. She hadn't wanted to appear as if she was trying too hard, but Lisa had insisted, doing her makeup again, and hanging a chunky gold "statement necklace" around Mabel's neck.

"We're not dining at the palace," Mabel grumbled. "It's more of a business meeting."

Lisa laughed. "Whatever you say. But I don't think the man who saved your life—and threatened to kill the guy who hurt you—would be taking you out to a nice restaurant for a business meeting."

"Technically, Linnea saved my life," Mabel muttered. She waved away Lisa's hand, which was wielding a tube of red lipstick. Lisa didn't understand. She'd always been little and cute, and guys had always liked her. Flirting came naturally to Lisa. Mabel had hoped for romance before and knew how that always ended. She wasn't going to break her heart over John Bigelow.

Although they'd planned an early dinner, it was dark when they arrived at Minutello's. No one sat at the bar, and only one other couple occupied a table near the front.

Mabel nodded at the other patrons' gray hair. "We're in time for the early-bird special with the rest of the seniors."

John smiled. "I figured at this hour we'd be able to talk in private."

They followed the hostess to a snug corner booth with high sides.

Mabel had already shared Darwin's confession about his grandfather's killing Walter, Jr., and confirming her theory about Margarethe. She was still in the dark about Helen and Devereaux. But for the next half hour, they exchanged pleasantries and planned their order.

When their drinks and appetizer—a huge platter of fried zucchini slices with a side of marinara sauce—had arrived, John cleared his throat. "You ready to hear what turned Darwin into a murderer?"

"Are you kidding? It's all I've been waiting for. I liked him." Mabel couldn't keep the hurt out of her voice.

John laid his hand over hers. This was romantic but also awkward, since Mabel was holding onto a greasy zucchini slice. This seemed to be a recurring problem.

"I'm sorry he hurt you." John gazed into her eyes.

Mabel glanced down at her cooling zucchini. "I don't get it. Almost everybody else hated me, but Darwin was my *friend*."

He patted her hand. "I'm sorry. Go ahead and eat. But yeah. I know he was. Don't forget he isn't your only friend in the world, though. Nanette's your friend too—right?"

"Yeah, I guess so."

"She is. And you know you've got Lisa and me," he said. "Anyway, here's what he told the police. Apparently, after Darwin's granddad... Can we call him 'Granddad?' It'll be easier. Granddad killed Junior, in what Darwin calls self-defense, right?"

She nodded, taking another slice of zucchini. So good.

"But he was still in the same bind—worse, in fact. Now he's not only desperate for money, but he's killed somebody. He'd have been an obvious suspect for both murders, if he'd been caught, so needless to say, he ran, and took the ax with him."

John paused as their salads arrived. He waited till the waitress was out of earshot before continuing.

"Here's where the story gets interesting. The cops were investigating the murders. They hadn't been able to build a strong case against anybody, though their favorite suspect seemed to be Edna."

"Mm-hmm…." Mabel stabbed a forkful of greens, tomato, and blue cheese.

"Granddad was questioned but they had nothing linking him to the scene. They kept coming back, and he was terrified he'd give himself away. As he thought about his situation, he decided he could solve his problems by blackmailing the Sauers, holding out what he knew about Margarethe."

"How was he going to do that? As soon as he admitted to being there, wouldn't the Sauers have turned him over to the police and tried to pin both murders on him?"

"He never identified himself and was careful not to give any information that would lead back to him. He had a complicated drop system for the money. He was never greedy, and he let them know enough to make it clear he was telling the truth about witnessing Margarethe commit the murder."

"They paid?"

John nodded. "For years. The Sauers were rich, and I guess to them, Margarethe's reputation was worth giving Granddad a comfortable little pension."

Mabel shuddered. "I can't imagine ever being comfortable—knowing you'd killed somebody—no matter the circumstances. And living the rest of your life as a blackmailer."

"Yes, but you have to remember it all started with his feeling the Sauers owed him something, right?"

"Did Edna and Violet know what their mother did? Before the old man approached them?"

"They knew right away. Edna discovered the bodies and ran upstairs—probably screaming—to check on her mother. She'd have seen the state her mom was in, and that bloody gown. She must've called Violet immediately and shared what their mother had done. They decided Edna would take the rap, knowing she had a good chance of beating the charges."

"And if they destroyed the dressing gown, nobody'd ever have to know."

John waited while the waitress moved salad plates and set down their meals.

"But did they honestly think their mother could've killed her own son?"

"What else could they think? Even with the murder weapon unaccounted for, nobody expected a second killer to show up. She was in such a state, they figured she'd snapped."

"Unbelievable. But about Helen—"

"Let's enjoy our food, okay? Then maybe we'll take a little drive, or go back to my place for apple pie, and I'll finish telling you what I know."

Mabel raised an eyebrow. "Is this a ploy for getting me to your place?"

He grinned. "Maybe."

Were they flirting? She felt herself redden. "Can't we have dessert here?"

"Ouch. You sure know how to dampen a man's self-confidence."

"I didn't mean it like that—oh, forget it. You're laughing at me."

He clasped her hand. "I'm kidding. I'll eat apple pie with you anytime, anyplace. 'My strength is as the strength of ten, because my heart is pure.'"

"Good grief." She focused on her plate and took a couple of bites. "Did you bake the pie?"

"No. I bought it at the Stotz farm market."

"Ooooh...they have good pies. We'll see."

For a while, they ate, and talked about Mabel's animals and her new career. "And so," she concluded, "I decided I needed to know something about being a volunteer, if I was going to write about it. That's what got me into this mess, and I'm not sure I can recommend the job to anybody else after this."

"There are lots of other volunteer jobs out there. I think you've got a great idea—don't give up at the first obstacle."

Mabel snorted. The "first obstacle" had been murder. "I'm picking something super quiet and boring next time. Maybe garden club."

"In all honesty, I would've thought the historical society was as benign as they come."

"Me too." Mabel fumed. "Oh, well, I can't say it's been boring. Losing my job was scary, and I miss the security. But, man, was life boring."

John grinned. "Embrace your new life. You have a chance most people never will. You can start over and do whatever you want. Follow your dreams."

She frowned. "I'm not sure I have any dreams. The writing thing seemed like a good idea, but now I feel like I'll never get anywhere. All these murders got me way off track."

He snapped his fingers under her nose. "Excuses."

She ate moodily. She didn't like being told what was good for her. Then, she laid down her fork and changed the subject.

"What about you? Are you going back to being a PI? Isn't that *your* dream job?"

John didn't answer right away. "Like I said, I'll go back in February, if everything works out. Meanwhile, I enjoy teaching. I'm only adjunct faculty, so I'll probably continue, even once I start up my PI business again."

Mabel chased the last morsel around her plate and sighed when it was gone. Delectable.

"Why do you have to wait till February?"

He stretched and looked around, then waved for the waitress. "You want coffee?"

"Are you diverting me?"

"Is it working?"

"Yes. But only for a minute."

They both ordered coffee—Mabel's decaf—and she added a slice of vanilla cream cake to her order. The menu promised it was sinfully rich, but light as a cloud. John shook his head. "So much for apple pie."

"We can split the cake."

John rolled his eyes.

As soon as the waitress had moved on, she tried again. "You were saying?"

"I wasn't saying. But we can talk about it later. My license was suspended, but it's no big deal."

Mabel's eyebrows shot toward her hairline. It sounded like a pretty big deal to her. "It was what?"

"I promise I'll tell you all about it someday. But it's a long story, and right now we have a lot more ground to cover, if you want to hear everything I found out about Helen and Devereaux and still get home for breakfast."

Mabel scowled.

"You're cute when you pout, but one major topic per evening, all right?"

Mabel brightened as the cake arrived. Nobody had ever told her she was cute before—especially when she was scowling. "I'm not going to forget this."

John sighed. "How well I know."

Chapter Forty-Three

MABEL LOUNGED IN JOHN'S DEEP ARMCHAIR. He'd told her to make herself at home while he warmed the pie. She kicked off her shoes, then gave one a cautious sniff. Not bad.

She curled up with her feet under her. Although she had no real intention of getting up, she called, "You need any help in there?"

"Nope. Make yourself comfy."

Mabel stretched, feeling luxurious. Her eye was caught by a glare from a magnificent poof of tortoiseshell fur, seated on John's fireplace hearth, her tail wrapped neatly around her haunches, tip flicking in obvious irritation.

"Oh, you've got a cat. I didn't see her before."

"Yep. Billie Jean. She hates you."

"She just met me."

"She hates pretty much everybody. Especially any ladies I bring home."

Billie Jean opened her mouth, showing pointed little teeth, and delivered a silent hiss.

Mabel hissed back. Billie Jean stalked away, tail swishing, her opinion of Mabel made clear.

"Major case of torti-tude there."

"Huh?"

"Torti-tude. Your cat has a classic case of tortoiseshell attitude. Most torties are raging individualists who tolerate humans grudgingly."

"Your cat's a tortie."

"Hey, I love torties." She considered Billie Jean skeptically. "Usually. Koi's an exception, anyway, when it comes to the dark side of torti-tude."

John returned, pie plates in one hand, and two full mugs in the other. As Mabel scrambled to clear space on the coffee table, her phone rang.

"This is Nanette. Did I call at a bad time?"

"I'm with…a friend right now. Was there something you needed?"

A gusty sigh nearly cleaned Mabel's right ear. Meanwhile, John held a hand up like a cellphone, mouthing, *Who?*

She covered the receiver. "Nanette."

"I'm so upset." Nanette's voice quavered. "They just reported *Darwin* has been arrested."

"I know. It's awful," Mabel told her. "I'm getting more info right now. Can I call you back tomorrow?"

"Don't wait. I won't be sleeping tonight, anyway."

Mabel finally managed to end the call. "Whew. I feel bad about Darwin. Nanette's taking his arrest hard."

"It's not your fault he attacked you. Or Helen. Or Devereaux."

"I know. But now I'm involved." A sudden thought struck her. "I'm a witness. I bet I'll have to testify, if he doesn't take a plea."

"'Fraid so." John grinned. "When you're on the stand, I'll come to court and be your groupie."

"Wow. I'm flattered. It's usually serial killers who get all the groupies."

"That's okay," he said generously. "You deserve it. I'm sure Darwin will get his own."

It hadn't occurred to her that some might call Darwin a serial killer. This would, at least, put a dramatic spin on her true-crime book, since she'd been all set to be victim number three. But if she wrote this story completely truthfully, she wasn't sure the details would all reflect well on her. She might need to think about this.

John snapped his fingers. "Mabel! Where do you keep going?"

"Sorry. I have a lot to think about. You were going to tell me about Helen and Devereaux's killings. Was it because he thought they knew something?"

"Not entirely. You know his grandfather had been blackmailing the Sauers. First, Edna and Violet were paying up, but after Granddad died, the blackmail stopped for many years, right?"

Mabel nodded, mouth full of apple pie. Yummy.

"Well, that's how it was for quite a long time. Edna died next, and then, Violet. But one day not that long ago, Darwin's father died, as well. While cleaning out his late father's attic, Darwin discovered the old man's blackmail records and the evidence he'd stowed away all those years ago."

"The ax with Margarethe's prints."

"Right. At first, he didn't understand. But when he started poking through a box of old photos at the Sauer house, he found the picture of Margarethe in the dressing gown, and realized it matched the bloody fabric the police had recovered from the crime scene."

"Like I did."

"Right. More searching finally turned up a confessional letter, of sorts, that old Granddad had written on his deathbed."

"Is that when he decided to blackmail Helen?" Mabel had trouble imagining it.

John nodded and sipped his coffee. "I believe him when he says he didn't want to pressure Helen. He was probably always quiet and law-abiding, but weak. He was desperate for money at the end. He'd been an instructor at the community college for decades, but when their funding was cut, a few years ago, he was older, and the economy was bad. He struggled to survive on part-time jobs and started volunteering with the historical society so he could at least feel useful."

Despite herself, Mabel felt a stab of empathy.

"Darwin sent an anonymous note about Margarethe, and naturally, Helen never suspected it came from him. If you believe him—and I tend to—when it came right down to it, he had a lot of trouble

resorting to blackmail. When he found Helen in the murder room that day, he tried to appeal to her sympathy at first." John grimaced.

"And she had none."

He shook his head. "So he pressed a little harder. Let her know that he knew all about her sainted ancestor—who was about to be honored at the big hospital gala."

"Helen went nuts?"

"Yup. She brandished the hatchet, which was out of the display case. They got into a tussle, and the old lady took a blow to the neck, but a heart attack finished her."

Mabel shuddered and pushed away her half-eaten pie. She needed a moment.

"Do you know what Helen was doing in that room?"

John shook his head. "She can't tell us. But Darwin said he'd sent her an anonymous note, letting her know Margarethe's hands weren't clean, and 'somebody' could release that information, if they wanted. Best guess—Helen wanted to go through what was in the murder room and archives, to see if she could figure out whether anything was missing or provided some clue to the identity of the poison pen writer."

"I'll bet she suspected Devereaux."

John winced. "I tend to agree. Her air of mystery about that upcoming tell-all book is why she died. Helen probably suspected her of a blackmail attempt—and so did Darwin."

Mabel made a mental note never to put herself in that position when she became a true-crime author. "I feel sorry for Devereaux and I feel kind of bad, because I didn't like her very much. Now, that all seems sort of petty." Although, a small voice in her head admitted, she still didn't much like her.

"Darwin finally admitted she showed up at the house the afternoon of Helen's murder, hoping for another peek at the back-parlor display. He had just killed Helen—or thought he had—and he told her the house was closed for the day. She seemed to pick up on his nervousness, and he realized later that he had blood on his sleeve."

"No wonder he thought she knew what he did."

"Who knows whether she saw the blood or not, but he decided he couldn't take the chance. He freaked out when she returned with the true-crime group, but she was probably still only trying to get another look at the parlor.

"So he drugged her and tried to make it look like she'd killed herself in the car."

John nodded. "He thought once she was found in the garage that way, everybody would assume accident or suicide. Since she was obviously overcome by carbon monoxide, he never expected they'd run a tox screen."

"Not a very smooth criminal…"

John patted the sofa cushion next to him. "Come sit by me?"

Mabel hesitated. Was he going to put the moves on her?

"I didn't finish my pie."

He laughed. "Bring your pie with you."

Mabel made her decision. She wasn't a boring, single, backroom lawyer anymore. She was a successful—or soon-to-be-successful—writer, who'd helped solve four murders. And she was dating a PI.

Wasn't she?

Mabel picked up her plate and mug and sidled over to the couch. "Now, tell me how you got suspended."

Instantly, a tortoiseshell fury erupted from under her seat and lashed out at her ankles with a blur of claws. Mabel screeched. Lukewarm coffee sloshed over her hand.

John jumped up to take her plate and mug and settle them on his end of the coffee table. He handed her a napkin, then shook his finger at Billie Jean.

"I love you, but you better respect my lady."

He slipped his arm around Mabel's shoulders. "Is your hand okay?"

"I'll live." It was hard to think, while they were snuggled up like this. She swallowed. "I guess I owe Linnea. I'm not sure what would've happened if she hadn't burst in when she did."

John laughed. "Since when she left, she was still threatening to have the health inspectors come check your house, I think that's pretty much a wash."

"I hope she doesn't decide to stay here—we're already like the Hatfields and McCoys." Mabel grimaced. "It looks like the State may consider that stupid swampy area the township wants me to fill in 'protected wetland.' So that still needs to be straightened out. But if she's really dragging the County into my house, it means I won't be rid of Acey for a while, either."

She shoved a gloomy forkful of pie in her mouth and felt a bit better. "I guess the original murder ax will be returning to the house after all these years." Mabel sighed. "I'm sure the true crimers will be back for that."

"Along with the missing hatchet. At least, once it isn't needed as evidence anymore."

"They recovered it?"

"Yeah. Darwin had it conveniently stowed in his attic, not far from the original ax."

In the momentary silence that followed, Mabel shifted, feeling she needed to fill it. But as soon as she opened her mouth to continue the conversation, John laid a gentle finger across her lips.

He planted a kiss at the corner of her mouth. "No more murder tonight. No Linnea. No axes, no hatchets, no swamps. I kind of hoped we could talk a bit about us."

"What about us?" Mabel swallowed hard and choked on her spit, setting off a coughing fit.

John thumped her back before darting into the kitchen to get her a glass of water.

When she'd recovered enough to breathe normally, he looked into her watering eyes and grinned. "All better now?"

She nodded and coughed.

"I was thinking with Helen's murderer locked up, I might need to come up with another excuse, if I wanted to see you again. But maybe I'll man up and skip the excuses. Would you like to come roller skating with me one night this week?"

Visions of Tommy Braddock's seventh-grade skating party flashed through Mabel's head. She shoved aside the horrifying image of her death grip on the railing while her feet shot out from under her and rolled madly in different directions.

Mabel coughed again and smiled at John. She knew Jen and the kids would help. Given a couple days, a capable person could learn practically anything.

"I'd love to."

AUTHOR NOTE

Dear Readers,

I hope you enjoyed "Mabel Gets the Ax" as much as I enjoyed writing it. While the book is solely the product of my overactive imagination, it does include snippets of real life, much the way a quiltmaker takes little patches from old clothes and joins them together. Let me tell you about a few of them.

Like Mabel, I spent many years practicing law before changing careers. I also live in an old (1875) Victorian house and grew up in a small western Pennsylvania town. My family, like Mabel's, includes animals—Elvis, who like Barnacle is a cattle dog (also known as a blue heeler), two little rescue dogs named Betty Sue and Louie, and a fluffy Maine coon cat, Cirrus. If you are interested in meeting them, please check out my website, Instagram, and other social media links below. Sometimes, it seems as if my animals have taken over my accounts, and I'm only a supporting character—exactly like in real life!

Volunteering has been important to me too. Among my many volunteer gigs, I've been involved in Australian cattle dog rescue, spent fourteen years on the Board of Education for a Christian day school, served on the board of a local symphony orchestra, and in the past few years, helped lead a Bible study at my church and sung in the choir.

All of this may give you an idea where Mabel came from, but how about the story itself? Years ago, our family visited Fall River, Massachusetts, site of the Lizzie Borden house. That story lodged in my imagination, along with another nineteenth-century ax murder that occurred in my tiny hometown. Somehow, those bits also worked their way into the "word quilt" I was stitching together.

Finally, some of you may be wondering about that story Mabel told her tour group. Did the murders at Frank Lloyd Wright's home really happen? Sadly, her account of the tragic deaths at Taliesin is true. You can, of course, learn more about both Wright and the Taliesin murders online. An excellent book on the subject is William R. Drennan's "Death in a Prairie House: Frank Lloyd Wright and the Taliesin Murders," published in 2007 by University of Wisconsin Press.

If you'd like to meet Mabel's Grandma and find out how Mabel met Koi the cat, I hope you'll read the prequel novella, "Mabel and the Cat's Meow." Please also join Mabel for her next adventure in volunteering and crime-solving in "Mabel Goes to the Dogs"—we've included a sneak peek at the end of this book.

And if you enjoyed "Mabel Gets the Ax," I would greatly appreciate your leaving a review, however brief, at Amazon.com, Goodreads, or other sites for book lovers. Reviews mean so much. I hope you'll also visit me online at one of the following sites—I'm looking forward to meeting you!

susankimmelwright.com
facebook.com/susankimmelwrightwriter
instagram.com/susankimmelwrights
twitter.com/SKimmelWright

DISCUSSION QUESTIONS

1. What is the significance of the book's title?

2. Do you believe women face unique problems in the work force, compared with men?

3. Why or why not? How about older or less physically attractive workers? Have you ever experienced workplace discrimination? If so, how was it resolved? What solutions would you suggest?

4. Have you ever volunteered? If so, what did you do? Was it a good experience—why or why not? Would you recommend it to others?

5. Have any of the scenes stuck with you since reading the book? Which are they? What do you think makes a scene memorable?

6. Mabel had a close relationship with her grandmother. Did you enjoy a close relationship with a grandparent or older relative? Do you think intergenerational relationships are important? Why or why not? Do you think today's technology is helpful or detrimental in building bonds between old and young?

7. Did the ending surprise you? If so, in what way?

Now, a Sneak Peek at Book Two

MABEL GOES TO THE DOGS

Releasing May 1, 2022

Chapter One

MABEL'S BEST FRIEND LISA HAD WARNED that the TV cameras would add ten pounds to her appearance, and anything with a pattern would strobe. Mabel's black pants, white shell, and black-and-gray tweed blazer looked sharp, if she did say so herself. And hopefully the generous scattering of dog and cat hair she'd brought from home wouldn't show up, but still…

"Excuse me," she said. The room's only other occupant, a fortyish woman with short brown hair and fresh, pink cheeks, looked up. "Do you have a lint roller?"

The big dog lying at the woman's feet thumped its tail. The woman smiled and shook her head. "Isn't that hair awful? It sticks to everything."

Mabel smiled back. "You're smart. Black clothes—black dog."

"I didn't actually plan that." She laughed and stuck out her hand. "Rachel Marciniak. This is Sammy—he's a coonhound. You might look in that basket over there."

Sure enough, Mabel found a lint roller, along with hem tape, safety pins, dental floss, Vaseline, and other emergency supplies for guests of WXAT's Country Morning show. Unfortunately, not much tape was left on the roller. Mabel did the best she could.

As she returned to her seat, she held out her hand for Sammy to sniff. "Mabel Browne. Is your dog going to be on the show too?"

"Yep. We're with Bartle County Canine Search and Rescue."

Mabel studied the dog's friendly face, with its reddish jowls and eyebrows. "I thought bloodhounds did that."

"Nope. Pretty much any breed can do search and rescue, but some dogs have more natural talent for it, especially nose hounds."

"So you find lost people?"

"We sure try, don't we, Sammy?" Rachel petted her dog. "Once we found a suicide victim, which was sad. But it's part of the job. Not all dogs do cadaver work as well as live tracking, but Sammy's multi-talented. Aren't you, guy? We've been lucky to locate a couple of lost hikers and that little boy who wandered off from the harvest festival last week."

"Wow." Mabel remembered the lost little boy. The search had gone on into the darkness, and it had been a damp night, with temperatures dipping into the thirties. "That must feel really good, to know you probably saved someone's life."

"It does. What are you being interviewed about?"

Mabel modestly lowered her eyes. "I solved the Sauer ax murder case," she said. "Maybe you read about it."

"I did!" Rachel's eyes widened. "Here I am, talking about Sammy and me, and you're the real hero. You nearly got killed, didn't you?"

"Twice," Mabel admitted with a little shrug. "My next book is all about it."

Mabel knew "next book" was a slight stretch. The only other "book" she'd ever written was a biographical booklet for the historical society.

"Wow, you're an author too." Rachel pulled a card from her pocket. "Put me on your mailing list when it comes out. I'll be looking forward to it.

Mabel accepted the card. "Sorry, I don't have any cards with me."

Again, this was a minor stretch. Mabel made a mental note—*order business cards.* What should they say? Maybe *Author, Speaker, Volunteer Expert.*

She thought about that last part. Maybe it sounded too much like she was offering to volunteer as an expert, instead of saying she was a writer who was an expert on the topic of volunteering...which, she also had to admit, was a slight exaggeration. Her short-lived gig as a historical society volunteer didn't exactly make her an expert.

This in turn reminded her she still needed to come up with her next volunteer job. After getting fired from her twenty-three-year career as a low-level attorney on the eve of her fiftieth birthday, Mabel hadn't been able to find another employer who could look past her age and forceful disposition.

Luckily, she had a nice severance package from her former law firm, along with a rundown house and a sizeable bank account, both inherited from her late Grandma Mabel. Relieved of the immediate need to take whatever subsistence employment she could scrounge up, Mabel had decided to reinvent herself by launching a glamorous new career as an author.

Her original plan had been to write about the benefits to seniors in volunteering. She'd gotten a bit detoured by the Sauer ax murders, but she still needed to keep that other book project moving forward.

"Nice talking to you, Mabel."

Mabel realized she'd zoned out and totally missed whatever Rachel had been saying. "Sorry. I'm not used to getting up this early. Guess I drifted a bit."

Rachel grinned. "That's okay. I know what you mean. We've got to go now. But listen. If you're ever interested in coming out with us, we can always use volunteer 'lost persons' for Sammy to practice on."

Mabel watched as Rachel and Sammy went to wait in the hallway for their interview. She'd be next.

Mabel took a deep, calming breath. Maybe she should rub some Vaseline on her teeth, so her dry lips didn't stick to them from all the smiling she'd be doing during her interview. That's what beauty contestants supposedly did.

On the monitor mounted high in the corner, the Country Morning hosts, Bee Novak and Doug Constantino bantered. Their teeth were unnaturally large and white. Mabel bared her teeth at the mirror. They looked almost yellow by comparison. She practiced smiling like the Mona Lisa.

"Well, this is looking more like Crime Morning than Country Morning, Bee. Cadaver dogs and ax murders. Is that a Halloween thing?"

Bee Novak giggled. "It certainly seems that way, doesn't it, Doug? I don't know about you, but I'm so excited to learn how these dogs do their important work. And Mabel Browne—facing down a killer?" She shuddered delicately. "How brave would you have to be?"

"I hope I never have to find out, Bee."

"Coming up after our news and weather break on the half hour, we'll be chatting with Rachel Marciniak and her partner, Sammy." Bee beamed into the camera. "Part of the team that located four-year-old Noah Poellot, who strayed from his family at the county harvest festival."

Mabel turned as she looked in the mirror. The right seemed to be her good side. She'd have to try to keep it toward the cameras.

The Morning news anchor, a baby-cheeked young man who Mabel suspected had grown his wispy mustache to make himself look more credible, read the local headlines, changing expressions to suit the subject. He frowned as he reported another missing person, an elderly nursing home patient, believed to have wandered off the night before.

Following the news segment, and commercials for the farm supply and Coffee Cup diner, the weather forecast came on. More cold temperatures and bouts of rain—Mabel hoped the missing old man wasn't somewhere out there in the elements.

The camera shifted back to Bee Novak and Doug Constantino. "And now please join us in welcoming Rachel Marciniak and her amazing dog, Sammy, to Country Morning."

Mabel watched the interview with interest. Bee Novak seemed to take the lead in asking the questions. None were very tough, but Mabel couldn't help admiring how relaxed and natural Rachel appeared to be on camera. She didn't rush her answers, Mabel noticed. She'd have to remember to take her time too. She tended to babble when she got nervous.

Why had she drunk all that coffee? It certainly hadn't helped her nerves. Did she have time to run to the restroom?

"So," Bee Novak was saying, "this missing person case. Is that the sort of thing you and Sammy might be able to solve for the police?"

Rachel smiled and shrugged. "Certainly, that's the type of thing we do. Sammy is very good at finding missing persons. But we'd need a place to start. When we did the search for little Noah, we knew he'd wandered from the picnic area at the park. We even knew which table his family had been using. There has to be a scent to follow."

"Could you start at the nursing home?" Doug asked.

"We could try, but if he stepped into a car or onto a bus, that would be the end of the trail. We aren't entirely sure when he disappeared, either. He could have traveled all around town for an hour or more, for all we know."

The entire interview only lasted about five minutes—maybe less. Surely, Mabel could be poised for five minutes. *Did* she have time to run to the restroom? No, probably not.

The green room door opened. "We're almost ready for you, Ms. Browne." The page held the door. "Would you please follow me, and we'll get a microphone on you."

Mabel passed Rachel and Sammy in the hallway. "Break a leg," Rachel said. "Don't forget to put me on your mailing list. And if I can ever answer any questions for your writing, give me a call, okay?"

"Thanks." Mabel blotted damp palms on her pantlegs. She tried to slow her breathing as someone attached a lapel microphone to her jacket.

The Country Morning set looked like a farmhouse parlor, right down to the view of autumn fields painted behind the fake window. Ivory duck slipcases covered the overstuffed chairs, and a coffee table of distressed pine held crockery mugs and a blue speckleware coffeepot. Only the blinding, hot lights spoiled the illusion of a visit to the farm.

"Welcome!" Bee Novak, looking shorter and tinier in real life than she did on the screen, pumped Mabel's hand with both of her own. "I'm so excited to meet you, you brave thing."

"Um, thank you." Mabel began to sit in the first chair, so her right side would be to the camera.

"Over here," a blue-jeaned young woman in headphones tugged Mabel to the opposite chair.

"Actually," Mabel said, "my right is my good side." Nobody seemed to hear her.

"We're on commercial right now." Doug Constantino shook her hand. "Have a seat and try to relax. Have you ever done this before?"

"Um, no. Only a couple radio interviews."

"You're going to be fine. Just try to enjoy yourself."

Mabel found a glass of water at her place and took a sip. Now that this was happening, she realized she wanted to be anywhere else. She was going to say something ridiculous. The camera was going to add another ten pounds to her already overweight frame, and she would look like a different species altogether from Bee Novak. What was she, anyway—a size 0? Was there something smaller than 0?

Suddenly, they were live. Bee beamed into the camera. "Welcome back. Today, we have the pleasure of talking to out-of-work lawyer Mabel Browne, who recently solved the decades' old mystery of the Sauer ax murders." She turned and focused her toothy smile on Mabel. "And welcome to you, Mabel. Doug and I are thrilled to have you join us in the farmhouse this morning."

"Um, thanks." Mabel was starting to sweat under the lights, and she had to quit saying "um." She frowned. "Actually, I'm an author. I did spend a number of years practicing law, but I recently made a career change. I completed a biography of Margarethe Sauer this fall, since leaving my law firm, and I'm working on a couple of other books right now."

"How fascinating." Doug Constantino looked anything but fascinated as he interrupted her. "Can you tell our viewers how you finally figured out Bartle County's case of the century?"

"One book," Mabel continued stubbornly, "is a nonfiction exploration of volunteering for seniors, and the other is a true crime book about the Sauer killings. And, of course, the more recent murders connected to them."

Bee leaned forward, touching Mabel's hand. "Let's talk about that. Actually, you nearly became one of the victims, didn't you?"

"That's right, Bee. The killer had me cornered. Twice."

"I'll bet that must have been terrifying. I cannot even imagine. This man had already killed two previous victims, but you escaped. Can you tell us about that? How did you survive?"

Mabel tried to look courageous but humble. She wondered if anybody she knew was watching.

"I didn't have time to be terrified." Mabel shifted in her seat, realizing that statement was not 100% true. She might not have had much time to think, but there had been plenty of time to be scared out of her mind. "All I knew was I didn't want to die. I knew if this killer was ever going to be stopped, it was up to me. The whole story is in my upcoming book, *Bloodstains*."

Bee and Doug seemed to exchange a look. Mabel was sorry, but she was simply not going to blurt out her whole story on Country Morning and spoil the best part of her book.

"Is it true you didn't press charges?" Doug asked.

"I'm sorry." Mabel sat back, arms crossed. "Since I'll be a prosecution witness for the murder trial, I can't comment on any specifics related to the cases."

Doug cleared his throat.

Bee smiled. "Of course. We understand and would never want to interfere with the upcoming trial. Can we get that archive photo up for our viewers, Ed?" Bee addressed somebody offstage. "The one of the crowds surrounding the Sauer mansion in 1939 after the discovery of the bodies?"

She turned back to Mabel. "Let's go back to the historic case then, shall we? I'm sure our viewers will be as fascinated as I am to hear how you came, after nearly a century, to solve the world-famous Sauer ax murders."

Mabel lowered her hand. She had been trying surreptitiously to wipe sweat from her upper lip. These lights were too much. Had Bee had her sweat glands surgically removed?

"Again, I'm so sorry, B. That's actually a fascinating, but very long story that's best told in my upcoming book."

This time there was no mistaking the irritated look passing between the two hosts. "Well, thank you, Ms. Browne," Doug said. "We will certainly all be looking forward to the release of your latest book."

"And Volunteering for Seniors," Mabel added. "That's just a working title at this point. It's a nonfiction handbook for seniors. About volunteering."

Bee reached across the corner of the coffee table to shake her hand. "Unfortunately, that is all the time we have right now. I'm sure we're looking forward to getting our hands on both your literary efforts in the very near future. Thank you for joining us this morning."

"And coming up in our next hour," Doug announced, "we will be treated to a live performance by the Grannies with Attitude hip-hop group. I hope I can rock out like they do when I'm that age. Or like Mabel here," he added a bit meanly.

Bee laughed. "Oh, Doug! You can't rock out like that right now."

Let Constantino be annoyed. Mabel tossed back her mane of still mostly chestnut hair. She hoped her former law school classmate—the one who'd fired her—had caught the Country Morning show.

As Mabel left the set, she had to squeeze past the Grannies with Attitude in the narrow hallway. *"Like Mabel," huh?* The youngest of the four women was at least seventy—old enough to be Mabel's mother. She had to admit, though, she was not and never would be half as toned as they were in their black leggings, ball caps, and Chuck Taylor high tops.

One of the Grannies offered Mabel a fist bump. Mabel fist bumped back.

"Proud of you," the woman told her. "We're showing younger people that growing older actually a wonderful thing, aren't we? It's all in the attitude." She turned to display the Grannies with Attitude logo on the back of her black moto jacket.

"If you're interested," another Grannie interjected, "we offer classes down at the Second Presbyterian church on Tuesdays at 7 PM. If you take to it, we can always use a few back-up members."

"Thanks." Mabel edged toward the door. "We'll see." Being recruited as a possible second-string Grannie, at barely age fifty, stung. Plus, she was forced to recognize the probability of her breaking a hip if she was foolish enough to try launching a hip-hop career.

Mabel felt around inside her pocket for Rachel's business card. Maybe she'd follow up on that instead. It would be exciting to add saving lives—or at least helping train dogs who saved lives—to her bio, along with capturing killers.

As she headed for the studio exit, Mabel imagined herself tramping through the autumn woods, wearing boots and flannel. Dogs baying like they did on shows about tracking escaped convicts, while Mabel scanned the bushes, searching for a lost person or maybe even a fugitive.

Or a dead body? An image flashed across her mind, reminding her of the last time she'd stumbled upon a corpse. She shivered and heard Grandma Mabel's voice in her head.

"Somebody just walked across your grave."

CPSIA information can be obtained
at www.ICGtesting.com
Printed in the USA
BVHW041149210621
610129BV00014B/230